Praise for *A Worthy Risk*
*Sovereign Liberty Series—Book 1*

*A Worthy Risk* has all the elements of captivating inspirational fiction: a noble-hearted heroine; an appealing, complex hero; wonderful supporting characters; swoony romance; family drama; and faith. Vividly portraying both England and the Colonies in the eighteenth century, T. Elizabeth Renich has written a sweeping novel that will appeal to romance readers and lovers of well-researched historical fiction.

—**Julie Klassen**, best-selling and Christy Award–winning author

An epic tale spanning continents, *A Worthy Risk* takes readers on an absorbing, stirring eighteenth-century journey replete with history, mystery, faith, and romance. T. Elizabeth Renich is a gifted writer.

—**Laura Frantz**, Christy Award–winning
author of *The Rose and the Thistle*

T. Elizabeth Renich is an exquisite wordsmith, researcher, and storyteller! Her skillful pen awakens all the senses, transporting readers into a riveting eighteenth-century drama in this hard-to-put-down novel. Huzzah!

—**Jenny L. Cote**, award-winning author of
the Epic Order of the Seven Series

Hot diggity! Bravo, Ms. Renich! This novel is reawakening the intrigue of our nation's infancy and the legacy of those who helped to nurture it!

—**Jaime Jo Wright**, award-winning and best-selling author of *The House on Foster Hill* and *The Vanishing at Castle Moreau*

T. Elizabeth Renich masterfully weaves solid historical research with creative historical fiction. Her stories highlight lesser-known events in American history in exciting and engaging ways.

—**Bobbi L. Graffunder**, author of *Hidden Places*

# A Worthy Risk

# A Worthy Risk

T. ELIZABETH RENICH

LOWELL
STREET
PRESS

Book Cover by Hannah Linder Designs

Library of Congress Control Number: 2025904142

Print ISBN: 979-8-9893386-5-8

Published in association with Books & Such Literary Management, 2222 Cleveland Avenue #1005, Santa Rosa, CA 95403

Printed in the United States of America

# Dedication

*A thank-you to my three Marcuses—*

Outward appearances may vary, changing over time while wisdom increases. More importantly, it is the heart, strength, determination, dedication, kindness, and valor that have proven memorable and lasting evidence.

I wanted my heroine to fall for a man she could respect and love. You three each provided inspiration, even if you did not realize it in the moment. I named my hero "Marcus" because I love how you love and lead your families, how your quiet and consistent integrity shines. God loves each of you more than I ever could, and I appreciate the individual influence through our respective friendships over the years. You have my gratitude for sharing insights and knowledge, and for being you.

Marcus Hermens, Mark Tornell, and Marcus Washington, I am grateful for each of you.

*And to my readers—*

I'm so glad you came along with me on this next adventure!

*—T. Elizabeth Renich*

.

*A Psalm of David*

Blessed is he whose transgression is forgiven, whose sin is covered.

—Psalm 32:1

# *Chapter 1*

*Bath, Somerset, England*
*Late October 1763*

The bribe worked.

Serenity Ravensworth had never doubted it would. Amos, like his older brothers before him, quite often could be persuaded to do her bidding if his mouth and belly were satisfied with flavorful fare.

Consuming the entire Chelsea-style bun without offering Serenity so much as a taste, Amos avoided her triumphant countenance. No matter. His acceptance of the cinnamon sweet treat removed any grounds for declining the invitation to accompany her to the home of their dear friends the Northcrafts, in Milsom Street.

Alighting from the Ravensworth carriage where it halted at a townhouse of honey-hued Bath stone, Serenity beckoned to her brother as he finished his last bite. "Come along, Amos."

A glum sigh preceded the impudent roll of flashing eyes. Amos wiped his mouth with the back of his hand and then wiped the hand down the side of his trouser leg, trailing sticky crumbs along the seam.

Serenity reached into the coach and retrieved Amos's forgotten hat. "Where is Grandee's sovereign coin?" she asked, for the sake of confirmation.

"Here." The uncommonly tall eight-year-old patted the shallow pocket of his brass-buttoned waistcoat. "Safe."

"As I knew it would be." Serenity ruffled her younger brother's unkempt locks, equally as black and shiny as her own, before he could swat her hand away. She dropped the hat onto his head. Though her junior by a decade and already as tall as her shoulder, he was proving trustworthy beyond his years.

"Here is a lovely surprise." Madelaine Northcraft opened the townhouse door wide, welcoming Serenity and Amos in from the soft grey October drizzle. "Jessa is down for her nap. Had I known you were coming, I'd have prepared tea. Come, I'll put the kettle on."

"Please do not go to any trouble on our account, Madelaine. It is my fault for not sending warning ahead of time." Serenity often confided in her long-treasured friend as she might have done an elder sister, if she'd had one. "You know I never wish to be a bother."

"And so you never are." Affection shone in Madelaine's smile. She took their hats and wraps, then pulled a chair in from the dining area and a stool from her sewing table, indicating they sit as she prepared a light repast.

Amos sat. Serenity did not. "That may soon change." She took a step closer to the elaborately carved wooden cradle near the hearth.

The darling child contained within slept on, undisturbed. Barely a week had passed since Serenity's last visit, but she discerned subtle changes in the girl of three months and impatiently wished naptime over so she might cradle the little one in her arms, harboring a wistful dream of being a mother herself.

With unsteady hands, Serenity retrieved spoons, a sugar dish, and tongs from the sideboard. The tinkling clatter of a china cup abruptly meeting its saucer drew Madelaine's attention.

"Serenity?" Madelaine added a small pitcher of milk to the table. "What is it?"

She released a slow breath. Madelaine knew her as well as Grandee did, and she could hide little from either of them. As a baronet's daughter, expectations for her future social position hinged on making a good match. Until that happened, Madeline and Grandee endorsed her heart's desire—to keep her family together. But with brothers here, there, and everywhere, Serenity—the lone Ravensworth sister among them—shouldered the responsibility to stanch the drifting. She petitioned the Almighty on behalf of all her brothers, though she feared Colson's choices carried an inordinate amount of detriment. For Gideon and Jonathan, she held every confidence in their ability to succeed as they pursued their livelihoods. Mystery and uncertainty yet shrouded Amos's prospects—unless the plan Serenity formulated could work. She needed it to work.

"Do you suppose Tyree would spare a moment to speak with me?" Serenity asked.

"Of course he will. Shall I fetch him from the shop?" Madelaine unlocked the lid of her octagonal cherry tea chest. She counted six teaspoons of Young Hyson green tea leaves into the pot and let them steep.

"Thank you, no. I— I'd prefer we go to him instead, if it's all the same to you." She cast a cautionary glance toward Amos, then back to Madelaine. The conversation was one better spoken out of Amos's earshot.

Serenity clasped her hands together, steadying their tremble. She raised her chin and squared her shoulders, determined to follow through lest her courage lapse. "Amos, would you mind keeping an eye on Jessa while Madelaine and I go to the shop?"

Guarded, Amos eyed the carved cradle and shrugged. "All right. I'll watch her. She's sleeping anyhow."

"I'll send Asher in to keep you company." Madelaine linked elbows with Serenity.

"We won't be long." Serenity mustered a brittle smile to mask her apprehension. "Should the baby wake up and cry—"

"She won't cry." Amos peered down at the napping infant and repositioned the light coverlet. "I'll be here for her."

Serenity squeezed her brother's shoulder and followed Madelaine out the rear door. Across the courtyard behind the townhouse, a joinery workshop stood tucked amid the mews. Madelaine's husband, master joiner Tyree Northcraft, expertly assembled pieces to form an intricate wooden bull's-eye window frame. Ten-year-old Asher looked on, learning.

Tyree glanced up, brushed his hands on his stained apron, and doffed his workman's cap. "Madelaine, my dear. Miss Serenity. What can I do for you?"

Serenity felt anything but the definition of her own name—in truth, the rapid racing of her pulse supplanted any trace of the serene.

Madelaine whispered in Asher's ear. Without resistance, her son took up his chess case by its handle and scampered out the shop door to meet his friend.

Serenity crossed the shavings-and-sawdust-strewn floor to a window-facing workbench, admiring the oval frame. "Oh, how lovely ... " Interconnected pieces took on the appearance of wooden lace, which would require precision in cutting the glass panes for completion. One slip of a misplaced chisel could ruin the elaborate work of art. Gathering her scattered thoughts, Serenity must make her reason for coming to see Tyree clearly understood, thereby eliminating any chance to shatter her prayerfully deliberated plans. "Is this for Grandee's place at the King's Circus?"

"Aye," Tyree said. "She has some very specific notions for finishing off that townhouse, your grandmother does."

"Grandee always knows what she wants." Serenity tried to imagine where, in the almost-finished structure, the beautiful window would be installed. "And she always knows how to attain it."

Madelaine laid an encouraging hand on Serenity's arm. "And what is it that you are wanting from us, Serenity? Or from Tyree?"

Fretting would solve nothing, but in sharing her ideas with the Northcrafts, she hoped they could provide a solution to her dilemma.

She blinked away the sting of unbidden tears and took a steadying breath. "I am unsure where to start—"

Tyree folded his arms across his chest, his stance wide. "Let's start with Amos. Is he finding trouble again? Is that why you brought him along this morning? Get him away from Fernsby Hall for a time?"

Unable to disguise her agitation and without forethought, Serenity picked up a chisel from Tyree's workbench. She defended her youngest brother. "Amos is a good boy with a good heart, and I don't want to see his spirit crushed."

Her fingers curled around the handle of the bevel-edged blade before she supposed she ought not meddle with the master joiner's prized tools. Serenity cast a silent "forgive me" at Tyree and returned the chisel to its resting place alongside a wrought iron holdfast.

"Has Colson started crowing over his own importance again?" Tyree asked.

Serenity fisted her hands. "He rarely stops—whenever he deigns to come home, that is. He spends far too much time in company with Lord Brentmoor, and the baron's influence is simply not good." She picked up a perfectly curled wood shaving. "Not long after our father sailed for Italy, Colson began spouting that portentous verse as a spiteful way to put each of my brothers in their rightful place. 'One for the land and one for the war, one for the church, and pray for no more.' There is a measure of truth in it, as applied to the older three. Colson is the son to inherit, Gideon is the soldier, and Jonathan will be ordained. But Colson harps on the 'no more' and vociferously wishes Amos had never been born."

"Words can build up or tear down, and whether for good or harm, their impact can be long lasting. Once spoken, there is no retrieval." Madelaine had resided at Fernsby Hall with the Ravensworths for a time—she knew Colson as well as his eldest-brother self-serving purposes.

Tyree shifted his weight from one foot to the other. "Colson has always blamed Amos for your mother's passing."

Serenity paced, heedless of the curly shavings littering the plank floor or residual sawdust collecting on her hem. "Amos was born before childbed fever robbed Mother of life, but to this day, Colson refuses to accept either the midwife or surgeon's explanation of the facts." She plunged her hands into her pockets and continued her lament. "As mean as he is, it surprises me Colson has not yet taken to calling Amos 'No More,' because he finds every opportunity to remind Amos his position in the line of succession inherits nothing. Amos is withdrawing. 'Tis rare I see his smile or hear his laugh of late. His tutor tells me he is falling behind because he does not apply himself to his lessons."

Madelaine's brow creased and she reached for Serenity's hand to lend comfort. Tyree's eyes narrowed in contemplation.

"Amos spends a good deal of time away from the house," Serenity continued, "for which I cannot rightly blame him. The stables are his escape. Our stablemaster says for one so young, Amos possesses a deft and canny way with the horses. But I fear he's begun to prefer spending time with horses moreso than people."

"Training horses requires special skill," Tyree said. "Riding and hunting are all good and fine, so long as he's a gentleman—which he will be, as he is, after all, a Ravensworth. But practically speaking, it won't do him any good if a fourth son can't afford to raise and keep horses of his own. In spite of primogeniture laws, young Amos might inherit an allowance from your father's estate, but Colson's expectation has always been the lion's share once the baronet's title passes to him."

Tyree's succinct outline of the dilemma was accurate and Serenity couldn't argue. Not when the scenario plagued her thoughts during the day and resulted in an increasing number of sleepless nights.

Her glance moved across the workbench with its chisels, wrought iron holdfasts, planes, gouges, hammers, and saws. Inhaling a fortifying breath, Serenity presented her case. "Amos will need to learn and master a trade, one in which he can earn a decent living, avoid future privation, and in time support a family of his own. I should very much like to see him settled into an apprenticeship before—"

"He's but eight years," Tyree countered. "You are not unaware, I'm certain, that most lads are closer to thirteen or fourteen years of age before a seven-year contract commences."

Serenity pressed clenched hands against her middle. "But under certain circumstances, can apprentices not start as early as age ten?"

"Our Asher is already learning his way in the shop, which he will one day inherit." To her husband, Madelaine said, "With all the additional building projects and commissions of late, you commented last night at supper that you might have need to hire another joiner."

"I meant an experienced journeyman." Tyree scratched behind his ear. "Taking on a second young apprentice—one even younger than Asher—is quite something else again."

Serenity paced the length of the workbench. "I have shared my concerns with Grandee, as I do with you now. Providing you will take my brother on as apprentice, we would pay for Amos's contract plus the annual wage of a journeyman to assist you."

She stopped and faced Tyree, restating her plea. "Until a few weeks ago, Amos has been curious and bright and a quick study." She fished in her pocket and withdrew a miniature elephant and a small hinged box. "See here. He carved these for my birthday. He likes to create things with his hands. Might that not be beneficial?"

Tyree glanced at Madelaine, whose petitioning expression mirrored Serenity's, but his answer held reserve. "I shall give you an answer by Monday next. I simply need to think on things, consider how best to proceed."

"If you do not agree to terms," Serenity's voice faltered, "I do not see another option." Should Tyree decline to take Amos under his wing, her youngest brother could end up fulfilling an apprentice's contract in a town farther afield or in a more distant shire, far away from Fernsby Hall. But if Tyree agreed, Amos could stay in Bath, an easy distance for frequent visits, and Serenity would be less alone. She refused to dwell overmuch on the notion, but logic forced her to acknowledge Grandee would not live forever.

"If not an apprenticeship with Northcraft Joinery, what about Kerrigan Shipping?" Madelaine suggested. "Surely Uncle Twitch could find work for Amos, when the need arises."

Serenity held tightly to the edge of the workbench, willing her knees to hold steady. Grandee had mentioned Uncle Twitch was due back from the Colonies soon, but the last thing Serenity wanted him to do was take Amos away to Virginia or Philadelphia on his next voyage. She bit her lip. "I— I would miss Amos fiercely if he sailed so far from me."

"We will think on it." Tyree enfolded Serenity's chilled hands in both his and Madelaine squeezed her shoulders, instilling hope.

"Thank you both." Serenity managed a wobbly smile. "Forgive me for burdening you. I would have much preferred to come here today solely to visit your little Jessamine—Grandee has already pronounced her an angel."

Tyree winked at his wife, and Madelaine led Serenity out of the shop, leaving him to finish the bull's-eye window frame in focused solitude.

"Jessa is indeed a sweet child, and you are no burden, Serenity," Madelaine insisted as they crossed the courtyard back to the town-house. "I know you want to do all you can for Amos, and you may trust Tyree will consider the best course for your brother. I will see that he understands how important it is to you. For now, let's have some tea, sit by the fire, and you can hold Jessa for an hour or more, if you like."

"Grandee sent along a gift for her. Amos has it in his pock—" Serenity halted before stepping over the threshold into the front room, observing a poignant tableau.

Asher knelt on one side of the cradle, Amos on the other, the wide-eyed baby girl basking in their undivided attention. Amos held an antique gold sovereign, which little Jessa reached for with perfectly formed fingers.

After kissing his infant sister's forehead, Asher scurried past Serenity when Madelaine quietly bade him back to the shop where his father waited. There was woodworking to be done.

Amos hadn't looked up when Serenity and Madelaine returned. His adoring attention remained unwaveringly on the little girl. "She is so very small. But she is strong. Watch." With a hint of laughter, he held out his finger and Jessa grasped it tight. When he held the sovereign coin just beyond her reach, she gurgled, following Grandee's shiny heirloom with her bright eyes.

Mimicking Asher, Amos leaned over the cradle's side and placed another kiss on the baby's downy-soft brow. Jessa cooed, eyes intent on Amos's smiling face. Her tiny hand reached forth to touch his cheek. From the look of tender wonder in his eyes, it was evident in that moment Jessa had captured Amos's heart.

# *Chapter 2*

*Bath, England*

From his position inside the coffeehouse, Marcus St. James could tell, even at this distance, the young woman he observed through the window possessed a tangible tenacity. She deftly maneuvered a makeshift pram—a combination of cart and cradle—dodging horses and their droppings, two carriages, and a wheelbarrow. Huzzah for her. She maintained her course crossing the street, drawing nearer to the coffeehouse, with several wrapped parcels in the shallow box underneath and what he deduced must be a baby in the cradle-like box on top.

Through leaded-glass panes, their glances caught and unexpectedly held. Amused, Marcus acknowledged her triumph with a wordless dip of his clean-shaven chin. She flushed. Prim smile set, she dropped a flustered curtsy. In haste, she turned, pushing the unpainted pram along the paved walkway, passing two elegantly clothed ladies—perhaps headed in the direction of Stahl Street for shopping or the Roman Baths or the Pump Room. It was the thing to do in Bath, taking the waters.

One of his three companions, Gideon Ravensworth, propped his elbow on the tabletop and concealed one side of his face with an open hand. To the two men with their backs to the street, Ravensworth hissed, "Do not turn around."

His cautionary order was directed at master joiner Tyree Northcraft and merchant Twitch Kerrigan.

Caught woolgathering, Marcus transferred his wayward attention from the fashionable ladies back to the ongoing conversation. He had no dog in the fight that brought these men together, and if he didn't excuse himself momentarily, he'd be late for his appointment with the tailor.

Not that Marcus was anyone's definition of a dandy. But he'd grown weary of his borrowed attire and determined to have at least one new coat before he departed Bath at week's end. The ill-fitting garment encasing his shoulders strained at the seams, was too short in the cuffs, and gaped in the front. He appreciated the loan from Ravensworth's limited wardrobe, but the smaller man's garb trussed up Marcus like a Christmas goose.

"What's the matter, man?" Kerrigan remained facing the crowded and smoky coffeehouse interior—where men of all classes mingled and exchanged ideas—but inclined his head, as if tempted not to heed the warning.

Northcraft's expression, too, displayed puzzlement.

"So much for clandestine operations." Ravensworth shook his head. "I just saw my sister outside—she's here in town."

"She is." Northcraft confirmed, unconcerned. "She was with my wife when I left home to join you here. Relax, Gideon. If your sister knew you were back in England, all Bath would hear her rejoicing."

Marcus hadn't clearly seen the faces of the two ladies walking toward the Pump Room, but they appeared more matronly to him. He thought Ravensworth said his sister was younger than he. Perhaps Marcus had been mistaken. Most of his recent memories were still fuzzy at best, and many he would choose to banish altogether.

Kerrigan glanced at Northcraft. "Did you not tell her we put in at Bristol?"

"I did not feel it necessary to tell her—yet." Northcraft savored the hot dark brew in his cup. "She came to see Madelaine and me yesterday. Scarcely an hour after she'd gone, I received word that you and the crew and cargo of the *Oceanna* had safely docked but two days ago. I needed to buy time before committing to a decision about Amos. I came to seek counsel from you and Gideon."

"And Amos is your brother, correct?" Marcus pieced together disjointed details.

Ravensworth drummed his fingers on the tabletop. "The youngest. He's but eight."

Right then. Marcus did recall Ravensworth mentioning the boy was judged somewhat of an afterthought, catching their parents off guard. "Gentlemen, it has been my pleasure, but at this point, I shall leave you to it." Tapping the trade card Northcraft had provided against his palm, he bowed, then reviewed the name and direction of the recommended tailor. "I've an appointment to be measured at the shop of Mr. Craddock."

"Are you set on turning down my invitation to come stay at Fernsby?"

Marcus donned his tri-cornered hat. Was it genuine concern or Ravensworth's gregarious nature that compelled him to extend his family's hospitality? "I appreciate the gracious offer, Ravensworth, but as I plan to be in Bath only a short time, I shall stay in town and be soon away on a London-bound coach. Your family will be engaged in welcoming you home. They needn't bother about me."

Ravensworth was not taking no for an answer. "If not to stay, then I insist you at least come to early supper before you go. I'll catch up with you later and confirm the particulars. I'll find you by half-past four."

"St. James." Kerrigan shook Marcus's proffered hand. "We'll be in touch."

"Soon." Marcus nodded.

In turn, Northcraft raised a hand in farewell. "Godspeed to you."

Half a block from the tailor's door, leaden clouds obliterated the blue sky, then unleashed a torrent. Breeze-blown, marginally drenched, and more uncomfortable than ever in his borrowed suit, Marcus let himself into Mr. Richard Craddock's shop with hopes of being measured in short order.

The tailor had the good manners not to remark on Marcus's towering height and less than adequate attire. Marcus detected in the tradesman's eyes that the price of his new coat was increasing to account for how much extra fabric, as well as additional time, would be required to complete the job. He was fortunate tailors, in his experience, charged by piece and not by stitches per inch.

Placing a low stool behind Marcus, Mr. Craddock grabbed a length of inch-wide paper tape along with his scissors and began recording Marcus's larger-than-average measurements with trade-coded cuts and notches along the length and edge. Nape to waist, shoulder to shoulder. Mr. Craddock stepped off the stool for underarm to waist, half girth of chest, half girth of waist. Back up on the stool, he marked nape to elbow, nape to wrist, and around Marcus's thick bicep.

When the shop's bell merrily jangled, the tailor stepped down to greet his next potential customer—the young woman with the makeshift pram, babe in arms wrapped so as to keep the rain off the little one. Standing in his smallclothes—sans coat and waistcoat, only a shirt and breeches—Marcus cocked an eyebrow in recognition.

She blinked. "Oh." Holding the child close, she dipped that little abbreviated curtsy again as a becoming blush stained her ivory-cream cheeks. "Forgive me for barging in, Mr. Craddock. I see you are busy ... "

Marcus bit back a grin, duly noting that while she held no tape or scissors, she had nonetheless taken her own incremental measurements of his frame, from his stockinged feet to the ribbon securing his queued hair.

She might have been about to apologize for such unabashed boldness, but her confidence resurfaced and she lifted her chin high, addressing the tailor. "I came straightaway from Mrs. Northcraft's. She is in receipt of your note and instructs me to say that she is able to offer assistance in the shirt-making endeavor you indicated."

"Ah, that is excellent news." With apparent relief, Mr. Craddock glanced sidelong at Marcus, then back to the young woman. "If you would be so kind as to inform her an order is forthcoming, I shall provide fabric and thread as soon as may be. It will be a rush job."

Over Mr. Craddock's head, Marcus scrutinized the young woman as the tradesman resumed measuring Marcus's forearm and narrowed hand.

Repositioning the baby onto her hip, she patted the child's back. "Very well. I shall let Mrs. Northcraft know to expect materials for the work. Good day."

The door closed upon her exit, and once the bell's jingling ceased, Marcus asked, "While you make my coat, Mrs. Northcraft will be making my shirts?" He wondered if that would be Tyree Northcraft's wife or another female relation.

"Yes, sir. In order to have everything finished on time." The tailor stepped back on the stool to measure the length between Marcus's nape to where the coat hem should fall. "Mrs. Northcraft is an exceptional seamstress, which is why I confidently consign piecework to her. The garments of her making will no doubt exceed your fine standard. I'll supply her with linen enough for three shirts?"

"Aye, three will suffice for now. And the young woman—who is she?" She looked familiar to Marcus for some reason, other than seeing her near the coffeehouse earlier.

"Why, that would be Miss Ravensworth."

"Ravensworth?" Marcus craned to catch another glimpse of her face, but she had retreated too far down the walkway and was weaving the pram amid pedestrian traffic like a salmon bent on an upstream swim. He had a certain appreciation for tenacity.

"Miss Ravensworth is the baronet's only daughter." Mr. Craddock's final measurement was Marcus's center front to hem. "There we have it." He pulled the pencil from behind his ear and labeled the paper tapes with Marcus's name, satisfied he'd detailed all the dimensions needed to produce Marcus's bespoke coat.

Shrugging back into the damp borrowed one, Marcus followed Mr. Craddock to his worktable and well-stocked shelves to select fabric. Marcus brushed aside the lengths of blacks and greys suggested by the tailor. On uncharacteristic impulse, pretending he wouldn't chastise himself later for his rash choice, he reached for a broadcloth of warm gingerbread brown. The exact color of the young woman's sparkling eyes. "Here. This will do."

# Chapter 3

*Fernsby Hall, Near Bath*

"She's gone again, miss."

Mrs. Todd, Fernsby Hall's housekeeper, met Serenity at the case clock in the entry as she came in from the stables. "Jean Collier has forsaken her post. Again."

"Foolish girl." Compassion laced Serenity's reluctant judgment. "Colson?"

"Has not been seen for several hours. Mr. Todd saddled his horse when Colson claimed he was going to meet The Lord Brentmoor at Claverton Downs."

"If that was intended as consolation, it is not." Serenity shivered with revulsion at mere mention of the baron. She peered through the window, down the lane toward the gatehouse her eldest brother commandeered as his domain. "I am not convinced Colson visiting the horse racing track with the baron is better or worse than his being back at the gaming tables."

Mrs. Todd stood arms akimbo, not putting her opinion into words.

It was common knowledge among the servants, as well as all the Ravensworth brood, that Colson was not the definition of discreet. As a matter of course, he possessed the bad habit of losing greater sums of money whenever there were the most people around to serve as witnesses, according to the gossips.

Serenity summoned a positive tone. "Thankfully, we have not heard any reports of any great losses ... "

"This week," Mrs. Todd muttered.

Serenity ignored the housekeeper's obvious disapproval, though she shared the sentiment. "Is my grandmother in the garden?"

"No, miss. Her ladyship is in the aviary with the ravens."

"Thank you, Mrs. Todd."

The competent housekeeper and wife of the stablemaster had served in the employ of Serenity's father, Sir Nicholas Ravensworth, since Fernsby Hall's completion. Unquestioningly devoted, each of the Todds was an acknowledged expert in their respective area. Mr. Todd governed solely in the stables as trainer, farrier, and horse doctor. Within the manor house, Mrs. Todd tolerated no nonsense— either indirectly from the family or directly from the staff.

Serenity dreaded the eminent sacking of Jean Collier, which would without doubt take place the moment the dairy maid reappeared. It would be up to Mrs. Todd whether to conduct private inquiries or, since Michaelmas was already past, wait until the next quarter's hiring day, after Christmas, to engage a replacement.

"You will keep an eye out for Jean?"

Mrs. Todd agreed she would and added, "Letter came by courier while you were in town. Thought you might wish to know. Her ladyship has already read it."

Yet Grandee had not disclosed said contents to the good housekeeper. "Very well. I thank you. I will see Grandee first, then I shall help Annie Daye with cleaning the carpets." It might feel good to release some tension by delivering a solid whack to dusty floor coverings.

Dismissed, Mrs. Todd returned to her realm below stairs, though not before Serenity caught displeasure in her expression. The housekeeper did not think it appropriate for the baronet's daughter to assist with chores—but Serenity would be responsible for managing her own household one day, which was why Grandee and Madelaine took pains with instructions for daily routines. Serenity believed she ought to master the basics.

Serenity ambled along the entry hall. Before Mother died and Grandee came to take charge of her and her brothers, Mrs. Todd had commanded a full complement of female staff, while Beckett, their butler, supervised the retinue of menservants. Fernsby was once a lively country house full of life and activity. Of late, with Father traveling on the Continent, Gideon off soldiering in British North America, and Jonathan away studying at Oxford, only a minimal crew was retained, and that meant instances when additional hands were required for certain tasks.

She slowed before entering the morning room, her glance drifting toward the wrought iron gates at the end of the estate drive.

For undisclosed reasons, Colson had transferred his things out of the manor and taken up residence in the gatehouse suite, pressing Beckett into service as his valet. Amos was mostly self-sufficient, and the lady's maid took care of both Grandee and Serenity. The cook, gardener, coachman, and two housemaids served them well enough. While the Ravensworths weren't yet required to undertake such economies, it was mutually agreed that until the older brothers stayed home on a more frequent basis, there was no call to increase staff until a true need arose. At the moment Serenity's contentment lay with things as they were—and precisely how she wished to keep them.

Serenity's maternal grandmother, Lady Aurelia, stood in the aviary surrounded by a small conspiracy of ravens. Perched on terraced branches in a semicircle under a half roof, these birds with ink-black feathers kept the silver-haired widow under keen observation. A week past, Grandee had introduced a *serinette*—a small French barrel organ encased in a wooden tabletop chest—letting the ravens become acclimated to the piece.

Removing the slatted sides, Grandee turned the serinette's hand crank in a circular motion, causing the organ's cylinder to generate a series of musical notes. She had a mind to teach one or two of the curious and intelligent Ravensworth corvids to sing.

Some in their society viewed ravens as symbols of ill luck, but not Grandee. She admired them, and Serenity wouldn't put it past her to succeed with the singing lessons. Grandee possessed that level of persuasion with people and creatures alike.

Most of the bright-eyed birds took flight at Serenity's approach, escaping through an empty skylight that allowed them to come and go at will. Two remained—those Grandee referred to as Loxley and Marian. Predominantly independent, the ravens favored human company on occasion and had learned they could earn treats at Grandee's hand if they stayed close.

"I'm here, Grandee." She leaned to kiss the cheek of a beloved face.

"Did you have a pleasant visit with Madelaine and Jessa, dearest?"

"Yes, while I was there, I did." Serenity elaborated on Madelaine cutting out a tool apron for Asher and Mr. Craddock's entreaty for assistance, as a new customer placed an order with finished pieces required at week's end.

Serenity blinked away the image of the broad-shouldered man from the coffeehouse in his shirtsleeves at the tailor's. "I took Jessa out in the new pram Tyree rigged." Serenity laughed. "I can only imagine what a sight my pushing that cradle-cart combination must have made. But it works—or at least we were doing well enough until the rain started. There's no covering or hood to keep the baby from getting soaked. I shall have to suggest that to Tyree when I see him on Monday."

"Sit for a minute, dearest."

Loxley and Marian gave Grandee leave to caress each of their feathered heads, but spying a bowl of butcher's scraps, they barely let her step clear before pecking greedily at the raw feast. "Or better yet, let us go to my cottage and have tea. There are a few things you and I should discuss before Monday." Assured the birds were feeding, Grandee beckoned Serenity to follow her out the morning room's side door.

Perched on a level rise, Fernsby Hall was the focal point of the Ravensworth estate. The long lane leading up from the gatehouse skirted a dormant formal garden, an iron lattice-work gazebo at its center. On the three sides of the triangular garden, at equal distance from the manor house, stood the stable block and Fernsby Cottage. Behind the cottage's landscaped yard, an ash grove sported autumn-hued leaves, and beyond the iron fence, a disheveled, wild parkland dissolved into more trees.

Serenity threaded her arm through Grandee's as the two traversed the brick-lined path leading from the manor to the cottage. "Is there bad news? Mrs. Todd mentioned a letter."

"Not bad per se. Rather... unanticipated." Grandee fondly patted Serenity's arm. "You, dearest, are the intelligent, beautiful, and only daughter of a baronet and have had, except for the untimely loss of your mother, a lovely life."

Serenity's steps faltered, then halted. "Is something in my lovely life about to change?"

"Life is always full of changes. Never doubt that. Challenges, surprises... At times the waters seem placid, and at others we find ourselves staring into the whirlwind without warning."

Admittedly, Serenity was not overly fond of either surprise or change—and neither was Grandee, according to her own confession, unless she was the initiator. "Has something happened to Father?"

"No, dearest. He is in Italy, by last report."

Impatience on the rise, Serenity faced Grandee. "Colson, then?"

"No, though it has been brought to my attention he and Jean Collier are absent from the estate. That will keep." Grandee prodded

Serenity, restarting their steps toward the cottage. "Recently you attained your eighteenth year and are of an age where you will come to learn—by choice or by circumstance—the world you think you know may not be truly thus."

Serenity touched the chain at her neck, curling her fingers around her sovereign pendant. Out of habit, she slipped the bezel-set antique coin from right to left and back to center again, repeating the agitated motion. Her heirloom gold piece was similar to the coin Amos had delivered for Jessa. "Grandee, please, you're scaring me."

"There is no immediate calamity." Grandee's loving smile chased away Serenity's unease. "Come inside, dearest."

The comfortable charm of Grandee's cottage contrasted with the aloof coolness at the manor. Grandee had come to Fernsby Hall for Mother's lying-in when Amos was born. Serenity's mother had not survived the ordeal, and so Grandee had stayed.

At Grandee's tea table, over currant scones and steaming cups of green Hyson, they enjoyed the first few sips in quietude. Then Grandee said, "Dearest, I know you have your heart set on a joiner's apprenticeship for Amos with Tyree at the Northcraft shop."

"Well yes. I thought you agreed with me that we would—"

Grandee blew softly into her teacup. "Do you trust Tyree?"

"Of course. I would not have sought his help if I didn't."

"But you lack trust in Twitch Kerrigan."

"He's ... " Serenity bit her lip. "I don't know. The man has the look of a pirate, but perhaps he could be trusted—you trust him."

"I do. Without question. He has been a most fortuitous business partner, and this family benefits greatly by employing him as factor. You are aware he is not really an uncle."

"We've always called him Uncle Twitch—even Madelaine calls him such. Why does he answer to a relational designation if he is not related?"

Grandee inhaled deeply, and Serenity wondered if her grandmother was cataloging in her mind what bits to tell and those to save for a later time. "To the Ravensworths, the man is no blood kin. As for Madelaine, well, we shall get to her in a moment. But if you think Twitch Kerrigan a pirate, let me persuade you to think again."

"I did not say he *was* a pirate—merely that he *looks* like one." Serenity envisioned the man's freckled visage, ginger hair and whiskers shot through with silver, sauntering gait, and air of unquestioned authority. An eyepatch was lacking to enhance her opinion, but it wouldn't surprise her one bit to learn he kept a brightly plumed macaw aboard one of his ships. "He seems to be quite at home sailing the ocean."

"A very useful aptitude in a merchant who also serves as ship's captain, when one considers he has investments and warehouses on both sides of the Atlantic to oversee."

Serenity traced the rim of her china cup. "If not related by blood or marriage, then how is he connected to our family?"

"By a good heart and shrewd business dealings."

"You are implying Uncle Twitch is utterly trustworthy."

"Not implying. Stating. The man overcame a rough start in life, and after all he's accomplished, I consider him a diamond of the first water. He is a man of character, one who may be counted on if called upon. You simply have not spent any length of time in his company to learn that firsthand."

"Because more often than not, he's sailing somewhere between here and the Colonies."

"True, and that makes him much missed by those in his familial sphere of influence."

Serenity could nod in easy acceptance or she could ask for clarification as to the reason why. "What do you mean he overcame a rough start in life?"

"If one judged Twitch Kerrigan by his present level of success, it might appear as if he has always been a member of the merchant class. But he was not. Twitch was once an orphan of the streets with no prospects or hope for a better future." Grandee broke a scone in half, tasting a bite. "My Sebastian, God rest his soul, used to say he found Twitch—but more likely the Almighty allowed Twitch to find my Sebastian—on a bustling market day amid a bit of mischief."

China cups clinked against respective saucers. "Not thieving ... "

"No, to his credit, and that arrested my Sebastian's notice."

Sebastian McCandless was a faceless relation to Serenity, known only by Grandee's tales of the legacy that belonged to a man deeply loved by her and still mourned.

"That first instance on market day, Twitch prevented an adolescent ruffian he associated with from picking my Sebastian's pocket. Before my Sebastian could offer thanks or reward, Twitch vanished among the crowd.

"After some weeks, my Sebastian spotted him again near Bath Abbey. That second occurrence, Twitch remedied a theft by making one of his gang return filched apples to a grocer's cart. My Sebastian perceived something good in the lad who, though living in squalor and temptation, owned a conscience and followed through on what was right.

"Admittedly, it took me longer than it should have to comprehend what my Sebastian wished to do. As you are aware, we had no son. Your mother was the only child born to us. Yet we had been blessed with much in material goods, and my Sebastian's kind-heartedness drove his desire to present a plan to the young urchin the next time their paths crossed." Grandee reached for the conical sugar loaf, pressed aside the blue paper wrapper, and snipped additional chunks off with the iron cutter.

Stirring her second cup of sweetened tea, Grandee explained the sponsorship at the Blue Coat School, which granted education and provided a favorable chance for Twitch to rise above his unsavory start. "As a scrappy young lad, he was savvy enough to grab the opportunity, determined to make the most of it. Later on, my Sebastian secured an apprenticeship for him with a blacksmith in Bristol."

Serenity tilted her head, imagining Uncle Twitch as a youth while Grandee relayed anecdotes from holidays spent at the McCandless estate. "But tell me—if he apprenticed as a blacksmith, how did he end up owning a shipping company?"

"Blacksmithing was Twitch's trade, but it was not his passion. The sea called his name."

"Twitch?" Serenity giggled. "Surely that cannot be his given name."

"It is not. His Christian name is Taggart, but he picked up the nickname in the aftermath of an accidental injury at the forge. The corner of his left eye was scarred, and the damaged muscles did not heal properly. When his Irish ire gets the better of him, that left eye is prone to twitch."

"And someone unkindly saddled him with the nickname." Serenity's hands balled into indignant fists. Her thoughts centered on Amos, the anticipated nickname of "No More" from Colson, and of Tyree's impending decision. Monday was two days hence. She earnestly prayed the Almighty would answer her prayers concerning the joiner's apprenticeship.

"If he minded about the nickname, you may be sure Twitch would have set the name-caller straight." With silver tongs, Grandee added an extra piece of sugar to her cup. "Two noted events happened in seventeen and thirty-three. My Sebastian made arrangements for our daughter—"

"My mother, who everyone says I resemble so much." Laurenda McCandless Ravensworth had oft been described a spirited beauty and the portrait over the fireplace in Fernsby Hall's library attested to that fact.

Grandee's glance softened. "You share her stature and her facial features, dearest, but ... "

"But?"

Grandee's troubled eyes focused on her tightly folded hands and regret laced her answer. "In spite of our best efforts and to our great chagrin, Laurenda demonstrated all the attributes of a spoiled hoyden."

Laid to rest in a Bath Abbey crypt eight years past, Serenity no longer heard Mother's voice in her memory. "Is that why you so rarely speak of her?"

"Before she married your father, there was little good to speak of. She was neither encouraging nor caring. You, dearest, are both. *Conniving* was an apt term to define her and Colson is no doubt her son."

Biting back a reconsidered word or phrase, Grandee clamped her jaw. When she spoke again, Serenity suspected the deliberate veering to a different subject altogether.

"Eighteen, dearest." Grandee laid her blue-veined hand atop Serenity's. "By that age, Madelaine had an anniversary as well as a child. Scores of young ladies equal to your age have had a London season and ardently dream of the man they wish to wed. Many become betrothed before they reach one and twenty."

"We discussed at length and decided against an expensive and extravagant season for me. I— I am not ready to marry." Serenity failed to muster any desire to leave family or Fernsby Hall for the pomp of London. She didn't require balls or society events to tell her what her duty was. She knew it by rote. A young woman of her station was expected to make a fortuitous match, produce an heir for her husband, and manage his household to satisfaction. Preparations included lessons in etiquette and deportment, emphasizing how to dress, dance, read, ride, and carry on conversation in company. Serenity invested time on the practical application of Grandee's and Madelaine's housewifery training and with Nancie Heath for cooking and baking. Serenity aimed to refine her skill level for running a successful household.

For two long years, she worried about Gideon off fighting and was thankful for random visits and frequent letters from Jonathan, a student at Oxford's Balliol College. "My efforts in the kitchen are improving, I continue to study about herbs and remedies, and I can plan a supper celebration right down to how to arrange fresh or greenhouse flowers for the table's centerpiece. There is much to learn still, but perhaps by the time you are finished with me, I might be ready to be a wife."

Setting down her teacup, Grandee let slip a resigned sigh. "That is not a subject we need concern ourselves with today."

"You started to say something about two events in seventeen and thirty-three before I interrupted. Will you finish telling me at least one of them?"

Grandee framed Serenity's face with her hands and kissed her forehead. "What I share with you, dearest, is because I believe you sensible enough to shoulder the truth." She sat back in her chair. "The two events ran concurrent.

"My Sebastian finalized a marriage contract with Sir Nicholas Ravensworth about the same time Twitch presented his proposal for a loan needed to purchase his first ship. His personal creed does not allow him to be indebted to a soul—it took Twitch three years to repay the loan and have enough surplus to pay cash for the second ship of his 'fleet.'"

A shudder spilled down Serenity's spine. Viewing lakes or rivers in nature or on canvas was agreeable enough, but utter qualm knotted her stomach at the very idea of sailing on a small seafaring vessel in a great, vast ocean. She found nothing enthralling about that whatsoever.

"With the *Adventuress* and the *Maid Morrow*, Twitch established connections in the Colonies and began his import and export enterprises. I am one of his chief investors and, due to his acumen, earned a tidy return. Your father also invested in Kerrigan Shipping and reaped rewards during the partnership. Twitch acquired the *Bluebird* and the *Oceanna*. Four summers ago, he commissioned a shipwright to build a custom vessel of his own design. He christened her *The Raven's Lady*."

"With prize money and pirate treasure?" Serenity laughed.

"Profits, dearest, not prizes. Remind me to give you a lesson in the difference between privateering and pirating."

"There's a difference?"

"Impudent girl. Of course there is and Twitch has his letters of marque to prove it."

"*The Raven's Lady*—did he mean that as a tribute to you, Grandee? He certainly knows of your affinity for the birds."

"I was honored when he told me his plan to signal his gratitude in such a fashion."

"Quite special indeed."

A wistfulness stole over Grandee's lined face. "After his first crossing to British North America and back, Twitch met a lovely girl from Bristol. He married his Amaryllis, and they soon had a charming daughter—"

Supposition rounded Serenity's eyes. "Madelaine! She is Uncle Twitch's daughter." A certain resemblance, more slight than overt, existed—but had not registered until this moment.

"Correct."

"But where is—what happened to his Amaryllis?"

"Upon returning to Bristol after one of his ventures, he found his wife had died while he was at sea, and his little daughter on the verge of being taken to the almshouse."

Compassion discharged Serenity's frown. "Until you stepped in and made Madelaine your ward."

"Madelaine was in leading strings and a pudding hat when Twitch initially brought her to me. He lacked all experience for raising a daughter."

"Madelaine and Colson are the same age." Was that significant? Each had twenty-eight years to Serenity's eighteen.

Grandee stilled, then licked her lips to moisten them before summoning a half smile. "That is also correct."

At mention of Colson's name, Serenity again reached for her sovereign pendant. She loved her brothers dearly, or at least three of the four. Colson's arrogance, bad manners, and foul habits rendered loving him most difficult. With Gideon, Jonathan, and Amos, affection came easily.

Catching herself fidgeting with the pendant, Serenity held the sovereign close to inspect the worn, embossed circle of precious metal. "Where do the coins fit into this story, Grandee?" Where did they come from? Amid talk of pirates, are they treasure, too? They are of great worth." Hesitant, she asked, "Is Uncle Twitch their source?"

Grandee retrieved a sovereign from her own pocket and held it on her flattened palm for Serenity to examine.

Comparing both Tudor coins, she found the gold pieces nearly identical.

"Twitch opted to receive a number of these as payment for an order once upon a time. He was told the gold sovereigns bearing the likeness of King Henry VIII dated back to 1545. Familiar with my fondness for old things and the enigmatic tales they carry, he gave me ten coins as a gift—presumably to cover what he judged an overdue debt.

"I insisted there was no call for him to reimburse kindness, but he insisted harder and refused to take them back. He said if I had no use for the coins, I should give them to my grandchildren."

Grandee rubbed the gold piece between her thumb and forefinger. "I found his suggestion a novel idea, and therefore, all my grandchildren have a coin as inheritance, each to do with as you please. An heirloom keepsake. An investment. A bit of financial security should such an unforeseen need arise."

Thoughts of what Colson—greedy as he was—might have done with his coin made Serenity shiver. Gambled it away? She didn't want to know. "And because Madelaine was all but blood, you bequeathed one to her, and another to Asher, and now Jessa has hers."

"Yes, dearest."

The mantel clock's ticking marked off several long moments, the tea in Serenity's cup having grown tepid. Without Grandee's connection to Uncle Twitch, the Ravensworths would not be in the standing they enjoyed. Grandee's story provided Serenity a glimpse of the man behind his customary gruff bluster. "Grandee?"

"Yes, dearest?"

"What does all this have to do with us now?" Serenity's thoughts tangled. "Or does it have to do with Amos and you are not specifically telling me why?"

"An illustration, dearest. The Almighty oftentimes places unexpected paths before us. He gives us free will to choose opportunities as they come."

Monday's opportunity was coming, along with its decision. Serenity mulled what Grandee shared, still curious as to what she hadn't. The subject of her mother had been skirted, again. On a shaky exhale, Serenity changed her mind about asking outright. Grandee would surely tell her what she needed to know when she needed to know it. If she didn't yet trust Uncle Twitch, she trusted Grandee.

After tea Serenity returned to the manor house and swapped her day gown for a faded work dress. She indeed found reward in beating Turkish rugs hung upon a clothesline stretched between two ash trees. Every hit dislodged a cloud of dust, inciting her own sneezes and those of the housemaid, Annie Daye.

Serenity beat one of the carpet runners even harder. Not only had the subject of her mother been closed, Grandee had neatly sidestepped sharing the contents of the couriered letter.

Was the lucrative shipping partnership more than what it seemed on the surface? Did Madelaine know Uncle Twitch was her father? She must... mustn't she? But if she did, she hadn't ever spoken of it.

Lost in rambling thoughts, Serenity's next backward step positioned her in the trajectory of Annie's carpet-bat swing. Serenity jumped aside, narrowly avoiding a sound hit in the head.

"Oh, miss!" The mortified Annie regained her balance. "I nearly thwacked you!"

"No harm done." Laughing, Serenity dabbed her brow with her apron. "I ought to have been paying better attention to the task at hand."

Gravel crunched under horse-drawn wheels, pulling Serenity and Annie's notice. A hackney cleared the stone gatehouse guarding the entrance to the Ravensworth estate.

"What on earth?" Not attired to properly receive unexpected company, Serenity might be taken for a servant rather than the baronet's daughter.

"Who on earth, more as like." Annie looked over her shoulder at the manor house. "Fernsby ain't fit for visitors, miss."

Bare hardwoods and shrouded furniture cluttered much of the ground floor. "No, it certainly is not." There was no help for it at this point.

On the far side of the hackney, as if playing hide and seek, a uniformed soldier urged his mount up the drive, cantering toward the house.

"I—Oh, gracious God Almighty!" Serenity breathed a ragged prayer as her heart jigged. Dropping the carpet bat, she hitched up her hem and raced the yelping hounds to meet the rider. "Gideon!"

"Hel-lo, love!" From his saddle, the middle of her three older brothers leaned precariously but managed to stay in his stirrups. He scooped her up and deposited her behind him. A groan-producing move he instantly seemed to regret.

"Gideon? Are you well?" Fighting to maintain her seat, Serenity wrapped her arms around her soldier brother, feeling him flinch again. "Gideon?"

"Just ease up, Sis. The ribs are mostly healed, but the s-strength of a hug like that s-still pains me."

Serenity wrinkled her nose at the odor of spirits on Gideon's breath. He'd been drinking and not just a few pints. What bad thing occurred, on the very day of his homecoming, to prompt his seeking liquid solace? She hoped his uncustomary action was an isolated incident and not an ongoing habit initiated on the other side of the Atlantic.

Such commotion brought Amos and Mr. Todd over from the stables. The stablemaster rounded up the baying dogs as Grandee appeared at the front portico. She descended the steps to the circle drive with Mrs. Todd on her heels.

Serenity dismounted at the block without assistance and held the reins while Gideon slid without grace to the ground. "You are hurt. Or drunk. Or both."

"Shuh-ush." Command slurred, Gideon playfully tapped the tip of Serenity's nose. "I'll be nice as ninepence." Dispensing a theatrical peck on her cheek, he weaved past her and into Grandee's waiting embrace.

"You are a wicked one, Gideon Ravensworth." Affection softened Grandee's scold. She might be as happy as Serenity to see Gideon after an absence above two years, but his unannounced arrival with company in tow cast them in a bad light as unprepared hosts. "Doubly so for subjecting your guest to such an impromptu introduction to this family."

The driver opened the hackney door for a single passenger to disembark, long legs unfolding, boots touching the gravel. The man from Mr. Craddock's shop paid his fare in pence.

Serenity winced. But *of course* he would be acquainted with Gideon—they shared the same soldierly bearing. She opened her eyes again to see he hadn't disappeared. The man acknowledged Serenity with the same dip of his chin as at their first encounter through the coffeehouse window, except his amused smile stretched wider.

Unrepentant, Gideon kissed Grandee's cheek and balanced his elbow on Serenity's shoulder. "Sur-pri-ise!"

"You know I'm not keen on surprises." But Serenity's pique melted like butter on a hot skillet. Unable to retain a shred of annoyance toward him, her gladness at his safe return bubbled over.

"I know." Gideon failed to restrain his glee. "And that's a vast under-state-ment." As if they were still children, he yanked the mobcap from her head. Her glossy black tresses tumbled past her shoulders. Holding the cap aloft, Gideon then tossed it to Amos, who approached with cautious shyness. "We-ell, he certainly sprouted. This one"—Gideon's chin pointed in Amos's direction—"this one'll be as tall as that one." He jerked a thumb over his epauleted shoulder toward his friend. "If you feed him right."

Grandee inclined her silver coifed head toward the tall visitor, attempting to defuse the prickly situation with a mute apology. Gideon's reckless imbibing eroded his manners.

Embarrassment burned Serenity's cheeks. With such a reception, she would not fault Gideon's guest if he judged their society ragged and in want of propriety.

She startled when Gideon pulled her arm, shifting her to stand before the man from the tailor's shop. She pushed her unbound hair from her eyes, pasted on a cordial smile, and peered up to meet the man's steady glance. Relief replaced her apprehension at finding empathy in his expression.

"St. James, allow me to present my sis-ter, Miss Seren-idy Ravensworth of Fernsby Hall. And this—this is my Grandee, Lady Aurelia. You've heard me talk about her before too. Remember?"

Gideon's friend and fellow comrade-in-arms bowed gallantly over each lady's hand. Grandee's was gloved. Serenity's was not. "Lieutenant Marcus St. James at your service. Lately of His Majesty's—"

"...of His Majesty's faith-ful gren-a-diers." Gideon's oblivion added to everyone's discomfiture. Without bothering to lower his voice, he said, "You think he's tall now? You ought to see him in uniform when he dons his bearskin cap. Puts him over sev-seven feet if he's an inch. No lie."

The lieutenant cut off Gideon's rambling. "Lady Aurelia, your grandson is not quite himself. Is there somewhere you'd like me to put him? Preferably where he can pass out and sleep it off?"

"One floor up, his room is the farthest down on the right of the staircase," Grandee directed. "Dearest?"

"Coming, Grandee."

"Mrs. Todd?" Grandee called upon the housekeeper.

"Nancie Heath will have strong black coffee on its way from the kitchen, my lady." The cook at Fernsby Hall always had a brewed pot at the ready.

The lieutenant stifled a grunt. "Come on, Ravensworth."

A harmonious groan suggested both men endured a significant level of pain. Serenity glanced back, half expecting to find the lieu-tenant had thrown Gideon over his shoulder like a sack of milled wheat, but instead he levered his shoulder under Gideon's and partially dragged him up the front steps as Gideon's functionality waned.

"Why didn't you alert us you were back in England?" Serenity chided Gideon.

"And miss...watching you...s-squirm? Where's the fun in that?" Gideon's bleary gaze met palpable displeasure in St. James's narrowed eyes. Gideon looked away. To Serenity, he confessed, "I owe this man my life, you know. He only owes me his arm."

Marcus St. James situated himself between Serenity and Gideon, terminating whatever her brother might have blurted out next. Serenity followed along toward her brother's bedchamber, where St. James unceremoniously dumped Gideon atop the duvet and yanked off his riding boots. Gideon was out before the coffee arrived.

St. James brushed his hands together and returned to the second-floor hallway. "It is my turn to apologize, Lady Aurelia, Miss Ravensworth. I was unaware this scoundrel had not forwarded any intelligence of his own arrival, let alone mine. He pestered me about coming out for supper, so I agreed in order to put an end to his emphatic persistence. However, I now count myself fortunate for having accepted. I feel as if I already know each of you to a degree from oft-repeated stories he's so fond of telling."

A teasing light in St. James's eyes and a barely contained chuckle earned reciprocal though short-lived smiles from both Serenity and Grandee.

"If you know my brother at all, Mr. St. James, then you will know this is not like him."

"I know your brother quite well, Miss Ravensworth, and agree this scenario is one rarely played out. Perhaps when he's had the chance to recover himself, he will explain what brought this about."

"Do you not know what's happened?" Following a loud snore, Serenity started toward Gideon's room.

Grandee halted Serenity's progress with a restraining hand, her characteristic calm reinstated. "Let us postpone the interrogation, dearest. We can, at the very least, feed the lieutenant as a token of our appreciation for seeing Gideon home and offer thanksgiving that no more serious trouble found him."

"I only wish I had located him sooner." St. James pulled the door closed, cutting off the sound of Gideon's snores.

Grandee proceeded to the grand staircase with an expectation Serenity and St. James would follow, but Serenity touched his arm and whispered, "Please, can you tell me anything?"

St. James leaned down, his soft reply tickling Serenity's ear. "I lost track of your brother while I was at Mr. Craddock's. His last known whereabouts were with Northcraft and Kerrigan, deep in discussion at the coffeehouse. They told me he left soon after I did."

Serenity's head tilted upward to meet the intense eyes of her brother's friend. She retreated a step and bashfully tugged her tingling earlobe.

Ever observant, Grandee cleared her throat. "Mr. St. James, do you care for cobbler or fruit tart? Nancie Heath, our cook, will want to know."

"I am not particular, Lady Aurelia. We soldiers are grateful for most anything other than campaign rations. Whatever graces your table will no doubt be perfectly delicious."

Serenity caught a glimpse of her unkempt reflection in the hall mirror and paused at her chamber door. "I shall change into a clean frock, Grandee. That way I shan't carry carpet dust into the dining room."

"Wise idea, dearest. Lieutenant?" Grandee extended a beringed hand, and St. James dutifully offered his arm. "While we wait for my granddaughter to rejoin us, I shall introduce you to the ravens."

# Chapter 4

The carpet runner lining the grand staircase muffled Serenity's ascending steps as she carried a water pitcher in one hand and a bowl of hot ginger tea in the other. She rested the pitcher on the hall table and, without knocking, barged through Gideon's door. She clunked her offerings atop the bedside stand. He didn't stir. His dark head remained buried beneath the goose-down pillow, snores abounding.

Forenoon light sifted through a gap in the dim room's draperies. Serenity stood over the rumpled bed, hands on her hips. She wanted to shake him. Except, now that Gideon was home she wanted to enlist his help in backing her goal of apprenticeship for Amos. Instead of the contemplated shaking—or dumping the water pitcher's contents—she delivered a hard yank on the ankle protruding from beneath the coverlet. Speaking his name did not incite awareness.

Gideon and Jonathan were her first heroes. Serenity respected and loved them with a protective bent, and in turn they doted on her unceasingly—at least until Amos had come along. That was when the three of them joined forces to make an adoring fuss over the youngest.

A fresh pang hit her heart. Two years ago, she was inconsolable when Gideon's orders sent him far away and Jonathan began his courses at Balliol College. Their ailing and reclusive father had sailed for Italy. Though she didn't miss him nearly as much as she did her brothers, Serenity had difficulty combating the abject loneliness their absence wrought.

Many a tearful time, either Grandee or Madelaine had dismantled Serenity's false notions with wise and gentle words, balm for her soul. The departures of Jonathan and Gideon could not be laid at Serenity's account. Those two were no longer boys but young gentlemen, carrying expectations to cultivate appropriate responsibilities.

This drunken stupor, however, proved irresponsible. Gideon knew better.

A second ankle tug, harder than the first, roused a grumbled groan, replete with recrimination. He pushed the pillow from his head and rubbed red-rimmed eyes.

"I brought tea." Serenity offered the porcelain bowl with a steady hand.

He flinched at the volume of her voice, then tentatively shifted into a sitting position and pressed his back against the headboard. "Thank you."

Her grip on the reins of impatience slipped. "What happened to you yesterday?"

Gideon sipped from the bowl slowly, offering no reply.

"Nancie Heath will be sending up buttered eggs and toast from the kitchen. You need to get some food in you."

He took another sip.

Oppressive silence settled between them. When they were younger, they'd held staring contests in which Gideon was usually the winner. This time Serenity claimed victory while Gideon studied the tea at the bottom of the bowl.

Not that Serenity wanted to win this round. If Gideon couldn't face her, how would he ever be of help? With an annoyed huff, she stalked to the window, ready to let in the noonday sun.

"Don't!"

Serenity obeyed his terse request and lowered her hand from the damask curtain, keeping it closed. She sat at the end of his bed, sliding her gold sovereign pendant on its chain. Waiting. Maybe he needed her help before he'd be able to help her in return. "Gideon, I'm not leaving you until you tell me what is wrong."

He cleared his throat. "If Grandee's ravens were white and I were Apollo, I'd cause them to be blackened all over again," he said cryptically.

Serenity searched Gideon's unshaven face and scoured her memories to match his abstract clue. The mythological Apollo—son of Zeus and Leto, twin brother of Artemis—was in Greek folklore representative of healing, medicine, poetry, archery, music, and, ironically, the sun.

According to legend, Apollo sent a white raven to spy on his beloved, and when the pale corvid returned to him with a report of her unfaithfulness, his unleashed fury scorched the raven's feathers from white to black.

"I was not aware you had an understanding with anyone." Serenity's astonishment brought her questions in rapid fire. "Were your affections engaged before you left for America? Who is she? Why did you not tell us?"

He hung his head. "Turns out it's better I honored her insistence for a secret engagement, for 'tis all a moot point now. When I went to surprise her yesterday, I was the one surprised. She married another. She did not wait for me as she promised she would and her husband wasted little time—she has a child on the way."

"Oh, Gideon. I am truly sorry."

"Don't be. It's my own folly. I never wanted to believe she was more interested in title and money. I stubbornly alleged I could make her love me for all my charm and good looks." Heartache tinged his jest. "But I am the second son—the 'one for the war' in Colson's dire poem. It doesn't matter I've returned, lived to tell the tale. Colson will inherit Fernsby—just ask him."

Serenity held no objection to being born the lone daughter in the Ravensworth lineage and not another son. She would have a dowry she could count on at least—providing she could land a good man for a husband. She curled her fingers around her sovereign coin. Every now and then, she uttered supplication to the Almighty on behalf of a man she hoped existed, but was in no particular hurry to find.

Melancholy was not one of Gideon's usual habits, and she attempted to stir up a bit of hope for her downcast brother. "What will you do?"

"Nothing for now, other than rest. Recuperate. Try to remove some of the horrific images that remain in my dreams by replacing them with fresh memories. Battles, charges, and massacres leave lasting impressions." His quip rang hollow. "Find a way to pave over a broken heart."

Serenity hadn't known when to anticipate Gideon's return since the end of the war, but she was grateful for this furlough. "How long before you must report back to service with the army?"

"Fighting the French concluded with a treaty and a royal proclamation. The army is sure to have more officers than peacetime needs. I am on half-pay until they call me back with a new set of orders or until I sell my commission."

"And your friend Mr. St. James, is he in a similar situation?" Serenity folded her hands and unfolded them beneath Gideon's perceptive stare. Although he indicated traveling plans to London, there was an implied sentiment that St. James was welcome to visit Fernsby Hall again at his leisure. "I— I presume you served together, which is how you know each other."

Gideon scratched his cheek. "I believe he is on half-pay, but he also holds a medical discharge." He broke off short of volunteering the reason why. He rallied a contrite grin. "I told you yesterday—he saved my life."

"So you did."

"Did he not tell you?"

"No. In fact, he spoke very little of himself. He steered Grandee to talking about the ravens. That filled all the supper conversation and then some."

"Did she introduce him?" Gideon obediently handed the empty tea bowl back to Serenity.

"She did. I came down from changing my gown and found him standing in the aviary. Stoic, entirely unflinching, even when Marian alighted on his shoulder."

"Goodness." Gideon arched a brow. "St. James passed muster that quickly?"

"Grandee always says the ravens are good judges of charac—" Serenity bit her lip. Whatever Gideon was thinking, that sudden, odd look in his eyes made her wary.

"—character." She emphasized with determination.

Gideon contemplated her in eerie quiet. He tapped a finger against pursed lips, and again they faced off, staring at each other in tetchy silence.

The ravens did not like just anyone and tended to fly off if they weren't impressed. Last night in the aviary, they'd stayed close. Grandee had conducted a congenial inspection of St. James during supper. Had her mild scrutiny been a test of some sort? Grandee did not bestow her good opinion without basis.

Was St. James truly a good character if deemed so by canny feathered corvids? Or did he merit approval on the strength of his service in the Crown's forces alongside Gideon?

His knowing smile spread, and Serenity was the first to look away.

"He'll be back." Gideon chuckled. "He's as good as his word."

"I thank you for the warning. At least next time, we'll be properly prepared for his company." She hopped down from the high four-poster, crossed to the window, and jerked the draperies fully open to let brilliant sunshine stream unimpeded through the glass panes.

Gideon squinted against the sudden brightness and rubbed circles at his temples. She did not feel sorry him. The residual pounding in his head was his own fault. He tossed his pillow in Serenity's direction, but the feeble throw fell short. She ignored his groan of protest as she sauntered out of the room on heavy feet.

Twice now Gideon mentioned St. James's rescue. Today may not be the day to beg for the story behind his assertion, but with her next batch of sweet buns, she'd willingly stake the bribe to wheedle it out of him. Before that, she needed to talk to him seriously about Amos.

Monday had yet to dawn, but Serenity felt the momentousness all the way to her toes. One way or another the plans for Amos's immediate future would be decided.

Late last night, after Grandee had departed for her lodgings at Fernsby Cottage, Gideon had knocked on Serenity's door, offering a mug of drinking chocolate as a peace offering. She had already forgiven his lapse in judgment, but he seemed to value hearing the words.

As they'd drunk their chocolate, she'd requested his help in pleading her case for Amos's apprenticeship, and she'd been disappointed he didn't seem to see things her way.

"Why are you so bent on this course of action, Sis? He's eight. If we had typical parental oversight, we might be discussing sending him to boarding school in London or a parish school in Edinburgh. We don't have those options since Mother is dead and Father has all but abdicated his influence."

Serenity had no ready answer. She didn't know how to explain why it was so important—she only knew it mattered greatly to her.

No one else cared as deeply as she for Amos's prospective outlook, and she desired to test available avenues—so long as they were near.

"Tyree Northcraft's decision will be based on sound reason, Sis. Might I suggest you keep an open mind, especially if Uncle Twitch is somehow involved. He may offer a practicable solution you haven't yet considered."

Serenity's trembling hands curled into fists. "A counterproposal?"

"Both are men of business and deal in risks they deem acceptable."

Serenity so wanted the best she could do for Amos. She drew up short when Gideon said, "Though your efforts to see him provided for are commendable, Sis, they may not be enough in the grand scheme of things. You are going to have to relinquish him. Let him explore—with guidance, of course—his most suitable option."

Given Grandee's recent revelation, if anyone owned firsthand experience with regard to making the most of unexpected opportunity, Uncle Twitch qualified.

Now, before sunup, Serenity scurried along the servants' hall below stairs. The chill of the worn pavers seeped through the soles of her knit stockings. As the days grew shorter, autumn mornings packed a brisk bite. Tiptoeing her way to the kitchen with a candle and her shoes, she found Nancie Heath engaged in the act of cooking. "You didn't wait for me." Serenity muffled a stout yawn. "How am I to learn if you've gone ahead and started?"

"I started three hours ago, miss. Too much to be done not to." Nancie Heath sent the maid, Annie Daye, to fetch more water from the well. "I delayed baking the sweet buns though, for isn't that the very thing you're wanting to make?"

"It is." Serenity slipped on her shoes and situated the leather backs over each heel. Ordinarily she donned footgear before her stays and petticoats, but today she didn't need shod footsteps to wake Amos or Gideon. That would ruin the sweet surprise.

She washed and dried her hands at the slate basin, hanging the damp cloth on a hook near the warmth-giving hearth. Above the basin, the east window perfectly framed Fernsby's parkland like a canvas capturing the shifting seasons, inevitable change in the air. The sun gilded sparse leaves and bare branches as it rose. It wouldn't be long before the bread dough, covered in a redware bowl near the brick oven, did likewise.

A lantern shone in an upper window of the gatehouse. Serenity's stomach flopped with a sickening thud. A sky-blue carriage with the Brentmoor coat of arms sat parked at the edge of the gravel drive. Had Lord Brentmoor been with Colson at the gatehouse though the night, or had he brought her eldest brother back from another evening's mischief?

"The young noble couldn't walk the distance from carriage to gatehouse," Nancie Heath said with honest disdain. "His lordship had to lend assistance to prevent his stumbling to the door." The cook paused, quick to repent. "Beg pardon, miss. That's terrible disrespectful of me to call your brother 'the young noble' in your hearing."

"Colson can demand respect all he likes, but he's done little to earn it." Serenity tied a temporarily spotless apron behind her back, and she said with an irreverent laugh, "My own brothers call him the same. Granted, the baronetcy will pass to him upon Father's death, and then he will insist we call him *Sir* Colson. However, Father is still living and Colson is not running Fernsby—yet."

"Waiting for a dead man's shoes." Nancie Heath set a sunny-yellow lemon and a punched-tin grater on the long trestle table that served as preparation and dining space. "Grate the lemon peel real fine—but first you'll need to grate two tablespoons of nutmeg."

Serenity took the small ceramic bowls from the cook and filled each as instructed. "I appreciate your making a second batch of buns with me in a week's time."

"Just keep in mind they's not true Chelsea buns, miss. I ain't got no written receipt for the like." Nancy Heath poured off brandy to leave plump currants in yet another bowl. "When I visited the Royal Bun House in Chelsea and tasted one for myself, 'twas easy to ken why folks line up for blocks to pay a penny apiece. I determined to create something near equal when I came back from London. Did my best to copy the flavors."

"If the quickness by which Amos devoured the one I gave him Thursday last is any indication, I am happy to report he had no objection to the counterfeit."

Nancie Heath produced a broad smile. "That one and his sweet tooth."

"'Tis a weapon I must make use of while I still can." Amos would soon grow wise to her tactics. Gideon and Jonathan had.

"Bribing young Amos again?"

"No, this time I hope to celebrate with him. That is why I need the whole dozen. Grandee, Gideon, Amos, and I will be guests at the Northcrafts for tea and amusements after dinner."

"Take them all." Nancie Heath ladled something in a kettle, then stirred up the embers in the hearth. She poured a bit of milk into a bowl and told Serenity the amount of sugar to add, stirring until dissolved. "That'll be for the glaze, when the time comes."

Attentive, Serenity listened to the cook's directives and performed each corresponding application.

Nancie Heath gathered ingredients for the filling. Brown and white sugar, more butter, more flour, a little cinnamon to go with the nutmeg. Serenity filched a currant and popped it into her mouth when the cook wasn't looking. Nancie Heath spread a generous layer of the filling over flattened dough, folded, added more filling, folded again, rolled, and cut.

Serenity transferred raw buns to a lightly floured tin tray. Half an hour later, Serenity slid the tray into the brick oven alongside the fireplace, a small cave enclosed by an iron door. She hadn't yet mastered how Nancie Heath gauged the level of heat or how long the duration, but once the cook proclaimed the buns ready, they emerged soft and light, smelling of warm nutmeg and cinnamon spice.

Well pleased, Serenity spooned the sugary milk glaze onto the top of each bun. "We ought to sample one, just to make sure they are good enough."

Nancie Heath knifed a warm bun into halves. "You tell me, miss, will they pass?"

"Mmmm ... Very much so." Serenity licked her fingertips. "Yes, these will pair quite nicely with tea later in Madelaine's sitting room."

# Chapter 5

*Near St. James's Square, London*

His arm ached.

Chest heaving and sweat drenched, Marcus St. James kicked free of tangled bed linens, nightmare decomposing. His ragged breathing slowed. The receding image of dense woods and sound of a waterfall's rush were gradually replaced by the reality of bookshelves and a barrel rolled over cobbles on the street below his window.

Two palmfuls of water against his stubbled jaw splashed cool, but not cold. Certainly not the iciness of wilderness rivers or streams. Toweling dry, he stared at the haunted face looking back at him from the mottled washstand mirror.

Like his arm, his heart ached, and in sorrow he cried brokenly, "Lord God, I know You are not finished with me yet. So evidenced by the fact I am the one still here."

To date, the Almighty provided neither answer nor reason for the ruthless sacrifice required in the lives of his father and older brother. Marcus found it difficult to come to grips with the knowledge he might never get to know this side of heaven. He'd ceased asking why somewhere on the return voyage aboard one of Twitch Kerrigan's schooners, but he was not yet capable of blind acceptance.

Dark speckles at the mirror's edge almost camouflaged the tribal markings on his upper left arm midway between the curve of his bicep and point of his shoulder. Even in dim morning light, there was no mistaking the marks were there.

Lifting his elbow away from his torso, Marcus re-examined the narrow band of overlapping feather tips encircling his muscles. The indelible blue ink had not faded, nor did it smear when he rubbed his thumb over it. Positioned immediately below the inked feather-tip armlet, a solitary feather was etched lengthwise on the near side of his arm, just shy of the bend in his elbow.

*Feathers.* He had no idea how he'd acquired the markings tattooed into his flesh, nor the when or where. Marcus tried in vain to conjure a memory of feathers from his mind's murky void. Nothing ... He fisted his hands and rubbed his eyes, disjointed thoughts tumbling. Feathers comprised wings, and wings could provide freedom or shelter. Or both.

"Hide me under the shadow of thy wings." A psalm or a prayer? As time created distance from that ghastly June day at Fort Michilimackinac, Marcus realized God had hidden him, protected him, and preserved his life—though the elusive details remained in a shaded abyss beyond his reach.

Another psalm chased through his mind. "Because thou hast been my help, therefore in the shadow of thy wings will I rejoice." Marcus sucked in a breath and released a measure of frustration at not being able to distinctly remember events in the wake of the massacre. Perhaps the gaps in his memory were their own form of divine protection.

Grey light filtered through angled blinds, enough to enable scrutiny of the pinkened scars near his elbow, caused by removal of embedded fragments of a razor-sharp agate arrowhead. The raised lump slightly above the joint had appeared after he'd returned to England, the swelling increasing since his visit to Mr. Craddock's shop in Bath. The rise beneath the skin, concerning to say the least, had not been there when he and Ravensworth had arrived at Fort Loudoun, near Winchester, where he'd been treated by the surgeon for a gunshot wound to his shoulder. Infection might have cost him the arm altogether but for Ravensworth's timely intervention.

Putting pain and jumbled thoughts aside, Marcus readied himself for the day ahead. He stood at the clothes press, a coat needed to complete his ensemble. He skipped the ginger-brown frock coat, though seeing it brought Ravensworth's sister to mind. He reached instead for one of midnight black with a mourning band basted onto the left sleeve—dark to match his mood.

Shrugging into the black coat, the sleeve felt uncomfortably snug. A matter that would have to be dealt with sooner than later, but not today.

The upcoming meeting with his uncle and cousin at the office of his father's solicitor would not be the reunion Marcus would have preferred. He would rather have been welcomed home at Oakleigh Combe, the ancestral country estate near Chipping Campden, his near relations rejoicing with happy relief over his safe return. His sister, Johnna, would have been as welcoming to him as Serenity had welcomed Ravensworth.

But Marcus was here in London, miles from the Cotswolds, facing the inescapable reality that he was now the last living male on his father's branch of the St. James family tree. No amount of wishing would bring his father or brother back.

⌒

*Home of the Northcrafts in Milsom Street, Bath*

The knot in Serenity's stomach tightened. In the Northcrafts' comfortable second-floor sitting room, she was more nervous now than when she'd initially put the apprenticeship notion to Madelaine's husband four days ago. She craved Grandee's wisdom and calm, but her grandmother was engaged in somber conference with Tyree and Uncle Twitch.

From across the modestly furnished room, Madelaine's encouraging glance conferred hopeful peace, making Serenity feel somewhat better.

Asher and Amos helped themselves to Chelsea-style buns from the tin ahead of their escape to the joiner's shop, and the adults gathered for tea and staid conversation. Tyree instructed Asher to teach Amos the difference between a chisel and a gouge.

Serenity took that as a positive indicator. For days, she'd prayed Tyree would agree and see things her way. She prayed now, pacing between the tapestry-upholstered settee and marble fireplace, lightly bouncing Jessa in her arms. She loved the little girl as much as Amos did.

Madelaine distributed cups of tea to Grandee, Gideon, Uncle Twitch, and Tyree. The tin of sweet buns emptied, much to Serenity's satisfaction. Grandee used a napkin to politely hide licking sweet glaze from her lips and a gracious nod signaled her approval of Serenity's latest baking endeavor.

Tyree called the meeting to order. "Not that I don't enjoy the company, but I know Serenity has been patiently waiting for an answer concerning young Amos."

Serenity trained her focus on Madelaine's husband.

"I agree with your assessment." Tyree's brow furrowed. "The boy will not inherit due to primogeniture law, and he will need to make his own way in this world. Therefore, I am prepared to sign him on as an apprentice—"

Serenity released the breath she held, until Tyree continued.

"—when he is ten."

"Two years from now?" Serenity searched the faces around the room, suspecting she wasn't getting the whole story. *Open mind, open mind, open mind.* Each word thudded heavy in Serenity's heart. Had Gideon's suggestion proved warning?

Uncle Twitch cleared his throat, adding to her alarm. "Between now and then, I'd like to take the lad with me to the Colonies."

Jessa's delighted squeal drew Serenity's attention. She untangled her coin pendant chain from the little girl's curled fingers. "But why?"

Grandee exchanged a glance with Uncle Twitch. "Dearest, please listen to the stakes Twitch is able offer."

"Very well." Serenity resumed pacing, patting Jessa's back between turns, and waited to be persuaded. Uncle Twitch earned Grandee's loyal approbation decades ago. A wink from Gideon bolstered her sagging spirit. "I— Please go on. I am listening."

"I have a wife in Philadelphia whom I adore, in spite of her dogged determination that she will never sail across the Atlantic or set foot on English soil." Uncle Twitch shoved his hands into his pockets. "Many years after the death of my first wife, I married Susanna. She and I have no children together. No one to take over our combined holdings on the other side of the Atlantic.

"Amos is young, and I'd like him to see British North America before any firm decisions are cast. If he is as quick a study as you indicated to Tyree, perhaps Amos might possess an aptitude for running a business."

"And if he has?" Grandee set aside her empty teacup and matching saucer.

"If I find he has the interest and the intelligence, I would change my will to include him."

"You mean to adopt him?" Serenity tamped down panic, pulling her sovereign coin from left to right, left to right.

"I won't ask him to give up Ravensworth, if that concerns you, but I could assign the benefits to him legally with properly drawn up documents."

Gideon emitted a low whistle. "It would be a rare and valuable opportunity for him, Sis."

"You support this?" Her objection was losing its grip. "You would have Amos sail so far from home?"

"I did, and I'm not terribly worse for the wear."

A disbelieving eye roll punctuated Serenity's irritation. She knew otherwise—French bullets and his broken heart notwithstanding.

Gideon discounted his past two years in America with battle-won injuries and tossed her a wry grin. "He's too young to be a soldier, so rest your mind on that score."

Pacing again, rather than face Gideon's logic, Serenity shifted her attention to Jessa's smile because in this moment she couldn't look any of the others in the eye without crying. "Ocean crossings . . . "

"Are a worthy risk." Uncle Twitch took a swig of tea, giving Serenity more time to ponder. "I've responsibilities and dealings here in England for the next month, maybe two, give or take. Depending on the calendar, I could delay the sailing until after the holidays, depart after Twelfth Night in the new year. Would that ease the notion of separation for you? Because the soonest I'd bring him back would be a year—at least—from when we sail."

"A year?" Serenity's knees buckled. Madelaine scooped Jessa from Serenity's arms as she sank onto the nearest footstool.

"Give or take," Gideon echoed, catching Serenity's hand.

"When Twitch brings Amos back," Tyree said, "if he's closer to ten than he is to nine, we'll revisit the apprenticeship, should Amos truly want to enter into the contract. I won't waste my time teaching skills to someone not willing or wanting to use them."

"We don't always get the choices we want, dearest." Grandee laid an arm around Serenity's slumped shoulders, straightening them with the unspoken admonishment to be brave. "That is when we must trust the Almighty will lead accordingly. Can you submit to His will if it does not coincide precisely with yours?"

Where was her faith? Serenity had prayed—before approaching Tyree with the possibility of apprenticeship and every single morning and evening and in the middle of each day since. The sought-after answer simply wasn't the one she wanted.

Requesting additional time to consider the options or ramifications of Uncle Twitch's plan served no valid point. She must allow Tyree, Grandee, and now, it seemed, Uncle Twitch and Gideon, were all in the decision-making together. For Amos's good. So why did it feel like she was on the outside looking in? They weren't conspiring against her. They saw the larger plausibility of an alternate plan.

Serenity conveyed acquiescence with a mirthless nod. "Amos going to the Colonies..."

Madelaine smiled. "It will open up a whole new chapter for him."

If Serenity viewed him as the hero of this unfolding story and put her trust in the answer to her prayers, all would be well in the end. *Please, God, that it would be so.*

A collective sigh settled in the wake of Serenity's meek resignation. "When shall we tell him?"

"Let me talk to him." Uncle Twitch smoothed his beard. "I have an order of tin awaiting payment and loading in Marazion. I'll take Amos with me to Cornwall, and he can have a few days on board and on the water."

Serenity's smile wobbled, but she joined her voice in agreement with the others as Uncle Twitch's idea gained unanimous acceptance.

Gideon drained and lifted his cup. "Here's hoping Amos is a good sailor."

Twitch threw his head back with a bark of laughter, wiping tears of hilarity from the crinkled corners of his eyes. "You had no problem on your recent crossing, so if he's cut from the same cloth, I believe he'll do quite fine."

"It is a comfort to know the boys will each have a secure future as the next generation of Kerrigan Shipping and Northcraft

Joinery." Madelaine smiled at Tyree and Uncle Twitch. "They have two exemplary men to look up to and learn from. That is something for which I thank the Almighty."

"Amen." Grandee raised her teacup in agreement with Madelaine's toast. "We ought also to thank Him for bringing Gideon home alive."

"Here, here." Tyree, Uncle Twitch, Madelaine, and Serenity saluted with china cups.

Gideon did not worry Serenity now that he was back where he belonged. No. It was Amos who had her apprehension.

*Chancery Lane, London*

Marcus walked from the St. James's Square townhouse to meet his cousin at his place of business in High Holborn. Completely engulfed in memories of his father and older brother, London's incessant bustle was lost on him.

Respected and decorated, whenever orders had afforded Caleb St. James time at home, he'd set duty and uniform aside to focus solely on family. He'd been proud Lucas and Marcus had followed his example to serve the Crown.

Corinna St. James, Marcus's mother, had had her hands full with four children in as many years. Marcus was born before Lucas reached a year old, then the twins, Matthias and Johnna, arrived a year and a half after that. Marcus's first taste of tragedy had come when Matthias was buried alongside their mother at Oakleigh Combe, smallpox claiming them both. Loss had forged a deeper bond of closeness between the remaining brothers, their father, and the little sister bereft without her twin.

No genuine rivalry stood between Lucas and Marcus, but contests knew few bounds—fishing, fencing, high marks on school work, riding, dancing, shooting, and whatever else. Competition spurred them in striving to be better. As they aged, that drive to keep improving manifested in drill, studies, and military instruction.

Marcus had followed Lucas's lead in pranks and policy, and he'd let Lucas believe himself the handsomer and smarter. Lucas had had a touch of sphinx in him, and he hadn't often changed his mind once made. But he'd told the best stories and tended to put everyone in his sphere at ease. He'd never taunted Marcus about the inheritance that would one day reside with him as the older of the two. Lucas had learned all he could from their father and had prepared to take over as viscount in their father's stead when the time came.

Army orders had sent them their respective ways in the King's service, until Marcus transferred to the Great Lakes Territory, where Fort Michilimackinac hugged the watery edge of the blue-green straits. It had been the first time—and the last—all three had ever shared a common duty station.

Marcus touched his fingers to his temple, an old scar inflicted by Lucas's miscast fishing hook now barely visible. He determined not to let memories of his brother and father or their sacrifice fade.

"Marcus!" Raphael St. James, Marcus's cousin just one year younger, emerged from the front entrance of the striking façade of Hamleys Noah's Ark toy store.

"This is where you work?"

"Yes." Rafe's strut mimicked a bantam rooster.

"Impressive."

"Thank you. Junior accountant. However, I am in line for a promotion. The department head has noticed the job I do. Seems all the studying to pass the oral exams at Cambridge is paying off."

Rafe, as all the St. James family called him, had taken a different career path from the soldiering one Marcus and Lucas had. Rafe employed his affinity for numbers to his advantage in his work and mental puzzles.

The cousins proceeded along High Holborn toward Staple Inn at Chancery Lane, arriving at a Tudor-style half-timbered edifice with its gabled dormers and leaded bow windows.

"I'm truly sorry about Uncle Caleb and Lucas," Rafe said. "They are missed."

Battening down a pang of devastation, Marcus managed without words to acknowledge the sympathetic sentiment.

"Remember that time fishing when we upended the skiff and Lucas came to rescue us?" Rafe asked.

"He—" Marcus swallowed. "Lucas didn't know to swim either. Our flailing almost drowned all of us that day." Uncle Kent had ensured all St. James cousins had swimming lessons after that episode.

"Ah, here's my father now." Rafe lifted a hand in greeting.

Marcus inwardly flinched. Never again would he be able to beckon his father.

Rafe shifted his stance, betraying his growing awareness and candid awkwardness. "I am sorry."

Kentwood St. James omitted the anticipated handshake and embraced Marcus. "We'd almost given up hope on you, my boy. Many a prayer answered to see you standing here today. I'd say that means the good Lord still has work for you to do."

On time for their appointment, the trio of St. James men met the Mr. Appleton of Plumtree, Starke, and Appleton at the solicitor's office entrance.

"You are the very likeness of your father." Mr. Appleton pumped Marcus's hand. "I am honored to make your acquaintance. I simply wish these were not the circumstances to have instigated our meeting. You have my condolences, Lord Oakleigh."

Answers to both the greeting and deference to rank went unspoken. *I should not be here. I have done nothing to merit any of this.* Marcus's fingernails gouged his palms. Lucas should have received the hereditary title from their father, the late Viscount Oakleigh. Marcus did not desire being saddled with all its formidable responsibility—entire estates he had no idea how to run or manage, people depending on his insufficient decisions. Too tense to pull up a chair and join the others at the long cherry table, Marcus leaned against the casement and stared out a leaded window overlooking the arch and courtyard below. He half listened to Mr. Appleton drone through the formalities amid the grief and confusion clamoring in his head. *Lord God, I cannot navigate this alone ... please, I need Your help!*

"It is not altogether out of the realm of possibility for a second son to inherit when an elder brother meets an untimely demise," Mr. Appleton said. The solicitor knew the St. James family history intimately, as he had been on retainer for going on three decades. Twice within as many generations, tragedies of war had disrupted the St. James lineage, devolving the Viscount Oakleigh title and lands to unsuspecting descendants.

It happened when Caleb and Kent's older brother Fletcher died at Falkirk Muir in the '45. Caleb had then inherited, which had put Lucas next in succession. When Lucas died, Marcus was thrown in, front and center, without the benefit of any of Lucas's preparation.

"If I hadn't come back ... " Marcus coughed to clear his throat. "If I had died in the massacre, then you, Uncle Kent, would have inherited the viscount title as well as Oakleigh Combe—as younger brother of my father, you would take over, with Rafe the next in line."

"But you survived." Uncle Kent clapped Marcus on the back.

"We are grateful for that miracle." Rafe's genuine relief mirrored that seen on Uncle Kent's face.

"Yes, a miracle." Marcus grasped for gratitude but fell short. *Oh, God, did You truly require both of them at once? Could You not have left one or the other and taken me instead?*

"By virtue of your survival," Mr. Appleton shuffled his papers and adjusted his spectacles, "you hold a unique position, Lord Oakleigh, inheriting as the second son of a second son."

The weight of responsibility descended on Marcus, balancing precariously on his broad shoulders. Everything his father stood for—including guardianship for the remaining bit of family—fell to him. Marcus felt adrift, overwhelmed, and, if he were honest, angry. He'd never wanted to end up in this role and didn't consider himself equal to the task. To his way of thinking, grenadier duties and fighting the enemy were easier, for that was where his experience lay.

"Caleb's service in His Majesty's Army began before he became viscount," Mr. Appleton continued. "He always claimed the life he had suited him admirably, and he wasn't willing to give up his military rank for a noble one. With both his sons following in his martial footsteps, he prudently put his affairs in order prior to shipping out with the 60th Royal American Regiment. A minimum of revised stipulations essentially assigned Kentwood St. James as acting viscount in his stead." From his file, Mr. Appleton pulled out a hand-drawn manuscript map of Oakleigh Combe.

Marcus reached for the map. A clear image of his grandfather—who'd styled himself an aspirant cartographer while he was alive—shook free from beyond the dark cavern of unremembered recent events. A draughting table came into view—pencils, paper, protractor, and compass within reach. Bent over the table, his grandfather spelled out place names on the map. Then his image dissolved into a wisp, swallowed by thickening fog, like the fog building outside the office's glass panes.

Uncle Kent's expression contained concern. The St. James men in this room were the end of the family line. *If anything happens to me . . .* Marcus filled his lungs with a shuddering breath and refocused on the business dealings at hand. Before his head or his heart shattered.

Mr. Appleton finished outlining the straightforward provisions of Caleb's will, which stood uncontested, as the terms were generous indeed. Oakleigh Combe and 640 acres were entailed. However, the remaining assets and more than a thousand acres plus the London townhouse were distributed among the remaining family, with Uncle Kent the designated estate manager.

As tactfully as possible, the solicitor indicated he had yet to receive anything official from the War Department confirming the deceased status of Marcus's father or brother. An unsavory formality.

"Receiving communiqués such as after-action reports or casualty lists in transit from the Colonies always takes time. We could, if you were agreeable, conduct a deposition," Mr. Appleton suggested. "An affidavit describing events from you, Lord Oakleigh, should temporarily serve to supplement the—"

"No." Marcus swiped beneath each eye to prevent the fall of burning tears. His icy tone brooked no rebuttal. "No. I— I cannot."

Uncle Kent and Rafe exchanged another apprehensive glance.

"I believe we have enough to go on for now, Mr. Appleton," Uncle Kent said. "None of us are under a time limit to take a petition before the Lord Chancellor or the Committee for Privileges. We can wait for documentation from the War Department, if that's what the law requires." Uncle Kent squeezed Marcus's shoulder and looked him in the eye. "It's all right, my boy. It'll be all right."

Marcus was far from believing that.

"Until then, what happens from here?" Rafe's attention to detail would prove beneficial—along with Mr. Appleton's knowledge of the situation—toward organizing the process Marcus didn't have the wherewithal to begin.

"As you and your father—the only other potential male heirs to the St. James fortune—are not contesting the outcome, there is merely the wait for the military report." Mr. Appleton hesitated before addressing Marcus again. "Of course, things would change should a son be born to Lord Oakleigh."

Marcus gritted his teeth. "Just St. James." The blasted tears welled again, and a nerve ticked along his clenched jaw. *A son of my own?* What was the legal jargon? *A male heir of his body, legitimately begotten,* or some such phrasing. His mind rejected the unfathomable notion. There would be no child, boy or girl, without a wife. And there would be no wife until the remnant pieces of his own life were in order first.

"If you don't want to be burdened with a title, you might try going back to the Colonies." Rafe chuckled with effort. "I have heard that due to a strong middling class, some there don't put as much stock in the like."

Marcus understood Rafe's intent to alleviate the pressing tension, but his cousin had no idea Marcus had given that very course of action preliminary consideration.

Mr. Appleton steepled his fingers on the table. "You are your father's son," he said with respectful admiration. "Caleb wasn't one for ostentation, and he determined to use his blessings to bless others. Perhaps you will do likewise."

A curt nod was the best Marcus could do at present.

"We shall reconvene at the end of the month," Mr. Appleton said. "I stand ready and able to draw up the legal documents as you should have need. There are, of course, certain things that will require signatures—from all of you—and witnesses."

"Thank you." Uncle Kent answered on behalf of the St. Jameses. "Should you learn something from the War Department prior to our next meeting, inform us, and we'll revise the appointment date."

"Very well." Mr. Appleton made a tidy stack of his case paperwork and closed the file. He shook hands with each of the St. James men and ushered them out.

The subdued mood of the three St. Jameses negated a stop at The Queen's Head. There was nothing to celebrate. Rafe and Uncle Kent declined Marcus's invitation to return with him to the townhouse. Rafe had an early start time at his office at Hamleys Toy Store the next morning, and Uncle Kent was eager to head home to his wife and four daughters. The Oakleigh Combe estate flourished under his management.

Marcus watched Uncle Kent and Rafe disappear into the evening's shrouding mist. He wasn't in the proper frame of mind to discuss anything further and wanted only to escape straightaway to his chamber, where he could pull the covers over his head in a feeble attempt to block everything out. His control was slipping.

Except for a handful of hired staff who lived in, Marcus resided alone at the townhouse. The place looked different, seeing it through his man eyes rather than those of the boy he'd been growing up here. The once-cavernous rooms seemed smaller, hollow without music, laughter, and family to fill them.

Heart heavy, he ascended the stairs to his suite without disturbing Featherstone, the manservant with overlapping responsibilities who'd served his father and now reported to him. Marcus kicked off his boots and tossed his coat over an armchair. Waistcoat and cravat followed. No taper, no supper... nothing but the resounding quiet coupled with a deep sense of inexplicable desertion.

Finally, Marcus did what he hadn't been able to do since the massacre in June. He lent free rein to his sorrow—he cried out the storm.

# Chapter 6

In a diminutive coffee room adjoining the counting office where Twitch Kerrigan conducted business and trade, Lady Aurelia awaited his return. One of the warehouse crew jogged down to the *Oceanna*'s mooring to fetch him, interrupting preparations for departure to Marazion.

While waiting, her lips moved in whispered prayer. Following Sebastian's death, Twitch had stepped up as counselor and confidant. Their trust, and keeping each other's secrets, was based on respect honed from long association.

The door opened with a brisk gust, then closed again. "My apologies, my lady. I did not remember you intended to be here today." Twitch doffed his hat. "We don't sail until the end of the week."

"Yes, I am aware, and Gideon, Serenity, and I will be here to see you, Amos, and your crew off."

"Are you well, Lady Aurelia?"

"As well as can be for one attaining as many years as I have." She removed her gloves and, giving way to the sour knot in her stomach, declined his offer for tea.

"Something is keeping you awake at night."

She put a hand to her cheek. Face powder failed in its duty to hide dark circles beneath her eyes.

"Is Serenity coming 'round to my taking Amos to the Colonies?" Twitch stroked his whiskered chin. "She doesn't like me much or trust me."

"She does not know you well. Give her time," Lady Aurelia said. "She is beginning to learn things are not always as they seem on the surface. It is good for her to make these discoveries, but not easy."

"She has you and my Madelaine for support." Twitch sat in the chair opposite hers and regarded her with squint-eyed intent.

"Between us, we will do the best we can for her." Lady Aurelia nodded.

Twitch crossed his arms, expression probing. "If not Serenity, it must be Colson."

Smoothing her skirt, Lady Aurelia asked, "Have you been conducting covert inquiries?"

"Whether I am in port or not, I will always do what I can to look after you, my lady. Should that include keeping watch on a wayward grandson with a malicious bent, so be it. Colson is out of hand."

"Yes." She met Twitch's frank gaze. "The Almighty blessed me with five grandchildren, plus your Madelaine. They have turned out rather well in spite of their uncommon upbringing—all except for Colson. He cares nothing for this family's reputation."

"He's imprudent, and his choice of 'friends' is questionable at best." Twitch sat back in his seat, crossing an ankle over one knee and clasping his hands behind his neck. "Tell me what you know of Lord Brentmoor."

"I have heard him described as a profligate, which was the politest of the terms. He has a plethora of vices and buries trouble by throwing money at problems. About a year ago, he returned to his family's country house near Gloucester, and now he routinely frequents Bath." Lady Aurelia narrowed her eyes, recalling other sketchy details. "A hushed-up scandal in Wales, or some such thing. But the timing coincides with when Colson started exhibiting his extravagant ways. Not yet a baronet, but he spends like a baron."

"Brentmoor exerts undue influence over Colson. Do you suppose that's because Colson cannot literally afford to go against the tide? Does he owe Brentmoor a ghastly sum for gambling debts, or does Brentmoor have something he threatens Colson with to keep him in line?"

"Aside from money, Colson does not possess anything Brentmoor does not already own. I believe the baron is bored, and Colson, while trying to make himself seem significant, is being manipulated out of sheer amusement."

Twitch's feet hit the plank floor. "Greed alone can be deadly—not to mention in combination with the other six sins spawned of bad behavior. When Colson loses at the gaming tables, he draws on account to pay what he owes, as if he's already claimed his inheritance. At his current pace, he'll deplete the Ravensworth coffers quickly."

None of what Twitch shared could be contradicted. "I am not convinced Colson is clever enough to find this depth of trouble on his own," Lady Aurelia said. "As you say, Brentmoor wields too much influence, and he makes it a practice to exploit Colson's weakness."

Twitch reached for an abandoned mug of tea, swirled the cold liquid, and tossed back the last bit without minding about the dregs. "I have seen his kind before, and it doesn't end well. Brentmoor possesses everything his money can buy, and in his position, he makes sport of taking what he wants—or what he can't have."

A shiver slid across Lady Aurelia's shoulders. "Precisely why his connection to Colson is so troubling."

"Colson's bad habits have increased since I've been away."

Lady Aurelia fought tears. "I should have done something before now."

"As if Colson would listen to you. Gambling is his addiction and money his siren song. Colson is his mother's son. Laurenda passed her penchant for reckless mischief on to him."

Consequences of Laurenda's abominable choices still emitted rippling effects, even from the grave. Lady Aurelia opened a decorative beaded bag and removed a parchment letter with a broken wax seal. The flourished, if shaky, signature belonging to her son-in-law, Sir Nicholas Ravensworth, substantiated the contents. "Sir Nicholas did the honorable thing in marrying Laurenda, but it cost him. His pride refused to let him nullify the marriage contract even when my Sebastian offered to release him."

Twitch's eyes widened as he scanned the pages. "Sir Nicholas has finally identified the sailor Laurenda ran off with ... The jack-tar is dead, but this is proof Sir Nicholas is not Colson's natural father."

Lady Aurelia nodded slowly. It had taken years before Sir Nicholas had found the means to forgive Laurenda for her rebellious dalliance and resulting consequences. Lady Aurelia commended him for that, as she was not quite certain she would have the strength to do the same, had she been in his shoes. "Laurenda fled to Scotland for her confinement. Colson's date of birth is recorded in the parish kirk."

Twitch released a low whistle between his teeth, digesting the degree of import and implication. "His findings prove Colson is not the Ravensworth heir he perceives himself as—Colson was born *before* Sir Nicholas married Laurenda."

Lady Aurelia bowed her silver head. The events had transpired long ago, but birds and curses tended to return to nest. "Fernsby Hall was still under construction, and he did not rush the workmen to completion. Three months after Colson's birth, Sir Nicholas followed Laurenda to Scotland. Witness of their vows are recorded in the same parish kirk.

"When Sir Nicholas sailed with you to the Colonies, Laurenda penned her confession in his absence—all but for the name of the blackguard who deserted her. She acknowledged her indebtedness to Sir Nicholas for not casting her aside. She begged mercy and declared her gratitude for his acting with honor because she had not." Dormant issues snaked their way into the light. Lady Aurelia was not yet prepared for this news to be made public.

"Colson was what, three, nearly four when Sir Nicholas brought them back to Bath to live with him at Fernsby?"

"He hoped enough time had passed for the whispers to dissipate."

Twitch refolded the pages and handed them back. "I feel sorry for Sir Nicholas. In spite of everything Laurenda did, and regardless of all he forgave, he was no fool. He chose not to correct the assumption Laurenda's son was his, and he covered them both with his name. Yet he quietly compiled proof her son had a different father, safeguarding his interests for his own offspring."

"There lies the crux of the matter."

Twitch heaved a sigh. "Gideon has no idea he is the rightful Ravensworth heir."

Lady Aurelia shook her head and plied a handkerchief to damp eyes. "None of them do. It took this long for Sir Nicholas to unearth the final piece of information for corroboration. True to that poem Serenity dislikes so much, Gideon became the 'one for the war,' while Colson insists he is the 'one for the land.' Colson is Laurenda's firstborn, but Gideon is Sir Nicholas's. I pray we can keep this under wraps for as long as possible."

"Which may not be long," Twitch said. "Will Sir Nicholas return from Italy to tell Gideon himself?"

Lady Aurelia blinked back more tears. "I do not believe we will see him alive in England again. His intent was to write and ... "

Twitch rolled his eyes, entirely unimpressed. "Brave enough to marry Laurenda but lacks courage to face his own firstborn." He pointed to the letter. "This will set Colson on his ear."

"It might have already done so." Lady Aurelia stared out the window, gazing beyond the forest of masts towering above ships clogging the docks. "If anyone wanted badly enough to find them, the details are attainable. One simply needs to know where to look. I have a sickening feeling Brentmoor may have discovered the truth and when most advantageous to himself, will use it against Colson."

"Colson cares nothing for you or his brothers and sister, but he is attentive to appearances. He will do all he can to avoid any such revelation to save face among his set. He'll want to prevent scandal for his own sake, to preserve his apparent place in society."

"When Sir Nicholas dies," Lady Aurelia covered the letter with her beringed hand, "this certification will cast aspersion on Colson's claim against the inheritance he so heavily counts upon."

"He is volatile, and Brentmoor's influence incendiary. Was Colson dallying with the dairy maid?"

"Yes, and she has since disappeared."

Twitch's left eye twitched. "I don't like the sound of that."

"I have engaged a thief-taker to gather information. I need to know what we are facing and determine how to proceed."

"Someone I know?" Twitch asked.

"He is new to the position but came recommended. He is concluding an embezzlement case in London, and afterward he will investigate Colson here in Bath." Lady Aurelia folded her blue-veined hands in her lap. "He assures me he will do what he can to keep the matter quiet."

"You trust him?"

"So far." The card she handed to Twitch revealed the thief-taker's name—or at least what he called himself.

"Oakley Lightfoot? Sounds like an actor's stage name."

Lady Aurelia inclined her silvery head. "I do believe he does some of his work in disguise, when required. As I said, he was recommended, and I liked his credentials. This Lightfoot is the grandson of an old business associate of my Sebastian's."

"Connections are good and fine, but if you are not satisfied with his results or his discretion, tell me, and I will delve into it further myself."

"I appreciate you." Lady Aurelia offered a belated smile. A London newspaper cluttered the corner of the table. "Anything of import in there?"

Twitch smoothed the insert flat. "King George has ruffled feathers with this." He showed her the heading: "By the KING, A PROCLAMATION." "The land acquired from the French after the war has been decreed off limits to the Colonists. It has been pointed out by those who hold sway that if the Colonists settle beyond the Alleghenies, it will be too difficult to regulate and tax them. Then there is the part about that swath of land west of the mountains being set aside for the native tribes already living in the territory. It doesn't tell what it means for any still living in the backcountry on the eastern side."

"England absorbed enormous debt in fighting the French for dominion over British North America."

Twitch folded the insert, crumpled the newspaper, and tossed both to the rubbish bin. "It was England's choice to fight. The objective to clear France out of the way is met. The Colonists' complaints pertain to troops still stationed there even after the treaty has been signed, and to a sudden enforcement of the Navigation Acts, which have been lax for a hundred years."

Lady Aurelia studied Twitch's weathered countenance.

"What?" He rested his elbows on the tabletop.

"You spend too much time away from England."

"In trade with her Colonies. The Navigation Acts ban goods from transportation on ships from any other countries and requires three-quarters of crew members to be Englishmen. English ships and merchants hold the advantage with the manufacturing industry. So long as the Colonies remain loyal and profitable, there is no cause for alarm. Word around the coffeehouses is that the war debt is bothersome because Parliament is sure to raise taxes. Some contend the expense of protecting the Colonies should be a charge laid at the door of the Colonists."

"Do you share that opinion? They are British subjects, the same as we."

"I can see both sides. The situation bears watching."

Lady Aurelia agreed. "Much like our situation with Colson."

Twitch leaned near and placed a comforting hand over hers. "Were I you, I might quietly arrange for a meeting with Sir Nicholas's solicitor and accountant. Shore up matters before either Gideon or Colson learns the true condition of their respective birthrights."

She had been thinking to do that very thing.

"I'll only be to Marazion for a few days. Once this personal business is settled and we are braced for the repercussions, your thief-taker can devise a course of action."

"I should like you to be with me at the meeting."

He gave a date by when he should return to Bristol. "Anything else, my lady?"

She dipped into her beaded bag again, this time producing a handwritten invitation to a small welcome-home supper for Gideon, scheduled two weeks ahead of Christmas. "I cannot remember the last time Fernsby hosted an event. It is overdue. Seeing as how you are in port and in the local neighborhood, I should like to see you at my table. Besides, it would do Madelaine and her family good to spend some time with you while you are here."

Twitch pulled an earlobe, like a shy schoolboy. "Madelaine's a good woman due to your efforts. Nothing to do with me."

"I beg to differ. She shares your good-heartedness, and that is more than enough." Lady Aurelia patted his callused hand and pointed at the invitation. "Come. That is an order."

"Aye-aye, my lady." Snapping a faux-naval salute, the twinkle in Twitch's eye returned, overriding latent regret. "But I won't shave."

"I know better than to ask it of you." She chuckled. "Besides, I might not recognize you if you did."

∽

*Near St. James's Square, London*

Marcus turned pages in the daybooks, not surprised by Featherstone's punctilious records for every operation at the London townhouse. All accounts were in order, columns of evenly printed numbers neatly tallied into fortuitous sums. Rafe couldn't have done a better job making sure expenses were proportionately fewer and income greater. To date, Marcus had gotten by on his education and commission, fully accepting second-son expectations. Even after continuing support of his father's charities, the interest per annum alone would keep him fed and clothed with a roof over his head for his lifetime. Unexpected nobility he was, which still made him cringe. Given his new title, he could go wherever and do whatever his heart desired. His resources, however, could not obtain his missing memories.

"Lord God," he rested his forehead on his clasped hands, "I am overwhelmed. Please guide me in what You want me to do." As he prayed, his thoughts slowed from a gallop to a canter.

Featherstone's impeccable ledgers detailed household, transportation, and clothing allowances. He'd sent off to the printer for ebony-trimmed mourning cards, gave Marcus the direction for a bootmaker's shop, and arranged another fitting for Marcus at a reputable tailor's establishment in nearby Bond Street.

Marcus did not regret the whimsical choice of ginger-brown broadcloth for his coat from Mr. Craddock's shop in Bath, but he added a black crepe mourning band stitched to his left sleeve, as he would have done with a uniform coat. The dark bit of cloth sat directly atop the concealed tattooed feather-tip armlet. His next coat would be of black fabric to satisfy London's societal dictates and to honor the passing of his father and Lucas, though there would be no formal funeral without bodies to be buried.

Upon his return from Bond Street, an envelope on an engraved silver tray in the entry hall greeted Marcus. The correspondence did not spell out his name but bore his title in copperplate script. *The Viscount Oakleigh.* Inside was a proper invitation to join the ranks at Boodle's, a club his father had frequented, but rarely, just enough to keep up appearances whenever home on leave from the army. In time, Marcus might enjoy a meal or socializing with other gentlemen and peers, but at present cultivating advantageous business deals or beneficial connections held no allure. He'd wait until Rafe came back from wherever he was and take him along for company. At some point Marcus needed to decide if he would disregard his discharge and return to the King's service. He shuddered at the thought. It was too soon.

Along with the note from the club, the silver tray contained several handwritten condolences and one conspicuous invitation for tea from a Lady Buxtram. Marcus couldn't dump them all in the grate to be burned, but he was almost thankful by virtue of his bereaved status to have Featherstone decline unwanted social obligations.

Marcus rubbed his eyes. The walls in the too-quiet townhouse inched closer, and in a mood as blue as the Wedgewood dishes in the china hutch, he went out again. Without a set destination, his feet took him from St. James's Square, across Pall Mall, and through St. James's Park.

In their younger years, Lucas—mischief glinting in his eyes— had boasted to Marcus and the twins that the square, park, lake, and even palace were named St. James in connection with their family.

When Marcus had repeated Lucas's tale to their mother on an outing to feed ducks and watch pelicans near Duck Island, she'd explained it was by chance, not blood, their St. James surname matched. Those royal and historic places had been named hundreds of years before their family ever resided at the townhouse near the square.

The memory of Lucas's unfounded claims concerning their name provoked half a smile, and, before he knew it, Marcus found himself at the Horse Guards barracks, near Whitehall. For a few minutes he paused, heedless of the grey morning mist, and observed the precision and drill taking place on the cavalry parade ground.

"What's this now? Lieutenant St. James!" A hearty greeting preceded the warm clap on his healed shoulder. "Bless my soul and forgive me, but we'd heard you died in British North America."

Marcus shook the hand of his former military instructor, Sir Rodney Westcott. "My father and brother were killed in the line of duty. I, however, escaped with my life, such as it is."

The knighted tactics teacher extended sincere condolences. "They'd want you to make the best of the life you have left, you know. Don't dishonor their sacrifice by feeling out of sorts that you've survived. Do something worthy in their honor."

Marcus blew out a heavy sigh. Sir Rodney knew of what he spoke, having lost comrades-in-arms to battle and coming back a lone survivor. "I don't know what to do."

Sir Rodney consulted his pocket watch. "I've time enough for a cup of coffee before my next class. Have time for a quick chat?"

"I'd welcome it."

Leaning on a cane, Sir Rodney defied his limp and led Marcus to the barracks coffeehouse. At a corner table offering only a smattering of quiet, they held their discussion over steaming cups, neither adding milk or sugar.

Without censure, Sir Rodney listened as Marcus haltingly put into words his apprehensions about returning to service full time.

England always needed soldiers—either militia on the domestic home front or regulars to fight abroad in the far-flung reaches of the British Empire.

A pending medical discharge had been in hand before Marcus left Virginia. Since returning, he was drawing half-pay. He hadn't sold his commission as of yet, but neither did he have interest in purchasing a higher rank.

"I will go mad if I don't have something to keep myself occupied." And his mind from turning back on itself in the frustrating search of the things he didn't remember. He drummed his fingers on the table's edge. "I haven't yet resolved what I can do. Maybe something to be useful, away from the front lines. Why did you become an instructor?"

"I carried home a French bullet in my hip—still do. Didn't trust the field surgeon, if you get my meaning. I'm quite partial to owning all my own limbs, and the limp is only pronounced when the weather's wet." Sir Rodney's dry chuckle held no mirth, considering England's damp climate. "I reckoned the knowledge I gained in service to the Crown could be useful to other soldiers taking the field. I felt it my duty to offer to teach a measure of preliminary defense."

Marcus took a sip and nearly burned his tongue. "I must confess, there were moments I believed I could hear your voice drilling pertinent points from classes past—all the way to the Great Lakes region."

Sir Rodney laid a small tablet and pencil in front of Marcus. "Show me. Where is that compared to New York?"

Marcus closed his eyes and envisioned the route marched overland as well as waterways skimmed from New York to Fort Michilimackinac—it was his journey back to Fort Pitt in the Ohio River Valley he didn't remember in its entirety. He sketched a hasty map, including rivers, the lakes—Ontario, Erie, Huron, Michigan, and Superior—as well as details gleaned from other maps, and recalled locations of former French forts turned English after the signing of the peace treaty ended the Seven Years' War.

Sir Rodney's raised brow conveyed the level to which he was impressed by Marcus's ability. He tapped the corner of the map. "Now where is it that the rumors had you dead?"

Marcus penciled a miniature stockade at the straits between Lakes Huron and Michigan.

Sir Rodney's sober nod suggested his mind was in contemplation mode. "There is more to your story, but I'm afraid I've no more time for discussion, as class begins in a few minutes. Let me think on this. I will see if there is any way the army can make use of your exceptional talent and be back in touch. Mapmakers—accurate and perceptive—are not always easy to find." He folded Marcus's map and tucked it into his pocket with the tablet and pencil.

"Thank you, Sir Rodney." The two exchanged another handshake before the tactics instructor excused himself and exited the coffeehouse to limp his way to his barracks classroom. Lingering over the cooling coffee in his mug, Marcus mentally reviewed the map he'd drawn. Had he walked to Fort Pitt—five hundred miles distant from Michilimackinac?

No. Impossible. Wasn't it?

# Chapter 7

*London*
*Mid-November 1763*

Visiting Boodle's wasn't Marcus's preferred method to pass another mundane evening, but Rafe enjoyed rampant hilarity in his casual scrutiny of well-dressed members. He invented comical anecdotes accounting for exaggerated expressions and gesticulations, mimicking voices in fictitious conversations, making Marcus squelch more than a few chuckles.

When at last Rafe was ready to leave, Marcus herded him toward the cloak room before he could change his mind.

Featherstone met them at the cloak room's entrance. "Beg your pardon, my lord, but I'm afraid I cannot let you go home."

Marcus was learning to ignore Featherstone's persistence in alluding to his new rank. "Reason being?"

"You're expected at your sister's house. Tomorrow."

"Featherstone, my sister lives near Oxford."

"Precisely."

Suspicion glinted in Rafe's green-and-gold-flecked eyes. "Is he in some sort of trouble at home?"

"Not yet, sir. And that's the way I aim to keep it."

"What is—"

"All the better it will be the less you know, my lord, if you take my meaning."

The resourceful manservant produced a prepacked valise and a small hamper stuffed with what smelled like a savory beef pasty or two. "I've been to the booking office and procured an inside seat for you on the last coach headed that direction." Featherstone handed over a printed ticket. "I took the liberty of sending an express to Miss St. James—excuse me, Mrs. FitzGerald—to let her know to anticipate your arrival. She must think you remiss for failing to come wait upon her, since she is so near her confinement." Featherstone paused his prattling. Then with a slight nod, added, "It makes perfect sense for you to visit your sister, as she is unable to travel at present. Do you both good to spend some time in company together, in shared mourning ... where as many people as possible may witness your presence in her home or on campus, perhaps."

"How long do I need to stay with my sister?"

"Oh, three or four days ought to do it," Featherstone calculated. "I shall send word when matters are resolved at the townhouse, then you may safely return. Unless you have plans to go on from Oxford to Bath?"

"Should I?"

Featherstone's expression turned speculative. "Yes, my lord, I think that might be a wise idea. Good, strong alibi staying with Lieutenant Ravensworth at his family's estate."

"There is need of an alibi?" Rafe swapped a puzzled glance with Marcus.

"It wouldn't hurt," Featherstone said.

Used to carrying out orders, Marcus accepted the coach ticket, the food hamper, and his valise. "Very well."

"My apologies for the inconvenience, my lord. Rest assured I will address and remedy the situation."

Marcus detected the manservant's genuine remorse. "I imagine you'll tell me what is going on ... eventually?"

"Let's just call it *protection* for the moment, shall we?"

Marcus quirked a brow, but there wasn't time to learn what exactly Featherstone was concealing.

"Take heart, cousin. At least he's not sending you north to Edinburgh." Rafe grinned. "Oxford's barely fifty miles—and what is fifty miles of good roads?"

"A safe enough distance, I suppose. Without meeting any highwaymen in passing." The hands on the face of Marcus's pocket watch indicated less than an hour before the coach would depart.

The handshake conveying Marcus's gratitude appeased Featherstone, who cast Rafe an imperative "don't leave him alone" glance. The manservant retreated through the servants' passage.

Rafe caught the gist of Featherstone's caution and earnestly played out the request. Together, the St. James cousins made their way to the coaching inn at Fleet Street, intentionally greeting and exchanging meaningless pleasantries with everyone who crossed their path. They were seen. They would be remembered.

In the cobbled courtyard, ostlers made quick work of changing out a spent team for a fresh one to pull the coach over the next leg of the route.

"It will be good to see Johnna again." Featherstone was right. Marcus should have called upon his younger—and happily married and expecting—sister and would have done so sooner if not for the business in London and, before that, Bath. Johnna would forgive him.

"Godspeed, cousin."

"Mind the front line." Marcus embraced the younger, only slightly shorter man, thankful for a trustworthy ally. "I'll return when I can."

"Not to worry. My father and I will meet again with Mr. Appleton should he require it. Otherwise, it's merely a waiting game here."

Oxford would save Marcus the boredom of the wait. "Send word to the FitzGeralds if you learn anything. Otherwise, I'll let you know if I decide to continue on to Bath."

⤳

*Home of the FitzGeralds, Near Oxford*

The parakeets occupying a suspended cage in the gilt-papered dining room were nothing but miniature, brightly winged things compared to Lady Aurelia's dark ravens. The fair image of Serenity Ravensworth at the serinette flashed in Marcus's mind's eye, then faded.

Dipping his quill, he scratched a hasty note addressed to Miss Ravensworth's brother, informing his friend he would be pleased to accept the gracious offer of room and board at Fernsby Hall for a few weeks. He should be there by Thursday next at the soonest.

Surely that ought to give Lady Aurelia and her granddaughter enough time to prepare for his arrival, thereby eliminating any hint of unwelcome surprise. Creasing the letter and tucking the bottom edge into the top flap, he melted sealing wax and stamped the blob flat with his father's signet ring.

Not wanting to dwell further on why the ring was now in his possession, Marcus's undisciplined thoughts returned to Ravensworth's sister, although she was not an altogether comfortable subject to dwell on either. An alluring image of her silky black hair freed from the constriction of her cap and flowing down her back toward her slender waist arrested his thoughts.

"Good morning." Marcus's sister Johnna swept into the elegant but pleasant room. "Have you helped yourself from the sideboard?"

Johnna, Mrs. Ian FitzGerald now, was no longer the definition of "little" in her current state. She was a twin, and Marcus wondered— if the girth of her was anything to go by—how possible might it be for her to carry twins herself.

"I know what you're thinking"—she laughed lightly—"but when the man midwife last visited to make sure all was well, he did not detect two distinct heart palpitations, only one. Consider: All of my brothers stand—stood … You stand more than six feet tall. My husband is also near the six-foot mark. What hope have I of birthing a short child?"

"Not much," he shot back, smile wistful. With Matthias, Johnna's twin, and Lucas both dead, Marcus alone remained to fulfill all duties of a brotherly nature.

Breakfasting together was a routine of old, reestablished during Marcus's stay. On this fourth morning, Johnna brought a London newspaper and poured hot drinking chocolate into a painted porcelain cup. "You might wish to peruse the advertisements."

Marcus scanned the newsprint with a cursory glance. Johnna had purposely folded the page in such a fashion that what she intended him to read was impossible to miss.

### FOUND

*Gold locket and single filigree pearl-drop earring discovered by a housemaid in a respectable residence near St. James's Square on Friday last. Locket engraved with the appearance of a family coat of arms not unlike the Buxtram crest. Both pieces safely stored at Coutts & Co. until owner can be proven and treasures returned. No reward required. Direct inquiries to D. Featherstone at No. 27 or bank authorities in The Strand. Unclaimed items will be auctioned and proceeds donated to a worthy charity.*

"Buxtram?" Marcus had heard the name before.

Johnna blew daintily on her chocolate before sipping. "The gossip columns not only report that you've met Miss Claudine Buxtram, eldest daughter of Sir William Buxtram, but have been seen in her company as well."

"A fortnight ago, after a meeting with Sir William, I was unable to gracefully disengage and thereby stayed for involuntary tea with his family. I will not make that mistake a second time. Ever since that afternoon, I have deliberately turned down every invitation that has come from Miss Buxtram's manipulative mother."

"Bravo, brother. All they're after is your newly acquired title and the inheritance that goes with it." Without apology, Johnna called a spade a spade.

"I would trade away the title and the money in an instant if it would bring back the rightful owners."

"But such a trade is not to be had." She laid a gentle hand on Marcus's forearm. "We might be orphans, but we have each other."

He nodded. "I am finalizing a trust with Rafe and Uncle Kent. Mr. Appleton, the solicitor, will have it drawn up officially and entered in the chancery court before ... before long."

Marcus wished he knew his sister a bit better as a grown-up, not merely as the pesky little pixie he'd not spent enough time with before he'd purchased his commission. Johnna seemed genuine and compassionate, content with her choice of husband and joyfully awaiting the birth of their child. She'd come of age and married with Uncle Kent's blessing while Marcus was away in the Colonies. "What are you thinking?"

"I remember when you used to hoist me up on your shoulders and carry me through the boxwood maze behind Oakleigh Combe. From that lofty perch, I felt as if I was flying."

He pulled one of her curls. "Wasn't that just yesterday?"

"No, brother, it was quite a while ago." She sobered, attention refocused on the lost-and-found column. "Featherstone served in Papa's employ for as long as I can remember. Lucas met with him quite a bit before his last set of orders. Now he reports to you. What is his role precisely? Is he the steward at the townhouse? Or butler?"

"Butler, steward, valet. The man keeps the townhouse in ready order, expertly ties a cravat, and, if I don't remain in England, will continue on in Rafe's employ."

Johnna let the mention about leaving England pass without comment, though Marcus knew she'd heard him. Rather she insisted, "The man deserves a raise."

"Why?"

Johnna pointed again at the found notice. "Do you not understand what he's done? He's cleverly called Sir William out and never had to issue an illegal challenge. Featherstone kept your name out of it and holds all the cards on your behalf."

"He was very insistent I leave town. If Rafe hadn't been with me to see to it, Featherstone might have put me on the coach himself."

"When I read Featherstone's express, the message made me so angry. Of all the underhanded—" Johnna caught herself before uttering anything unladylike. "I happen to know for a fact Claudine Buxtram shows off every new piece of jewelry her father has ever bestowed upon her."

"Is that not a common practice among young ladies?"

"Some do, but others of us are more discreet." Johnna demurely touched the amethyst brooch adorning the black velvet ribbon circling her throat, a gift from their late father.

"Two seasons ago, at a ball I attended before I married Ian, Claudine Buxtram made a rather condescending display of her pearl filigree earrings and new locket engraved with her family's coat of arms. Her father was knighted for some serviceable good deed in honor of the King, and her mother made the most of their unexpected elevation in society."

Marcus listened, re-examining the newsprint. "There is only one housemaid—I don't even know her name. But I do know she lays the fires in the grates and tidies my bedchamber each day."

"Her name is Jenny. It is she who found the treasures in your room and dutifully turned them over to Featherstone."

"If she hadn't, they would have made quite an incriminating setup." Marcus swallowed the rising bile. He didn't want to believe a woman he barely knew could be so malicious toward him, but he was discovering otherwise. "The housemaid has done me a great favor. I think I'll see about an increase in her wages too."

The implication of the carefully worded advertisement unsettled him. Absent Featherstone's interference, things might have gone very wrong for Marcus. As events stood, if Sir William wanted his daughter's jewels back, he must privately contact Featherstone or publicly apply to a banker at Coutts & Co.

"Those pieces were found in your home because they were left there—by design, Featherstone indicated—and my money is on Lady Buxtram as the instigator," Johnna said. "Featherstone turned the tables on her—and has since dismissed the accomplice without a character reference."

"Accomplice? Someone working at the townhouse was in on it?"

Johnna's smile dimmed. "It was the coach driver. That's why Featherstone sent you to us by way of public coach line rather than in the traveling chariot."

"All this over some jewelry?"

"No, Marcus. The jewelry is beside the point. It's about your name—the Viscount Oakleigh title. Surely you realize you will be a sought-after prize." Johnna's expression held pity concerning his apparent naïveté. "According to Featherstone, Claudine Buxtram herself was in your room—in your bed—waiting to be found along with the jewelry."

Marcus's disgust rose another notch. "Conniving bit of baggage."

"Claudine likely acted on what her mother prompted her to do. Should you have returned home from the club, and Claudine discovered in such a compromising position, you'd have been coerced, in the firmest of gentlemanly demands, to do the honorable thing and marry her."

"Then I thank God Featherstone intercepted me. I shall indeed see his loyalty rewarded."

"I look forward to seeing how he plays out the thwarted scandal." Johnna's eyes, the same green gold as Marcus's, lit with a canny smile. "I imagine he'll invent something ... memorable. Meaningful. A cautionary tale serving to squelch any other such misguided maidens and their meddling mamas casting about for rank or fortune."

"Featherstone suggested I return to Bath for a time." Marcus tapped the sealed note to Ravensworth against his fist before he walked into the entry hall and set it on a familiarly engraved silver tray that matched the one at the London townhouse.

"You have friends there in Bath?" Johnna followed him into the airy hallway.

"Fellow officer and his family. The Ravensworths of Fernsby Hall. They have offered me a place to stay, if I have need while I'm in that part of the country." He rotated his shoulder and straightened his swollen left arm as far as it would go. Bath was a spa town, and he meant to arrange for hot- and cold-water treatments while there.

Johnna smoothed a hand over the pronounced swell of her abdomen. "Well, I am thankful I had you for a little while all to myself. It has done me good to see you, brother."

"You will see me again."

"I will if you stay here in England and are present to meet this little stranger when he or she arrives." Shifting her weight from one foot to the other, she folded her hands atop her distended belly. "You will make a wonderful uncle, and I daresay an exceptional father when that time comes." Before he could voice objection concerning any sentiment about his needing to produce a son, she reminded him, "You are welcome to stay with us here if you have no wish to remain with the memories at the townhouse near St. James's Square."

Should Marcus sire a child, he would strive to emulate his own father in examples of childrearing. Marcus also admired Tyree

Northcraft's unabashed affection for his children. His son, Asher, was following in his joiner footsteps, and his daughter, sweet little Jessa, made the dimple in Marcus's cheek deepen. He wondered, if Johnna birthed a little girl, could she be as sweet? He remembered Jessa in the arms of Ravensworth's sister, then coughed to defuse that line of wayward thinking.

"Eventually," Marcus said, "I plan to sail back to the Colonies. I have unfinished business there."

"Business, such as claiming the land you were granted for your military service?"

"Two thousand acres in the Ohio River Valley."

"That you cannot touch."

His brows lowered. "What do you mean?"

"Are you not aware of the King's Proclamation? King George has decided it is in the political best interest of the Crown to constrain British settlement. All the land England acquired from vanquishing France on the western side of the Allegheny Mountains is off limits. It is reserved for existing Indian tribes—or so Ian has discovered. Both Ian and his brother invested in the Ohio Company years ago and had purchased Crown land for resale, intending to turn a profit. They lost their entire outlay."

In Europe, less than a quarter of the population owned their own land. Landlords sustained estates with rents from tenants. In the Colonies, more than half were freeholders, independent to employ their own choices and make good on the risk. They could raise crops, plant a family ... "I am at a loss to understand how promised land can be revoked by the stroke of a royal pen."

He took Johnna's hand, pulling her in his wake across the hallway into her husband's library. Ian FitzGerald, a don at one of the colleges at Oxford, was sure to have a map of the Colonies of British North America somewhere. Finding none, Marcus took up a pencil and began drawing on a clean sheet of foolscap.

Mesmerized, Johnna watched as within a few minutes Marcus sketched rivers, mountains, forests, forts, towns—all from memory. He deliberately left off fields of battle, but he highlighted the area where he had intended to stake his claim. Intrigued at his artwork, she asked, "Have you given any thought to contracting Papa's friend at the Bureau of Ordnance?"

Marcus glanced up from his map. "No." Atticus Bartholomew hadn't remotely crossed his mind, but he gave pause as his sister's suggestion held merit. In fact, Sir Rodney was acquainted with Atticus Bartholomew.

"Hmmm ... " Johnna tapped her forefinger against her lips. "You should arrange an appointment to see him at the White Tower when you are back to London. He may relish a visit from an old comrade's son, someone familiar and who would share sympathies. Sometimes telling stories enables a way to work out the grief."

Johnna hit closer to the mark than she knew. Marcus had his stories, but they were sorely lacking in too many details to be of use to anyone. Therefore, his grief remained reburied—and his alone.

⌒

Johnna rapped on the open chamber door the next afternoon. Marcus bid her enter as he set about preparations to depart for Bath on the morrow.

"Did you make a decision on the nursemaid?" he asked. His sister had interviewed three potential candidates that morning, hoping to find someone to live-in. Johnna was sister-less and motherless, though Ian's second cousin from Bourton-on-the-Water planned to stay and assist through the duration of Johnna's confinement and delivery.

"I did. She will meet with Ian in the morning, and if he approves, we shall hire her. Ian's cousin arrives on Monday—you will just miss her. Although, given the recent turn of events in London, perhaps it best there is no one else staying here until you've gone. No unnecessary fuel for gossip and fewer tongues wagging."

That night, however, Johnna entered her travail. By suppertime the following evening, she and Ian named their new baby daughter Corinna St. James FitzGerald, to honor Marcus and Johnna's deceased mother. Upon his sister's request, Marcus altered his plans to stay in Oxfordshire two days more. The extra time enabled him to become better acquainted with his precious niece. He was extremely proud of Johnna, and told her so.

One of Ian's students at Balliol College was among a string of visitors who dispensed congratulations for the new mother and babe. Ian made the introductions, and Marcus shook Jonathan Ravensworth's proffered hand.

"I served with your brother Gideon."

"Were you with him at Bushy Run?" Jonathan's inquiry conveyed a touch of awe. "That was a desperate fight."

Marcus stilled, mind devoid of any recollection of said place or action. "N-no." At least he didn't think he had been. Frustration tightened his jaw at yet another missing memory.

"Speaking of Gid ... " Jonathan dug through his coat pocket until he produced a creased envelope with Serenity's name and direction at Fernsby Hall. "I've been meaning to post this letter to them, but I keep forgetting."

"I leave for Fernsby come morning. I could take it with me, if you like."

"Thank you!" Jonathan placed the letter onto Marcus's palm. "That will make Sis very happy. Grandee too."

Marcus nodded with a grin. Jonathan Ravensworth resembled young Amos in appearance, with a temperament a shade more serious than carefree Gideon. Jonathan's contagious smile was a precise replica of his sister's.

# *Chapter 8*

*For the Lord God omnipotent reigneth ...*

The steady sway of carriage suspension straps combined with murmured conversation between Gideon and Grandee lulled Serenity into drowsiness on the road home from the concert at Bath Abbey. She still heard infiltrating strains of Handel's oratorio called *Messiah.* The entire audience rose to their feet as the choir accompanied the musicians, repeating the refrain: *And He shall reign forever and ever ... Hallelujah! Hallelujah! ... King of kings and Lord of lords, forever and ever, Hallelujah! Hallelujah!*

An annoying poke in the ribs from Gideon stirred her back into wakefulness. Through the window on her side of the carriage, she viewed Mr. Ralph Allen's magnificent country house as they drove past. Located roughly a mile distant from the Ravensworth estate as a corvid would fly and separated by dense parkland, Prior Park shone brightly against the night, illuminated by the twinkling glow of countless lanterns.

Fernsby's gatehouse stood dark as the horses and carriage ascended the drive, though their father's study burned bright with candlelight in every window.

Unable to stifle a broad yawn, Gideon jested, "Company at this hour? I'll go investigate."

As habit dictated, Grandee checked on the ravens while Serenity intended to look in on Amos, but Gideon's exclamation arrested her steps, and she followed his voice to the study door.

"Have you gone mad?" Gideon marched into the room's chaos. "What are you looking for?"

Papers and ledger books, receipts, statements, and cards were strewn haphazardly across their father's otherwise orderly desk. Down on one knee, Colson attempted to yank open a locked lower drawer in the massive walnut piece. The brass handle would not yield.

"Where is the family Bible?" Colson ran a shaky hand through his wild auburn hair. "I know we have one."

Gideon and Serenity shared a shrug.

Grandee glided into the study, regal and commanding. "The family Bible, Colson? Whatever for? Were you trying to discover if my birth date is divulged by the frontispiece family tree?"

"Or were you actually wanting to read it?" Even as she spoke the wishful sentiment, Serenity doubted the Scriptures were her brother's intent.

Gideon's chuckle burst out unbridled. Colson opted to pay required fines for nonattendance at Bath Abbey and had been doing so even before their father had departed for Italy. He did not darken church doors any oftener than he must, not even for the sake of appearances.

Staring up at Gideon with no trace of familial affinity in his angry blue glare, Colson sneered, "Still playing the returned prodigal?"

"That is indeed a Bible story, but not an altogether applicable one in this case."

"You sound like Jonathan." Colson's observation wasn't a compliment. But then he put forth a new idea. "Hold on … suppose we *do* kill a fatted calf in your honor—a belated welcome home of sorts. To celebrate."

Gideon and Serenity both failed to mask their surprise, and Grandee said, "An excellent notion, Colson. Truth be told, I have already begun making preliminary arrangements for exactly such a fête. Gideon's safe return is an answer to many prayers, and we shall rejoice with our friends. What, pray, were you intending to celebrate?"

"Things..." Colson faced off with Gideon. "We could host Gideon's party along with a hunt, and a gala. Perhaps by then Serenity, too, might have cause for a festive event."

Gala? Serenity's head swam with the overwhelming amount of work anticipated to make Fernsby's manor house presentable for such a gathering. Additional staff would need to be hired, not to mention the enormous quantity of food and drink, for Colson would go all out to try to impress. But exactly *whom* was he trying to impress?

"What are you really up to?" Suspicion laced Serenity's query.

Grandee and Gideon paused, equally interested to learn the reply.

"Too early to tell." Colson smirked at Serenity. "Name the date, Sis. We may all have something to celebrate the night of the party."

Colson sauntered from the study, abandoning the inflicted disarray. Seconds later his bellow for Beckett preceded a resounding slam of the front door.

"A welcome-home party?" Marcus St. James materialized from the shadows of the grand staircase.

"St. James!" Gideon flattened a dramatic hand over his heart. "Good to see you at last. I was beginning to think you'd lost your way back. How long have you been here?"

"About an hour. Beckett allowed me in, told me I was going to have to wait if I wanted to see the family, as they were out." He kissed Grandee's hand, then acknowledged Serenity with an appreciative tilt of his head and a polite bow. "Your oldest brother didn't appear to be in the mood for company, so I chose to watch while I waited."

That interested Gideon. "And... what did you observe?"

"Definitely searching for something of import. Kept muttering about coins, a Bible. A letter inside of a Bible."

"He shall find neither." Grandee's icy decree preceded a more pleasant, "Do tell, Mr. St. James, how did you find London during this season?"

"London was...London. My father's estate issues are ongoing, amongst other things. I did not stay long. I traveled to Oxford to visit my sister and her husband for a fortnight. She has given birth to her first child and made me an uncle." Large hands held apart, roughly the length of a swaddled newborn, he said, "She's such a tiny little thing." The pride-induced grin transformed his expression from serious to besotted.

Serenity presumed there was a good deal more than met the eye with this grenadier friend of her brother's. "As Gideon informed us of your return, we have prepared the guest suite above the stables for you. You'll discover a resplendent prospect from the window facing the stream."

"You are very kind."

Marcus's eyes glinted with amusement, but then his seriousness returned. Serenity felt his glance skim her features, tallying details of her claret-colored frock and coiffed hair. She willed her hand to remain at her side rather than reach above her ear to ensure no curls had escaped their confines at this late hour.

"I'm pleased you accepted my offer to stay." Gideon clapped Marcus on the back.

"I can pay a fair price for the lodging. The coach passengers complained of few vacancies to be found at any of the inns or taverns in town and how expensive it would be even if there were any rooms to let."

"Nonsense. Any friend of Gideon's is welcome." Grandee sent him a disarming smile. "However, if you feel the need to give money away, might I suggest a donation to the Blue Coat School instead? They are sure to do something useful with the funds."

"I thank you for your hospitality, and I shall consider your suggestion."

Serenity pushed aside the bed coverings, sleepless. A light in the stable block had her making haste to pull on a work dress and a pair of sturdy boots, then she wrapped herself in a thick shawl. When she stepped into the hall on tiptoe, she found Gideon's bedchamber door closed, but Amos's stood wide open. Oil lamp in hand, she exited the main house and passed through the garden parterres to the stable.

The flame flickered as she slid the stable door open, closing it behind her. A lantern glowed in the second stall beyond the tack room. "Amos?"

He looked up for a moment at the sound of his name, then resumed application of the curry comb to the coat of one of the Cleveland Bays.

"Couldn't sleep?"

He shook his head no.

"Me either." Serenity perched on the lid of the feed box. "Except for mealtimes, I haven't seen much of you since we were at the Northcrafts."

"I know."

"Are you angry with me?" Serenity tipped her head, meeting his eyes. "Do you find me interfering?"

He scowled. "No."

She patted the box lid, inviting him to sit beside her. He did and leaned his dark head against her shoulder.

"Sis?"

"Yes, Amos?"

"Will you be disappointed to learn I want to go to the Colonies with Uncle Twitch?"

"No," Serenity answered. "I simply wanted the best I could do for you. I thought working with Tyree and wood and Asher could be an agreeable resolution. Familiar." *Close by.*

"Asher is going to inherit his father's shop and he has a coin and he has a grandfather in Uncle Twitch, who has already made a provision for him in his will."

"You have one of Grandee's coins as well," Serenity reminded him.

"Yes, I know. But unless I go with Uncle Twitch—farther than Marazion—I will inherit only what I can learn."

Serenity could not argue against truth. "What appeals the most to you about the Colonies?"

"Uncle Twitch told me if a man is willing to work, he can make a way for himself. There's a strong middling class, wherein titles and inheritances aren't quite so important. He has worked hard to make his fortune and is highly respected. He will teach me how to do that."

Serenity picked at her shawl's hem. "Uncle Twitch conducts extensive business across the Atlantic. His warehouses and mercantile shops are spread between multiple towns in several of the Colonies: Philadelphia in Pennsylvania; Baltimore in Maryland; Alexandria, Richmond, York, and Williamsburg in Virginia; then Charles Town in South Carolina. He could use someone like you, willing to work and make a way for yourself."

"I know. He told me."

"And does that appeal to you?"

Amos nodded his assent, eyes sparkling, until he added softly, "But who will watch over you while I am away?"

"Oh, I'll be all right here with Grandee. I know you will pray for me, and those prayers will sustain me. The Lord is my strong tower and in Him will I put my trust."

"And will you pray for me?"

She gave his hand two short squeezes. "Every. Day."

"Grandee will move into her new townhouse while I'm away."

"If Tyree is able to get everything finished, I believe she's hoping to move in after Christmas and Yuletide."

"I wanted to help Tyree and Asher install that bull's-eye window on the second-floor landing overlooking the rear garden. The fronts of those townhouses are all required to match, Tyree said. But the backs of the buildings are not, you know."

"I know." Serenity held on to a scrap of gladness at Amos's retained display of curiosity concerning aspects of joinery. Having an alternate plan could prove beneficial. She chided herself for not paying heed to her own admonition now that the dream of keeping her family together was dashed.

"You should go stay with Grandee when she moves to the King's Circus. That way she won't be lonely there, and you won't be by yourself here at Fernsby. And you would be closer to Madelaine and could help keep an eye on Jessa."

"An idea worth looking into." Serenity didn't want to think about it at present—or why Amos didn't think Gideon would be at Fernsby. "What will you miss most, besides Mr. Todd and the horses?"

"You, of course." He bestowed a one-armed hug. "And ... Jessa." Pulling a small wooden horse from his pocket—his latest carving— he handed it to Serenity. "What if she forgets me before I get back?"

"There is that chance." She wouldn't lie to him. "But then perhaps that means you'll have to introduce yourself again when you return. Maybe you can write her a letter and Madelaine will read it for her."

Amos shrugged. "I will go see her many times before I leave. I already know you and Grandee won't forget me."

Serenity tousled his black locks. "Never."

Amos sat up straight. "Do you think a ship's cook can make sweet buns?"

"You'll have to ask." Serenity giggled softly.

"Sis?"

"Yes, Amos?"

"What if I don't belong in America either?"

Serenity swallowed, wondering that herself. "You cannot come to a determination one way or the other until you have seen the place for yourself. I think you are quite brave to take the chance. Uncle Twitch will have a lot to teach you."

"Gideon's been to America. Maybe I could ask him some things."

"Good idea."

"I'm going to take Gideon and Mr. St. James riding tomorrow after church."

"That would be a fine time to ask. Mr. St. James has been to America as well. He might prove an additional resource."

"Does Mr. St. James hunt?"

"I don't know. You'll have to—"

"—ask him." Amos's eye roll insinuated she should have learned that much about Gideon's friend by now. "Colson's talking about a hunt party."

"It was initially Grandee's idea to host a welcome home for Gideon, but Colson is manipulating it for his own purpose."

"Do you mind if I put him on Sparrow?"

"Colson?"

"No, Sis. Colson has his own horse. I mean to let Mr. St. James ride Sparrow. He has such long legs, but Sparrow is the best mannered."

Such *very* long legs. Serenity remembered the image of St. James standing on Mr. Craddock's stool at the tailor's shop, and her cheeks grew warm. "Y-yes, Sparrow is a fine choice for him."

Amos rested his head on Serenity's shoulder again while she admired the carved horse he'd made for Jessa. They sat, without additional words, in quiet company together.

At a later time, Serenity would look back on that conversation in the stable as the night Amos settled in his young mind that he was going to America to learn what he could learn. His decision made, she resolved to be brave enough to let him go.

At the top of the stairs leading to the guest quarters above the stable, Marcus concealed his presence in shadow. He did not wish the brother or sister below to hear him or have them know he'd overheard them. Serenity had such a heart for her younger brother and, with the exception of Colson, was close to the older ones as well—as Jonathan's letter would illustrate. Marcus must deliver that missive to her on the morrow, as he'd promised.

Serenity and Amos's poignant exchange made Marcus doubly glad he'd stayed longer with Johnna and Ian and their little Corinna. Time with loved ones was a precious commodity, and it was his desire to hold on to the remnant of family he had left for as long as possible.

# Chapter 9

*Home of the Northcrafts in Milsom Street, Bath*

"Have you always known?"

Madelaine's stitching stalled at Serenity's blurted question, and before she could answer, Asher bounded in from the joiner's shop, sent by his father to find out what time dinner would be served. And were creamed peas or fried beets on the menu?

When Asher departed, Madelaine resumed slipping the threaded needle in and out of the fine linen, completing a hem on a custom-sized shirt. "Twitch made the proclamation himself once when he was in port. I was eighteen, your age, and he thought it time I should understand he was not my uncle, I was not an orphan, and I was indeed loved. With deep regret, he confessed he'd not been the kind of father he believed I deserved."

"So you had no inkling?" Serenity persisted, picking through a basket of scraps, stacking small piles of like-colored swatches and counting the pieces needed to make a patchwork pocket.

"None." Madelaine bit off the thread and stuck the needle into her heart-shaped red felt pincushion. "He wasn't certain how to break the news, so it just tumbled out in his blunt, no-nonsense manner. He apologized for lengthy absences—essentially running away—and not supplying active influence in my life while I was growing up. He claims his gratitude knows no bounds that I favor less of him and more my mother."

"Do you remember her?" Each year that passed blurred reminiscences of Serenity's own dead mother and further faded the sound of her voice. Of the five Ravensworths, Colson was the one who'd inherited her coloring. The rest shared their father's dark hair and brown eyes.

"I have no memory of my mother at all," Madelaine said. "My earliest recollections of tenderness and caring belong with Lady Aurelia."

Serenity's thoughts still snagged on Uncle Twitch and Madelaine's relationship to him, and any attempt at subtlety failed. "So he went to sea to forget about you, about being responsible for you?"

"No, no. He's never forgotten me. He simply didn't know what else was to be done with a daughter during the midst of his own grief. He was immeasurably grateful Lady Aurelia stepped in when and how she did."

"Have you ... forgiven him?"

"Entirely." Madelaine rethreaded her needle and resumed her stitching. "Twitch Kerrigan did the best he could with what he had to work with at the time. Since then he's done quite well for himself. Recently he detailed the provision he has made for me, Tyree—though that one possesses his own measure of pride—and for both Asher and Jessamine. It is in his power to do now what he was financially unable to before."

Serenity stopped sorting fabric scraps and leaned forward in her chair. "Do you find it odd that he made the offer to all but adopt Amos and take him to the Colonies?"

"No. On the contrary. I've learned when he perceives a problem, he steps up with a way to resolve it. Working with Lady Aurelia for so many years has rubbed off. He is exceedingly generous and kind—so is she. Serenity, Twitch may look and sound gruff, and many are put off by his cut-and-dried ways. He certainly isn't one to cross, and woe to them who do. He is wily, shrewd—can be ruthless in business matters, but only when he has to be. He's very good at what he does, and beneath his windswept bluster lies a good heart."

"That's what Grandee says."

"Are you double-checking for your own knowledge or on Amos's behalf?"

"Perhaps both." Serenity didn't want to admit her alarm at how fast the days on the calendar were passing. Seventeen and sixty-three would be spent in less than two months. She couldn't prevent the weeks from edging away any more than she was able to harness the tide upon which Uncle Twitch's ships would sail. With Amos. Away and across the wide Atlantic.

Jessa stirred in her cradle but did not waken. Her bow lips found her thumb, and her other hand curled around the wooden horse Amos had carved for her. Perhaps Serenity could persuade Amos to sit for a miniature before he left with Uncle Twitch. In fact, she'd request two—one to keep for herself and the other for Jessa. Amos might like that idea—even without needing sweet buns to sway agreement.

"Tell me about the lieutenant, this Mr. St. James." Madelaine fixed her focus on folding the finished garment—which was nearly as tall as she was—while she gauged Serenity's expression.

Serenity shrugged. "He's Gideon's friend."

"I know that much." Madelaine grinned. "What else?"

"That shirt is for him, isn't it?"

"You recognize his measurements already? Interesting." Madelaine bit the inside of her cheek but then laughed. "He sent a message to Tyree indicating he intends to return to Bath in the near future, and would it be too much trouble for me to have four shirts waiting for him?"

"He has returned. Two days ago."

"The tenor of his note caused me to suspect we might see him again prior to Christmastide. By good fortune, I have all four shirts completed."

"Will you invite him to your Twelfth Night festivities if he remains at Fernsby with us that long?"

"Yes, I'm sure we could. Tyree and I would not want him to feel left out. No doubt Gideon would encourage us to include Mr. St. James as well, were I to ask his opinion."

"Oh, no doubt." Madelaine's curious gaze made heat rise in Serenity's cheeks. Her brow furrowed as she confessed, "I cannot figure out Gideon's angle with regard to his fellow grenadier. He would know if St. James is naturally serious all the time or only occasionally. And what causes such deep sorrow in his eyes?" Given enough time, she intended to coax the information out of Gideon.

"Why don't you ask him yourself?" Madelaine sallied forth before Serenity could answer or rebut. "Mr. St. James and Gideon served together?"

"Yes." Serenity remembered how she'd told Amos to ask questions. Perhaps she should as well. St. James seemed an intriguing character, to say the least. "They were in the Great Lakes region, beyond the Colonies, in territory taken from the French at the end of the war. I have gleaned few details, as neither seems willing to speak of it. Scant specifics paint an incomplete tale of having had each other's backs for the past two years, fighting a common enemy together, and each owes the other for getting them through severe scrapes. Both have made mention of a reciprocated saving of arms and lives. Thick as thieves. And ... "

"And?" Madelaine prodded.

Serenity shrugged again. "And the ravens like him."

"Do you?"

"Well ... " More heat suffused Serenity's face, all the way to her hairline beneath her beribboned cap. "I don't know enough about him *not* to like him."

Madelaine's laugh was merry. "Fair enough."

Serenity cleared her throat and steered toward another topic. "How is Asher getting on with his work in the shop?"

"Much to his father's proud delight, Asher has taken to joinery like a duck to water. Tyree has indicated Asher has an eye for the smallest of details and his calculations are consistently proving true. 'Measure twice, cut once,' so they say."

"Did the bull's-eye window get installed in Grandee's townhouse?"

"Not that I've heard as yet, but it must be happening soon, because he needs it in before the plasterer comes to finish the ceilings and molding in the entry hall, dining room, and drawing room."

"Amos did mention he'd like to see that."

"I'll ask Tyree if he's scheduled a time and day. You could come along for the installation or wait to view the completed project, though I think you'd enjoy a tour of the place better once it's free from sawdust and construction debris. It will be beautiful."

A breathy coo rose from the carved cradle at Serenity's feet, within reach of the warmth given off from the hearth fire. The little girl's bright eyes were open wide, and she wriggled beneath her pink coverlet. "Well, there you are."

"She may be in need of a change," Madelaine warned before Serenity picked her up. "I can feel it's time for her to feed."

Madelaine discarded Jessa's wet linen tailclout before diapering her again with a dry one. In her freshly donned gown, Madelaine folded Jessa in a knitted blanket to keep off the November chill. Once filled with nourishment, the baby was momentarily content.

"You observe so intently." In anticipation of an air bubble, Madelaine draped a cotton cloth over her shoulder to minimize any spillage while she patted Jessa's back. "As if trying to memorize each step of what to do."

"It's a long time ago now since you and Grandee took care of Amos after my mother died. I remember holding him and feeding him from a bottle when instructed, but little else."

"You have ample time to learn, and, if you take to the basics of childcare as thoroughly as you have done with your baking and cooking lessons, you will manage just fine."

"I do not want to just manage." Serenity crossed her arms. "If I am to do it, I want to do so right."

"I know you have decided to forgo a season and have no desire to be presented at court."

Serenity lifted her chin. "I have no interest in being paraded through the marriage market to be judged or salivated over like a prime cut of meat."

"Have you given any thought to how you plan on meeting a man for whom you'll one day cook and bake and bear children?" Madelaine asked. "Is that why Gideon brought St. James to visit, do you suppose? Lady Aurelia would not expect you to remain at Fernsby forever—but she will only sanction a match if the man is deemed worthy. Has something happened to cause you to reconsider wanting to be a wife?"

Serenity chose her words, trying to make Madelaine understand. "Yes...no." She sighed. "I— I believe one day I would like to be someone's wife—providing the someone is a man I could respect and grow to love and care for." She added in a forlorn whisper, "Is it too much to wish to be wanted for myself, as a partner and helpmate— like you are to Tyree—and not merely the means to fill or restore dwindling family coffers?"

Madelaine squeezed Serenity's hand. "I've been praying the Lord will bring you to such a man when the time is right. There's no rush, not as far as I can see. Besides," her laughter bubbled, "you haven't any notion as to how much preparing the Almighty must do to that man before he is ready for *you*. Whoever he is, he will have to prove a worthy risk."

Serenity giggled too, then expelled a dramatic sigh. "For now I shall keep at my household lessons until such a time as then.

Nancie Heath gave me her old copy of *The Art of Cookery Made Plain and Easy*. I am happy to report I can plan and prepare a full week's worth of menus. Beyond that, I run out of fresh ideas and start repeating, but I learn as I go. As for babies, they are a bridge to cross on another day but not this one."

At the sound of a melodic chime, Madelaine passed Jessa to Serenity, wiped her hands on her apron, and crossed into the next room to greet the visitor at the front door. "Why, Mr. St. James, how nice to see you again."

Serenity's heart did an odd little skip and she straightened her shoulders. Even without the blatant heralding of his name, she instantly identified St. James's resonant voice. Because it sounded as if he were smiling, she did too.

"My apologies, Mrs. Northcraft," St. James said to her friend. "When there was no answer to my knock, I let myself in. Twitch Kerrigan gave me the direction to find you."

"You indeed have the correct house number. My sewing room is right this way." Madelaine bid St. James to follow her into the well-lit, well-organized space furnished with built-in shelving, cupboards, and drawers, compliments of her woodworking husband. "Tyree's joinery is in the mews out back, which is where he and my son are, and my good friend is visiting this afternoon."

The doorframe connecting the parlour and Madelaine's work-room seemed to shrink as Marcus St. James filled it from top to bottom and side to side. His eyes held no surprise at finding Serenity here, and the recognition forming his smile was genuine.

Serenity dipped a half curtsy, and over the top of Jessa's downy head, she met his steady gaze. "Good day, Mr. St. James." She ignored the furtive look Madelaine shot to her behind St. James's back.

"I've come to fetch the shirts I ordered and ... " St. James caught himself staring, and his neck stock bobbed when he swallowed. "And offer Miss Ravensworth an escort back to Fernsby, if she has need."

"I came in the phaeton," Serenity said. "However, if you are returning directly, you might tie your horse at the rear and we could make the drive back together."

"I should like that."

Madelaine collected the bespoke garments. "I trust Gideon has convinced you to stay for a proper visit this time?"

"He has, and assured me of a most hearty welcome by all his family and acquaintances." St. James bowed to Madelaine, then held his hands out to Serenity. "May I?"

A tad slow in understanding he wanted to hold Jessa, Serenity reluctantly turned the baby girl over to him. Little as she was, Madelaine's daughter looked even smaller in his big hands. Jessa's fingers curled around a covered button on his wine-colored waistcoat. Anchored tight with silk thread, the button could not be pulled lose or stuck into her mouth.

"A good day to you, young miss." St. James was perfectly at ease with the baby. His inane chatter brought forth Jessa's delighted squeal. "She favors you, Mrs. Northcraft, though I also see a marked resemblance to her father in the shape and sparkle of her eyes. Wouldn't you agree, Miss Ravensworth?"

Serenity's "yes" was nigh unto inaudible. Less than a quarter of an hour ago, she had agreed with Madelaine she was in no hurry to find a husband, yet here she was inspecting the specimen before her with certain admiration. St. James was Gideon's friend, she reminded herself, and pressed a palm against her stomacher to quell the quavering nerves in her middle.

When he smiled at her again, a warm chill inched along the nape of her neck. Whatever sadness she'd noticed before was absent, replaced with dancing gold flecks in his amused green eyes.

The pull of their silent exchange broke when Asher entered from the shop, making a beeline toward Madelaine. "Papa asks you to bring a length of felt, plus your shears, if you please."

"You may tell him I'm on my way," Madelaine said to Asher, then tossed a spirited grin over her shoulder to Serenity and the man at her side. "I'll only be a moment." Madelaine gathered and departed with the items Tyree requested, leaving her four-month-old daughter to serve as chaperone.

"You like children." Serenity initiated conversation in the quiet wake of Madelaine's exit. Watching Jessa rather than meet St. James's studious glance, she anticipated a need and retrieved a cotton cloth from the worktable.

"Aye. Little ones seem to have a special knack for drawing a body in with their antics and innocence." He accepted the cloth from Serenity's outstretched hand and wiped drool from Jessa's chin.

"You are on your way to becoming a dab hand at that." Serenity counted the easy rapport Amos had with Jessa a special gift. It pleased her to learn St. James possessed a similar gifting.

St. James walked the perimeter of the sewing room, as if on guard duty, while Serenity stood alongside the worktable, out of his way. Straight to the corner, quarter turn, straight to the corner, quarter turn. "My sister insists Corinna is too young yet to know how to be anything but delightful. Then I tease a reminder that all that delightfulness could change as Corinna gets older, for Johnna is her mother, after all, and has her moments."

His jest was underpinned by obvious love for his family, another something they shared in common. The strength of that familial love formed a lump in her throat at how much she would miss Amos when he went away with Uncle Twitch.

St. James tucked Jessa into the crook of his arm and hummed a segment of a military-themed song, "O'er the Hills and Far Away."

It was a melody Gideon too had a habit of singing on occasion. Softly Serenity put words to a stanza as St. James continued humming. "'Then fall in lads behind the drum, With colours blazing like the sun, Along the road to come what may, Over the hills and far away ... '"

St. James joined his voice to Serenity's by harmonizing the chorus. "'O'er the hills and o'er the Main; Through Flanders, Portugal, and Spain; King George commands and we obey; Over the hills and far away.'"

Had he been staring at her the whole she'd been lost in the lyrics? Picking at the lace edging her sleeve, she couldn't decide whether his thoughts conjured past campaigns or if she might be the cause of his intent focus. "I—" She gave Jessa her full attention, affectionately brushing her pudgy cheek. "I intend to be a doting auntie to this one."

"I shall take note so I can learn to become a doting uncle." St. James shifted Jessa to his other arm, holding her securely as she sat up, smiling and jabbering. Being as tall as he stood, she was a long way above ground level, which afforded her a vantage point quite different from her usual view of the room. She kicked and wriggled, reached toward the shiny brass candleholders on the mantel, and patted Marcus's jaw.

The baby's emphatic cooing preceded a drooly grin, and her eyebrows shot up while she seemingly gave an account in untranslatable gurgles. Serenity and St. James laughed as they sang—in harmony.

Jessa batted a rattle from Serenity's outstretched hand, knocking it to the floor with a clatter. Serenity stooped to retrieve the toy, wiping it with her apron. As she straightened, she had an unobstructed view down the length of the hall and through the open rear half door.

Madelaine looked into the face of the man who tenderly held her shoulders. Tyree dipped his head the same instant his wife stood on tiptoe, and they met in the middle to share a kiss.

Rattle in hand, Serenity turned back toward Jessa and bumped into St. James standing directly behind her, observing the same view.

"They are so in love." Serenity tamped down a spark of envy. She couldn't deny she wanted that bond of mutual affection with a husband of her own.

St. James wasn't looking at her now but focused solely on Jessa. Did he want similar things? Where did he rank love and family, affection and belonging? Gideon adamantly testified his friend was neither married nor spoken for.

"Those two set an example to aspire to." St. James anchored Jessa close as she reached toward her parents in a long stretch.

The wistful sincerity in his voice prompted Serenity to let him in on a bit of mellowed history—nothing either Madelaine or Tyree wouldn't themselves confess, if asked. "They eloped to Gretna Green."

"Truly? Do tell."

Perhaps St. James possessed his own romantic streak. "Madelaine was Grandee's companion, and Colson—" Serenity hesitated, frowning.

"Let me guess. Your oldest brother thought she was pretty enough to trifle with but not suitable enough to be his bride."

"She wouldn't have accepted Colson's suit even if he'd had the gall to ask her! Madelaine only ever had eyes for Tyree Northcraft. *That* is what pricked Colson's pride the most. She cared not a whit for him—or who he thinks he is—and paid him no attention whatsoever. Tyree stole Madelaine away in the dead of night and Grandee did not stop them. In fact, she helped them. Oh yes, they love each other very much indeed."

Madelaine retraced her steps from the shop, her color high. Her glance traveled from St. James to Serenity, then to Jessa, and she offered an embarrassed little grin. "The felt was needed for the lining. Tyree is helping Asher build a Shut the Box game within a small hinged chest. It's to be a going away present for Amos, so you must keep quiet about it."

"We'll not say a word," St. James said conspiratorially, including Serenity in his assurance to Madelaine. "I suppose we should be setting off for Fernsby. How much is my bill of receipt for the shirts?"

As St. James relinquished Jessa back to Serenity, Jessa burped loudly and liquidly.

Madelaine snatched up the cloth and caught most of the milky spit-up—except for one lengthy string stretching precariously to St. James's broadcloth sleeve. "Oh! Not your new coat!"

In short order, Jessa was cleaned up and put to rights. The coat sleeve, spared from staining, would dry without retaining the lingering odor of sour milk. St. James confirmed to Madelaine no harm done and followed her to the desk to settle their business transaction.

St. James secured his horse behind the phaeton and handed Serenity into the conveyance. She scooted aside to make room when he climbed up to the upholstered seat, taking up two-thirds of the bench. He reached for control of the reins the same instant she did.

"Mr. St. James—"

"I know you are capable of driving yourself," he brushed aside her objection, "but it would be my honor to take care of it for you in this instance."

She acquiesced with a slow nod and whispered, "Thank you." Her shoulder fitted neatly between his and the dimpled leather seat-back. Rather than him riding back to Fernsby with her, the situation somehow transposed to her riding back with him.

"Comfortable?" he asked. "I am sorry to crowd you so in this little vehicle."

"I am quite comfortable." The warmth of his nearness was like a protective shield blocking the rushing breeze that increased in strength and chill as the horses picked up speed. At her next breath, she smelled ... peppermint.

St. James navigated the team and conveyance past medieval alleys and through a maze of streets lined with buildings in various stages of construction—some lately finished in fashionable Palladian style, others yet being roofed and trimmed in local honey-hued Cotswold limestone. Clear of Bath, the open country landscape glowed with remnants of autumn's burnished colors.

She peeked at him from beneath her linen market bonnet's brim. The farther they traveled from Bath, his seriousness returned, and she tried to think of something to reinstate his smile. Not knowing when an opportunity to have his undivided attention might again present itself, her tenacity prodded her to speak into the silence.

"Gideon has mentioned more than once that you saved his life. That sounds very heroic to me. Will you tell me the tale?"

Quiet met her query. A nerve ticked along the set of his jaw. His hands tightened on the reins, and he replied hoarsely, "Not today, Miss Ravensworth."

# Chapter 10

*Fernsby Hall, Near Bath*
*Early December 1763*

"Were you expecting company?"

"Other than you, no." Serenity joined Madelaine at the unshuttered library window.

A shiny blue carriage drawn by a matched team halted alongside the gatehouse at the lower end of Fernsby's tree-lined lane. The horses tossed their heads, and their stamping belied a lack of patience and apparent desire to continue onward. A liveried driver nodded at Colson's instruction, and the carriage trundled forward on its ascent toward the manor.

The case clock chimed eleven. Nancie Heath rolled a tea cart into the library and angled it toward the table facing a wall of Palladian windows with light streaming in from the sunlit aviary. Handing a lidded silver container to Serenity, the cook said, "They be the scraps you were wanting, miss."

"Oh yes, thank you for saving those. The ravens will be most appreciative." Attention lingering on the blue carriage, Serenity set the covered dish on the corner of the table without another thought.

The richly appointed equipage—bearing the Brentmoor coat of arms emblazoned on the door panel—continued up the incline.

Madelaine smacked the closest chairback. "The audacity." The ravens' squawking interrupted her agitated tirade. "What brings him here, do you suppose?"

Serenity shivered and rubbed her arms to generate warmth. "I have intentionally avoided the baron at the Assembly Rooms for the past few weeks. Why would he come all the way up here when he's seen Colson at the gatehouse? Colson knows Grandee went into t—" Tardy realization dawned. "She left Fernsby Cottage early, I thought into town, for an appointment of some sort."

"Do you suppose Colson was still abed when I arrived and so believes you here alone?"

"Gideon and St. James have gone to the Pump Room and the mineral baths," Serenity murmured as she watched the baron emerge from the carriage and climb the portico steps. "Or I think that's where Gideon said they were headed."

"Where is Amos?"

"Not in the schoolroom with Mr. Atwater today. Very likely he's occupied with Mr. Todd at the stables."

Beckett stood in the hall scant minutes later, announcing, "The Lord Brentmoor to see you, miss. If you are at home."

So close was the baron on Beckett's heels, he stepped into the library before Serenity could offer any form of civil declination. "Good day, Miss Ravensworth. Uh, and good day to you as well, Mrs. Northcraft."

Bestowing a flustered bow, the baron exuded artificiality while seeming to adjust his original design for arriving sans invitation.

"Lord Brentmoor." Madelaine eyed the baron with cautious curiosity.

Into the stilted silence, he said, "I see you ladies were about to partake of tea. Have I come at a bad time, or may I join you for refreshment?"

Serenity and Madelaine exchanged a mute glance, sharing joint assessment of the intruder. *Brash* would be putting it mildly.

Not wishing to appear as unwelcoming as she felt, Serenity practiced Grandee's lessons in courteous hospitality. "I shall request Nancie Heath bring another cup and saucer."

"No need to trouble yourself, Miss Ravensworth. I shall take care of that." With a deferential nod, Beckett headed toward the servants' stairway.

Pouring steeped tea from the pot, Serenity gave her own cup and saucer to their guest, then attended to Madelaine's. Assorted china plates boasted scones with clotted cream and marmalade, fresh butter, and panna cotta served with berry compote.

The Lord Brentmoor reached toward the covered dish on the corner of the table, and Serenity made no effort to stop him from lifting the lid.

"Ah!" The baron upset the dish of raw pulled-chicken remains—some with bits of skin and feathers still attached—causing a clatter. The contents spilled down the front of Serenity's fawn-colored frock, leaving behind traces of blood as the grisly bits rolled down her skirt and onto the floor.

Surging to his feet, Lord Brentmoor bumped the edge of the table, disturbing the full cups. Tea overflowed the shallow saucers, soaking the lacy tablecloth and linen napkins before pooling on the surface and dripping to absorb into the Turkish carpet below.

Brentmoor's pale expression darkened to furious red, and he muttered an oath under his breath.

Madelaine pressed her hand against her lips to stifle a laugh, while Serenity stooped to avoid eye contact and gather the remnants of the corvids' treat. From the aviary, a raven mimicked, *"Whatsthisnow?"*

Lord Brentmoor scowled, seeming unable to determine whether he'd understood the feathered query or if his own understanding was in question.

Serenity retrieved the stringy meat off the floor and put it back into the silver bowl. "Excuse me." She maneuvered around the tea cart and placed the container on the ledge of the aviary's open half door. Removing the lid, she showed the bright-eyed birds the scraps within.

The ravens patiently refrained until Serenity moved aside, at which point the nearest three delved in to devour with thick, lethal beaks.

Lord Brentmoor dared follow Serenity, halting beside her, an action to which Loxley took immediate exception.

Unfolding his blue-black wings to their full four-foot span, the raven swooped away from feeding to take a protective stance on the overhanging branch arched above Serenity's head. The penetrating glare combined with a menacing *croak* forced Lord Brentmoor into prudent retreat.

Failing to disguise his increasing ire, the baron returned to the chaotic table, where Madelaine plied whatever dry linens she could to mop up the unchecked tea spillage.

Incessant and loud, the ravens' disproving scolding continued until Serenity shushed Loxley, tapping the silver bowl to remind him what he was missing. The others were not saving him any. Each of the birds fended for themselves.

"Go on, Loxley," she whispered with a gentle rub on his scruff. "I thank you for your defense."

"Oh my." Madelaine took in the dark-red splatters marring Serenity's skirt from waist to hem.

Serenity's attempt to wipe away the bloodied smudges made matters worse. Forcing a charitable smile, she found an apology. "I must change and look into getting these stains out. But do feel free to finish your tea, Lord Brentmoor, if you are so inclined. I shall inform Beckett you are welcome to stay—with the ravens—until you are through and trust you will see yourself out." To Madelaine she said, "Mrs. Northcraft, I shall need your assistance, if you don't mind."

"Of course." Madelaine righted her overturned teacup.

The baron sputtered an objection. "But we have not yet discussed the upcoming hunt gala."

Serenity wanted to laugh at such a lofty title applied to the event. "Gideon's homecoming supper, you mean? It will be held in two weeks' time. I suppose you are on Colson's list of guests?"

"Of course. But ... "

"Then I am sure you will also join him in commandeering your eligible lady friends for the dancing. Good day, Lord Brentmoor."

The heat of his anger bored into Serenity's back, which she'd turned on him, and she linked arms with Madelaine. "Do you have any secret treatment to work bloodstains out of this fabric?"

"I have something we can try." Madelaine steered Serenity away from the library. "But I cannot make any promises it will work to satisfaction."

〜

*Deck of the* Oceanna, *Bristol Docks*

Twitch Kerrigan extended a welcoming hand to Ravensworth and Marcus as each crossed the *Oceanna's* gangway from dock to deck. "What brings you two to Bristol?"

Though several weeks had elapsed since the last time Marcus stood on the deck of a ship, he acclimated easily to the gentle rocking as the water lapped the schooner's hull. Kerrigan had told him on the crossing from Alexandria, in the Virginia Colony, that Marcus would have made a tolerable sailor.

"I've something I need to get your perspective on," Ravensworth said.

Kerrigan cast a guarded glance toward the passageway ladder. "My pardon, Gideon, but I'm in the midst of a meeting belowdecks."

"It has to do with Colson—I wouldn't have troubled you otherwise. No doubt Grandee has confided to you that my brother is banking on an inheritance that isn't yet his, and at the rate he's going, he'll have it squandered before my father is cold in his grave."

"Stay here. Let me see if the business is finished up." Kerrigan descended backward down a five-stair ladder into the schooner's lower realm.

While they waited, Ravensworth asked, "You're not still put out about missing a session at the mineral baths, are you?"

"Coming here was a more urgent matter." Marcus rotated his shoulder, extended his elbow, and flexed the fingers of his left hand. "I can bear the soreness a day or two longer, but I am truly hoping the warm mineral water might resolve the aching." He'd experienced a temporary relief after visiting the Warm Springs north and west of Winchester in Virginia. The penetrating heat had helped somewhat, and perhaps like treatments in Bath would garner similar results. The swelling in his elbow was not getting any better.

Kerrigan beckoned Ravensworth and Marcus to come to the salon below. Ducking to clear the short lintel, Marcus was caught off balance—not due to the motion of the schooner but because he locked eyes with a well-dressed blond man sitting at Lady Aurelia's left. It was all Marcus could do to compose an expression of placid equanimity. What on earth was his cousin doing here? In this company?

Lady Aurelia, occupying the seat at the head of the table, was the lone stately woman present for what apparently had been a discussion of some duration and consequence. Marcus acknowledged her with a deferential smile and hoped the wordless exchange between himself and his cousin would escape her notice, but he doubted it. For even in their short acquaintance, he'd learned Lady Aurelia possessed keen powers of observation.

Kerrigan went around the table so that Ravensworth and Marcus were introduced to the other men in attendance: Braden MacDougall,

Kerrigan's factor in England; Alton Grierson, solicitor; and "Oakley Lightfoot," from the Bow Street magistrate's court in Westminster.

"Lightfoot." Marcus gave Rafe's hand an extra-hard squeeze, which the younger man surely felt, though refrained from flinching.

"Lieutenant. Allow me to thank you for your service to our country." The belated sentiment was more than polite verbiage and laced with meaningful sincerity.

"Don't mention it," Marcus commanded. "And what, may I be so bold to ask, is *your* service?"

"Mr. Lightfoot is one of Sir John Fielding's thief-takers." Lady Aurelia's sharp glance shifted between the two men.

"A Bow Street Runner." Grierson referred to the investigator by the name less favored among those in the position. Runner or thief-taker, either term still described a member of the organized policing force paid for collecting and revealing pertinent information, which often led to apprehension and prosecution of wanted criminals. Evidence gathered by these men in Fielding's employ successfully brought scores upon scores before the magistrate for judgment, thereby keeping the streets of London a bit safer. Marcus wondered that Rafe's duties brought him so far from England's capital city on the Thames.

"A case Mr. Lightfoot was working on led him to this shire, and he has concluded that what seemed to be two different matters are in truth linked." Lady Aurelia seemed to have read Marcus's mind. "I have engaged him to dig deeper into his initial investigation. He has recently discovered information pertaining to the Ravensworths that has some overlapping similarities with his previous cases."

Marcus quirked an eyebrow and clamped his jaw to curtail shocked gaping, which might have otherwise followed discovery of his cousin in these unusual of circumstances. He would not call his cousin out—not with so much at stake in this moment—and Rafe nodded in what Marcus interpreted as relieved gratitude.

"I should have known you were already taking precautionary measures." Ravensworth slid into the banquette, seating himself closest to his grandmother. "You are aware then that the banker in Bath confirmed Colson came to him for yet another five hundred pounds. Said it was needed to cover the most recent amount he owed to The Lord Brentmoor. Reportedly, the baron told Colson the next time it would take more than hard currency to settle his debt."

"What else could Lord Brentmoor be after? He must realize Colson won't inherit the Fernsby estate until Sir Nicholas is dead," MacDougall said.

"But Sir Nicholas has a daughter who has a dowry." Kerrigan's low voice was laden with speculation, and his unwavering gaze settled on Marcus. "An attractive, unmarried daughter."

Lady Aurelia pursed her lips, as if suppressing annoyance.

Ravensworth appeared to mull Kerrigan's statement. "What are you suggesting?"

Lady Aurelia spoke before Kerrigan could put his unsavory estimation into words. "As much as I try to love all my grandchildren equally, Colson has been a challenge all his life. Moreso since now his greed and gambling are proving detrimental."

All at the table knew as much, Marcus included.

Lady Aurelia turned a multiple-paged document with a broken seal face down on the tabletop. "Sir Nicholas orchestrated an investigation with his contacts in Italy. If the theory is proven, it may usher in a host of uncertain consequences."

Marcus's powers of observation sensed correlation between Lady Aurelia's vague language and her failure to look directly at her grandson.

"Mr. Lightfoot has corroborated evidence Brentmoor has purchased all of Colson's debts and Colson is solely at Brentmoor's mercy."

Of course, Marcus's accountant cousin would incorporate numbers into his search.

"If Brentmoor holds all of Colson's debt, and he knows Colson may not have access to funds to repay because Father still lives ... " Ravensworth's incomplete thought trailed off.

Marcus and Rafe exchanged a quick glance. This was not merely about Colson spending money that wasn't yet his. There was more to it—perhaps much more—and Lady Aurelia was working with this group of men to assure measures were in place before the Ravensworth house of cards came crashing down.

From his own limited experience, Marcus knew the wheels of hearings and proof and decisions turned with agonizing slowness when answerable to committees of Parliament. Primogeniture verdicts tended to side with established peers of long-standing pedigree than award a case that could rock the proverbial boat. Proving his own viscount title was on indefinite hold until Mr. Appleton had all his documentation assembled. Was Lady Aurelia running out of time in Colson's situation?

"I suspect," Lady Aurelia said, "Lord Brentmoor has more than enough means to leverage against Colson. If at all possible, I should like to avoid the threat of scandal." She blinked back the unshed tears clogging her throat, and Kerrigan laid a comforting hand on her shoulder.

Marcus scanned the collection of faces around the table. "Who is left at Fernsby if we are here? Is Seren—Miss Ravensworth—is she alone?"

"No." Lady Aurelia shook her elegant silvered head. "Serenity mentioned Madelaine was coming for tea."

"We're going back." Ravensworth and Marcus swiftly rose to their feet.

Marcus met Lady Aurelia's troubled expression. "Pray."

"Care to ride along, Lightfoot?" Ravensworth extended the invitation.

Marcus gave an imperceptible nod to Rafe. Oakley Lightfoot acquiesced.

Kerrigan offered his arm to Lady Aurelia, whose face paled in alarm. "I'll tell your driver to take you back in the carriage immediately."

Her eyes conveyed gratitude and silent prayers shot heavenward.

It was but thirteen miles to Bath from Bristol, but even that could be too much time.

⤳

*Fernsby Hall, Near Bath*

In his role as Oakley Lightfoot, Marcus's cousin jotted notations in a sextodecimo-sized book as Miss Ravensworth reiterated the brief visit by The Lord Brentmoor earlier in the day. Marcus mutely thanked God for Madelaine Northcraft's presence. What he'd gleaned concerning the baron, he hadn't liked, and he wouldn't trust the man any farther than he could spit.

When Miss Ravensworth relayed Loxley's protectiveness, Marcus asked Lady Aurelia, "Can that be? Would the ravens actually guard her against an intruder?"

Lady Aurelia rubbed the ruffled scruff of first Loxley, then Marian. "Ravens are territorial. I believe they recognize faces, voices. I once observed a raven pull the tail of a fox hound to divert its attention so a second raven could swoop in and steal its food when the hound was not looking. I cannot vouch for their guardianship. However, it would not surprise me. The corvids are clever—and they know who feeds them." Meeting Marcus's eye, she lifted a brow in an undisguised dare. "They mate for life."

When Lady Aurelia unabashedly winked at him, a roguish smile tugged at the corners of Marcus's mouth. His smiled widened when Miss Ravensworth whispered a chiding "Grann-dee ... "

Rafe kept plenty of distance between himself and the aviary. "I certainly wouldn't want one of those ravens coming after me—a bite from one of them could inflict considerable damage, if they were determined to be mean."

"They didn't mind you when you first arrived, Mr. St. James." Miss Ravensworth referred to his initial visit to Fernsby Hall. "They seem to accept you as well, Mr. Lightfoot."

Confirming Miss Ravensworth's remark, one from the conspiracy of corvids ventured from the aviary and perched on the high back of Rafe's chair. The black-feathered, keen-eyed, thick-billed bird tipped its head to scrutinize the blond man with curious intent, not malevolence, and added a raspy croak to signify approval.

Marcus trusted the Ravensworths, and he could tell his cousin wanted to but could use assistance in breaking the proverbial ice. "Mr. Lightfoot, Lady Aurelia mentioned another case you were working on that led you here to Bath. Tell us, if you are at liberty to do so, what are you hoping to find during your investigation?"

Flipping through his notes, the thief-taker turned back a handful of pages before landing on a previous entry. He cleared his throat. "I was consigned to investigate the case of a missing dairy maid. I followed a lead indicating she worked most recently here at Fernsby Hall."

Miss Ravensworth sat forward on the edge of her seat. "Her name was Jean Collier."

"She disappeared the day Gideon arrived home with Mr. St. James," Lady Aurelia said.

Abandoning his post at the window, Ravensworth turned his attention from the gatehouse to the company before him. "No one has seen or heard from her since?"

"No." Lady Aurelia and her granddaughter shook their heads.

"Perhaps I can ferret out some information," Rafe offered. "Discreetly, of course."

"Perhaps." Lady Aurelia covered a small yawn, signaling the end of further discussion. "Are you lodging in town, Mr. Lightfoot, while you are conducting your investigation? Where should we send word should we need to contact you?"

"I've taken a room at the Bear Tavern."

Lady Aurelia nodded. "I understand their dining room features a palatable menu. Nonetheless, we shall expect you to join us for dinner after Sunday service. Unless you have other obligations?"

"None that I am aware of, my lady." Rafe cast a sidelong glance at Marcus. "In fact, I should be delighted to escort you and Miss Ravensworth to Bath Abbey on Sunday, if you'll allow me."

Marcus curbed the glower he almost shot at his cousin. He needed to make certain Rafe understood the ground rules if they were going to maintain this charade in which they found themselves embroiled.

He couldn't honestly fault Rafe for noticing Ravensworth's only sister or for wanting to spend more time in her company—Marcus conceded he wanted that very thing. Miss Ravensworth was indeed Sir Nicholas's comely daughter with a dowry. A singular creature who talked to ravens and with the serinette, cajoled the birds to "sing," or so she dubbed the cacophony.

Marcus eyed Rafe's lingering observation of Lady Aurelia's granddaughter. Did it matter if Rafe took an interest in her? The strange feeling twisting his gut indicted the affirmative. Mayhap she was starting to matter more than he cared to acknowledge. Thoughts of her weren't yet a full-blown invasion, rather more like a recurring scouting party assigned reconnaissance to test the lay of the land. Marcus ordered his wayward thoughts and dismissed the absurd notion, but when he looked away from Rafe, he found Ravensworth watching him with open conjecture. He shook his head, but Ravensworth knew him too well.

# Chapter 11

*Home of the Northcrafts in Milsom Street, Bath*

Before the end of the week, a package with the Brentmoor seal affixed arrived at the Northcrafts' townhouse, along with a note addressed to Madelaine. She was all astonishment to find twenty or more yards of hand-painted silk taffeta accompanied by organza for ruffles and lace for trim—all procured at Lord Brentmoor's expense and couriered by express from London.

During Serenity's next visit, Madelaine read the brief decree aloud: "I want you to make a splendid gown for Miss Ravensworth to replace the one I inadvertently ruined. Do you estimate it can be done in the space of time left before the hunt gala? I wish to see her wear it that evening. If this cannot be achieved, please let me know at once, and I shall engage another seamstress to see it done up properly."

Serenity simmered as she rocked little Jessa, who found the bevel-edged coin pendant hanging from the gold chain around Serenity's neck. "Presumptuous arrogance. He and Colson are just alike."

"Do you find his increasing attentions a bit odd?" Madelaine asked. "Mayhap it's my imagination, but since you turned eight and ten on your last birthday, Brentmoor seems to have set his attention on you."

"He is not a man I could respect or love." Nauseous bile burned the back of Serenity's throat. "Besides, I have the new sacque-back gown you made for me. I shall wear that to Gideon's homecoming supper, thank you very much."

"A word of advice?"

"Certainly." Jessa tugged at the pendant chain, and Serenity eased it from the baby's firm grasp.

"Don't turn your back on him again. Always make sure you can see him coming so he cannot catch you off guard."

Madelaine's unspoken implication spurred a prickle up Serenity's back. She held Jessa closer to glean a measure of warmth to ward away the sudden chill. "I will endeavor to not be in his company at all."

"Shall I send the taffeta back with regrets?"

"I want nothing from him." Serenity saw Madelaine's smile diminished by a sobering thought. "What? What are you thinking?"

"A year and a day—it's been about that since his wife's funeral, hasn't it?"

"I— I don't know." Serenity could not recall with clarity. "I likely didn't pay attention because it did not directly affect me."

"If I remember right, the procession was duly elaborate. Yet there were . . . whispers. The Lady Brentmoor was healthy enough one day and dead the next." Madelaine paused. "Gideon is aware of the baron appearing for tea?"

"Yes. Gideon has been staying close to the manor. Mr. St. James is installed in the guest quarters above the stables."

"Good. Because the more I think on it, 'tis rather troublesome how Lord Brentmoor showed up on a day when Colson believed you would be home by yourself. It pains me to say it but I believe Colson is mixed up in this somehow."

"Colson owes the baron money. An exorbitant amount of money."

"That cannot bode well for the rest of you Ravensworths."

Serenity sighed. "But I thought Colson paid off his recent losses."

"If it isn't money, what other motive could Lord Brentmoor have for blackmailing your brother? Is he angling for you?"

Stunned horror rounded Serenity's eyes. "Dear God, I hope not!" She placed a soft kiss on Jessa's flushed cheek on the heels of her quick prayer. The distasteful notion that Lord Brentmoor paid her any notice at all made her skin crawl.

"Please take this as the precaution it is meant to be." Madelaine reached for Serenity's hand. "Perhaps it would be best if you not drive into town by yourself. For a time. Either bring Lady Aurelia or Amos along with you, or Mr. St. James, for that matter. If no one is available, send word, and I'll have Tyree or Asher accompany me out to you. Although Fernsby is hardly more than two miles beyond town proper, with that lengthy stretch of solitary road in the countryside, I wouldn't want any ill to befall you."

Serenity fumed but gave her reluctant assent. "At least until we can figure out what is going on."

∽

*Fernsby Hall, Near Bath*

Shifting shadows in predawn light beyond the kitchen window slowed Serenity's birch-twig whisk to a stop in the salt-glazed bowl of batter. Did the nondescript forms originate with human or beast? She wiped her hands on her flour-dusted apron and cracked open the exterior door, a chilly draft slicing into the fragrant warmth. Marcus St. James walked two saddled horses to the top of the stone steps. A boyish grin lifted the corners of his mouth. "Might you spare time for a ride?"

Throwing a quick glance over her shoulder, Serenity bit her bottom lip to stifle a giggle as Nancie Heath conspiratorially shooed her away.

"I reckon sunrise would look glorious from the top of Beechen Cliff," the cook snorted. "Go on. You go with the grenadier."

"I'll be back," Serenity promised, discarding her apron. She ascended the handful of stairs up from the basement kitchen and pulled her shawl close about her shoulders.

St. James had taken the time to have Annie Daye locate Serenity's hooded cardinal, and she was thankful for that as she wrapped herself in the heavy red woolen cloak.

"Your gloves are in my pocket." St. James lifted his elbow so she could retrieve them.

His thoughtfulness earned Serenity's smile.

"Need a leg up?" He squeezed his eyes shut and shook his head as if embarrassed by his inelegant query.

"Thank you, but I can manage," she quipped, biting back a coy laugh. Their conversation plumed against the still-dark and frigid December air. Serenity gathered Sparrow's reins, leading the Cleveland Bay to a low wall bordering the kitchen garden. From there she mounted her sidesaddle and secured her skirt beneath her. "You have been out early these past few mornings." Only after the words were spoken did she realize her confession of keeping track of his whereabouts on the estate.

St. James's triumphant grin confirmed he noted her offhand comment. "I've obliged Mr. Todd in exercising the horses and ridden out on each mount except for Crusoe. Amos has been saving him for last."

"Crusoe is a fine horse for a hunt—or a race. That thoroughbred goes from walking to galloping with nary a breath in between."

"In truth, I prefer your Sparrow. She anticipates, has a smooth gait and a sweet temper—most of the time."

Serenity imagined him mentally adding *much like her mistress.* He'd not uttered the actual words. However, the implication came with a wink.

"I've enjoyed riding her when she is not with you driving into town."

Serenity's smile dimmed. "I have not gone to town in days. It's more than a week since I've seen Madelaine and Jessa." She attempted to keep the sadness out of her voice, but his expression revealed he'd heard. He likely knew she stayed at Fernsby because, along with Gideon and Lightfoot, they agreed this temporary—and safe—solution best.

"Jessa is a sweet child." St. James let Merchant, an Andalusian-Friesian, keep pace with Sparrow.

"Madelaine and Tyree will bring Jessa and Asher along to Gideon's homecoming at week's end. They will come out that morning to help put the finishing touches on the festoons, food, and fashion."

A muscle along the side of his jaw ticked. She thought he was about to say something, but changed his mind.

Silence flooded the space between them as the distance from Fernsby increased. A mile or so farther on, St. James beheld the brightening sky and quoted with reverence, "'Blessed be the name of the name of the LORD from this time forth and for evermore. From the rising of the sun unto the going down of the same the LORD's name is to be praised.'"

The horizon's purple-edge paled, and shades of light pink and mauve gilded the dispersing clouds. "Why haven't I seen you at services at the Abbey since you've come to Bath?" It seemed to Serenity that a man who memorized Scripture shouldn't be a stranger to a pew on Sundays.

"Mayhap you don't see me for worship because you don't attend the services I do."

She studied his rugged profile. "Are you a . . . Dissenter?"

The broad line of his shoulders lifted and settled, the shrug substantiating his own indecision. She listened to his explanation, for he apparently gave matters of faith deep consideration. "I've attended Presbyterian services in Edinburgh and Anglican sermons at various Church of England locales. I've gathered with Methodists, Baptists, and Moravians, here in England and in the Colonies. Whenever I have not been near enough to go to a church building, I remind myself Jesus is in my heart always. I believe in Him, I study His Word, I adhere to the Ten Commandments to the best of my ability—which falls far short of the mark—but am convinced God's grace is more powerful than the ancient law. I've been labeled a nonconformist, but that isn't wholly accurate either. I love God, am thankful He sent His Son to die for me, and that His sacrifice has covered my sins. I am forgiven, so I strive to live my life in a way that brings Him honor and glory." St. James paused in his discourse, admitting, "Some days, that proves easier than others. All I can do is the next right thing. And pray. A lot."

Serenity couldn't disagree. In fact, most of his sentiments were articulations quite similar to her own beliefs. "You might enjoy discussing theological ideas with my brother Jonathan."

"Ah yes, the 'one for the church.' I met him when I was in Oxford visiting my sister. My brother-in-law is a don at Balliol and tutors your brother in his studies."

"Jonathan will be here for Gideon's homecoming as well. He is three quarters into his coursework, and, by the time he is three and twenty, will graduate and be ordained." The last bit of darkness gave way to a blue of the palest hue as the sun's golden light ascended and caused Bath's honey-colored limestone buildings to gleam.

Situated in a natural bowl with hills and ridges all around, and with so many trees having shed their leaves, the panoramic view of Bath was extensive. Pointing over the tallest structures and church spires to a hill beyond the town, St. James asked, "What is that?" He grimaced, pulling his left arm close to his side.

He withdrew a collapsible field glass from his cowhide knapsack. Extending it to viewing length, he closed one eye to focus. Handing the instrument to Serenity, St. James pointed with his right arm instead. "Look, and you'll see what I'm talking about. Straight across to the other side."

Serenity held the field glass to one eye and closed the other. "That's the sham castle—a folly. It was built last year by the same man who owns Prior Park, Mr. Ralph Allen. He used to be the post-master and served as mayor for a time. Would you like to see it up close?"

"If you wish. I have no objection to taking you there."

On their way, St. James had Serenity laughing at several of his amusing tales of military life while in uniform, along with a few relatable pranks executed with Gideon's provocation. The sun crept higher by the time they arrived and dismounted, tethering the horses at a kissing gate.

From foundation to parapet, the sham castle proved a fascinating edifice. Entirely constructed of local Bath stone, the pointless struc-ture all but served as an eye-catching piece of advertising for quality building materials available from Mr. Allen's quarries.

"Some say it was built to improve Mr. Allen's view because it makes an impressive prospect from his townhouse in Bath." Serenity tipped her head back, beholding the rounded turrets on either side of the empty entrance. On both ends, two square towers stood like sentries. Though there was no roof, no windows, and no door, the medieval-themed folly evoked images of King Arthur and Knights of the Round Table at Camelot.

St. James offered his right arm, and together they strode through the doorless arch, marveling at the scaled-down castle. The front of the folly was elaborately decorated, but the back was flat, like a paper cutout, devoid of any detail. Returning to the front, St. James exam-ined the solid portals through which bows and arrows might have been employed in defense had there been actual openings instead of stone. Out of the corner of her eye, Serenity saw a telling shudder steal over him and suspected its cause was due more to some dark memory than the cold air surrounding them. In resounding silence, he turned on his heel and stalked back to the horses.

Following a few steps behind, Serenity witnessed his struggle with an unnamed emotion, one which he seemingly forced aside.

"Are you hungry?" he called, retrieving his knapsack and untying a blanket roll. On the sunnier side of the folly, he folded the blanket double and spread it atop the browned grasses.

She accepted his implied invitation and sat down beside him. "Did you coerce breakfast from Nancie Heath in advance?" Her laugh echoed.

"She did not dissuade me when I helped myself to rolls with bacon and cheddar, and a bottle of cider to share." He held a single tin mug. "We've only one of these, so whichever of us gets it leaves the other drinking straight from the bottle." He pretended to ponder, then gallantly relinquished the mug to her.

Taking the drinking vessel from his outstretched hand, Serenity wondered at the shadows dulling the sparkle in his eyes. Something pained him, and she couldn't decide if he bore a physical ache or one lodged in his heart.

They sat propped shoulder to shoulder, nibbling on breakfast and sipping cider, taking in the view. His mellow song enhanced the bright morning. "'Christ the Lord is risen today, Alleluia! Sons of men and angels say, Alleluia!'"

Serenity added her soprano. "'Raise your joys and triumphs high, Alleluia! Sing ye heavens and earth reply, Alleluia!'"

"You know the words."

"Grandee sings when she waters the plants in the conservatory. With the ravens picking up tunes, she'd much rather teach them hymns than sailor's sea shanties."

Their smiles matched, but he sobered. "I think the ground is frozen. Or my backside soon will be." He gained his feet and offered her a hand in assistance. "Sun might be up, but there's not much warmth in it."

Agreeing the ground in summer might prove more favorable for picnicking, Serenity placed her hands in his. Pulling her to stand, he flinched. He muffled a groan in denial of obvious pain.

"What is the matter, Marcus?"

"Just..." He drew in a breath between his clenched teeth. "Something that should have been healed by now." Favoring that left arm, he collected the remnants of their breakfast picnic and dumped them into the saddlebag. "We should go."

If the sun held little warmth, his tone held none, and the camaraderie between them dissipated like the layers of fog in the valley below. Serenity compared his reaction this morning to that of their ride back to Fernsby in the phaeton. That time, he'd snuffed out their conversation after declining to answer her direct question. This time... She glanced back toward the folly. Something about the sham castle or was it the pain in his arm? Uncertain whether she was supposed to initiate further conversation or if he preferred his brooding solitude, Serenity chose to let him stew in whatever juice he was mulling. She'd inadvertently addressed him by his given name without permission, but that was how she thought of him. Marcus. If he heard her, he hadn't objected—and whatever it was he hadn't said before remained unsaid.

∼⌒

*Fernsby Hall, Near Bath*
*Mid-December 1763*

"We should head back so we have time to dress for supper. Then the dance will come after." Amos slowed Gwinna to a walk and gave the mare's neck an affectionate pat.

Astride Sparrow, Marcus halted parallel to Amos's mount. No doubt the lad was looking forward to the elaborate supper spread more than the dancing. Nonetheless, Marcus and Ravensworth had taken pains to teach the boy figures to a pair of the easier country dances so he would, at the very least, be able to stand up once with his sister and again with his grandmother.

The ash grove's trees stood denuded, barren branches reaching heavenward under the December sky. The breeze ruffled the carpet of dried leaves across the withered grasses of the hills and parkland. Gazing along Beechen Cliff and the ridges bracketing Bath, Marcus prepared for Amos's certain disappointment. "I am not going to supper, and I won't be there to dance."

"But why ever not?" Disbelief widened Amos's eyes. "Nancie Heath has had Annie Daye and the other servants working this whole week making all manner of good things to eat. Serenity contributed to the menu too, not just Grandee. And if you don't go, how will you see the new dress Madelaine made for her?"

Marcus smothered a chuckle. "A new dress, you say?"

"Do you think Serenity pretty?"

"Your sister is very pretty indeed. Wouldn't you say so?"

"Yeah, except I'm her brother and I'm partial to her, but I don't stare at her half as much as you do."

A retort died on Marcus's lips. He could not in good conscience lie to an eight-year-old. "I ... suppose ... you could say I keep an eye on her. Someone should be charged with the duty, as it seems she is generally up to something."

"Oh, she is. She does her best to look after me, and I was glad when she started learning how to cook. At the beginning, some of her attempts weren't so tasty, but she's doing much better. My favorites are the sweet buns."

"You'll have to alert me the next time she makes a batch." Marcus's sweet tooth flared with a new craving.

"She would save one for you if you asked her to."

"I like your confidence, Amos."

"She'd save a dance for you too, you know."

"I told you, I'm not going to supper or the dance."

"But you didn't tell me why not." Amos shifted in his saddle. "So why not?"

"I have already had this discussion with Gideon." Ravensworth objected much the same way Amos was doing now, but Marcus wouldn't change his mind. The excuse was duly true and convenient. "I'm in mourning. Save for your companionship, your brother's, and that of Lady Aurelia and your sister, I am not much for mingling in society these days."

Amos dipped his chin in understanding, but he ventured, "Is it true your father and brother died in the same battle?"

Marcus's reply registered at low volume. "Yes."

"You must miss them."

Affirmation came in the form of a mute nod.

"Gideon and my father went away at the same time. I was six, and I missed them greatly. My father's been in Italy to a more favorable climate that wouldn't aggravate his consumption so much. I wish he would come home and put Colson in his place."

"Colson's not much fun as an older brother?"

Amos shook his head and crossed his arms, like a defensive shield. "Colson's mean. And sneaky. Like a fox set on getting at the hens in the coop, by whatever means suit his purpose." He rubbed Gwinna's neck and coarse mane. "He's always quoting that stupid poem because he thinks it matches us. 'One for the land,' because Colson'll eventually get control of Fernsby. 'One for the war,' since Gideon is a soldier. 'One for the church,' like Jonathan after he's ordained. And 'pray for no more.' I'm the 'no more.' The unwanted one."

"Are you certain about that?" Marcus squinted, exaggerating his depth of thought. "What if it doesn't mean just sons? What if Serenity is the 'no more' since she was born a sister in the string of brothers?"

Marcus leaned over to locate the tender ticklish spot beneath the boy's ribs. Amos's high-pitched glee broadened Marcus's grin.

"I hadn't thought of Serenity." Amos maintained his seat when Gwinna sidestepped to avoid Marcus's reaching hand. Catching his breath, he asked, "What made you think of her?"

Marcus swallowed, not about to admit to himself that she traipsed into his thoughts at too frequent intervals—and he certainly wasn't going to confess it to the boy. "In my family I was born the second son, but I became the youngest son when my brother Matthias died."

"That makes you like Gideon and me combined."

"Something like that, but since my older brother, Lucas, is gone now, that makes me both the eldest and the only brother. The older I get, the more I learn life has lots of complicated things in it.

"Don't let Colson and his dire poem get to you, Amos. Just because your overbearing older brother strives to cast the rest of you into a coincidental pattern in a few lines of ancient poetry for his own self-serving purpose doesn't make it true. Don't give him leave to prevent you from pursuing your own heart's desire."

Amos blinked, then rubbed his chest right in the center. "What's a heart's desire?"

"Something you want. Usually very much."

Gwinna stamped a hoof and tossed her mane while Amos pondered. "I want to go to the Colonies, but I don't want Serenity—or Jessa—to forget me while I'm gone."

Marcus did not let on he'd overheard Amos's previous conversation with Serenity. The boy's young mind lingered on the troubling idea. "You can rest assured your sister will never forget you. Ever. I cannot stake any guarantees on Jessa, as she's just too tiny to tell. I have limited knowledge of little babies."

"Probably so until your wife has one." Amos punctuated his simple logic with a shrug.

Marcus choked back a cough. He'd given hardly a thought to a wife or ensuing children—until recently—when his newly devolved title and financial status seemed to make it a public matter of import whether he produced an heir or not.

Amos regarded Marcus afresh. "You know, you could make an offer for Serenity ... "

Marcus bit his tongue. Hard.

" ... for I am certain she would prefer you to Lord Brentmoor."

A furrow creased Marcus's brow as he turned in his saddle. "What makes you say that?"

"I saw him corner her at the theatre a few weeks ago. Serenity shies away like Sparrow would when she doesn't want to take the bit. There's something not nice about him—too much like Colson."

"Oily jackanapes." Marcus prevented himself from uttering worse.

"I heard Colson tell Brentmoor that Serenity's dowry was worth a small fortune, and Brentmoor told Colson he'd be willing to take her to get the money."

Amos's revelation soured Marcus's stomach. "Have you mentioned this to Gideon?"

"Do you think I ought to?"

"Yes. We should find Gideon as soon as may be." He gave Sparrow's sides an accelerating kick, not looking back to see if Amos followed. A second, more urgent kick sent Sparrow into a full gallop back to Fernsby.

# Chapter 12

Marcus stared at the chessboard, at his cousin, then out the wide window of the apartment the Ravensworths graciously provided for his use. Comfortably furnished and well stocked, he had few immediate needs. Even the bedstead proved accommodating—long enough for his long legs. In his opinion, the greatest appeal was proximity to friends who kept his mind anchored in the moment and not drifting toward the vague, shapeless nothing clouding his memories.

The largest structures of the Fernsby estate—manor, cottage, and stable block—formed a three-sided frame for the terraced garden and its gazebo. During spring and summer, tree leaves impeded the line of sight between buildings almost equal distance from each other. At this time of year, the view was unimpeded through the naked branches. From this second-floor perch, he'd watched the comings and goings of deliveries and staff and the arrival of invited guests.

Rafe executed his next strategic move. Marcus contemplated his. "Tell me again, why are you here?"

Exasperated, Rafe rolled his eyes and scooted his chair away from the table. Picking up the diagonal corners of the chessboard, and without toppling a single piece, he set the game aside.

"Excuse me, it's my move." Marcus held a bishop.

Rafe plucked the ivory chess piece from Marcus's hand and set it with the others. "Were you not paying attention when we were part of this same discussion on the *Oceanna*? Lady Aurelia hired me to investigate Colson and the precarious situation his gambling losses have created. He's backed himself into a desperate corner, and he's reckless enough to commit desperate acts."

"Exactly what does that have to do with being a junior accountant at a fashionable London toy store?"

Rafe plopped back down onto the chair opposite Marcus. "Once I finished at Cambridge, I looked for a job. I accepted a junior accountant position at Hamleys. Steady work but a mite staid and dull. I wanted to do more, to help people."

The St. James family exhibited a generational penchant toward service and duty entwined with compassion.

"I started dabbling in detecting and later fed gleaned tips to Bow Street. The magistrate and runners acknowledged my findings showed merit. I contributed solid leads that led to solved cases. I accepted the odd thief-taker assignments here and there when they needed part-time assistance. If a full-time position becomes available at some point, I shall apply." Rafe shifted in his seat. "Between now and whenever that may be, I keep working at Hamleys. A few months ago, I came across a concerning number of discrepancies in the toy store's accounting books. When I brought them to the notice of the senior accountant, he requested my help in solving who was behind the embezzlement. I was encouraged to stay on. Undercover. The culprits were apprehended. The successful resolution earned the gratitude of both the senior accountant and the owner.

"Not long ago, the senior accountant came to me at his wit's end. His niece had run away, and he hired me to locate her. My search for the niece is what caused my path to cross with Lady Aurelia. Jean Collier was last known to be working at Fernsby Hall. She was seduced by Colson, then disappeared."

"And what else?" Marcus stared at Rafe until his cousin broke eye contact.

Caught, Rafe's guilty smile flashed, and he confessed. "Lady Aurelia has employed me to investigate you."

Marcus crossed his arms, mildly affronted. "She doesn't trust me?"

"Lady Aurelia doesn't trust *anyone* where her dearest grand-daughter is concerned, and even though you are associated and in good standing with her second grandson, she wants to make abso-lutely sure. It's my understanding your name has been thrown into the ring as a potential suitor. Her intent is to establish—before anything goes anywhere—if you are worthy."

"Oh, this is rich." A rumble of laughter escaped Marcus. He slapped the tabletop, as if relishing the most amusing of jests. "Have you reported to her? Does she know who I am?"

"No." Rafe slowly shook his head. "Not yet. I've had to be rather ... circumspect."

"Aye, I'd imagine so. Otherwise, she'll find out who *you* really are."

Rafe conceded the point, sat in his chair with ankle crossed over knee, and steered the conversation back to its original course. "The leads in the Jean Collier case had grown cold until I discovered she was last seen in Colson's company at Claverton Downs." Something outside, beyond the window, captured Rafe's attention. "Well, if that isn't speaking her into existence, I don't know what is."

Marcus peered through wavy glass panes. No otherworldly spec-ter of a deceased dairy maid, but Miss Ravensworth approached on the bricked path from the manor, probably straight from the kitchen given she toted a medium-sized hamper on one arm and carried little Jessa Northcraft in the other. "Stay put."

Rafe snapped a silent salute, obeying the terse command.

Marcus descended from the guest quarters on stairs leading to the stable block's ground floor. He pinned Ravensworth's sister with a quizzical look.

She halted in the alley dividing the rows of stalls, empty save for Sparrow, the Andalusian-Friesian, an Irish Draught, and an Irish Cob. All the thoroughbreds and the other Cleveland Bay participated in the hunt. These remaining four equine heads extended over their respective stall doors, nickered their various greetings to her, and observed with interest the human interaction. The air smelled of straw, horse sweat, and leather—and crackled with an undercurrent of muted awareness.

"Are you daft, woman? You'll sully that skirt here in the muck."

Miss Ravensworth swung the covered basket aside, shifted Jessa farther back on her hip, and leaned to examine the hem of her day dress. "No harm's done."

"To what do I owe this pleasure?" Without asking and ignoring the twinge of pain in his left arm, Marcus took Jessa from Miss Ravensworth. His relieving her of the hamper left her with empty hands.

She clasped them behind her back and fidgeted under Marcus's lazy scrutiny. "Amos tells me you are foregoing supper and dancing because you're in mourning."

The black armband sewn onto his coat sleeve reiterated the subtle reminder.

"That, plus I never received a proper invitation. As host of the event, the invite should rightly have come from Colson."

"But Grandee invited you to supper and—"

His funny faces captured Jessa's attention. "I occupy the guest suite at Gideon's behest, but I have the distinct impression I'm the last person Colson would wish to see at Fernsby this evening."

"Why?" The stable's interior light slanted to shadow his features but revealed hers to his unhurried perusal.

Before he formed an answer, she pointed to an unfamiliar mount in the stall nearest the tack room. "Whose horse is that?"

"Hired from a hostler in town. As more guests arrive, so will there be more carriages and mounts." The contents of the hamper smelled good enough to make his mouth water. "What's in here?"

"I brought a sampling of supper, since you refuse to join us."

"You are very kind. I thank you for your understanding."

The flash of her eyes told a different story, making him want to believe Miss Ravensworth would miss dancing with him as much as he would with her.

Jessa squealed, insistent on having her share of the conversation, contently gurgling first at Miss Ravensworth, then at Marcus.

"Stay close to Gideon tonight. Or Jonathan." Marcus willed her to trust him enough to honor his suggestion. "Amos tells me you have a new gown for the occasion. I should have liked to have seen you in it."

A rosy blush stole across her cheeks. She met his bold inspection without flinching. "Madelaine is waiting on us back at the house," she whispered.

Marcus returned Jessa with reluctance and repeated his caution. "Remember what I said."

"I wish you would tell me why, but very well."

Marcus let Miss Ravensworth suppose he, like her brother Gideon, was accustomed to having orders obeyed.

In the distance, the hounds barked a discordant ruckus, surging past Mr. Todd, who served as huntsman with his horn, then raced beyond the collection of riders. The pack veered as a clotted mass toward the stream.

"They must have taken up another fox's scent. They lost the first line about an hour ago."

"Colson and all his friends?"

"Jonathan went out with them. And Amos."

Marcus leaned down to confide in her ear. "I saw you out there this morning. Riding in disguise with the first group. Would you have done so if Jonathan and Amos were not there to cover for you?"

"No." An emphatic shake of her head, reason in her tone. "I used to go along with them on occasion, but Grandee has decreed this would be my last time."

"You cannot mean she doesn't want you to ride?" Marcus hoped that was not the case, as he had deliberations in progress for another early sunrise excursion.

"No, of course not. Riding is essential. She insists she doesn't want me going out hunting with strangers from now on."

"Wise woman, your grandmother. Did Gideon know of your antics?"

"When we were younger, it was his idea initially. It was a lark, but we are not children anymore." The growing din outside caught her attention. "I don't know where Gideon has gone. I have not seen him since breaking our fast this morning."

Marcus sincerely expected his friend was following up on Amos's disquieting report.

The hounds' baying grew even louder. Overhead, several ravens circled above the rowdy canines. Something bigger than a fox had been found. Much bigger.

⁓

Sentimental nostalgia spawned the original impetus for what Lady Aurelia intended as a simple homecoming supper. A grateful welcome back for a returning soldier. A gathering of those she held most dear. An experimentation to assess Serenity's domestic achievements.

Colson's true motives for appropriating plans and elaborating the event stayed unknown and suspect. While the day's hunt started off well enough, the unexpected incident at the footbridge set things to unraveling.

Lady Aurelia briefed Mrs. Todd and Beckett, pushing the supper start time forward by a full hour. Better to keep the attention of Colson's guests occupied rather than linger aimlessly or verbalize unfounded speculation. She shouldered responsibility, took a calming breath, and mustered her most hospitable countenance.

Praying with all her might, she ceased wrestling against the tempting impulse to nullify the rest of the evening, as its outcome might yet be salvaged. To concede would give Colson the satisfaction of wrecking the celebration, and that she refused to allow.

She lifted her head with an imperious tilt to her chin, determined to play her part. No one need know how close things teetered on disaster's precarious edge.

Outside, Oakley Lightfoot assisted the constable with a report and removal of the deceased dairy maid's remains before nightfall halted their labors. She had to trust their promised discretion would hold. The *Bath Herald*, along with other local newspapers, often printed sensational details of criminal activity. The Improvement Acts dealt with regulation for Bath's watchmen, but the reason thief-takers like Lightfoot had jobs was because victims of crimes had to pay for information and prosecution. Catching a criminal in the act of committing said crime, then delivering them personally to the magistrate's court remained the surest way to attain justice.

Lady Aurelia's appetite suffered. Aside from food, she had no stomach for Colson's invited guests—a dubious set with The Lord Brentmoor leading the charge. Perhaps a masquerade might have been a more fitting scenario. Between Colson and Brentmoor, they concealed false pretenses strewn amid lies and deceit.

Beckett, garbed in the ceremonial black and red of Fernsby Hall's designated livery, announced supper ready to commence. Lady Aurelia exercised forbearance while waiting upon Colson. As host, his duty was to lead her—the hostess and senior lady in attendance—to the dining room and place of honor at the head of the elaborately set mahogany banquet table.

Colson bestowed an obligatory kiss on her cheek, then moved to take his place at the table's foot. His condescending acquaintances filed in to their corresponding seats.

Shimmering beeswax tapers set in crystal chandeliers pooled their glow with that from the brass candelabras adorning both crackling fireplaces. Deepening twilight caused the room's flickering interior to repeat unendingly as a mirrored reflection in the expanse of panes.

Twitch accepted the offered place at her left hand, and Madelaine and Tyree scooted into the chairs on her right. Lady Aurelia shared with them concealed amusement as they observed the baron's foiled attempt to maneuver a seat next to Serenity.

Gideon and Jonathan strategically flanked their sister, right and left, leaving the baron's only choice to settle for the seat across the table. A deep cut-glass bowl at the top of the epergne boasted a classic arrangement of white winter roses, holly, ivy, and evergreen. The bouquet created a beautiful—and useful—screen. Serenity cleverly ensured the thick floral barrier stood between herself and The Lord Brentmoor.

Irritation flared over his miscalculation, as he'd not accounted for the height and breadth of the sterling-silver centerpiece.

From where Lady Aurelia sat, it appeared two separate dinner parties converged in the same dining room by sheer happenstance, attendees categorized into distinct groupings. An illusory atmosphere displayed cheer and good spirits, yet impressions were faulty. All was not as it appeared on the surface.

Tactless and sullen, Colson carried an air of shock about him, and he failed to introduce any of his crowd—numbering a dozen and clad in prescribed finery. Attempted conversation proved fruitless, as they made no effort to join in polite discourse. Gossipy whispers persisting since the hunt's abrupt end did not escape notice.

Gideon blithely ignored those dour dispositions and regaled his immediate listeners with tales of his tamer experiences in America.

It comforted her to observe his anticipation as he eyed the various dishes properly arranged down the table's length. His gaunt appearance upon returning home from his stint in the Seven Years' War worried her. Between campaign rations, healing wounds, and a broken heart she wasn't supposed to know about but for Serenity's whispered confession, Lady Aurelia continued to petition the Almighty for Gideon's full and complete recovery.

The first course, served by a combination of Fernsby's own staff and temporary hires, consisted of gravy soup with chicken and bacon, giblet pies, Scotch collops, roast beef with horse radish and pickles, and a fine boiled pudding. Madelaine, Twitch, and Lady Aurelia were the outnumbered few who enjoyed the stewed mushrooms. In truth, she was surprised Serenity remembered to include mushrooms on the menu at all given her unmitigated aversion to them.

Twitch met Lady Aurelia's eye. The quirk of Jonathan's brow and Gideon's intent gaze suggested they too monitored the frosty words Lord Brentmoor and Colson exchanged—a modulated venting of the former's spleen. Unease from Colson's end of the table threatened to subdue the family. She entreated well-read Tyree to relay a story to lighten the mood for Gideon's sake.

Lady Aurelia listened to Tyree's animated retelling but also remained distracted by the sobering discovery of the former dairy maid. The poor girl had been done in, murdered, if not on Fernsby's grounds then somewhere nearby, and recently deposited near the stream's footbridge. Had the macabre unearthing, today of all days, after the girl had gone missing weeks before, been a message of sorts—or warning?

Beyond the rim of her goblet, her scrutiny fell upon her eldest grandson. Colson squirmed, guilt etching his forehead above angled scowling brows. Though she wished it otherwise, it took little imagination to jump from gambling debts to blackmail and violence. Colson represented a full-fledged problem.

As staff removed soiled first-course linens and dishes prior to lay-ing out clean settings and implements for the second course, Serenity nodded approval for Mrs. Todd to proceed. She then leaned toward Jonathan and whispered a directive.

"Never fear, Sis," he assured with a nod. "I can follow instructions."

At the conclusion of the second course, Gideon administered a one-armed hug about Serenity's shoulders. "Sis, I am impressed with all you've done in putting together this homecoming."

Serenity's color was high, reveling as she did in the unaffected adoration of her nearest brothers. "Grandee, Madelaine, and Nancie Heath helped me a great deal. We all wanted you to know how much you are loved and how much you were missed."

Serenity nudged Jonathan with her elbow. He dutifully raised his goblet of punch. "A toast for my older brother: May God grant health and happiness to you now that you are back here where you belong, and may He continue to protect you when you wander afar. Welcome home, Gid."

"Thank you, Jon, and thank you each for being here for me." Gideon cast a sly glance at Serenity. "I shall take the liberty to add, though he's not present and sends his regrets, a toast to honor St. James."

"Hear, hear!" Madelaine hastened to lift her goblet with the oth-ers. "We are indeed thankful you brought Mr. St. James as a new friend into our lives. Even in such short acquaintance, he has had a favorable impact on us all."

The rim of Lady Aurelia's goblet clinked when touched to those on either side of her. She sipped her punch and mulled an uncomfort-able certainty. As veteran grenadiers, Gideon and St. James could be transferred as needed to other units or seek staff appointments if desiring to continue with soldiering. Decisions such as these would be made with serious consideration of potential ramifications, but likely not before the new year.

"Trusted friendships are rare and cherished, are they not, dearest?" The budding attraction between the grenadier and her granddaughter was noted and not unwelcome. Gideon would not object if anything substantial came of their association either.

Lady Aurelia spied Amos and Asher on the grand staircase, peeking over the newel post with shameless guilt and stifled chuckles. Their gazes centered on the buffet and the cleverly crafted marzipan hedgehog displayed among the desserts. Two distinct spoon marks verified their deliberate sampling of the confection before its arrival in the dining room.

The spoon marks attracted Serenity's attention as well. Her initial mortification gave way to exasperated amusement. Lady Aurelia glanced away, lest they each unleash a bubbling torrent of unchecked laughter.

Beckett rounded from the butler's pantry and escorted his young charges upstairs to Amos's bedchamber. Madelaine agreed it easier to leave Asher and Amos reading or playing with toy soldiers rather than insist on their participation at a dance they wanted no part of.

Lady Aurelia committed Amos into the Almighty's keeping. Again. Her youngest grandson had a wide variety of lessons to learn under Twitch's expert tutelage. She simply had started to miss the boy already, and departure loomed but a few weeks hence.

Lord Brentmoor stood and struck his crystal goblet with his knife handle twice, discharging a solid bell-like tone that quieted the swirling discussions at both ends of the table. "Friends, I should like to share my good news. Another toast for congratulations and felicitations is quite in order. This very afternoon, I settled a most fortuitous deal with Mr. Ravensworth." He offered a half bow to his host.

Colson slouched lower in his chair as the baron went on. "You see, I have obtained his endorsement for my endeavor to charm his lovely sister and secure her consent to becoming the next Lady Brentmoor."

Confusion, shock, and astounded gasps delayed a smattering of applause from the far end of the table. Stunned silence descended at this end, until Twitch sputtered a dry cough.

Face ashen, Serenity gripped the hands of Jonathan and Gideon. All eyes were upon her—some in sympathy, some in expectation—awaiting reply.

But words failed her.

# Chapter 13

*Fernsby Hall, Near Bath*

"Dearest." Lady Aurelia conjured a soothing smile for her grand-daughter and silently willed her to believe all would be well. To her relief, Serenity's breathing resumed.

Delicately clearing her throat, Lady Aurelia masked disbelief with a magnanimous thread of a smile. "This is news indeed, Lord Brentmoor. When, pray, did you plan to apply to my granddaughter directly to see if she would be amenable to entering into an understanding? I was not aware you had written Sir Nicholas to offer your suit."

"Father is not here." Colson sneered and thumped his chest. "*I* gave Brentmoor my permission."

"But *you* are not her keeper!" Gideon tossed his crumpled napkin aside.

Serenity's urgent tugging on Gideon's arm prevented him from instigating a long-anticipated fight.

"You are not in control of her," Lady Aurelia said.

"Nor are you in control of her dowry." Twitch's smooth voice exposed the transaction Colson and the baron were truly after.

Serenity lifted her goblet to her lips and took a small sip. Lady Aurelia suspected she was buying time, corralling tempestuous thoughts, attempting to formulate a courteous but conclusive response.

Madelaine offered no profound advice in spoken words to her friend but communicated calming reassurance. Lady Aurelia had no doubt their urgent prayers matched, dispatched heavenward with all haste.

"Sis?" Jonathan squeezed Serenity's hand. "What say you?"

With willowy grace, Serenity stood, chin raised in dignified determination. She had never looked more like her free-spirited mother than she did in this moment. One by one she faced Lady Aurelia, Gideon, Jonathan, Madelaine, and Tyree—and she bestowed an inclusive nod to Twitch. Her timorous smile expressed comprehension of their durable support.

Inhaling a fortifying breath, she turned to The Lord Brentmoor, smile ebbing. "I thank you, my lord, for the high compliment of your intended proposal, but I have no plans to be married at present."

"Serenity!" Colson pounded the table. China, crystal, and silver clattered.

Shards of temper glittered in the baron's ice-blue eyes. His face turned a red darker than his hair, a shade almost rival to Gideon's uniform coat.

Serenity added, "Besides, I am leaving England. For several weeks now there have been plans afoot for sailing to the Colonies in British North America. I have decided I will be on that journey."

Gideon rose to stand at his sister's side, clasping her hand in his own. "Sis . . ."

Lady Aurelia was grateful for Twitch's presence and relied on his strength as a steadying force. Serenity's pronouncement didn't seem to startle him any more than it did Tyree, though it certainly surprised Madelaine.

"I am relieved to learn you have arrived at a choice, dearest. We shall discuss it further at a later time." Lady Aurelia pasted on a rallying smile. "Colson, why not escort your guests to the drawing room until the musicians are ready to begin?" This night was already interminable, and the sooner it ended, the better for them all.

His friends took the hint and followed their host's directions to the location of the drawing room. However, Colson stayed, and The Lord Brentmoor continued to occupy his seat, making a show of boredom and inspecting his fingernails. "Perhaps you need explain to your sister the deal we closed is not merely a suggestion."

Tyree, Gideon, Jonathan, and Twitch created a barrier around Serenity.

"Go to my cottage." Lady Aurelia lowered her voice, which shook as much as her hands. She wanted Serenity out of the middle of this outlandish muddle. "Make haste and lock the door."

Serenity blinked.

"No." Gideon suggested a counter option. "Go to the stable instead. St. James is upstairs. Tell him I sent you."

Lady Aurelia nodded in agreement and stroked Serenity's pale cheek. "Then you'll be in company, dearest."

Head high and back ramrod straight, Serenity exited the dining room. Beneath her courageous veneer, Lady Aurelia presumed her granddaughter's insides a jumbled tangle of nerves.

Too warm near the fire, Lady Aurelia moved to a half-open window to breathe in the crisp night air. With tears streaming, Madelaine joined her.

"Never fear. I shall speak with her." Oh, she grasped what Serenity was about, impulsively seizing on an expedient escape and thereby removing herself from conflict. But did Serenity comprehend what heartache such a lengthy separation would wrought? Lady Aurelia and Madelaine would be bereft by Serenity's long absence—if she truly meant to go.

To Colson, she said, "If you and your band of friends cannot maintain a charade of civility, I am asking you take them now and go. Before any more trouble erupts. You have done quite enough."

"She has no idea what she's doing! How *dare* she!"

"How dare you is the better question." Praying for the good Lord's guidance, Lady Aurelia locked gazes with Colson again. "You leave her be, and you ensure Brentmoor leaves her be. Do you understand?"

Colson reared, shaking off the hand she laid on his arm. "Oh, I understand—far more than you do! I gave my word to Brentmoor," he pointed in the direction of where the baron lounged in his chair, "and she had no right to break the promise!"

"A promise you had no right to give." Jonathan spoke unvarnished truth. "What were you thinking, speaking out of turn on her behalf? You have no grounds."

With reckless disregard, Colson heaved a vase at his younger brother. Madelaine screamed. Agile and with quick feet, Jonathan dodged the projectile. Porcelain shattered against the wall. Water and flowers rained down.

"Colson Ravensworth!" Lady Aurelia's pity warred with utter exasperation.

"Why do you insist on calling him that still? Have you not divulged the entirety of the situation to him?" Twitch asked.

"Not as yet. I had hoped to before tonight, but as you see, such has not been the case."

Colson stopped prowling. "What situation?"

Twitch started to speak, but Lady Aurelia held a finger to her lips, for Gideon and Jonathan would also be significantly impacted by the eventual revelation. "Tomorrow will offer plenty of time to unravel your predicament."

Colson's tantrum smoldered. "My predicament is this: I can't pay what I owe! Brentmoor must be repaid."

"You may do what you will with your mother's money. I have already instructed Alton Grierson to bring a bank draught for you." Lady Aurelia slipped her hand through her pocket opening.

"Mother's money?" Confusion burned in Colson's narrowed eyes.

"Your mother left you an inheritance."

Greed jostled Colson's anger. "Then why haven't you let me have it?"

"It came to light only recently." Lady Aurelia heard practice strains of "Sir Roger de Coverley" floating from the drawing room. "Be warned, Colson—it will not be enough to settle your debt with Brentmoor, nor with the tailor or the bootmaker in town, or any residual card sharps either."

"Then I'll cover the shortfall with Father's money."

"If you mean Sir Nicholas's money, then I am sorry to advise you there will be no future access for you from his accounts." The room was suddenly hotter than Nancie Heath's bake oven, and all carefully laid plans rendered askew.

"This is preposterous!" Rage mounted in Colson, and he speared Jonathan and Gideon with a menacing glare. "I suppose *they* could access the accounts if they had need."

Lady Aurelia sighed. Out of the corner of her eye, Twitch's nod of encouragement bolstered her decision, and she reluctantly concluded tomorrow would not arrive soon enough after all. "Yes, of course there are provisions and allowances for Gideon and Jonathan, and even young Amos. They are Sir Nicholas's legitimate sons."

The bald implication behind her staunch declaration drained the color from Colson's contorted face. "What—"

Twitch positioned himself between Lady Aurelia and her grandson, anticipating Colson's next volatile reaction.

"Now is not the most opportune moment to go into the matter, but," Lady Aurelia produced a letter from her pocket and handed it to Colson, "once you read this, it will explain all. It is your mother's confession. She wrote it after she married Sir Nicholas."

"The letter exists." Confounded, Colson shook with fury and swore with venom. "Brentmoor has dangled his high-handed hints over my head for months, threatening disgrace upon the Ravensworth name, but I assumed he was bluffing. Here you've had it all along."

Lady Aurelia recollected the night Colson had ransacked Sir Nicholas's desk. It stood to reason he had been looking for proof to deny Brentmoor's assertions. "That letter serves as confirmation. Take it. You will need it in order to claim the money she left you. Mr. Grierson, Sir Nicholas's solicitor, has his instructions, along with a duplicate of the original."

"You're all in this together—out to ruin me!" Colson hurled another vase, this one colliding with a gilt-framed mirror, its spider-web cracks breaking into jagged pieces. He knocked over a chair in a scramble to reach Gideon.

"You have ruined yourself." Gideon would not back down. "You're all greed and arrogance."

"We'll see where loyalties lie now, won't we?!" Colson grimaced, anger resurfacing.

"Loyalty? Can you properly define that word?" Jonathan asked. "Your loyalty hasn't been with this family for quite some time. Always out for what you can get—and then you can't manage to keep it."

Lady Aurelia swayed. The chair Brentmoor occupied was empty, and no one had seen him depart.

Twitch pulled her arm through his. "Let's navigate through the rest of tonight. Tomorrow we'll discuss all this and its repercussions in the cold light of day."

"Until then, you'd do well to be on your best behavior." Taller than his half brother, Gideon straightened his broad shoulders, emphasizing the implicit warning.

"You have no idea what Serenity has done." Colson jabbed Gideon's lapel. "She's going to be the death of all of us!" Colson quit the room in a fury and barreled into Beckett. The sparkling wine intended to celebrate Serenity's engagement popped like a gunshot, its ejected cork slicing across the room.

Fernsby's front door opened and closed. Ravensworth's sister crossed the portico, lantern in one hand, gathered skirt in the other, selecting the path leading toward the stable block. "What is she doing?"

Marcus pulled on his cloak and descended the apartment stairs two at a time. He intercepted her at the garden's wrought iron gazebo.

"Seren—Miss Ravensworth. Is all well?" He ducked to see her face by the light of the cressets lining the bricked walkway.

"I—" Her breath caught, and her eyes roamed his face. "Gideon sent me."

Marcus looked toward the brightly illuminated house. Music floated from the drawing room, where shadowed forms of the dancers continually shifted, not allowing for an accurate count. From the dining room, angry voices carried.

He couldn't see Rafe, but his cousin moved in stealth close to the house, conducting reconnaissance, hoping to glean any scrap of useful information.

Without a hamper or baby in tow, Serenity wrung her empty hands. Marcus unclenched his fist, hesitating before gently touching her shoulder. It was one thing to seek him out in the afternoon with Jessa as chaperone, but after sundown quite another. Ravensworth would not send her to him without reason. Marcus ought to consider it an honor his friend thought so well of him—enough to entrust his precious sister to Marcus's care.

One step more brought the toes of his boots in contact with the tips of her embroidered slippers and erased the distance between them. Lavender mixed with vanilla scented her skin and hair.

"Amos was wrong. You don't look pretty in your new gown—you are beautiful."

She bit her lower lip to rein her smile and kept her eyes trained on his face. "I thank you, Mr. St. James. It pleases me to hear you say so."

In spite of the night's dropping temperature, her cheek was warm and soft beneath his fingertips. His heart tripped. Resting his hands on her satin-encased shoulders, he angled her in the cresset light. A sheen played along the fabric's surface. Ribbons and pearls were woven into her raven-black tresses, and the sovereign bezel pendant adorned her neck.

He took note of the smallest details, in case she flitted into his dreams. She was lovely in her frock with stripes of green, grey, and copper, embroidered roses and ivy tendrils, neckline and elbow-length sleeves edged in frothy cream lace. The feminine ruffles offset the straight pleats draping from her shoulders and formed a short train at her heels.

"Do I pass inspection?" Her arched brow and teasing sparkle in her ginger-brown eyes made him grin.

"Can you dance in this fine raiment?"

"I can." Her lilting laugh provoked his deeper chuckle. Accompanied by music filtered from the house, Marcus bowed. Serenity curtsied. She followed his lead and placed her smaller hand in his. They circled a half turn to the left, a step back, then circled to the right, shoulders brushing. He couldn't stop looking at her any more than she could stop looking at him.

"Are you going to tell me why you've come looking for me? You seem a bit troubled."

She faltered mid-step in their nonsensical dance. She shivered and rubbed her arms, sputtering, "I— I have turned down a proposal of marriage." Her fists clenched, jaw set. "And I have an awful feeling someone is going to pay for it."

Marcus removed his caped cloak, her announcement as jarring as a punch to his gut. He bundled her within the heavy woolen folds.

"I don't want to be a baroness. Most certainly not Brentmoor's." Tears balanced on her lower lashes. "His first wife ... she was with child before they wed and didn't live to see their anniversary. The baby was stillborn, and the baroness died rather suddenly. Not a very appealing prospect, wouldn't you agree?"

"Not in the least." His tone softened. "What is it that you want, Seren—Miss Ravensworth? Of what do you dream?"

A leading question that had her covering the stain of blush on her cheeks with both hands. She forced a laugh, glancing toward the cold light of the moon. "Mayhap we have similar dreams?"

"Perhaps."

She shook her head, bewilderment in her expression. "I told them I was going to go to the Colonies with Uncle Twitch and Amos." The hand holding the coin necklace shook. "I don't know if I am truly prepared to do that. I would be near Amos, though far from Grandee, Madelaine, Jessa, my brothers, and ... " She stopped shy of saying "you" aloud. But her eyes conveyed what her spoken words didn't.

Marcus licked his lips. Was it possible the growing attraction between them was mutual? It would be short lived if she decided for leaving. That was then, and this was now. He pulled her close, and she willingly accepted the invitation of his embrace. Little chance she wouldn't hear his heart pounding with her head resting against his chest. Ingrained in his nature was the urge to guard with his life the people most important to him.

He bent his head lower. Her breathing slowed. "Serenity?" His fragmented question lingered. She raised up on tiptoes to decrease the last bit of distance separating their whispers.

Marcus heard Rafe's noisy approach before Miss Ravensworth did, and he prudently stepped aside. She shivered when his arms no longer encircled her.

She looked as disappointed as Marcus felt, but then she flashed a brave smile. "Ah. Mr. Lightfoot."

"Oh bother!" The teasing light in Rafe's eyes belied his hinted apology. He made no effort to conceal his speculation as to what might have happened but for his ill-timed return.

Marcus didn't doubt they would have covered that last quarter of an inch to kiss if not for Rafe's interruption. Marcus bit down on his lower lip to arrest the sting of want. Might she have kissed him back?

Doffing his cocked hat, Rafe flashed a droll grin. "Carry on. Don't mind me."

"Too late, Lightfoot." Marcus crossed his arms. "What happened? The ruckus coming from the dining room—everyone all right?"

Rafe met Serenity's questioning expression, then turned back to Marcus, voicing a cryptic reply. "The house of cards has toppled." He asked Miss Ravensworth, "But you already know what the trouble is, don't you?"

"Aye." Tenacity flared in her luminous eyes, acknowledging the leveled charge. "And I started it."

Another crash, shattering glass, splintering wood. Another scream.

"That cannot be good." Rafe stated the obvious. "St. James?"

Marcus felt the pull in both directions. Stay with Miss Ravensworth or go fight as he had done so many times before alongside her brother?

She decided for him, pushing against his arm. "Please go! Gideon and Colson will be at each other's throats! I will wait for you at the stable."

Marcus pressed a hasty kiss on her forehead. "Hurry. Go upstairs and bar the door behind you."

## Chapter 14

*Fernsby Hall, Near Bath*

Lightfoot and St. James sprinted toward the manor house, scrambling through intermittent pools of light and darkened shadows. Serenity hugged the caped cloak tight around herself, worrying her bottom lip. "Dear Lord, please don't let my brothers kill each other."

Fernsby Hall sparkled brilliantly against the inky night, and Serenity recalled bygone galas her mother had orchestrated, when acquiring an invitation to one of Lady Ravensworth's gatherings had been a coveted award.

Serenity and Jonathan used to hide on the grand staircase—much as Amos and Asher had done tonight—with hopes of glimpsing glittering ladies and dapper gentlemen. Their little supper this evening didn't hold a candle to those elaborate parties and the outcome of this one had not gone by the script. She gathered her skirt plus Marcus's peppermint-smelling cloak and followed the cresset-lined path toward the stable.

A shadowy form separated from the boxwood hedge, startling Serenity.

The Lord Brentmoor maneuvered himself between her and the manor, snuffing out her view of the house lights and cutting off egress toward the garden. "Miss Ravensworth, might I have a word." The request was civil enough, though its undertone sent a rattling chill snaking down her spine. He offered his arm.

She ignored the gesture, advancing past him toward the stable block. "Beg your pardon, my lord. I must attend to an important errand. Pray, excuse me." Though still wrapped in St. James's cloak, it no longer yielded any warmth. Her stomach roiled, her teeth chattered, and the short train of her sacque-back gown swept the flagstones.

Incensed, Lord Brentmoor stomped on the dragging fabric, halting Serenity and upsetting her balance. His arms banded around her, averting a complete tumble.

"The sooner you learn not to turn your back on me, the better off it will go for you." He spun her to face him, casting aside her borrowed cloak. "We can have a wedding or not. It makes no difference. I'll have you and your dowry one way or the other. I already own Colson. I'll own you as well."

"Leave me be!" Serenity squirmed to dodge his mouth. Lord Brentmoor's brandied kiss landed near her ear.

He latched on to her chin and forced her to face him.

Her pinned arms were useless in creating space between them. Fear stuttered her breathing and spurred her pulse. She wriggled and kicked, but Serenity's voluminous skirt and underpetticoats proved an obstacle in Brentmoor's favor. The blow she aimed at his shin was too hampered by cloth to be effective. "You're hurting me."

"Get used to it." Wicked light ignited in Brentmoor's eyes. Crushing her against himself, his unwanted kiss found its mark.

Furious flailing minimalized duration and impact. Brentmoor's rising dissatisfaction proved meager reward. The more she struggled, the tighter his grip. Bones might snap should she continued to thrash. She stamped her heel down atop his instep. Hard.

The baron's backhand connected with her jawline. Serenity's head snapped, a burst of stars distorting her vision. Through her smarting tears she recognized Colson at the stable just a short distance away. Watching. Doing nothing. Offering no form of rescue whatsoever.

"Gid-e-on!" She belted out a yell that carried on the cold night air. "A-mos!"

Brentmoor slapped a palm over her mouth to muffle her distressed cries. She bit down with enough force to break the skin—an action which earned another dizzying blow.

Dazed, Serenity tripped and fell forward. Her head smacked against a stone paver. When the air returned to her lungs, she leveraged herself into a sitting position. Blood seeped and dripped from the gash on her forehead. Brentmoor scooped her up and flung her over his shoulder, knocking the wind out of her a second time.

Upside down, her head throbbed in time with the cadence of the beating of her heart. Serenity frantically prayed someone would hear her screams and follow the trail of her blood—before it was too late. *Lord God, I need Your help! Be my shield...*

Hauling Serenity to the stable, the baron dumped her onto a bed of straw piled in a corner adjacent to a vacant stall. Like a wolf stalking vulnerable prey, he prepared to strike. Without wasting words, Lord Brentmoor's feral glare betrayed malicious intent, and he made short work of removing his velvet coat.

"Mar-cus!"

Lord Brentmoor's distorted face was a dark mask of lividity. Dragging Serenity upright, he shook her shoulders. "No one is coming! Colson will keep them occupied." He cupped the swollen side of her face with a cruel hand.

Serenity twisted away from his next attempt at kissing the corner of her mouth, where blood mingled with her tears, and she braced for another blow.

"Such a pretty face." Pulling the ivory combs free with his bloodied hand, he destroyed her elegant coiffure, discarding satin ribbons and ignoring the broken string of pearls absorbed into the straw beneath their feet.

Back pressed against the stable wall, Serenity's breath hitched when Lord Brentmoor brashly traced the lace edging her bodice. "Don't!" Avoiding his scandalous pawing, her plucky command dripped ice. The throbbing in her head increased, and her vision blurred. Tears streaked her face.

Amid their tussle, the baron swore as a number of pins securing her stomacher to her stays and jacket were set askew. The sharp pricks jabbed his groping fingers. Belligerent, he clawed at the striped fabric, tearing it away to expose a slender shoulder. Serenity's struggling resulted in additional damage to her once-beautiful gown. "To think"—he rent another seam to shreds—"if you'd accepted my offering of higher-quality material, it might have made it more difficult for me to rip it off of you."

*Loathsome.* Combined with her blood loss, Serenity was on the brink of retching. *Lord, God, please ... help me, please ...*

The baron jerked her coin pendant hard against her neck in an effort to break it, but the clasp did not give way and the strong chain held, digging into her skin. He curled his fingers around her throat, and she shuddered at his snarl. "You. Are. Mine."

The crisp metallic click of a flintlock pistol brought to half cock disrupted Lord Brentmoor's foul course of action, and his bruising grip on her slackened a fraction. Serenity's shove to be free of him proved futile.

"She is not yours, Brentmoor. Nor does she wish to be."

Marcus St. James. *Thank You, Lord God! Oh, thank You.*

Thick tears spilled from her lashes, and she tasted salt in rivulets mingling with congealed blood. Her marred cheek was puffy and bruised. Shifting Serenity's position, the baron used her as a shield to keep St. James at bay.

With deceptive calm, St. James set the firing mechanism of his pistol into full cock. Serenity immediately appreciated the grenadier's imposing physical presence and training, which clearly unsettled Brentmoor.

St. James had killed before, under orders and in the line of duty. The baron, almost a head shorter than the soldier and at least two stone lighter, registered the uncomfortable fact. "'Twill be a blemish on your exemplary military record if you shoot me."

St. James's pistol did not waver, his emotionless aim steady. He did not confirm or deny the sarcastic jibe. Nor did he so much as glance her way. His aim focused solely on Brentmoor.

Colson burst into the aisle between the stalls, spewing a vulgar string of profanity. Grabbing the nearest shovel, he swung it like a cricket bat.

"Marcus!" Serenity's hoarse whisper came too late.

Inflexible iron connected with St. James's left arm. The jolt and shock drove him to one knee. He dropped the pistol. The ball discharged, reverberating into the night, and wedged into a post near Colson's ear.

The gun's sharp report served as a warning signal. Gideon and Amos arrived breathless at the stable door. Mr. Todd snatched the shovel from Colson before he could strike St. James with a second blow. The stablemaster restrained Colson against the stall wall, the length of the shovel handle across the chest. Gideon pinioned Brentmoor against the tack room door.

Amos collected Marcus's weapon. Oakley Lightfoot returned, a readied pistol of his own in one hand, a glinting dagger in the other.

Freed from Brentmoor's clutches, Serenity gathered the tatters of her ruined gown to her bosom in a failed attempt to hide her quilted stays. She staggered forward, but St. James drew her close, his right arm curling around her shaking frame. She rested her cheek against his left arm, and his coat sleeve absorbed the continued flow of crimson oozing from the wound on her forehead.

St. James collected her to himself but his left arm hung at an unnatural angle.

"Amos." Serenity lifted her head and voiced a ragged whisper. "Go fetch Dr. Graham. Be quick."

"Sis?" Amos's innocent eyes widened as he viewed her injuries. "You are hurt." His chin quivered in sympathy. A resolute nod and her youngest brother dashed away to do her bidding.

Once the boy rode out, Gideon delivered a well-aimed hit, dropping the baron into momentary oblivion. Leaving Brentmoor sprawled where he lay, Gideon approached Colson with a murderous look. He shoved his older brother's shoulder, forcing Colson's head back until he collided with the stall wall. "What have you done?"

Unable to escape Mr. Todd's detention, Colson looked up with angst-filled eyes, his declaration a nasal whine. "You don't understand!"

"No! I don't!" Gideon shoved Colson again, harder. "How could you stand by and fail to protect our sister?! You all but served her up to Brentmoor on a silver platter!" Gideon rammed his fist into Colson's aquiline nose. A second blow followed and a third.

"Ravensworth, stop! Deal with him later. Take your sister out of here." Marcus's pain threaded through his clenched teeth. "Todd, lock these two in the tack room. Lightfoot's a lawman—he'll take charge of things from here before the rest of us do something we'll regret."

Lightfoot gave a brusque nod and aided the stablemaster in securing Colson and Brentmoor.

"You can't keep us like this." Colson's crunched nose trickled blood.

Ignoring Colson's pathetic objection, Marcus cradled his damaged arm close to his torso. He repeated his terse directive to Gideon. "Ravensworth, see to your sister."

Her brother tried to wipe away the blood on Serenity's face with a handkerchief but only succeeded in smearing it more. He draped his uniform coat about her, covering her ruined dress but not staving off the shivers settling across her bruised shoulders. He scooped her up in his arms, as he did when she was a little girl to torment her, but now his hold guarded her. "I'll take her to Grandee's cottage. There's been enough trouble at the manor."

Serenity tugged her brother's arm. At her silent request, Gideon paused in front of St. James. A strange mix of comfort and righteous indignation blazed in his gold-flecked green eyes. His roiling anger was not directed at her but at the circumstance, and her instinct affirmed he would fight on her behalf if called upon—because he cared. "I—" Crestfallen, her voice was reduced to a raspy whisper. "I don't know what led you back, but thank God you returned when you did."

"Illogical as this may sound, it was the ravens. They flew in and out of the aviary, squawking and croaking something fierce. Between their shrill alarm and your screams, we turned back."

Lightfoot's expression held accordance with St. James's account. "One even seemed to be shooing us along, as if pointing us toward the danger."

"The ravens." An involuntary smile reopened the cut at the corner of Serenity's mouth.

"I'll see her settled, then I will be back. Don't start without me," Gideon said to St. James and the thief-taker.

Dazed but not reeling, Marcus was beyond caring if Gideon or Rafe witnessed his slipping control. Between nauseous waves of pain, he vowed, "I'm going to kill Brentmoor."

"No, you're not," Ravensworth countered, having returned a scant quarter of an hour later.

"If I thought him worth the trouble, I might help you, but he's not," Rafe added.

Ill at ease, friend and cousin inspected Marcus, concern reflected in their eyes.

Rafe cast a cursory appraisal at Marcus's distended elbow and the blood saturating his left coat sleeve. "Amos fetched the doctor for Miss Ravensworth's sake, but he should take a look at you too, St. James. That arm doesn't look good."

"Doesn't feel good either." Marcus gritted the telling confession, but his fleeting thoughts were filled with agonized worry for Serenity's injuries above his own. "She ... the blood. It's hers ... not mine."

Acting as Lightfoot, Rafe assumed charge and issued orders. "Ravensworth, take St. James to Fernsby Cottage. Mr. Todd and I will deal with Colson and Brentmoor."

A suppressed whimper sounded behind the tack room door. Ravensworth's chin dipped in a quick if hesitant nod. Marcus guessed Ravensworth wrestled against doubt but relented to inevitably place in the thief-taker the same trust his grandmother had. "Do whatever you need to do."

"Count on it." Rafe spoke to Serenity's brother. However, the message was meant more for Marcus's benefit.

Marcus stumbled forward. Ravensworth situated his right shoulder under Marcus's, throwing an arm around his waist to steady him. His wry grin accompanied his quip, "Just like old times in America."

"Not open for discussion." A rush of disturbing recollection swamped Marcus, buckling his knees. Smoky battlefields, bullets, shot, shell, musket volleys, blood-stained bayonets. And arrows. Ravensworth had redeployed on new orders, while Marcus had stayed at Fort Michilimackinac with his father and brother—until the massacre and its indistinct aftermath. He straightened and spat, "Leave off, Ravensworth."

"Grandee calls me the definition of muleheaded more often than not. You have me beat by far."

Marcus replied with an unintelligible groan. He followed Ravensworth's lead, one foot in front of the other.

Backed up to the ash grove, Fernsby Cottage sat on the crest of a low hill, the third segment of the triangle-shaped yard shared with the manor house and stable block. Ravensworth ushered Marcus inside. "Grandee moved here after my mother died, filling in as maternal substitute to us five motherless grandchildren. At present, she's at the manor executing duties as gracious hostess in Serenity's stead, bringing the party to its overdue conclusion and answering questions as truthfully as circumstances allow. As soon as Colson's guests take their leave and the Northcrafts and Twitch are settled in, she'll join us. Jonathan has first watch."

Marcus scanned the room for Serenity. "How is your sister?"

"With the doctor now."

Theophilus Graham, Lady Aurelia's personal physician, had apprenticed as a surgeon before taking his education further by attending the medical college at Edinburgh, where he earned the title befitting a doctor. Certification lent him credibility with the nobles and gentry, even though he served equal time in the realm of hands-on surgery. Dr. Graham wielded needle and thread with practiced precision. Cleansed of blood, Serenity's forehead boasted six even stitches closing the vertical ragged-edged gash. A final snip of his scissors echoed on the heels of the physician's caution. "The headache may linger. The bruising will darken, appearing worse before it gets better." He placed a hand to her forehead alongside the bandage, feeling for rising temperature. "I'll check the stitches again before I leave."

Dr. Graham finished tending Serenity's miscellaneous scrapes and cuts. Purpling marks inflicted by Lord Brentmoor's ruthless hands caused Marcus's ire to rise.

Serenity's sad eyes mirrored the flickering candlelight. Realization quashed her alarm. "The blood soaking your coat sleeve is mine. But your arm—the one that hasn't healed properly."

"Ssshhhh." Marcus's concern was all for her. "The doctor will set me to rights next."

"I am grateful you returned when you did," she repeated.

Marcus thumbed away a tear tracking down her pale face. He too was thankful beyond words. He wished to restore the rosiness in her cheeks and put the sparkle of laughter back in her eyes. He did not like the wan, haunted shock lurking beneath her lowered lashes.

Dr. Graham expressed a request for Miss Ravensworth, if she was able, to make a pot of willow bark tea, and while she was occupied with that task, he peeled off the sleeve of Marcus's coat to examine the damaged left arm.

Removal of the soiled linen drenched with blood and sweat revealed the bone decidedly broken, though not jutting through skin. Not finding a corresponding wound, Dr. Graham deduced, "The blood was hers and not yours. Right then." He examined the aggravated and protruding lump and concluded it the original source of the persistent swelling.

"I'm afraid I'm going to need to open you up after all, and then the blood *will* be yours. But without being able to see what is going on beneath the skin, I can't fix this correctly. And cutting you open will hurt," Dr. Graham warned, unfastening his leather case. From velvet-lined trays, he selected the appropriate surgical implements and knives required to perform the procedure.

Marcus downed the tea Miss Ravensworth prepared, praying relief from pain would come. Soon.

Dr. Graham offered Marcus a three-quarter-inch wooden cylinder measuring a palm's breadth or an equal length of double-strapped leather to bite down on, but he declined both, opting instead for a chunk of willow bark to chew on.

Ravensworth headed off Amos's approach to the cottage with an order to bring back a decanter of rum from Sir Nicholas's study. Dr. Graham rinsed Marcus's arm with the amber liquid to stave off putrefaction, but would offer none to drink until after the procedure when risk of alcohol-thinned blood was past. Marcus knew hurt from previous experience. The ingested willow bark helped to dull the incredible level of pain endured through the physician's effort to repair the wound but did not eradicate it entirely.

Before Marcus could object, Dr. Graham expediently cut away the rest of the sleeve of the fine custom-made shirt Marcus had commissioned from Madelaine Northcraft. Naked all the way to the shoulder seam under the chandelier's glow, the stark blue feather tattoo seemed more pronounced than ever against his bare skin.

While it was not altogether uncommon for sailors or prisoners to be tattooed—or any number of warriors belonging to various native tribes—titled second sons were usually not.

Curiosity flitted across Miss Ravensworth's face, her glance ensnared by the singular markings. She frowned with uncertainty, puzzled, and retreated a step. Pain-induced misgivings had Marcus assuming her slow blink and hard swallow equated to unmitigated revulsion.

The good doctor, having set Marcus's dislocated elbow, commenced with surgery. Stanching the blood as much as possible, he none-too-gently investigated the swollen lump below the joint, angling his probe deeper until it came into contact with metal. "How long, exactly, have you carried this bullet?"

Physical and mental agony assailed Marcus, and he bit back a cry. "Since ... Ju-une." He retracted his arm and minced an oath, neither proving effective in quelling a surge of escalating discomfort.

"I'm not finished." Taking the decanter from Ravensworth, Dr. Graham beckoned to Marcus to return his injured limb. "I need your cooperation to get this right."

Marcus's nostrils flared as he blew out a breath. He tossed his head back when the burning sting of rum washed over the deep incision, and an involuntary anguish escaped.

Miss Ravensworth scooted her chair nearer to Marcus, edging closer than propriety might dictate under routine circumstances.

Marcus mustered a measure of renewed fortitude but it fell short of her tenacity on his behalf. A single gentle squeeze relayed warm comfort from her hand to his larger one. Almost with apology, she whispered his name before easing her fingers from the vicelike grip transferring enough force to crush her delicate bones.

"Forgive me."

"No harm done." She flexed and curled her ringless fingers.

"No. I'm sorry I didn't get there sooner. To stop Brentmoor from hurting you."

"Bruises and scars will fade in time." Miss Ravensworth studied her folded hands. "Though he intended far greater harm, he was thwarted in his plan." She winced. "Let's not talk about that."

Marcus refrained from placing a reassuring hand on her bowed head, unsure if she might shy at his touch. He retreated from the stilted conversation with unspoken assent to honor her hoarse command. He was grateful she stayed near and not adversely affected by the amount of blood in the midst of Dr. Graham's procedure.

Dr. Graham withdrew a dented .69 caliber lead ball from Marcus's arm and held it up for inspection under the suspended candle lights. "There is no earthly reason this didn't shatter the bone on impact." Dropped from the grasp of medical forceps, the bullet clanked into a metal dish.

The disturbing sound brought another flash of foggy memory, transporting Marcus back to the Great Lakes wilderness...A native woman from Michilimackinac, Wakwi, leaning over him in gathering darkness, mercilessly digging into his wound with her knife, trying to see by only the flickering light of a dancing fire...She removed an embedded arrow shaft and withdrew three pieces of broken arrowhead that had pierced his flesh. *Had she not seen the bullet, or had it proven too difficult to extract and so she'd left it to heal over?*

Ravensworth let out a low whistle. "How could that get missed?"

Dr. Graham offered plausible theories. "Low light, position of the muscle, too much blood. Perhaps the surgeon found something else in the wound?"

"Possible." Ravensworth scratched his jaw. "It wasn't the first time or the last that St. James was shot. Colson might have done him a favor dislodging that ball with that makeshift cudgel."

Though light-headed, Marcus refused to show himself weak— any more than he already had. He breathed deeply, filling his lungs. "Stranger things have happened on a battlefield."

"I'll have to take your word for that." As he had with the gash at Miss Ravensworth's hairline, Dr. Graham plied his needle and another length of silk thread to close Marcus's incision with three times as many stitches. "There. Almost as good as Mrs. Northcraft's handiwork."

"Not quite." Marcus pulled a grimace. "But it will do."

To Miss Ravensworth, Dr. Graham said, "Watch him closely over the next few days. There is risk of infection. Fever." The physician sized up his patient. "Though it seems he's survived the like before, I certainly don't want to lose him on my watch." Following Ravensworth out, Dr. Graham turned to add, "Continue to ply him with willow bark tea for now. Leave the rum to his choosing, if the pain gets too much. If fever comes, send for me immediately."

Once more Miss Ravensworth's gaze skittered over the tattooed feathers on Marcus's arm before her gaze collided with his. Were the markings off-putting to her? Or maybe it was the gore of the wound after all. Mayhap she simply didn't wish to spend any more time than necessary in his company. Or maybe his pain propagated too many lies of self-deception.

"I shall endeavor to be a model patient."

She returned his level glance, eyes dulled by ache. "I shall try to follow instructions. For your sake."

So be it.

# Chapter 15

*Fernsby Cottage at Fernsby Hall, Near Bath*

Twelve chimes.

Marcus awoke after but an hour or two of rest, stitched arm hugged close to his chest, legs dangling over the end of the tapestry chaise lounge.

He was not alone.

Across the width of a tasseled Turkish carpet, Miss Ravensworth perched on the damask sofa, legs tucked under, head braced on her palm, elbow propped atop the bolster. Watching. Him.

Fragrant vanilla mingled with lavender. Freshly washed, her damp hair bound in a long glossy plait, free of matted blood and specks of straw. A bandage encircling her head concealed a row of spiky stitches. When she rose to add more wood to the fire, the flames illuminated her battered visage in golden light. The bruises on her face, neck, and wrists would soon darken to rival the deep purple of her dressing gown.

"What are you doing here?" His query came out as raspy as a raven's croak. He pinched the bridge of his nose, willing the persistent throb in his left arm to leave off.

"Following instructions." Reseated on the sofa, she pulled the bolster onto her lap and folded her hands into a tight knot. "Is it true?"

"What?" *That I could have killed him for hurting you? That I care for you?*

"Gideon has all but insisted Colson should challenge Lord Brentmoor to a duel."

"It is a brother's duty to defend his sister's honor."

"Colson doesn't have any honor!"

"Not from what I've seen."

"How do I stop this?"

"You don't. You would do well to leave it alone and let it play out."

"Come what may?"

"Come what may."

She shook her dark head, fighting fresh tears born of incredulity. "I do not know what it is about Colson. I don't understand why he is always so distant and difficult. His meanness has reached new depths and afflicted us all, yet he is still my brother."

"Not fully—only half."

She leveled a bemused stare. "What are you saying?"

A small groan escaped Marcus as he shifted his weight from one hip to the other on the narrow tapestry chaise. "Remember the night we found him rifling through your father's desk?"

Confusion furrowed her brow. "Yes."

"He was in search of an important letter."

"How do you know this?"

"Gideon's been piecing it together."

"Piecing *what* together?" She wasn't following, and her puzzlement increased a notch.

Marcus licked dry lips. Observant, Miss Ravensworth poured a ceramic mug of cool water. He raised himself on his good elbow and reciprocated her intent glance. When she touched the rim of the mug to his mouth he partook of several soothing ounces. "Much obliged."

Lady Aurelia's light tread swept her into the cottage sitting room, still arrayed in an exquisite silver ballgown. "I trust I'm not interrupting, dearest."

Miss Ravensworth set aside the mug. "Of course not, Grandee."

"St. James, you look like you are already feeling a mite better. I imagine carrying a bullet would be most uncomfortable." Lady Aurelia seated herself on the tufted red leather wingback chair nearest Marcus. She reported on a sigh, "The last of Colson's guests have finally departed. Twitch and the Northcrafts are staying. Oakley Lightfoot and the watchman are dealing with Brentmoor and Colson, although the magistrate will likely do no more than order house confinement for each until this business is sorted out." She did not provide any further detail and turned her attention to Marcus. "Truly, how is your arm?"

"Throbbing like the dickens."

If Lady Aurelia noticed the feather-tipped tribal tattoo, she abstained from comment. For now. "How much do you know, St. James? For clearly you know something."

"As bits and pieces came to light and details emerged forming an alarming picture of Colson's depredation, Gideon needed to vent his ire. I am his friend. He knows I am the trustworthy sort."

"Indeed." Lady Aurelia paused, offering her granddaughter a chance to concur.

But Miss Ravensworth did not.

For some reason, that stung. He reminded himself their association spanned but a few weeks and allowed the fact to serve as provisional balm. They were acquaintances by definition, and his head warred with his heart over the unfamiliar yearning to reinforce this tenuous connection.

Marcus directed his answer to Lady Aurelia, aware Miss Ravensworth hung on every word that was news to her. "I was with Gideon on the way to Bath when he stopped to pay a visit to Sir Nicholas's solicitor. Alton Grierson mentioned he'd had a letter couriered here to Fernsby Hall. Said letter stated Sir Nicholas's health is failing, deemed too ill to return from Italy as such an arduous journey would be too taxing. It also disclosed that Sir Nicholas hired someone to track down the man who impregnated your daughter prior to her marriage."

Miss Ravensworth sat up straight, eyes blazing, ready to refute. But her indignance wilted when Lady Aurelia confirmed rather than challenged his blunt statement.

"Laurenda was ill used by a smooth-talking jack-tar on liberty from Bristol and taking a holiday in Bath."

Marcus nodded. "Somehow Lord Brentmoor learned of Lady Ravensworth's indiscretion prior to her vows, and he is aware Colson is not Sir Nicholas's firstborn son."

Lady Aurelia squinted her eyes, pondering. "I would surmise the disclosure came from Veronica, The Dowager Lady Brentmoor—the current baron's mother."

"Why the baron's mother?" Miss Ravensworth asked.

"Old grudges fester," Lady Aurelia answered. "Before she married this Lord Brentmoor's father, Veronica, Lady Brentmoor, once had designs of her own on Sir Nicholas Ravensworth, but he was a mere baronet."

Marcus let out a snort of disgust. Evidently, he was not an isolated victim of conniving society *femme fatales*.

"Lady Brentmoor married above her station for the sake of title and wealth," Lady Aurelia continued, "and is one of the few who would remember Laurenda fleeing to Scotland. It took a good while for Laurenda and Sir Nicholas to settle into the marriage and reconcile, but at length they learned to love each other in their own fashion."

"Nigh unto seven years." Miss Ravensworth whispered the calculation. "Gideon is seven years younger than Colson." She swiped at the moisture collecting in her eyes and sniffed into her handkerchief. "How long do you suppose Lord Brentmoor has had access to this knowledge?"

Lady Aurelia inclined her head. "I would venture the better part of a year, dearest. My guess is Colson gambled recklessly and lost heavily. The baron, it seems, has been using the potential scandal against Colson as a way to manipulate him."

"Blackmail him, you mean," Marcus put in.

"Hmmmm ... I suppose that is not too strong of a word when one considers the string of Colson's inexplicable actions over the past twelvemonth." Lady Aurelia stood, brushing wrinkles from her silvery skirt. She pressed a hand to Marcus's brow, then skimmed his stubbled cheek with the backs of her tapered fingers. "Warm, but not overmuch. I'll send Annie Daye for more water. Willow bark tea is what will render the most benefit to you at this point. And that goes for you as well, dearest."

*Fernsby Hall, Near Bath*

Grandee found Serenity curled up in the big leather chair at Sir Nicholas's desk as the sun still struggled to make an appearance.

"My father is dying."

"Yes, dearest. Most people diagnosed with the white plague invariably succumb to the disease within five years. Some call it consumption. Dr. Graham calls it tuberculosis. When the coughing fits increased, your father took measures to put his business affairs in order, had documents witnessed and filed with his solicitor, and decided to try a climate more healthful than England's. His physician in Italy prescribes a *lana, letto, latte* regimen derived from healers in Roman times."

Serenity straightened in the leather-upholstered seat. "Lana. Letto. Latte? What does that mean?" She knew a little French, less Spanish, and didn't understand Italian.

"Warmth, rest, and good food," Grandee replied, sympathy in her eyes. "It is said milk, sea travel, and higher elevations provide relief, albeit temporary. His condition worsens, he rallies, then worsens again. A body can withstand only so long such a pattern with that hacking cough and spitting up blood, so it is a good thing your father's physician is not prescribing bleeding and purging."

Grandee squeezed Serenity's hand, then placed a letter into her palm. "I've maintained correspondence with him. He asked this be passed along to you when he is dead. I intended to honor his wish in that—until things changed last night. It may contain disclosures needed sooner rather than later. You may find a request for forgiveness in his written lines, and it will be your choice whether or not to give it."

Serenity touched the raised "R" in the wax seal. Jonathan once conveyed a story from Matthew's Gospel of Peter asking Jesus how many times he was called to forgive a brother who sinned against him. "I am going to have to make the choice to forgive Colson as well."

"We all will, when the dust settles." Glancing through the windowpanes where clouds obscured dawn's sunny salutation, Grandee's focus shifted to the stable block. "After you retired in the wee hours of this morning, St. James was installed in his quarters. I daresay he is more comfortable recovering in a bed where his feet do not hang so far over the edge. Madelaine pulled the first shift and brought Jessa along. He chafed over not being able to hold her because of his bandaged arm, but at least her entertaining antics amused him to the point of genuine smiles. The laudanum and tea rendered their desired effect, and Amos had charge of the baby holding."

"Amos loves little Jessa."

"Madelaine's daughter is a sweet child to be sure, and I love her too." Grandee stood behind the desk chair and laid her cheek atop Serenity's dark head. "But I love you more, dearest, and, praise the Almighty, no further harm befell you last evening. I am sincerely appreciative of His divine protection, for it could have ended far worse."

"I do not doubt it within His power to have sent the ravens to get Marc—to catch St. James's attention." A deep blush suffused Serenity's averted face as she toyed with the wadded handkerchief in her lap.

Without further comment on Gideon's grenadier friend, Grandee tapped the envelope on Sir Nicholas's desk. "Do with that what you will."

The envelope bore Serenity's name in Sir Nicholas's recognizable script. "He never asked us to come," she whispered. She tried in vain to remember the day they'd said good-bye to him at the dock in Bristol. In truth, it was the day Gideon had shipped out to the Colonies in service of the King's Army, which entirely overrode the details of her father's departure. Serenity had been more afraid of her brother not returning. She had not realized at the time she might never see her father alive again.

"I believe your father would rather you remember him as he was." Grandee raised a beringed hand toward the portrait of him hanging above a curio case. "And that, in a small way, is a blessing of its own."

Serenity pressed Grandee's hand to her unbruised cheek. "Death is part of life. I accept that, even though I don't like it."

Grandee bestowed a sage smile. "To be absent from the body is to be present with our Lord. His Word assures salvation when we believe in Him. His is a promise of life eternal, in His glorious presence."

"That promise is one I look forward to someday." Serenity sighed. She tucked her father's letter into her pocket, deciding it would keep.

"I shall go to the kitchen and see what Nancie Heath suggests for St. James. He'll need fortifying sustenance so he can gain strength back in that repaired arm."

"Indeed." A knowing smile played at Grandee's lips. "When Lightfoot returns, he will share a debriefing with us all."

"Amos and Gideon want a challenge, but I don't think Colson is man enough to go through with it."

"Would you want him to?"

Serenity lifted her shoulders in a shrug. "In many aspects, Colson is a stranger to me. A duel would be meaningless, but the men will not see it that way."

"No. Not when there is honor at the heart of the matter. You must realize they take championing you seriously. You are their only sister."

How likely would death claim a brother before it did her father?

# Chapter 16

*Fernsby Hall, Near Bath*

With the precision of recurrent guard duty, Lady Aurelia, Annie Daye, Mrs. Todd, Madelaine, and Miss Ravensworth rotated turns sitting with Marcus after surgery. Miss Ravensworth's assignment most often followed Lady Aurelia's, and Marcus suspected her ladyship administered laudanum sparingly into his tea, enough to make him drift off, and thereby pose no coherent threat to correctness. Marcus wished she wouldn't. Next time, he'd request she please stick to the willow-bark tea without the additional ingredient. Due to his military training, he preferred awareness of his surroundings. Something niggled at the back of his mind about unnatural sleep.

Cracking open his eyes, Marcus found Ravensworth volunteering a stint as watcher.

"If you were expecting my sister, I'm sorry to disappoint you."

Marcus moved his head from side to side as he emerged from another prolonged nap. "I knew you weren't her. She smells of lavender and vanilla. You don't."

A wink accompanied Ravensworth's amused chortle. "Astute observation."

"What do you want?"

"Just doing my duty. I assured Grandee I would cover for her because her appointment in town ran long." Ravensworth put a palm to Marcus's forehead. "You don't feel feverish, which is good. I'm also instructed to unwrap the bandage and ensure there's no pus or reddening around the stitches."

Marcus was relieved when Ravensworth found neither at the incision site at his elbow. His continued prayer was that healing would come swiftly so that when Dr. Theophilus Graham drove out to check on him, the stitches could be removed.

Rewrapping Marcus's arm, Ravensworth's curious glance lingered on the inked feather armlet and the larger feather on his inner arm. "Still no memory of how you came by those markings?"

"Leave off, Ravensworth."

His chuckle boomed. "When will you understand that I only want to help? If I were missing eight weeks and five hundred miles from my life, I'd be bothered by that!"

Marcus pulled the blanket to cover his bandaged arm and its mysterious tattoos.

"All right, I'll leave off. For now. I honestly think talking through things might serve you better than bottling them up. You know I'm here for you."

Silent, tense moments passed until Marcus nodded. Ravensworth was a good friend.

"If you don't wish to talk about your time in the Great Lakes Territory today, let's talk about ... my sister."

Marcus rubbed his jaw, uncomfortable he'd quit the frying pan to land in the fire. "What about her?"

"Amos says you look at her quite a lot. I've noticed the same myself."

Marcus wasn't prepared to discuss his thoughts about Ravensworth's sister, but that didn't deter his friend.

"I want to thank you for defending her. Grandee and I were trying to get Serenity out of the house because we thought the danger to her was inside. The Fernsby estate has been a safe haven for my family until Colson's residual depredations shattered all the illusions."

Ravensworth sat forward and rested his forearms on his thighs. "The implications revealed the night of the party ... Like you, I am not the second son I always believed I was. In an instant," he snapped his fingers, "perspectives altered irrevocably."

"Is Colson in hiding?" Marcus asked.

"He hasn't left the gatehouse that I know of since the revelation. I imagine he's hoping to stay clear of Brentmoor, but we all know there will be an eventual reckoning, in whatever form that takes."

"I wasn't as much help to your sister as I should have been if—"

"But you were there. Your presence prevented her suffering a more disastrous outcome. She took the brunt of his beating but fought against him, so he reaped nothing beyond an errant kiss or two. Barring your arrival at the scene, the rest of us would have been too late. And I would have wanted to kill him myself had he ... "

"I know. So would have I."

Ravensworth scooted back in his seat. "You like my sister." It was not a question.

"Tell me the truth. Is she the reason you brought me here?"

Ravensworth paused before answering, considering his explanation. "Mayhap I didn't realize it when I first invited you to visit, but yes, I'll own it. She will be a credit to the man who loves her."

Marcus held his breath. Ravensworth wasn't here to caution him against formally courting Serenity—he was encouraging it. The notion gained precarious traction. "I—" He sounded like her, about to respond to an inquiry requiring added thought. "I can't say I'm ready to go down that road just yet. Too much confusion still, too many missing pieces." Too obscure. His faulty reasoning could only undergo so much scrutiny in the light of day.

"So be it. If she really is set on going to the Colonies with Amos and Uncle Twitch, she'll leave England and you'll remain here. Who knows? She might find some nice Virginian—"

"Leave off." Marcus ground his back teeth and tasted a surprising pinch of jealousy.

Ravensworth stood, chuckling, and brushed his hands together. "Do you talk to Serenity when she's here on duty and you're awake? Read? Sing?"

Marcus heard her sweet voice in mellow echo of hymns and the military ballad. *On the road to come what may, O'er the hills and far away.* "She reads to me. We talk." She prayed over him when she thought him asleep, but Marcus kept that treasure to himself.

"Good to know." Ravensworth rocked on his heels, stuffing his hands into his coat pockets. "Rest as much as you can. You're starting to mend."

"Another debt of thanks to you."

A wicked grin spread across Ravensworth's face. "Oh, don't thank me just yet."

⌒

Checking St. James's bandage was not one of Serenity's sickroom duties. That fell to Grandee or Mrs. Todd. Serenity's job was to read, bring the occasional meal tray, and help him eat, but most of the time, she watched him as he slept. His brow and skin blessedly cool and absent fever.

When Gideon napped on the library sofa, everything about him relaxed and he resembled the boy he used to be. But St. James didn't relax—his eyebrows always knit, every muscle wound taut. He didn't appear refreshed upon waking and she wondered what caused his restlessness. It took time for his focus to engage upon waking, for him to actually see her instead of his disagreeable dreams.

This afternoon she brought a tray with broth and fresh-baked bread. The warm, yeasty aroma stirred his stomach to growling and his eyelashes spread open. "Mr. St. James."

"Miss Ravensworth." His deep voice resembled Loxley's croak. She lifted his head so he could drink from the glass of water. "Miss Ravensworth." His repeated greeting sounded more like himself.

St. James sat up, and Serenity stacked the pillows behind him. She placed the wicker tray on the bedside table, dishes and utensils arranged for right-handed usage. "Mmmm... Did you make this bread?"

"I did." She situated her chair so the more bruised side of her face was turned away from him. The lady's maid could only do so much with her hair in an attempt to hide the bandage at her forehead. "Where did we leave off?" She flipped the pages to locate the bookmark.

St. James relieved Serenity of the book. "I don't want to listen to someone else's story. I cannot concentrate today. Can we simply... talk a bit?"

"Of course." Serenity's cheeks burned under his deliberate perusal. "Anything particular you would care to discuss?" She lifted her chin, meeting his intent gold-flecked green eyes and conducting a reciprocal study of him. He was alert and smiling and the handsomer for it.

She held her breath, saying nothing when he took her small hand and enclosed it in his callused grasp. She did not withdraw or object as he raised her hand to his mouth. Watching for a sign of reaction, he boldly kissed the back, turned it over, and kissed her palm.

"You like cooking things, baking sweet treats," he said.

"Yes." Serenity blinked, reaching for her sovereign pendant with her opposite hand. "And that is significant how?"

"Your brother told me of a time when you left gingerbread biscuits in the oven too long—they came out charred, hard as rocks, and beyond salvaging. Then there was another instance when you mistakenly substituted salt for sugar."

She tugged her hand loose at the mention of that first batch of biscuits gone bad and crossed her arms with an embarrassed *Humph!* "Gideon has been telling tales on me."

"In truth, it was Amos who tattled."

"Oh?" Serenity primly smoothed her checked linen apron over her quilted petticoat. "Well. It may be some time before I make sweet buns for him again if he cannot learn to keep a confidence."

St. James's chuckle rumbled. "You'll make them again—for any of your brothers—as soon as you need something from them enough to stake the bribe." He bit into the second slice of bread. "After I started interrogating him, Amos hadn't much of a choice."

"Your point?"

"You didn't give up learning how to cook due to early mishaps. You carried on. As a result, your culinary efforts bring delight to all who taste your creations."

Her eyes narrowed, uncertain where St. James's line of flattery would lead. "So?"

"Your tenacity spurred you to try again, to trade a failed attempt for one with more satisfactory results."

Serenity watched his mouth as he spoke, pondering what might have been had he kissed her at the gazebo, before ...

"Are you brave enough to let me impart a better impression of kissing to override Brentmoor's mistreatment of you?"

St. James offered the chance to redeem that which the baron stole and sullied. Challenge glinted in his eyes. Dare she?

Marcus waited to see what she would do. As Ravensworth's sister, he banked on her spirited tenacity to prod her toward taking the risk. His aim was to help her heal and forget, which required he tread with care so as not to jeopardize her fragile trust. If he were honest, he'd admit a selfish desire to make a new memory of his own to replace ... to replace whatever he feared he couldn't remember.

"Brave enough?" She cocked a haughty brow, bunching her apron in clenched fists.

"Aye. Are you?"

The proverbial gauntlet lay between them. A scant moment's contemplation and all hesitation on her part dissolved. She framed each side of his stubbled jaw with her hands. He didn't breathe, just stared into her ginger-brown eyes, anticipating her decided course of action.

She leaned closer. He curled his fingers around her nape. They both experienced the instant jolt of connection when their lips touched. Curiously. Softly. Tenderly.

Marcus exhaled incrementally, not wanting to startle or disrupt her as she acclimated to the feel of his mouth, letting her lips tarry against his for a minute ... or two.

Their mouths parted, ending the kiss—a shade reluctantly, he thought. Her eyes snapped with sass, her whisper all but inaudible. "I am not afraid of you, Marcus St. James."

Her declaration caused his heart to sing. "Good thing, that."

The gravity of their situation colored her ivory cheeks a rosy pink and raised her chin to its determined angle. She'd initiated a kiss between them, albeit with his ... encouragement.

"Serenity—"

A creaky footfall at the stairwell made them jump. Marcus released her hand. "That will be the changing of the guard." He checked his timepiece. "Punctual as ever."

"I— I should go fetch more water, ice ... or ... something." She toyed with her coin medallion, flustered, and pushed a wayward curl back under her cap. His mollified smile arrested her fussing. "You look like you've solved some ponderous riddle to great satisfaction."

"Truth be told," he said without apology, "I had been wondering."

"Wondering about what?"

"About what it would be like to kiss you." His audacious wink lacked sheepishness.

"And?" The warmth in her ginger-brown glance rivaled the hearth's dancing flames.

"And I liked it. Very much."

She touched her lips. "So did I."

Upon the candid admission, she exited the guest chamber in haste, as if suddenly needing to rescue a kettle off a crane before its contents boiled over.

"Oh, dearest, there you are. Is St. James awake?"

"Yes, he is." Marcus heard Serenity's reply to her ladyship. "I'll return for the tray later."

He propped his head on the fist of his good arm, unable to contain his grin until retrospection trampled his euphoria. *What had he done?* If he possessed a lick of sense, he'd not do that again, no matter how much he wanted to—not until he had a better grasp on his life and where he was headed.

Ravensworth might approve of Marcus's interest in his only sister, but he'd maim, if not kill, Marcus if he believed she was being trifled with. Of that Marcus held no illusion to the contrary.

∽

Rubbing sleep from the corners of his eyes the next morning, Marcus awakened to a sharp rapping against the stable's apartment door and Lady Aurelia's urgent greeting. "St. James?"

"Yes, my lady." He tugged the bedclothes up from his waist to his chest. "Come in."

Her ladyship stood behind the bedside chair. "Good morning. Your cousin has arrived and asks if you feel up to joining us in the library."

*Your cousin.* Marcus scrubbed a hand over his face, expelling the air from his lungs. Asking forgiveness would be most expedient. "Lady Aurelia..."

"Your color is better today." She touched an experienced hand to his forehead, seeming gratified to gauge no exceeding warmth. "Thankfully, you do not seem to have a fever. What say you?"

Marcus ducked his head, pinned by her knowing gaze. He should have realized sooner the connection between himself and Rafe could not remain undetected. "I was unsure how long the charade could last. When did you figure it out?"

"That is not important at the moment. What is important is that I know you were not directly lying to me, yet neither were you open with the entire truth. This discussion, however, must be tabled at present, as there are bigger fish to fry."

"What's happened?"

From a bureau drawer, Lady Aurelia retrieved a clean shirt and shook out the wrinkles before tossing it over. "Amos will be up to help you dress."

"But is everything all right?"

Lady Aurelia shook her head. "Colson is off the hook for having to issue a challenge to defend Serenity's honor. Brentmoor has stolen a march and sent his own challenge instead. He is claiming fraud and offense for breach of promise. The written missive all but called Colson out as a liar. Brentmoor's second delivered notice a few minutes before Lightfoot arrived."

"Dear God." Marcus exhaled a fragmented entreaty.

"Precisely." Lady Aurelia found the water pitcher empty. "If you do not feel strong enough to come down, please do not. Simply send Amos back with your regrets. Though it would be encouraging if you were there. I believe Gideon—as well as my granddaughter—would welcome your presence."

"I can be ready with some assistance."

Lady Aurelia's mouth formed a tremulous, sad smile. Concern sprouted in Marcus, and he ached for her decisions and carefully constructed plans gone awry. Her kind and understanding expression held a fondness Marcus felt lucky to have won and not forfeited, in spite of himself.

"St. James, I must admit you are burrowing your way into the heart of this family."

"Your family are likewise charting their own place in mine."

Lady Aurelia nodded in acknowledgment. "We shall talk, you and I. There is much to be discussed."

⌒

Amos delivered the refilled water pitcher to Marcus's quarters along with a brocade banyan. The informal flowing India-inspired garment was loose fitting, easily donned over his shirt and breeches. With the banyan, a coat sleeve was not required to fit over Marcus's wrapped arm. Madelaine, bless her, had lengthened the hem with an additional layer of trim to account for his height. She'd also fashioned a muslin sling to cradle his damaged wing.

Marcus gripped Amos's shoulder as they left the stable for the house, ambling along the brick path through the garden gazebo. He wasn't entirely steady, as a headache pounded at his temples while holding his throbbing arm close.

Rafe was the first to make eye contact with Marcus when he arrived at the library. His cousin's demeanor conveyed a trace of warning. Marcus tried to relay assurance, though he wasn't yet sure what penalty Lady Aurelia might exact for their sin of omission.

Twitch, Jonathan, Gideon, Serenity, and Tyree welcomed and greeted him, commenting on his health and best wishes for continued recovery. Serenity's bruised and swollen half smile verified that supporting the Ravensworths was the right thing to do.

Serenity sat closest to Lady Aurelia and to the aviary. They would have the ravens for an audience.

Madelaine joined the company after assigning Amos and Asher care of Jessa for the duration of the briefing. Lady Aurelia signaled Rafe to begin.

"Most of you know I am a thief-taker operating under the name Oakley Lightfoot." Rafe inclined his dark-blond head to the Northcrafts and Jonathan. "I report to Sir John Fielding out of Bow Street. Most of the time I work undercover and am not strictly confined to London.

"Two of my recent cases intersected and led me to Bath and here to Fernsby Hall. The first was the disappearance of Jean Collier, a masquerading dairy maid who was a runaway from Mayfair. Her uncle employed me to locate her. Regrettably, it was her body found by the hounds during the recent hunt.

"A second case was presented to me by Lady Aurelia. At her solicitor's suggestion, she engaged me to quietly look into Colson's gambling and other misdeeds.

"I shall try to make this as succinct as possible. Should you have any questions, feel free to ask."

Tyree spoke up. "Do you know who murdered Jean Collier?"

"Yes and it was not Colson, though it was intended at first blush to make it appear he was the culprit. Colson's greed blinded him to the extent he was in over his head with the wrong sort. Brentmoor used him for sport, playing on his compulsive gambling habit and growing richer because of it. The deeper Colson's dilemma, the rasher his actions. When he failed to deliver on promises he should not have made, Brentmoor called in favors starting with having the dairy maid killed." According to Lightfoot's notes, Colson cared for the girl and was completely undone over her passing. He admitted fathering her unborn child. "At some point, he expressed a desire to marry her, but without follow-through. Colson's words likely were meant to persuade her to give in to him, not actually change her name."

Lady Aurelia closed her eyes and pinched the bridge of her nose. Marcus guessed she was thinking Colson was cast from the same mould as his mother. On the battlefield, Marcus had received a harsh introduction to the face of evil in a common enemy. What devastation for her ladyship and the Ravensworths to suffer an enemy within their own connections.

Lightfoot enumerated Colson's gambling debts and described how Brentmoor planted marks by insidious means to goad Colson into betting with or against higher and higher stakes. Out of desperation, Colson went so far as to put up Fernsby itself—and lost.

Twitch's jaw dropped at the revelation. "He wagered the deed to Fernsby?"

"Before or after selling Serenity out to that brute of a baron?" Gideon cracked his knuckles.

"The transaction would not have held up under legal scrutiny. The documents were forged," Lady Aurelia said in a tone meant to impart calm. "Colson has added counterfeiting to his list of debatable accomplishments."

"What will happen to them?" Serenity paced a short track at the aviary door. "Anything?"

Prejudice didn't set well with Tyree. "Colson is the assumed son of a baronet, and Brentmoor holds the rank of baron. Brentmoor is equally as guilty of wrongdoing as Colson, if not more so."

Lightfoot approached Serenity. His troubled eyes lingered over her purple bruises and bandaged head wound. "It's a nuanced business, the unsavory realm of crime and punishment. It pains me greatly, but I must tell you plain: There likely won't be any. Punishment, that is. Pray, forgive my bluntness, Miss Ravensworth, but from scenes I've witnessed to date, a charge of attempted rape against a powerful peer such as Brentmoor would be dismissed without—*ahem*—certain evidence, which, unless proven by means of ruthless interrogation..." Lightfoot hung his head. "Miss Ravensworth, if you were to take the stand in a courtroom, you would do so alone. There would be no one present to prevent a heap of verbal abuse, and the unfortunate experience would reduce your reputation to tattered shreds."

"That is not right," Serenity said through clenched teeth. Indignation curled her trembling hands into fists.

"No," Lightfoot lamented, unable to disagree. "The law is far from perfect, and sinful humans farther still." He met Marcus's gaze, as if to clarify somehow. "When I can't find right in certain situations, I doggedly seek it in others where I can."

"This is unconscionable!" Gideon said. "Brentmoor deserves sentence but will get off scot-free. And he knows it."

"There will be no punishment for Brentmoor's cheating or doing away with Jean Collier either, will there?" Twitch asked.

Lightfoot faced the bearded merchant. "Murder is a different category—a corpse is admissible evidence. I am in the process of assembling a stronger case. It must be solid or it won't have a chance. If I can prove it, Brentmoor will have no claim to 'privilege of peerage.'"

"What about Colson?" Jonathan asked. "I'm to be his second in the duel."

Lightfoot's shoulders raised and settled in a hesitant shrug. "Dueling exists outside the law."

"No!" Serenity's objection reverberated. "Jonathan, what are you thinking?"

"Yes, Jon, what are you thinking?" Colson braced an arm on either side of the library door, his scornful glance encompassing each of the gathered. "Seems all this jury room lacks is an accused."

"Since you are here, we are no longer lacking." Serenity marched to confront her half brother and slapped his arrogant face with all her might.

The blow connected on point. Colson rubbed the reddening welts surfacing along his cheek and exercised his jaw from side to side.

Marcus thought Gideon might applaud Serenity's feisty action, and he wouldn't have been alone in doing so.

"I'm surprised, Jon, that you aren't pushing 'Thou shalt not kill' rather than fill in as my second."

Jonathan, nine years Colson's junior but the taller of the two, protectively moved Serenity behind him. He loomed over his older brother until Colson retreated a step. "You need me, for no one else will volunteer to stand on your behalf. All your so-called friends have abandoned you and remain entrenched in Brentmoor's camp."

Colson flinched, unable to dodge the cutting harshness of Brentmoor's absolute betrayal.

"I am not an ordained man of the cloth yet," Jonathan added, "and in this particular instance, my conscience doesn't wrestle my desire to see right triumph. You are guilty of many things, brother. I prefer to let the Almighty sort it out between the two of you. Until then the dictates of chivalry demand satisfaction between gentlemen." He shook his head. "That you lied and cheated to essentially sell our sister into a promise of matrimony with a monster like Brentmoor in order to distribute her dowry to cover your debts is inconceivable. You are indeed the accused in this room."

Colson rolled his eyes. "You, of all people, advocating an illegal practice."

Jonathan poked Colson in the chest. "With matched smoothbores, God will have His judgment. You brought about this travesty, now you'll fix it—or die trying."

Colson spun on his heel, but before he cleared a step, Gideon grabbed him by the lapels to forestall his retreat. "I *wanted* to be your second."

"You can't, Gid," Jonathan said. "You remain a commissioned officer, and if you're found out, it won't go well for you."

"He's right, Ravensworth," Marcus said, "and you know it. A duel could get you cashiered."

"You think either of you could stand up to Lord Brentmoor?" Colson sneered and shoved past Gideon. "Do you know how many duels he's won?"

Jonathan released a steady breath. "I don't have to beat Brentmoor. My responsibility is to serve as witness should he kill you."

Colson's complexion paled.

Twitch cast an affirming glance to Gideon, who retrieved a gleaming mahogany box trimmed with polished brass inlay and fixtures. He opened the lid.

All present viewed two well-crafted pistols and corresponding powder flasks nestled within neat compartments lined with green baize. In addition to the guns themselves, the box contained accompanying rods for cleaning and loading, flints, spanners, a bullet mould, and a ready-made supply of .50 caliber balls.

Jonathan spoke into the thick silence. "You are the challenged, Colson. Brentmoor, as challenger, will send no letter of apology. He intended to ruin Serenity after she refused his offer publicly—an offer that never should have been announced or even entertained. His actions avowed if he was not to have her, no one would.

"As challenged, you choose the weapons and the ground. Brentmoor retains the choice of distance. I, along with whoever is Brentmoor's second, will set the terms for time and firing."

Colson's cocky arrogance dwindled. "He will kill me."

"You might have considered that sooner before your willful recklessness endangered the rest of us." Lady Aurelia stood at Serenity's side, protective arm about her granddaughter's shoulders. "Actions produce reactions and reactions always have consequences."

# *Chapter 17*

*Fernsby Hall, Near Bath*

Feeling older than his nineteen years, Jonathan's heavy heart weighted his descent on the grand staircase the following morning. Serenity and Grandee met him at the bottom step with consecutive hugs, and he treasured the infusion of reassuring love that lifted his spirits. He collected his cloak, hat, and gloves, and the box. Out of the corner of his eye, he spied one of Father's walking sticks propped in the umbrella stand next to the hall tree. His fingertips brushed the engraved *R* on the brass cap. The ebony stick measured the exact height for him.

"We have been praying," Grandee squeezed his hand, "and will continue to do so."

"I'll take all the prayers you can spare. I must make sure nothing goes awry or be called into question—afterward—whatever the outcome might be."

Mr. Todd brought up the carriage, silently offering his services as another "unofficial" witness.

Jonathan was grateful for the additional support. Over his shoulder to Grandee and Serenity, he said, "Pray for Colson most especially. Brentmoor will not relent, though I must believe he will honor the code as a gentleman. I fear Colson is in no way prepared to meet his Maker."

Mr. Todd halted the carriage at the gatehouse. Jonathan briskly rapped the monogrammed head of the walking stick against the iron-studded portal. "Colson. The time has come."

Beckett swung open the door for Jonathan to enter and offered a note. "For her ladyship."

A packed carpetbag resting on a bench in the narrow entry hall incited Jonathan's frown. "No. If you are thinking to resign your position here at Fernsby, you will need to seek an audience with my grandmother. You know quite well she administers household matters in my father's absence. I have my hands full enough with my brother's immediate circumstance. Take responsibility for yourself."

The former butler bowed, picked up his bag, and headed up the hill toward the manor.

Colson's obsession with appearances and what other people thought had him sporting his most expensive suit, embroidered waistcoat, and clocked silk stockings. Silver shoe buckles glinted in the cold morning light upon his exit from the gatehouse. A sudden gust tore at the ribbons securing his clubbed powdered wig and threatened to upend his black felt hunting hat. Donning cape and gloves, he cast a contemptuous glance at the mahogany box on the carriage seat. Jonathan suspected Colson's efforts to quash his mounting anxiety had proven ineffective.

Jonathan climbed to the seat opposite his brother. Mr. Todd clucked to the team and the horses pulled the equipage forward. "Colson, you have an equal chance of coming out of this alive or dead. Either way, I recommend serious repentance before we arrive at the field of honor you have chosen. God loves you more than you can fathom. At the same time, malicious wickedness is something He does not accept. As Grandee said, there are consequences to bad choices. There are stories of sin calling for a blood sacrifice to atone."

"Look no farther than when Cain killed Abel and was marked for it."

Jonathan's brow lifted. "Seems you have been listening to random sermons here and there. Had you listened more closely, you would have heard how Jesus became the sacrifice for our sins. You still have time to ask His forgiveness."

Colson waved off Jonathan's remark. "If I die, you move up in the pecking order."

Jonathan searched his brother's red and swollen eyes. "The money and inheritance have always been an idol to you. Not so to me."

"The 'one for the church.' Too holy and above such mundane things as money."

Jonathan folded his arms across his chest. "It saddens me to see how obsession and greed have corrupted you, brother. As for inheritance, should I receive anything at all in Father's will, I shall put it to good use toward helping others."

"Of course, you would."

Jonathan ignored Colson's biting sarcasm. "I would have rather volunteered to stand up as best man on your future wedding day than serve as your second today. Yet here we are."

The carriage made a brief detour to the home of Dr. Theophilus Graham. Grandee's physician toted a disapproving scowl along with his medical bag. "This has all gotten rather messy. How did this come about?"

Colson sat mute. Jonathan filled him in. "Colson failed to challenge Brentmoor for his disparaging treatment and insult against our sister. His cowardly inaction created a window of time Brentmoor used to issue a challenge of his own. Should Brentmoor win, he alleges he will dismiss Colson's debt and consider satisfaction met."

The physician stared straight ahead, resigned to his role in the ordeal. "With terms agreed upon, can't back out now." To Colson, he warned, "You, sir, will be judged by your comportment during this affair of honor. Try not to disgrace yourself any more than you already have. You have caused trouble enough for your family and they deserve far better. Knowing them, they will weather your scandal with grace—as they have done before."

Jonathan doubted if Colson even heard the admonition.

Rising sun dispelled shadow and fog, granting perfect clarity in the secluded field screened by a stand of trees in view of Beechen Cliff. Visibility, or lack of, was ruled out as a contributing factor in the outcome.

Lord Brentmoor's second, a man Jonathan had met briefly at the homecoming supper, examined the fine brace of pistols. "These are exceptional. Ever been used?"

"No. My father acquired them thinking he might have to defend his wife's honor once upon a time. Ironic her firstborn son is the one who will break them in."

"As you and I have been selected as the men of sense and judgment to oversee these proceedings, in this good light and on this good ground, let's get it over with," Brentmoor's second said.

With synchronized movements, Jonathan and the other second inspected and prepared the weapons. Patch. Ball. Powder. Each delivered a readied pistol to the respective combatant.

The agreement called for single shot, first blood, fire at leisure.

More than three seconds elapsed with neither Colson nor Brentmoor firing. Dr. Graham suggested the duel commence upon the drop of his handkerchief.

Brentmoor and Colson took positions ten yards apart, pistols cocked. The physician released the square of snowy-white linen.

Pistols barked in unison.

A frosty breeze cleared away smoke from spent black powder. Jonathan spotted blood—spilled on both sides.

Colson's unsteady shot had grazed Brentmoor's cheek, leaving behind a swath the width of a lead ball. Blood rushed to fill the surface in place of the missing skin. There would be a scar.

The calculated shot fired by the baron was the more accurate and destructive of the two. Colson's body had jerked on impact and Brentmoor coolly lowered his pistol.

Eyeing Brentmoor with glazed incredulity, Colson pressed his hand to his wounded abdomen. His fingers came away bloodstained. The ensuing ruby flow absorbed into his elaborately embroidered waistcoat. Defeat sank Colson to his knees.

"Satisfaction is received." Lord Brentmoor pressed a kerchief to his bloodied cheek to stanch the trickle. He returned the gun to his second by way of an overconfident pitch. He said, loud enough for all witnesses to hear, "Such a pity to waste good powder on a fatherless profligate." Without sparing a glance at his victim, Brentmoor stormed from the field toward a closed carriage, opting to wait inside while his second wrapped up the grim details.

Dr. Graham conducted a cursory examination of Colson's wound while Jonathan and Brentmoor's second cleaned and repacked the pistols in their elegant mahogany case.

The matter stood closed.

Jonathan hoped never to have cause to be party to another duel. Once in a lifetime was more than enough.

~

All through the night and into the sequential morning, Serenity's earnest prayers swam in sorrow. At this point, there was nothing she, Dr. Graham, or anyone else could do. The infection spreading in Colson's gut would hasten his demise. 'Twas only a matter of time.

Hand on the doorknob of the sickroom, Serenity filled her lungs, silently petitioning the Almighty for courage to do the right thing. The man languishing in the four-poster bed—the brother with whom she shared only the blood of their mother—had manipulated events, put her in harm's way, and brought shame to their whole family. She struggled to understand the motives for his depredations and she struggled to release her hurt. *Vengeance is Mine, saith the Lord.*

Her half brother opened eyes brimming with pained disdain. His reluctant acceptance of her offer of water was devoid of thanks.

"Colson?"

Unblinking, his cold stare traced the intricate design in the plastered ceiling overhead.

Serenity wiped a tear from her bruised cheek and sent an aching appeal heavenward. *Lord God, I cannot do this in my own strength. I plead for Your help to do as the Scriptures instruct.* She swallowed queasy distress and declared in a whisper, "Colson, I want you to know ... please believe me when I say I forgive you."

"Get. Out."

She didn't linger to be told twice. Colson would answer for his actions in judgment. Pausing at the end of the bed, she looked once more at the prone figure of the man whose greed surpassed good sense. "As you wish. Shall I send Mrs. Todd?"

Zero acknowledgment.

"Good-bye, Colson." Retreating to the door, Serenity exhaled a ragged sigh and again swiped at misting tears. Her heart felt free of the pressing stone weight now lifted. Turning back, she whispered another prayer on Colson's behalf, "May God have mercy on your poor, wretched soul."

# *Chapter 18*

*Fernsby Hall, Near Bath*

Gideon joined Serenity in the library after dinner the next afternoon. Lingering embers, duller grey than glowing orange, gave off little to no heat. December's bluster lashed the trees outside, shaking persistent leaves loose while rain rattled against the expansive Palladian windows.

"There you are. How are you holding up, Sis?"

The lifting motion of Serenity's one-shouldered shrug pulled at stiff muscles. "Well enough. Is he ... "

"Dr. Theophilus Graham will handle Colson's final arrangements. He and Uncle Twitch have it all worked out and will execute Grandee's orders. Quiet. No fuss. No scandal. Jonathan said something about washing hands and shaking dust off feet."

Gideon hunkered down on the tufted footstool near her chair, his usual amiability subdued. "There's still more to come before resolution can be had. The past few days have answered questions—and raised others."

"More loose ends." Serenity agreed, contemplative. "Am I a horrible sister because I feel more freedom than I do remorse?"

"No." He gently cupped her discolored cheek. "You are an extraordinary sister—my favorite—and Jonathan, Amos, and I are blessed to claim you as ours."

"Favorite? By default, as I am the only one you have. But thank
you for saying so." Serenity sighed. "Have you been to see St. James
again?"

Gideon expelled a heavy sigh of his own and rested his elbows on
his bent knees. "Sis, I'm worried about him."

"Why? By last report, he showed no signs of fever."

"His injuries keep mounting and the memories to go with them
are waning."

"I don't understand."

"When you first asked me to tell you the story about St.
James saving my life, I suppose I was trying to shield you from
unpleasantness."

Serenity tipped her head, studying him. "I am not a little girl
anymore. Life contains many unpleasant things, as we have had
ample proof of late. By the Almighty's grace, we pick up the pieces
and move forward."

"You sound like Grandee."

"That is a treasured comparison. Are you moving forward?"

Gideon answered, but not with reference to himself. "That's part
of St. James's problem. He cannot find some of the pieces that would
enable him to move forward because he cannot remember what happened." Gideon scooted the footstool closer, covering her hands with
his. "St. James is a good man, true friend. I have almost lost him
twice. My desire is to help him, but he refuses to talk to me."

"Do you know what happened to him?" Serenity envisioned St.
James's feather tattoos. Next to his prayer book on the bedside table,
a porcelain dish held a broken arrowhead and the musket ball Dr.
Graham had recently removed from his damaged arm.

"I have compiled as much information as I could unearth. I cling
to the hope that by sharing the details with him, he might recapture
more of his elusive memories. He keeps things locked away tight, and
I am not convinced that is constructive for his state of mind."

"What is to be done?" Serenity asked. "How can I help you help him?"

Genuine relief tinged Gideon's smile. "I have an idea, but it could be costly. If I tell you what I know, would you be willing to share it with him? He shuts me out, but ... "

"But?"

"But he holds you in high regard. He's fond of you."

She wasn't so sure. Marcus had been increasingly distant since they'd shared that kiss. Serenity lowered her eyes, not wishing Gideon to see the impact of his words. It was bad enough she blushed at the remembering.

Gideon focused on the immediate dilemma. "His regard for you could be useful because you could serve as emissary to elicit St. James's confidence. You are like Grandee in that way too." He cracked his knuckles, the nervous habit betraying his agitation. "Mayhap coming from you, the words would provide solace, where mine have failed."

"I cannot help him if you don't tell me what happened to him."

Gideon weighed his decision and nodded once, adding with caution, "There are no half measures. All or nothing. You and I could both lose his friendship if he doesn't take to the idea. He's a stubborn man."

She curbed her grin. "Is there not an adage about said pot calling a certain kettle black? You are a stubborn man too, Gideon. Your similarities are likely why you befriended each other. If we don't try, we will have failed him for sure."

Gideon stood, hands clasped behind his back, and paced. Serenity thought he might be trying to judge the most logical place to begin. "The summary is this: He survived a massacre at Fort Michilimackinac during Pontiac's Rebellion. And then he disappeared. For eight weeks, no word—he was absolutely unaccounted for. His name was not listed among casualties or the dead. The Battle of Bushy Run brought an end to the siege at Fort Pitt. I was injured and taken to the hospital there to have my wounds checked by the surgeon. Which is where I found St. James." Gideon shook his dark head, still amazed. "Sis, Fort Pitt is five hundred miles from Fort Michilimackinac—and he has no idea how he got there."

Serenity plaited her raven tresses but didn't bother pinning the thick mass into a knot at the back of her head. She donned a ruffled cap, letting the braid trail halfway to her waist. She had not been able to sleep last night after listening to Gideon relay his collected information concerning St. James. He'd started haltingly at first, afraid he might run her off with portions of the story. But she had listened without flinching. She was almost glad he'd told her all he had—her rampant imagination painted more gruesome images than those Gideon had shared. "All or nothing, no half measures with him," he'd reminded her, then winked. "No half measures with either of you." For St. James's sake as well as hers, Gideon had deemed the risk worthy, and with methodical description, he pitched into his unsavory oration, then awaited her reaction.

"I understand now why he wouldn't wish to discuss it," she had replied in a dry whisper. "It's a lot to bear."

"He's a soldier."

"That doesn't mean his heart is disconnected from his head. He thinks deeply and feels as much as you or me." Or so she had observed in the hours she spent with him as he recuperated.

Gideon met her at the case clock in the entry hall. Outdoors, with the storm blown over, the sun pinkened the eastern sky. "Do you want me to go with you?"

She pondered. "I appreciate your offer, but please let me try on my own first. All right? If you truly think he will listen, mayhap it will go easier if he only has me to face." She wouldn't back down from this challenge, because she wanted to help him, enough to risk the coming consequences. Come what may.

"Sis?"

She tied the ribbon of her red wool cardinal beneath her chin, waiting.

"Are you fond of him?"

She bit back a smile, declining to answer and praying Gideon didn't detect the quickened cadence of her heart. Fond of him? *Yes.* Last night, after mulling all Gideon had shared, it had occurred to her that her decision to sail for the Colonies could be impacted if she let herself care too much. What she was about to do was for St. James's sake.

Across the garden and yard, she kicked at downed branches and strewn leaves left by the storm's wake. She climbed the apartment stairs, then knocked on the open door. "St. James?" She set the bucket of water and the hamper, prepared by Nancie Heath, on the small dining table.

St. James lay sprawled across the bedstead, random movements jerky, agitated. Sweat matted his loose hair against his forehead and neck. One tentative touch confirmed his temperature on the warm side, though that could just as well be the result of his tangle with the bedclothes, not infection. Dr. Graham was expected to remove his stitches on the morrow, as well as hers. She dipped a towel cloth into the bucket to bathe his face. His eyelids fluttered open, and in half a breath his fingers encircled her wrist like a vise.

She stilled, casting an inquisitive glance at his strong hold on her arm, then met his confused frown. He unhanded her with a swift release. He blinked three times in succession before his focus registered.

"Good morning," she said with a shy smile.

He ducked his head. "Morning."

"You felt warm to me. We don't need a fever to find you."

"No fever."

"I brought breakfast."

"Not hungry."

"Thirsty?"

He nodded.

She turned to get a drink for him. "Wait ... Don't go."

"Just to fetch some water, or there's milk from the springhouse, if you prefer."

"Water."

He drained the glass, let out a calming sigh, and leaned back against the rearranged pillows.

"I didn't sleep very well last night either." She pulled a fan-backed Windsor chair next to the bedside table. "Did the storm wake you?"

"No."

*Oh, Lord, please smooth the way. Make it plain if I should tread this path with him or not.* She picked up the copy of Defoe's *Robinson Crusoe* but didn't open the cover.

"Don't want to hear someone else's story." His bleary eyes closed, and he sank down farther into the mattress.

"All right. In that case, I have a different story to tell you, but it's a hard one."

"Tell."

"Before I start, I need you to agree that you will listen all the way through to the end." She gave him an out.

Tension coiled through his tall frame, like a hunter's trap waiting to be sprung. He nodded his acquiescence.

She prayed again, for grace in the telling and for Marcus to receive the words in the spirit of their intent. A fortifying breath, then she began, for even though his eyes were closed, she sensed he heard her every syllable.

"Dr. Graham will be here tomorrow to remove your stitches and redress your wound. As you continue to progress, we continue to pray the incision heals without difficulty and the break mends well. It is his professional opinion the dislodged musket ball somehow worked its way along the muscle beneath the skin's surface. He calls it providential that when you were initially shot, the elbow didn't shatter." Did this battle-tried warrior give credence to how closely the Almighty must have been shielding him to keep him alive throughout his ordeal?

"Gideon accompanied you on a schooner from General Amherst's headquarters at Montreal to Fort Michilimackinac." She echoed Gideon's French pronunciation, which sounded like *Mish-eh-la-mack-inaw*. "I've only just learned to say that, so please don't ask me to spell it."

His lips quirked, which revealed he was indeed listening.

Maintaining her one-sided conversation, Serenity forged on. "Arriving at the fort overlooking the straits, Gideon received new orders from Captain Etherington and Lieutenant Leslye. Gideon was to organize an exploration along the St. Clair River to learn if vessels larger than canoes or bateaux could safely travel the waterway leading to Fort Detroit. Gideon was surprised you weren't tasked with going, given your eye for detail and rough-sketched maps. His plan was to leave with a handful of assigned soldiers and a pair of sailors, and they would carry dispatches for the garrison commander when they departed the next day. Rumors of hostilities with the Indians had been brewing since the treaty putting an end to the Seven Years' War, but news of the siege of Fort Detroit hadn't yet reached Michilimackinac. After his briefing, Gideon visited your quarters to share what became a last supper of sorts with you, your father, and your older brother. His name was Lucas. Is that right?"

An involuntary shudder raised gooseflesh along St. James's arms.

Serenity followed her instinct and curled her fingers around St. James's to impart a measure of comfort, however small. This recovering man had fought for the Crown and nearly died. In service, he'd traveled hundreds of miles across newly acquired territories of British North America. Serenity had never yet left England's shores, but she would, though now was not the time to dwell on that. The large hand she held squeezed back.

⌒

If Marcus hadn't known Serenity's recited narrative as truth—an accurate chronicling of events in which he himself had been an active participant—he might have written it all off as a fanciful plot of an adventure novel. A morbidly captivating one at that.

"Gideon was three weeks gone from Michilimackinac by the second day of June."

Her soft inflections lulled him, luring his repressed memories in a direction he didn't want to go yet couldn't help but follow.

"Only later did he learn what happened on that day. How Captain Etherington and Lieutenant Leslye opened the fort's Land Gate for the Ojibwe warriors, who had invited them to come out and watch a *baggatiway* game played against Sauks, supposedly in honor of King George's birthday."

*Who had told the Ojibwe the date of the King's birthday?*

"A war cry signaled the attack and the match turned lethal. By design, the baggatiway ball sailed over the palisade, aimed at the officers, and sent hundreds of Indians rushing the Land Gate. Indian women lined the outside wall, and as the shrieking warriors ran past, they distributed the tomahawks, war clubs, hatchets, knives, and guns concealed in the folds of the heavy blankets they'd worn during the match."

*Of course, hiding weapons would necessitate wearing heavy blankets on such a sultry day ...*

Serenity used the towel cloth to wipe his temple. Sweat? Tears? Both mingled together. He couldn't block out the next part of the story. The worst part—or so it had seemed at the time.

"Warriors surged through the gate, surviving English officers taken hostage. French traders and their families were not beset. Only soldiers wearing red coats in the fort were summarily cut down," Serenity's voice dropped to a choked whisper, "shot, stabbed, scalped."

Marcus tensed under the quilted duvet. His breathing grew shallower still.

*Absolute chaos ... piercing battle cries ... a felling shot followed by merciless clubbing ... left for dead by war-painted Indians bent on annihilating the English. Nowhere to hide ...*

His father had had no time to reload his musket before he was killed. His brother had fought bravely, one against too many, until butchered before Marcus's eyes.

*Lucas ... bleeding out, soul and spirit escaping ...*

Marcus commanded himself to breathe.

And remember.

Badly hurt and unable to move his battered body, he'd played possum for the duration of the attack, praying not to be discovered. The tactic preserved his life until darkness shrouded the fort and all the bloodied carnage contained within its walls, as well as some without. Marcus hadn't been put under the knife and his scalp remained miraculously intact. Pain seared his heart afresh. He could do nothing to bring back his father or his brother, not then nor in this moment.

"The attack was spent in under an hour." Serenity's voice startled him from his macabre reflections. Ravensworth—and now his sister—possessed an account of the events. Even so, neither of them comprehended the full extent of what happened to him, that day or afterward. Those dark hours were his alone to bear.

"Gideon said it was from Michilimackinac that you disappeared. Did you know ten forts were destroyed and fell over the next month? Perhaps not until much later, as witnesses were few and survivors fewer still. Seeds of rebellion were rooted in a vision seen by a Delaware named Neolin, but the coordinated uprising was planned

by the Ottawa Pontiac with war councils, wampum belts, and alli-
ances of several tribes. Their common mission was to kill as many
English as they possibly could. Michilimackinac was the fifth fort
targeted by Pontiac's warriors."

*After, amid the carnage, by the light of the moon, Wakwi sought me,
rescued me...* The woman's face and braided hair flashed, then blurred.

"Detroit, Niagara, and Pitt outlasted their respective sieges. I did
not ask Gideon how he broke through the siege line after the Battle
of Bloody Run near Fort Detroit, as I am certain that is another long
story for another day. But he did tell of being wounded at Bushy Run
in relief of Fort Pitt. Shortly following that engagement, the siege
lifted. At both Detroit and Pitt and everywhere in between, he asked
anyone and everyone who crossed his path if there was word of you.
Who might have seen you last? Though you are hard to miss and not
easily forgotten, he learned nothing, as there was no trace. With no
confirming evidence of your death, he earnestly prayed you still lived.
God alone knew what had become of you."

Marcus caught her familiar lavender and vanilla scent, and he
imagined a moist sheen in her eyes, as she sounded on the verge of
tears. For him? For her brother? Marcus's exhale came out ragged.

"Gideon struggled during his recovery. Infection found him
at the stronghold on the point where three rivers converge—the
Allegheny, the Ohio, and the—here is another Gideon had to teach
me pronounce—the Monongahela." *Ma-non-guh-hee-la.*

"The regimental surgeon threatened to take Gideon's arm off
to prevent the infection from spreading further before you—on a
blistering August day—inexplicably showed up at Fort Pitt, seemingly returned from the dead to the land of the living, back from the
wilderness."

*Inexplicably miraculous...God preserved me in the wilderness...Lean
not unto thine own understanding...His ways are not our ways, they are
higher...Wakwi...keening, crying...her tears washed his wounds...*

"How you traveled the miles—overland, by water, or a combination of the two—from Fort Michilimackinac to Fort Pitt was anyone's guess. A mystery. Gideon suspects you were brought there deliberately by someone ... in order to be reunited with your own kind."

*Wakwi could have killed me, but instead she made me well and let me live ...*

"Between your prayers and whatever concoction was in the poultice applied to Gideon's wound at your direction, both caused my brother to heal and remain whole. Gideon said after the Battle of Bushy Run and the arrival of Colonel Bouquet's reinforcements, you were debriefed but unable to supply any useful information concerning the massacre at Fort Michilimackinac because you maintained you didn't remember.

"Several days later, Gideon received new orders. You went with him this time. The small detachment trekked through the Virginia backcountry toward Alexandria, where you were to board a transport ship home to England. Before reaching Winchester though, your party was ambushed. One scout was killed outright and, in the next instant, you launched yourself between Gideon and a distantly aimed long rifle. I am not glad you were shot, but I confess I am grateful for your action on his behalf. Without your intervention, my brother would not have come home."

*I couldn't save mine, so I saved yours. By the grace of God.*

"A man down and moving quickly, Gideon dressed your wound as best he could. He had a hard time getting the graze to stop bleeding.

"Your shoulder was inflamed by the time you reached the Warm Springs. The mineral waters with their medicinal properties offset infection. After a few days' delay, Gideon deemed you well enough to travel. With the others, you left the springs to keep going toward Winchester and what remained of Fort Loudoun."

*Fort Loudoun ... one of a string of defensive installations on Virginia's western boundary ... designed and established by the leader of the Virginia*

*militia, Colonel George Washington ... built on high ground on the out-*
*skirts of the frontier settlement called by an English namesake. Winchester.*
*Nothing about the primitive colonial town remotely resembled its counterpart*
*in England.*

"At Winchester, near the fort, a surgeon treated your shoulder and
lingering lacerations. He examined the arrowhead wound at your elbow
and found it healing over. Nothing gave him any indication a musket
ball from the massacre remained in your arm. It was overlooked. Dr.
Graham necessarily carved new scars to go along with your old ones."

Marcus opened his eyes. Serenity bowed her head, her raven hair
loosely bound in a long silken plait hanging in front of her shoulder.

Pieces of the broken agate arrowhead rested in her cupped palm.
Fragments removed from his arm, the one marked with the feather
tattoo. Between her opposite thumb and forefinger, she held the
biggest of the three pieces for closer examination, turning the flat,
highly polished razor-sharp stone this way and that. "What you have
been through, Marcus ... "

His name from her lips sounded like *Mar-kiss* ... And he
upbraided himself for wanting to kiss her again. Every grain of dis-
cipline he possessed brought to bear so as not to repeat the action.

He was through listening to her—no, to *his* tale. "Leave the
pieces be."

"As you wish." Resolute, she returned the agate fragments to the
porcelain dish. "I— Is there anything else I can do for you?" She was
polite.

He was not. "No. You've done quite enough."

She had taken tormenting memories that for several months had
lurked in the murky corners of his mind, held at bay by dint of will,
and thrown them out into stark light. She caused him to think. And to
feel ... The cultivated numbness of his mind and heart gave way to an
ache that had not diminished in the least, and he wasn't able to deny
its existence any longer. *Nowhere to hide ...*

"I'll leave now." Tears shimmered in her ginger-brown eyes. "Thank you for honoring my request to listen."

*Gideon said...*

Ravensworth had his moments, but in the end, he proved loyal. A trustworthy fellow combatant. His sister was but trying to help, as was her wont. Truly, Marcus understood her part in this— Ravensworth set her up because he rightly assumed Marcus would comply with her request.

Marcus hesitated half a beat, heart pounding. Cautiously he extended his hand, and she placed hers in his. He discerned a different warmth in her touch, one born of caring.

"Come back later?" Marcus didn't want to be left to tame the memories alone.

"Count on it."

She was indeed related to Ravensworth.

# Chapter 19

*Bath Abbey, Bath*

Resonant bootheels announced another visitor in the otherwise empty abbey. Unrushed strides along the stone-paved aisle brought the intruder to the pew where Serenity sat, but she did not lift her head or open her eyes until her prayerful petition concluded, punctuated with a scarcely audible "amen."

Marcus St. James held his hat in both hands. From his lofty height, he appraised her. She scooted over to make room beside her on the wooden bench, but he instead entered the pew one row ahead and sat facing forward toward the jewel-colored window beyond the altar. The breadth of his shoulders obscured all else from view.

"I owe you an apology, Miss Ravensworth," St. James said in a tone so low Serenity strained to hear him in the quiet.

Her heart thudded. She didn't believe he regretted their kiss. Mayhap he regretted his gruffness, for he'd acted like a curmudgeon during more days of this past week than not. Her prayers included a sincere request the Almighty would continue healing his wounds—quickly and completely—and restore his good humor.

"My mother would be appalled at my manners—or lack thereof—and my sister . . . " He shook his head. "May I beg your forgiveness?"

"Upon my word, Mr. St. James, trust you have it—but I owe you an apology as well. I tread on ground I knew you did not wish to travel. Gideon said—"

"Yes. Your brother, my friend, understood I needed help. He calculated I would turn him away sooner than I would you. He was right," St. James admitted. "Your tenacious narration restored some of the missing pieces, though not all. Until I can acquire the remaining lost bits, I am at loose ends, not yet at peace with it."

Leaning left, she sought to catch a better glimpse of his square-jawed profile. His gold-flecked green eyes focused on the barrel-vaulted ceiling, where sunshine cast scraps of color through panes of stained glass. His damp honey-brown hair fell unrestrained between his shoulder blades, telling evidence of where he'd spent his morning hours. "You've been to take the waters again."

"Aye. A warm tumblerful at the Pump Room prior to a long soak at the King's Bath." He tentatively rotated his shoulder and straightened his left arm once before again cradling it against his side. "Gained some benefit, I think." From his right coat pocket, he withdrew a length of black ribbon and held it out to her. "I can't yet reach with this injured arm of mine to put my hair in a queue. Would you mind tying it for me? Please."

Mischief in his eyes melted her surprised hesitation. The abbey was vacant. They weren't sharing a pew. The ancient walls would not tattle. Serenity coyly gathered his hair. It was clean and thick and soft. "Braided?" she whispered.

"No, it's fine to leave the tail unbraided."

Hearing the smile in his voice and with hands steadier than she credited, she accomplished his bold request by tying the ribbon into a simple knot, then combed through his mane from nape to shoulder-length ends with her fingers. "There you have it."

"Much obliged."

"Happy to assist."

He balanced his good arm along the back of the pew. "I interrupted your quiet time."

"I had finished praying."

"How does one go about getting included on your prayer list?"

She studied his face, regarding his serious appeal. "You are already on my list."

"Good, because you are on mine as well."

Fidgety in his pew, St. James faced the nearest abbey wall. He studied a few of the etched memorial stones, settling on the one that mattered to her.

The ledger panel in memory of her mother, Laurenda McCandless Ravensworth, held a brief inscription. Etched below the dates of her birth, death, and age appeared the words *Beloved as Daughter, Mother, and Wife.* Given what Serenity now knew concerning her mother's history, the roles were conspicuously listed in their chronological order for all the world to see. Colson's unlamented remains rested in the crypt as well. In time, his name would also be hewn into the stone marker.

"For what it's worth, please accept my condolences on your brother's passing. Lady Aurelia wisely opted for a quiet burial. It's hard to eulogize someone who has done nothing praiseworthy."

"He will hardly be missed." The uttered realization saddened Serenity. "Truly, it is more of a sense of welcome relief knowing he can't inflict hurt on us anymore."

"For that I am thankful." St. James's keen inspection skimmed her fading bruises and lingered on her mouth.

"So am I." She glanced down at the kid gloves on her lap, then returned his unwavering glance. "How did you know I was here?"

"Madelaine. I stopped by the Northcrafts' after the King's Bath to convey my regrets for being unable to accept her invitation to their Twelfth Night gathering. I wanted to hold Jessa once more as well as bid Madelaine and Tyree and Asher good-bye."

"Good-bye?" Dread widened Serenity's eyes.

He nodded. "Gideon received word of my sister's impending arrival. Johnna will be here after Christmas with little Corinna. I gather your brother Jonathan made a report of my injuries to her upon his return to Oxford. Johnna deems it best to collect me and take me back to her own home, where she can keep an eye on me— though I sincerely doubt she can dispense any better treatment than I have received at Fernsby thus far, thanks to the professional care of Dr. Graham and the tender ministrations of the ladies deployed by her ladyship—and you."

Beneath a tremulous smile, Serenity absorbed Marcus's words. She wanted to believe Gideon when he said St. James held her in special regard, but reminded herself that saying good-bye to him now would mean she wouldn't have to do so again when she sailed for the Colonies. Her gaze landed on the silk mourning band encircling his left sleeve. The fabric concealing his tattooed skin didn't hamper her recollection of the indelible feather-tip armlet she knew was there. "Do you—"

"Will you—" he began at the same time. "Please, you speak first."

"Will I what?" Serenity hedged, wondering if the inked markings were one of the bits and pieces he couldn't place.

"Will plans for young Amos alter since Colson no longer wields that dreaded poem or threatens dire predictions against the remaining Ravensworth brothers?"

"No, the agreed-upon plans are going forward. Amos will sail with Uncle Twitch and work with him in the Colonies," she answered. "Have you plans to search for your missing bits of memories?"

"I don't know if I can plan with determined specificity. No forecasting the when. Every now and then, without warning, a sound or a scent will spur a string of consecutive recollections. But when hazy images sharpen then dissolve before I can latch on to them or make any sense of them, my frustration slips its restraint." He scrubbed his face with his hand and exhaled an exasperated sigh. "Once my sister gets her fill of my brooding presence, Johnna will pack me up and ship me back to the townhouse in St. James's Square. There Featherstone, my steward, is keeping matters in line until I return. I have army connections in London—associates of my father's—who might be able to help me weather or at least wade through the residual trauma."

Serenity detected no immediate hint of a repeat visit to Fernsby Hall. The thought depressed her, until she acknowledged she might not be there much longer either. "I—" She cleared her throat and pasted on a bright smile. "I will indeed be praying for you, Marcus."

"I'm counting on that."

⌣

*Fernsby Hall, Near Bath*

"Good afternoon, St. James. Am I interrupting?"

Marcus relaxed his at-attention posture at identifying the poised female voice as Lady Aurelia's. He offered his hand, should she need it, to ascend the last three steps at the top of the staircase. "Good day, my lady. To what do I owe the pleasure of your company?"

"A wish to convey my earnest gratitude." A twinkle in Lady Aurelia's eyes accompanied her sanguine smile. "My granddaughter was humming when she returned from town today. She mentioned crossing paths with you on her way to visit Madelaine and Jessa. 'Tis the first time I have heard anything light-hearted from her since ... "

"Since before the homecoming gathering," he finished her incomplete sentence. Ravensworth confirmed to Marcus his grandmother's approval. She liked him—quite a lot, in fact. But Marcus reminded himself Serenity had made her decision to leave, and from what he knew of her, she would keep her word and sail off with her tenacity in tow.

Lady Aurelia sat upon the chair he indicated. "You spoke with her."

A single nod. "I needed to apologize."

"And she accepted your apology?"

"She said she did."

"You may take Serenity at her word."

"Yes, my lady." He offered a differential dip of his chin. "I believe I can."

"May I take you at yours?"

"I will not lie to you."

Lady Aurelia arched an inferring brow. "You should have told me Oakley Lightfoot and your cousin Rafe are one and the same."

"Yes, I should have," Marcus agreed. "Now I will apologize to you for the omission. It was not intentional at the outset. My cousin's undercover investigating talents were unbeknown to me at that time."

Lady Aurelia waved his words aside as of little consequence. "He has concluded his investigation of you and reported his findings to me, Lord Oakleigh." She emphasized his seldom-used title, making him aware she knew exactly who he was, though she did not press for explanation, choosing to wait until he was ready to disclose his situation. "He is still working the Jean Collier case, seeing it through to completion."

"Rafe has bulldog tendencies."

"Evidently, a common trait in your bloodline." Lady Aurelia placed a copy of *Robin Hood* and a portrait miniature on the dining table. "You may pack those with the rest of your things." She pointed to the leather valise and cowhide knapsack atop the coverlet, his folded shirts, frock coats, smallclothes, and shaving kit waiting to be added in. "You are eager to leave us and return to your sister's home?"

"Gideon and Amos tried to persuade me to stay longer, but I believe it wiser if I go."

"That did not answer my question." Lady Aurelia scrutinized him. "What are you running from?"

"Not running," Marcus said. "Redeploying."

"So you say."

"I am curious, my lady. Why did you hire my thief-taker cousin to investigate me? What were you hoping to find?"

"Nothing." Lady Aurelia ticked off items as she would a daybook list. "No debts, no wife, no children, no unsavory habits. Nothing more than good breeding, good connections, good character. Your military service record is a bonus. I ought to be content and satisfied with the favorable outcome." Her laugh dwindled. "You may deem me presumptuous, but for my part, I construe it as preemption."

Her ladyship took her responsibility of looking after Serenity's interests very seriously. Marcus understood why Serenity took on responsibility for Amos in like fashion.

"We shall miss having you with us."

"And I you. All of you."

Lady Aurelia tilted her head to the side, like Serenity sometimes did. "What, besides your healing arm, pains you so? Grief over your father and brother? Or Serenity?"

A grin tipped Marcus's lips. "I know you read your Bible, Lady Aurelia. Are you familiar with the story in the twenty-fourth chapter of Genesis, where Abraham instructs his trusted servant to acquire a wife for his son Isaac?"

"Yes, now that you mention it. Does the story hold a particular revelation for you?"

"I am intrigued by the way Isaac was out in his fields praying when the caravan arrived and his father's servant brought Rebekah from a faraway land. Nowhere in the passage do I see that Isaac was looking for a wife. He had been in mourning, grieved on account of his mother's death. Arrangements were made on his behalf. Did he know that? Was he in agreement? The Scripture doesn't overtly tell or infer. What it does say was that once Rebekah arrived, Isaac took her to wife and he loved her."

"Are you bent on waiting on God to bring you a woman of His choosing?"

"Are you intent on helping God by offering Serenity as a candidate?"

She did not counter his accusation, and her laughter betrayed her attempted machinations. The matter of importance was that they shared an undeniable partiality for her granddaughter.

Lady Aurelia sobered. "Curiosity has killed a number of cats, and I ought to be more circumspect, but I will hazard anyway because I want to know the answer: Have you ever been in love, St. James?"

Rather than an instant reply, Marcus studied the oval water-color-on-ivory miniature by Gainsborough, an attractive rendering of Serenity. The artist captured the alluring flash and fire in her eyes, the innocence in her smile. Strands of pearls threaded through Serenity's glossy ebon tresses, and a raven stood guard, perched behind her shoulder. He closed his long fingers around the edge of the brass filigree frame, concealing the beguiling countenance.

In dense silence, Marcus tucked the portrait miniature into his waistcoat pocket. Clearing the hoarseness from this throat, he uttered a terse declaration. "I have been loved."

Raising her hem, Serenity halted an instant before her slipper attained the bottom stair. The rich timbre of St. James's voice drifted from the guest suite. "I have been loved."

She stepped back rather than upward. Her cheeks burned, mind galloping like wild Exmoor ponies.

Grandee spoke. "That sounds like a lamentable confession. Care to elaborate?"

St. James's bootheels struck the plank flooring above. The anguish in his voice plucked Serenity's heart, her feet rooted to the straw-covered stable floor. She debated leaving or staying, unsure which might be the more regrettable, wondering if any more of his missing memories were restored since sharing Gideon's information about the massacre.

Frustration laced his reply. "I don't ... know ... exactly. Because I cannot remember! Even after Serenity's storytelling, much still eludes me. The gnawing fear permeates ... What if I never recapture the missing bits to make enough sense of what happened?" His pacing restarted. "I know the events of before ... and then after. But those five hundred miles and more than eight weeks of my life are shadowed, unclear. The disjointed memories I do possess are raw and vague at best."

"Why not start with what you do know and leave the missing bits for a later time?" Grandee suggested.

St. James unleashed a burdened sigh. "There was a woman, Wakwi. Ojibwe, I think. After I reported for duty at Fort Michilimackinac, I saw her in a backyard garden of one of the trader's houses, speaking with my brother. Lucas knew her. When I confronted him ... he did not confirm with words, but his mannerisms marked him as a man in love. That one instance, when my gaze locked with hers, it was jarring because her eyes, they ... were blue ... "

St. James continued, "I saw her again on the day of the massacre. When Lucas fell, I spied her on her knees in front of the guardhouse beside his prone body. Our glances held amid the horror, each of us devastated, until in the next breath, I went down under the braves' beating."

Grandee remained quiet, and St. James must have felt encouraged to keep talking. "I hadn't the strength to move because of the inflicted pain. I thought I was dying, so I pretended I already had. I know not how much time passed, but when I came to, the sun was long down. And the blue-eyed woman came hunting for me. She and a man—a priest from Ste. Anne's church—hid me in a cellar for the rest of that night, and maybe one more? Then they loaded me onto a travois and dragged me away from the storehouse near the Water Gate. Clear of the palisade walls, we were swallowed into darkness. When I asked for water, she gave me a cup and urged me to drink. I must have slipped into mind-numbing oblivion again. Had she wanted to, she could have left me to die or killed me herself, but she did not. She tended me, helped me heal . . . and she called me by my brother's name."

"Do you favor your older brother?" Grandee asked.

"To a degree, but she was there when Lucas was killed. She had to know I wasn't him," St. James insisted.

"Not necessarily," Grandee said. "Consider this: A highly traumatic event and an apparent connection to your brother—one of such substance she grieved his death deeply. If you resembled Lucas enough in her eyes, suppose she transferred that connection to you?"

St. James expelled another troubled sigh. "Mayhap."

"Do you suppose that her reason to come back to rescue you?" Grandee asked.

Serenity knew of being rescued, and she couldn't deny it was after St. James's heroics on her behalf that caused her opinion of him to alter. He wasn't merely Gideon's friend—he was a man she cared about. He had been rescued by the woman at the fort. Did he care for her?

Another "I don't know" was St. James's answer to Grandee's question. "There were horses in a stable where we hid, but after that the days and nights blurred and blended from one into the next. Whenever I regained my senses, either due to the demands of my personal needs or quenching my thirst or making me eat, she was there. Her voice was the only clear one apart from the others ... " He stopped, as if what he'd said registered afresh. "There were ... other ... voices."

"But you don't know whose?" Grandee asked.

"No," St. James answered, "but if there were others, and she wasn't alone, that would explain—otherwise how could she have moved me? We would have left tracks any scout could follow. She had to have had help, as I am far too tall and heavy for her to maneuver as dead weight. And whenever I asked for water, she gave me drink ... and I slept. Each time I woke ... we were never in the same place as when I slipped out of awareness."

"Sounds to me as if she was intentionally dulling your senses to help you rest or alleviate the pain," Grandee said.

"I don't know. If that be the case, I was foxed with some mighty potent herbs ... " St. James spoke as if the possibility hadn't previously entered his thoughts. "She would have had ample opportunity ... How simple it would have been for her to add something to fortify her medicinal berry juice concoction."

"A significant dose of valerian root could potentially keep you in and out of awareness—or belladonna," Grandee said. "If knowledgeable with herbs and their effects, she might have administered varying dosages by design. As she moved you and time passed, she might have needed to keep you quiet to lessen the risk of being discovered. Or prevent capture. You made mention of hearing other voices."

"Never near, merely murmurings. Possibly in French. But Wakwi's voice was always closest, and other than my brother's name, her language was unintelligible. Her expression and caring were in her ... touch." He coughed to clear his throat. "I know you've seen the inked feathers ... "

Of their own volition, Serenity's fingers clutched her left arm at the equivalent level of the markings he bore.

"If the potency of the herbs dulled my senses to the extent that I was tattooed without knowing it in the moment or remembering the incident after the fact, then how do I know what else I did or didn't do under the influence?"

No immediate answer came from Grandee, and St. James's voice rasped. "I have begged God to forgive me. Over and over."

"For what precisely?"

"For whatever it is I can't remember doing!" he barked. "We had no common words for conversation. What if... what if I tried to relay gratitude for tending my wounds and keeping me alive with more than a kiss?"

"Something in those shadowy memories of yours prompts you to believe that?"

"I told you," St. James said, "she kept calling me Lucas. She acted as if I were Lucas. Her familiar manner with me implied he was very dear to her."

"Therefore, you are determined to punish yourself with guilt over an act which may or may not have happened?"

Grandee issued the query most likely to goad St. James toward reason. It was a tactic Serenity had been subjected to on occasions when Grandee had applied her seldom-errant wisdom.

"Wakwi marked me as hers with a feathered tattoo, and I can't even remember the when or the where," St. James replied.

"That must have been quite the shocking discovery. I cannot imagine," Grandee said.

No response from St. James, and Grandee continued, "You told me earlier you apologized to Serenity and she accepted said apology. Why do you think the Almighty will not grant your request for the forgiveness you seek from Him? In his first letter, the Apostle John wrote, 'If we confess our sins, He is faithful and just to forgive us our sins, and to cleanse us from all unrighteousness.'"

St. James emitted another exasperated sigh. "That much I do know."

Grandee offered another morsel of well-meaning advice. "You are your own man, Marcus St. James, and I don't need to remind you that actions have consequences, but maybe you will want to refrain from telling this part of your story until you make peace with it. Particularly in Serenity's hearing."

"I have not told another soul besides you, Lady Aurelia. Certainly not your granddaughter, nor Rafe, nor Johnna—not even Gideon. Your investigation of me would be incomplete if I did not confess."

Serenity pressed a fisted hand to her mouth, stifling a feeble cry and rising bile. She blinked, feeling ill, as tears spilled. Grandee had Marcus St. James investigated? To what end? What did Grandee suspect him of? Did she not trust him? Only a few short weeks ago, Grandee had emphasized everything was not always as it seemed.

Treading softly away from the stable's staircase, she accepted that truth and infused starch back into her spine. Her trust in the Almighty undergirded her tenacious choice to banish rankling thoughts of undefined actions in which St. James had or had not partaken. Mankind was born with a sin nature, of which existed daily proof.

Serenity knew St. James as a man of integrity. A forgiven man— in spite of all she'd learned about him since Gideon's initial introduction—including what may or may not have happened to him in the miles stretching between Fort Michilimackinac and Fort Pitt. All she needed do was convince her hurting heart of the same conviction she held in her head.

Marcus's heart plummeted at the sight of Serenity leaving the stable block, shawl pulled tight about her shoulders, swiping at tears and trudging across the lawn toward Fernsby Cottage. To his rear, the apartment door stood open, leaving the sour knowledge she'd heard from his own lips confession of the story he hadn't intended to tell.

With a gentle blue-veined hand, Lady Aurelia covered the fingers gripping Marcus's left arm, circling the hidden feather tattoo. Compassionate understanding shone in her eyes.

"While you might approve of me, my lady, I can only imagine what Serenity must think. Whatever good opinion she may have had of me is ruined," he said.

"I will speak with her."

He doubted it would do any good, but he didn't dissuade her.

"Do you love my granddaughter?"

He swallowed against the lump in his throat to speak the truth. "I think I could. In fact, I might be halfway there."

Lady Aurelia's shrewd glance measured his uncommon lack of confidence. "What of her dowry?"

"You are in possession of Rafe's report. You know I inherited the Viscount Oakleigh title from my father, along with Oakleigh Combe. I have no need of Serenity's dowry. I'd love her without one."

"I believe she cares a great deal for you," Lady Aurelia said. "More than she may yet realize. Will you tell her?"

"Which part?" He faced a considerable mound of roiling confusion. "That I love her? No, not at present. She is not ready for all this ... Neither of us is. Besides which, I have other matters requiring immediate attention. It may be best all the way around to just leave off until things are better settled."

"One day soon perhaps?"

"We both need time to sort things out." Veiled vexation directed inwardly at himself remained.

Sympathetic and with an impressive degree of insight, Lady Aurelia commanded him as a loving mother might a repentant son. "Do stop punishing yourself, Marcus."

"I have tried. I still feel guilty and it haunts me."

"You have repented—you said so yourself."

His lips pressed together in a grim line. Whenever he came into Serenity's sphere, he measured himself unworthy of her.

"Forgiven," she repeated the resolute reminder. "By the grace of God. You would do well to remember that."

Self-loathing reversed his belief in Lady Aurelia's assurance. And what of Serenity? Could she—would she—forgive him?

"Marcus?"

"Yes, my lady," he answered dutifully. "I will remember that I am forgiven."

"Then act accordingly."

# Chapter 20

*Evensong, Balliol College Chapel, Oxford*
*Late December 1763*

Ancient languages comprised part of the university curriculum, and Jonathan Ravensworth had attained satisfactory progress thus far in his education. However, tonight, the choir's lyrical Latin incantation of the Magnificat proved purely untranslatable to him. His lanky physical frame occupied an aisle seat, though his troubled mind winged miles beyond the chapel's stone walls, the quadrangle, porter's lodge, and Broad Street.

The past few weeks had wrought varying degrees of distress, and he'd lost more than half a stone due to lack of hunger and infrequent meals. Too often, he relived recent events in dreams—those during the day as well as those that robbed him of peaceful nighttime slumber—from the cruel attack on his sister to the duel that killed his half brother to the shocking alteration of his third-son status to second born. He parried a mental barrage of new questions and doubts as to whether he was indeed meant to be the "one for the church."

Then came the unsettling announcement that Mr. FitzGerald faced a charge of regulatory noncompliance and probable dismissal from his position as don and academic fellow, going down at the end of the Michaelmas term. With each added wave of disturbance,

Jonathan commiserated with Serenity's heart-felt desire to retain familiar things as they stood. Except that time marched forward and change had its own way regardless.

Jonathan blinked to refocus, then skimmed the bronze-crowned eagle lectern and the mullioned windows' deepening colors as daylight waned on the second-to-the-last day of December. Sights and sounds of the Gothic chapel normally filled him with joy to be in the house of the Lord, but in this instant, they did not penetrate his cold soul. He clung to the promise that God would never leave him or forsake him, but heaven help him, he would keenly feel the absence of Mr. Ian FitzGerald's guidance.

Since Jonathan's arrival at Balliol, Mr. FitzGerald had tutored all his scholars not only in requisite coursework but also in how to live out the gospel message in practical application amid daily life. Helping the less fortunate, visiting the sick and imprisoned, sheltering, feeding, and clothing the poor. *And the King shall answer and say unto them, Verily I say unto you, Inasmuch as ye have done it unto one of the least of these my brethren, ye have done it unto me.*

Oblivious to The Reverend Canon's spoken prayer, Jonathan lifted a silent one of his own. *Lord God, am I not where I am supposed to be in Your scheme of things? If You are varying my path, leading elsewhere, please show me what service it is You desire of me.*

He remembered sitting, nervous but eager, in the Sheldonian Theatre during matriculation, hearing from the gowned vice-chancellor how time would pass quickly, to not be afraid to try new things and learn from mistakes, to give his best. Sir Nicholas deemed it no small thing to have a son at Oxford, and Jonathan also wanted to make Grandee proud. The transitory notion that he might not participate in graduation after completing his degree shook him. After ordination, the church was his intended vocation, though he had no idea where an eventual living might be had. *Thank You, Lord God, for Your unconditional love and forgiveness. Without them I cannot serve You in a manner worthy of Your glory. How shall I be Your witness? What do You want me to do?*

Unclasping his tightly folded hands, feeling reverted to his fingers. He scooped up his thick Bible and ducked out the back of the chapel the minute the evensong service concluded.

A bracing chill in the darkening night made his eyes water and, like a slap, crystalized his rambling musings. Jonathan's long stride carried him through the high-walled garden and down Magdalen Street toward St. Giles' to the Eagle and Child, where he thrice weekly taught basic lessons to a young lad Mr. FitzGerald targeted as a worthy project.

Under signage displaying a bird and baby, Jonathan crossed the threshold of the hundred-year-old public house. Closing the door on the winter night, he nodded to the barkeep and settled onto a bench at a table within range of the hearth. Henry, a spindly boy of a dozen years who did odd jobs for the proprietor, delivered a pot of steeping tea and two bowls, promising Jonathan he would return in a quarter hour.

Jonathan's fingers curled around his bowl of steaming tea, relishing the warmth as he waited. The taproom of a public house offered little in the way of privacy, and he didn't intend to eavesdrop on the pair of men at the next table. However, the low susurration of their voices pulled Jonathan's hesitant attention. *War debt. Land taxes. Cider Act. Mob riots. Lord Bute's army of 10,000 troops left stationed in America.* Their hissed whispers reeked of monarchical plotting over a proposed fiscal contribution expected of the Colonies. *Parliament. Molasses. Smuggling.* Grenville, Bute's successor as First Lord of the Treasury, conducted business affairs on behalf of the King and collected from the House of Commons suggested measures to raise revenue to assuage the cost of war. The hushed allusion to festering tensions between Britain and her subjects living in the Colonies hinted at an impending threat of deeper divergence.

For all Jonathan knew, these men might have been elected Members of Parliament or governmental clerks engaged in Crown business. If he didn't have kin intending to risk the Atlantic crossing themselves, it wouldn't have mattered to him whether these strident issues were to be debated in Parliament or not.

Sipping his tea again, Jonathan sought to relegate the men's discussion to the taproom's perpetual din, but their buzzing continued floating within his hearing. Their talk touched on resurrecting the 1733 Molasses Act, which applied taxes to molasses, sugar, and rum of non-British foreign colonies. Then they referenced the disposition of the 1740 Plantation Act and its regulation of naturalization for non-English-born citizens.

He heard their commentary on initial debate for a Currency Act, which would impose restriction on the individual Colonies for issuing their own paper money since British merchants preferred payment in specie backed by gold or silver rather than anticipated tax collections or land mortgages with rate fluctuations. According to speculation, the Colonists might well view said act as an attempt by Parliament to extend control over the disparate financial systems from one colony to the next.

Establishment of admiralty courts in Halifax, Nova Scotia, faced stern opposition due to exclusion of trial by jury—an English right with origins in the Magna Carta. Uncle Twitch indicated most Colonists were proud of their Britishness, simultaneously asserting their right to the same liberties and privileges as any other English-born subjects—with the right of governance through their own representatives and legislatures to enact and enforce laws and taxes of their own consent.

Unsettled, Jonathan shifted in his seat and shook his head to discard the notion of an affirmed rift in philosophy between Crown and Colonies. His immediate concern was instructing young Henry to cipher and spell, and so he concentrated on the upcoming lesson rather than politically charged matters.

Both he and Henry enjoyed their mutually anticipated sessions. Henry's determination to press through his struggles and not give up served as Jonathan's reward. He emphasized the importance of learning, explaining that education could aid Henry's attainment of a different lot in life, much along the lines as the opportunity from which Uncle Twitch benefited with Grandee's backing so many years ago.

*Learning... that is what I am here for, is it not, Lord God? Until the unsavory episode of Colson's duel, I thought I was to graduate Oxford, be ordained, but if not, I pray You clearly redirect my steps.*

Fifteen minutes later, Henry doffed his apron and hung it on a peg near the bar. His puckish smile thawed Jonathan's heart. Henry scooted into the booth beside Jonathan and reached for *Cocker's Arithmetick.* He opened his exercise book, resolute to work through the assigned calculations with a black-lead pencil. The boy always chose arithmetic first, to get it over with. He liked far more the time they spent drilling with *The Child's New Spelling Primer.* Jonathan couldn't fault Henry for that as he too loved words that formed sentences that wove into stories. Conversely, he reminded the lad that knowing the use of both numbers and letters to his advantage would serve him well in the long run.

*Stay put.*

The directive wasn't audible, yet Jonathan heard its echo in his heart nonetheless. He rubbed his chest, his glance rising from Henry's exercise book to the ceiling beams, and he strained to hear something, anything out of the ordinary above the pub's usual hum.

*There are plans for your future. Fret not. I am your hope. You are forgiven, redeemed, and loved, for you are Mine. I have called you by name.*

Only a "carry on" seemed absent, Jonathan pondered with a low chuckle. So he would do from this very moment. He pulled two tomes out of his bag—*The Life and Death of Tom Thumb the Great* and *A Description of Three Hundred Animals.* Henry's eyes lit up, reverently touching the bumpy spines of the leather-bound volumes.

"Whichever one you choose, you keep. The other I shall send off to my youngest brother," Jonathan said

"The one going away on a ship?" Henry asked.

"Yes, that one." Jonathan cleared the emotion collecting in his throat. His sister would be colony-bound on the same ocean-faring vessel. He felt no desire or call to leave England. His adamant discharge of an unthinkable possibility bordered on denial—that once they separated from the English shore, he might never see them again.

He tapped the exercise book. "Before reading, we will first complete the arithmetic, hmmm? Let us suppose a schooner sails from Bristol and travels one hundred nautical miles a day toward Philadelphia. We shall estimate British North America is more than three thousand miles distant. How long would it take the ship to arrive at the Pennsylvania colony, factoring in a week's worth of foul weather?"

Chair legs scraped against floorboards as the unspecified men at the next table settled their account and departed with their palpable agitation. Jonathan restated the mathematical problem, but he didn't expect a precise answer from Henry due to several other variables. Mayhap he'd be wise to leave the navigating, as well as the impending increase of customs duties at Colonial ports, to Uncle Twitch.

*Home of the Northcrafts in Milsom Street, Bath*
*January 5, 1764*

"Marcus, do stop worrying. You know your friends are not going to turn us away." Johnna FitzGerald bounced little Corinna in her arms as Marcus tucked the blanket closer around the baby to keep off the cold. "Even from short acquaintance, they do not seem like the type who would rescind an invitation once issued. Or leave us to the elements." With a laugh, she dropped the brass knocker against the door again, and this time it was opened in greeting.

"St. James, Mrs. FitzGerald, please do come in." Tyree Northcraft beckoned them from the stoop into the townhouse's hospitable warmth. "We understood you had returned to Oxford. What brings you back to Bath?"

Johnna replied before Marcus could. "He did return to Oxford." Her laughter inspired others to do so with her. She handed Corinna to Marcus so she could shed her wraps. "It's my fault he's back so soon. It isn't a very festive mood at home now, and when he mentioned your celebration ... I do hope you'll forgive him for reconsidering your Twelfth Night invitation and for extending it to include me and my daughter as well."

"Of course." Tyree took Corinna so Marcus could shrug free of his cloak. "My wife and all in attendance will be pleased to see you both and this little miss again. You've arrived at a good time—the games are in progress. Supper has been had, but we'll get you a plate if hungry, and we have wassail or tea to offer."

"You are very kind." Johnna smiled brightly, following Tyree into the sitting room. To Marcus, she whispered, "I told you." And she had. The silent command in his sister's expression indicated all he had to do was relax and enjoy. Holding Corinna, however, gave him something useful to do. A quick glance upward caused an impish grin, and Johnna said with a wink, "Mind the mistletoe, Marcus."

From dawn of Christmas Eve, ivy garlands, evergreen boughs, and holly sprigs bedecked the Northcrafts' townhouse. By this evening, Twelfth Night, the scent of diffused wintergreen mingled with the smoky remains of the nearly-burnt-down yule log. Early on the morrow, all the Christmastide decorations would be destroyed in the flames so as not to usher any ill luck into the New Year of seventeen and sixty-four.

Candlelight flickered and glowed while Twitch, Madelaine, Asher, and Tyree progressed through a game of hearts with candid merriment.

Near the hearth, Amos entertained little Jessamine. The baby girl had grown tall enough to stretch the length of his lap. She lay on her back, contentedly staring at him. Her small fisted hands— one gripping a block with the letter *J* carved upon it—could not quite reach him. Amos clasped Jessa's stockinged feet together, and she gurgled with rapt glee at his silly face-making.

The kindred company assembled in the sitting room exhibited a harnessed tenacity, each determined to carry on and move forward, collectively relegating recent unpleasant events into the past. Change was afoot, and not only for the Ravensworths. Marcus contemplated the degree of adjustment looming in the weeks to come, for not only himself but likely for Johnna and her husband as well. He located Miss Ravensworth before she spotted him, and when his presence registered, he enjoyed the gratification of mellow delight designing her smile.

Lady Aurelia took interest in Johnna's explanation as to her husband's current predicament. "Oxford has a rule—not one consistently enforced—that dons, tutors, and fellows are not allowed to marry. However, there are a number of them who are married and for years the powers that be have ignored it. Ian was appointed to his position before he met me, didn't deny knowing the rule, and he married me in spite of it. Now he has been called out. He's remained behind at Oxford to plead his case, see if there might be any exception in order to keep his standing. But that may take a miracle."

Over cups of spiced cider, Johnna said, "My husband doesn't teach for the money. He does it because he has genuine rapport with his students, and they look up to him for positive guidance. Your Jonathan is one of Ian's scholars—we have him in common." Johnna shot a smile at Miss Ravensworth, and Marcus shot a warning at his sister, wordlessly cautioning her not to rush her fences by expressing a wish to have additional family members connected between their two families.

"Ian instills and perpetuates a respectable example of a higher calling and moral character in a place frequently known for its lack thereof," Johnna said. "If his appeal is denied, I am not sure what other options he has."

Lady Aurelia's eyes narrowed. "Hmmm. I shall think on this, pray about it. I always find it interesting to wait and see what the good Lord is doing in due course. Sometimes He brings people into one another's lives for very distinct purposes."

Marcus had no doubt Lady Aurelia would look into potential resolutions on Johnna's behalf regardless of the appeal's outcome. She would find a way for Ian to have options.

Lady Aurelia served a steaming cup of Lapsang Souchong to Marcus. He traded Corinna for the hot beverage, blowing on the smoky black tea to cool it prior to taking a sip.

Patting Corinna's back, Lady Aurelia asked, "In the meantime, what of your course, St. James?"

His shrug pulled coat seams tight across his shoulders. "Like you, my lady, I am deliberating and praying."

A message recently delivered to Marcus from Atticus Bartholomew in London required a great deal of serious consideration. By design, no doubt. And only this very morning did Marcus decide he was ready to honor the request the letter contained. He simply hadn't yet disclosed to anyone his decision.

"Come join us, you two," Johnna entreated, playfully escorting Ravensworth and Marcus to the varnished inlaid table where she and Miss Ravensworth sat talking. "Providing you're up to a friendly game of Goose, that is."

One game called for another. Johnna's competitive nature harmonized with Marcus's. Anticipating a second swift victory—her marker a handful of spaces away from the finish position at number 63—she arched a saucy honey-blond brow in Marcus's direction. Somewhere along the line, the friendly game of Goose had evolved into a contest pitting brothers against sisters. Johnna and Miss Ravensworth were in the lead over Ravensworth and Marcus—at least for the moment.

The game board with its coil of numbered spaces 1–63 offered distinct instructions to cause actions and reactions among the players. No one had yet landed on space 42, the Maze, which meant the player must return their marker to number 29. Any spaces detailed with the picture of a goose doubled the number of spaces to advance. Spaces that bore pictures of the Inn, Alehouse, Prison, and Death also carried consequences and sometimes dictated an additional stake to be paid.

Johnna shook the dice, spilled them across the board, and groaned. She pouted as she advanced her marker the total spaces of her roll, until she landed on number 58—the space showing the skeleton representing Death, which required her to move back to the beginning and start over.

"Oh!" the girls lamented in unison.

"Poor Johnna." Ravensworth crossed his arms over his chest and grinned without sympathy.

Johnna jabbed her brother's ribs. "What are you laughing at? You are still in Prison," she pointed to space 52 as a reminder, "and will stay thus unless Serenity's next roll rescues you."

Miss Ravensworth cupped both dice, whittled by Tyree's pocketknife, dramatically drawing out her turn. She giggled when a five and two showed. "Seven!" The exact number of spaces needed to free the marker belonging to Marcus while simultaneously causing hers to remain until someone else's roll might rescue her.

"See?" Marcus taunted his sister as he held out his scooped palm, with an aside to Serenity. "I am in your debt, Miss Ravensworth, for rescuing me."

With a slight nod, she acknowledged his veiled inference to a matter between them far beyond the boundaries of the board game. "Happy to oblige." Their glances tarried, and he decided Ravensworth's sister had a competitive nature equal to his own sister. Eyes sparkling with mischief, she dropped the dice one by one into Marcus's hand. He lowered his head to hide his smile, appreciating that tenacity of hers.

"You ought to make him pay a fine, Sis, unless you are content letting him off easy."

Miss Ravensworth's glib smile held a challenge. "Oh, I've little doubt Mr. St. James will contrive something to reciprocate."

Marcus felt his neck heat as he sat tongue-tied and unprepared to offer a witty retort. He sat up straighter in his chair, the elbow jab to his ribs from Ravensworth no less subtle than Johnna's delicate kick under the table. "Right. I'll get to work on contriving."

Stifling mischievous grins, Johnna and Ravensworth looked at each other, then at Marcus, then directed a sharp glance at the beribboned mistletoe bough suspended at the sitting room arch. A blush suffused Serenity's cheeks when their glances shifted from Marcus's face to hers with silent implication.

At the card table, a boisterous cheer signaled the last round of hearts with Asher the winner. Forfeits and mistletoe were momentarily forgotten. In two more turns, Ravensworth sailed past his sister's marker, leaving her stuck in Prison. He set his marker down on space 63 with a triumphant smack against the board, reveling in victory.

Both the sisters applauded Ravensworth's accomplishment, acknowledging their defeat with grace.

Curtailing any suggestion of a third game, Miss Ravensworth collected Amos while Madelaine collected Asher, and the four marched toward the butler's pantry, where the boys hoisted the heavy Great Cake with its elaborate decorations and sugared icing, ceremoniously conveying it to the dining room. Brushstrokes applied with feathered tips and freestanding marzipan swans adorned the crowned top of the cake. As Madelaine cut generous servings for her guests, the speculation increased on who might find a silver coin, dried bean, or dried pea baked into their slice.

Tyree read the pertinent lines from Herrick's poem describing an English Twelfth Night feast:

"'Now, now the mirth comes,
With the cake full of plums,
here bean's the king of sport here;

Beside we must know,
The pea also
Must reveal as queen in the court here.'"

Tradition did not visit Marcus on this instance. Madelaine and Johnna were crestfallen when Ravensworth found the bean in his cake and no one found the pea. Had Marcus located the bean amid candied citrus rinds and madeira-soaked currents hidden in his slice of the rich dessert, he would promptly have been pronounced King and encouraged to solicit Miss Ravensworth's favor as Queen for the revelry. But 'twas a moot point.

Dabbing the corners of his mouth with an embroidered linen serviette, Ravensworth broadly winked at Lady Aurelia, inviting her to play Queen to his King. He initiated the mock court proceedings, which prevailed merrily for the remainder of the festive evening with her by his side. Ravensworth's first decree as king was an order for more refreshments and to clear furniture to make room to dance.

Amos relinquished Jessa into Serenity's keeping on his way to obey. Marcus heard him say to her, "Take care, Sis. You're practically under the bough. What if St. James catches you?"

Marcus met Serenity's wide eyes without flinching and his heart thudded. *What if?*

Only on special occasions did Twitch play his fiddle, and on this night, in the wake of the lively dance tunes, he performed songs of the season—a mellow rendition of "The First Noel," which melted into Bach's "Jesu, Joy of Man's Desiring," followed by the traditional "Coventry Carol."

When the final note evaporated, Marcus prayed aloud into their midst. "Father God, we are thankful to be gathered together tonight and we commit our lives and our plans for this New Year into Your hand. Lead us where You can use us to do the most good and bring glory to Your holy name. Let the coming changes strengthen us rather than break us, and please illuminate our path as we seek Your truth. We strive to serve You, Lord, and we ask for favor in our endeavors. Thank You for sending Your Son to earth—so celebrated by this recent Christmastide—to provide the way for us to be redeemed and forgiven, that we may one day spend eternity with You, and to be reunited with those loved ones who have gone before us. We thank You for Your unfailing lovingkindness. In the mighty name of Jesus, we pray. Amen and amen."

# Chapter 21

*Bath, England*

The walk after the Twelfth Night party from Milsom Street to Grandee's townhouse in the King's Circus wasn't but half a mile, but to Serenity, the dark cold seeped bone deep. Gideon and Amos led them along the paved walkways, their brotherly banter creating steamy wreaths above their heads in the frigid air. Johnna FitzGerald, with sleeping Corinna bundled in her arms, walked beside Grandee, exchanging pleasant whispers with her. A few paces behind, St. James and Serenity brought up the rear of the procession, taking advantage of the small amount of privacy the position afforded.

St. James captured Serenity's hand with unabashed daring, gloved fingers entwined and hidden from plain view amid the voluminous folds of his black woolen watch coat. She stole a peek at him, curious and pleased about the soothing squeeze he administered, though his resolute jaw did not dip in her direction. He didn't look at her directly, as his vigilant eyes scanned the all-but-empty cobbled streets, assured no danger lurked in the shadows.

Mrs. Todd kept candles burning as well as fires in the grates. She collected wraps and coats and made sure no one was in want of anything else before she and Annie Daye retired for the evening. It gladdened Serenity to see the housekeeper wearing the new brooch she and Grandee had given her on Boxing Day.

Family and guests dispersed to their respective chambers after an extended round of good nights, and as doors closed one floor above, Serenity and Grandee made their way to the aviary. Loxley croaked *Wishyouhappy*, and Marian mimicked Grandee's variation of *newyear*.

"I wish you happy as well, Grandee." Serenity placed a kiss on her grandmother's cheek. "Together we shall endeavor to be."

"Bless you, dearest."

"You'll not stay up too much later?"

Grandee patted Serenity's hand and stifled a yawn. "I am not far behind you."

The long day had contained much activity. Serenity's eyelids drooped heavy until her head nested in her pillow and wakefulness pounced. An hour later, unable to sleep, she tiptoed down the stairway to fix a bit of warm milk, if there was any. Like the Todds, Nancie Heath had relocated from Fernsby Hall to the townhouse within the past week, as Fernsby Hall was likely to be closed up for a bit. While Serenity hadn't yet had opportunity to cook or bake with Nancie Heath in the new basement kitchen, she knew the lay of the land well enough to possess an inkling of where to find the few ingredients she needed.

A footfall on the landing startled her. "Oh! Marc—Mr. St. James..."

"Shhhh." He rested a finger against his lips. "Can't sleep either?"

"No. I—" Serenity tugged her shawl close about her shoulders, covering her modest dressing gown. "Care for some warm milk? You are welcome to join me."

Acceptance implied, he gestured for her to lead the way.

He paused at the bull's-eye window Tyree had crafted at Grandee's request. She halted beside him. It was a work of art on its own merit, even if it was too dark to see through at the present hour. During the day, the oval window overlooked the planned back garden and framed a stunning view of the hills surrounding Bath.

"If I ever build a place of my own one day," he whispered, "I shall want a window like that in it."

"It's a favorite feature of mine as well," Serenity said. "Tyree matched it exactly to Grandee's specifications, as he did with the aviary."

"Northcraft's handiwork is top notch." St. James traced his fingers along the oval window's painted edge. "Do you suppose the ravens will take to this as their new home?"

"Grandee will talk them into it, I imagine." Serenity laughed. "I am not sure if they all will come along, but Loxley and Marian seem sufficiently familiarized and content settling into their new habitat."

She descended the servants' stairs, padding through the kitchen passage by the light of a single candle. St. James followed.

Aware of his nearness and silent surveillance, she procured a pair of clean earthenware mugs and a small pitcher of milk. His hand on her arm stalled her motion and she met his serious eyes.

"You have been in my thoughts so often since that day you overheard my conversation with Lady Aurelia at the stable. Please tell me I haven't lost all favor with you."

"No, you have not lost all favor."

"I am relieved to hear you say it." He expelled a breath, shoulders relaxing.

"Is my good opinion so important to you?"

"It is. I don't know the words in explanation when I hardly have my own understanding ... "

"There is no need to explain." She stirred the embers to life and poured milk into a sauce pan.

Serenity had confided her inadvertent eavesdropping to Grandee, and Grandee's sage caution was to consider she had not heard all, nor did she comprehend the entire depth of context, maintaining Serenity had no grounds to argue or judge that which she'd had no part in. Serenity licked suddenly dry lips. "You have lived more life than I have, seen far more of the world. You are not accountable to me for anything that transpired before we were introduced. That is not fair." *And it is between you and God, whatever it is.*

"Thank you. I have no wish to cause you pain."

Grater in hand, Serenity rummaged in the spice drawer until she located the nutmeg. It wasn't the uniform he once wore or the courage it represented that drew her to this man. Nor was it his friendship with her brother—although, without Gideon, no friendship would exist between them. She liked him. Being with him, hearing his voice, sharing his faith. She liked singing with him and appreciated both his intensity as well as his gentle ways with little Jessa or Corinna. He was a man of his word, pleasing in form and appearance. Doubt assailed when she feared not being able to make him forget the woman from the fort. But that phantom woman was not here, not in this moment. Serenity was flesh and blood and with him now.

"I have received word from London," he said. "Not 'official' orders, but I am being presented an opportunity I cannot pass up. It would be for me, in a manner of speaking, a situation similar to young Amos's chance to learn from Twitch, only my position will be as a draughtsman at the White Tower, making maps for the army's Bureau of Ordnance. I will work and study with Atticus Bartholomew, one of my father's old friends. He has agreed to give me a chance, and I am willing to give it a go, see if mapping is indeed a niche I can fill."

"What of Oakleigh Combe?"

His chin lifted, eyes glittering in the kitchen's low light, and Serenity guessed St. James chided himself for not taking into account Grandee would share information she deemed in the best interest of all parties concerned.

He exhaled on a shrug. "Uncle Kent has been managing Oakleigh Combe since before my father's regiment was transported to British North America. The estate prospers because of him, and I do not want to spoil or hamper that. Should he or Rafe need me, they'll know where to find me."

"So you will draw maps." Serenity recognized the fortuitous offer as one that would allow St. James to postpone an immediate decision on plans to accept his medical discharge and resign his commission outright or re-enlist again for whatever assignment he might be dispatched. Or deployed. Gideon told her red-coated British troops were still stationed in the Colonies—amid a growing number who disputed the wisdom and challenged the need of a standing army since the war with France was over. His Majesty's army had orders for duties, including reinforcing former French forts and protecting frontier settlements in the backcountry. They were also to carry out enforcement of the King's Proclamation, attempting to prevent settlers from staking claims on the western side of the Allegheny Mountains, disrupting a precarious accord with regional native warriors. She wondered where those mountains might appear on a hand-drawn map.

"Mapmaking is a prized skill in military operations."

Listening to the low timbre of his words, she supposed St. James meant to convince himself as much as persuade her.

"To fight in scouted territory with an advantage, commanders rely on surveyors and mapmakers to convey where bridges or fords are, and to locate civilian-occupied villages to avoid." His expression grew animated as he explained the new challenge awaiting him in London. "Quartermasters must know where roads already exist or should, and surgeons the safest places to establish field hospitals. Cavalry requires sources of forage and water for their mounts. Artillery needs the high ground. All of that—and more—can be identified with a good map."

"A mapmaker would serve in a position on a headquarters staff?" she asked. At peace since the treaty ending the Seven Years' War, how long would England remain so? There was no way to tell when the next time the Crown's forces would be ordered to fight to preserve or enlarge His Majesty's empire. When that happened, St. James and Gideon could both be called back into active service.

"If it came to campaigning, time and duty would be spent between surveying in the field and producing maps in camp. My assignment in the Drawing Room will begin with duplication of existing maps previously surveyed, checking for accuracy, possibly hand tinting."

The milk simmered, and Serenity divided the warm white liquid between the two mugs. "Here you are, Mr. St. James." With ground nutmeg flakes added, she tapped his mug with hers in toast. "To mapmaking."

"You may call me Marcus, you know, at least between the two of us. Given what we've weathered together, don't you think we can dispense with stilted formality?"

"I— we could." A grin preceded her admission. "I do think of you as Marcus more often than St. James anymore."

"I like it best when I hear my own name on your lips."

"Remember I am leaving too, Marcus. I have committed to going to the Colonies with Amos and Uncle Twitch for a year at least." Her recent prayers had not clearly indicated she should do anything to the contrary.

"I haven't forgotten." He sipped and licked away the milky residue.

She brushed his cheek with her fingertips and with the pad of her thumb erased a leftover smear of milk from his upper lip.

A spark of surprise diffused into awareness. As he done before, he captured her hand, turned it over, and traced her fingers. In the next breath, he brought her palm to his mouth, planting an unhurried kiss in the hollow of her hand.

"What will become of us?" She hadn't intended to utter the question aloud, but neither did she wish it unasked. Aside from permission to call him by his given name, he offered no assurance or proclaimed any feelings beyond friendship.

Marcus released her hand. He stepped past her, placing his emptied mug near a cutting board. "God alone knows what will become of any of us. I remind myself His ways are higher than ours, and His timing will work out according to His will. Come what may."

"Come what may," she echoed in a forlorn whisper.

His eyes flashed and he reached for her. She inched closer and felt the slight tremor in his hand as he caressed her cheek.

"Serenity ... " He framed her face in his hands but slowly shook his head, deliberately denying them both of what might have been.

Disappointment cut even deeper than the night in the garden when Rafe had interrupted them. Removing herself from the circle of his arms, she shivered absent his warmth. She offered a silent petition to the Almighty on behalf of this man. Unsettled and unsure, and until he obtained satisfactory resolution to his elusive questions, Marcus would not be fit to move forward unless he could forgive his own past. Difficult as it might prove, and with no guarantee of a happy outcome, she surrendered him into the Lord's safekeeping. Guarding her heart at this point was little more than a belated, futile action. Resigned, she stiffened her spine and sipped again from her mug. "When do you report to the White Tower?"

He clasped his hands behind his back. "Johnna, Corinna, and I will depart for Oxford after we break our fast on Friday. Johnna can be impulsive—coming here was an impromptu and welcome diversion. But my sister misses her husband and Ian misses them. Once she and Corinna are safely back where they belong, I shall continue on to London."

"I see."

"Amos told me you will be leaving at the end of the month."

She blinked back stinging tears. "Uncle Twitch has confirmed that with me, yes."

"Serenity, you and I ... " He lifted broad shoulders in an aggravated shrug. "We are not traveling synchronic paths. Current intentions may run parallel, but they do not yet intersect. I do not foresee a change in my circumstances anytime soon, and it will be a year, at least, before you return to England."

"My head knows this." Her choked whisper punctured the quiet surrounding them. Her heart suffered the harsh tug of impending time and distance. Madelaine had said something about God having to prepare a man if he wasn't yet ready for her. The Almighty had His work cut out for Him in Marcus's case.

Marcus pulled her back into his secure embrace, clutching her close. Beneath her cheek and palm, his heart thudded. She did not object to being held by him.

*Stalemate.*

⌣

Marcus pounded the ceiling to indicate to the driver their readiness to depart. Johnna blithely waved farewell through the traveling chariot's window until the corner of another Palladian-style building cut her sight line to the Ravensworths and Lady Aurelia and their answering chorus of farewells.

Relaxing against the upholstered seat cushion, Johnna released a conclusive sigh. "Good people, those Ravensworths."

"Yes." Marcus firmly fixed his attention upon his darling niece instead of facing Johnna's grin. "Seems Corinna is hungry."

"I like her. Very much. I'll tell you plain. I believe she would be a good match for you." Johnna handed over a pewter feeding vessel along with her unasked-for opinion.

"First you applaud Bartholomew's offer, suggesting how good it would be if I did something useful with my drawing talents, and now you've changed your mind in order to foist me onto Ravensworth's sister instead?"

Johnna's eyebrows reached her hat brim. "*Foist?* There's a strong, descriptive word." Her gold-flecked green eyes sparkled with intrigue. "Must those two things—drawing and Miss Ravensworth—be mutually exclusive? Any valid reason why can't you have both?"

Marcus looked over the top of Corinna's lacy bonnet. "She's leaving for the Colonies and has no viable reason to stay here in England."

Johnna folded her arms. "You are in foul frame of mind because good-byes have never been your forte. To my way of thinking, if you don't provide a reason for her to stay, then why should she? If there is truly no hope for the two of you ... Well, I think there is, and I will keep hoping still. Anyone with eyes can see you care for her. Tell me you are not such a numbskull that you won't admit it to yourself—or *do* something about it."

"In case it didn't register, let me say again—she's going away," he shot back, equally terse. "Leave off, Johnna. It's for the best. Believe me when I say I've surrendered her to God's keeping."

Johnna scanned the scenery beyond the window glass, clearly trying not to laugh outright. For all Marcus knew, she would insist *surrendered* another strong and descriptive word.

⌒

*Fernsby Hall, Near Bath*

The aviary stood empty; the ravens having flown. Orange-hot fire crackling in the fireplace and the mantel clock's ticking were the only sounds in the library. When Twitch coughed, Lady Aurelia startled, and Gideon, gripping the chair arms tightly, lifted his head to look up. She folded her hands in her lap, comforted by Twitch's silent support, waiting for Gideon to speak.

Twitch winked at her. Once again, she waived her pride to retell the story of Laurenda and Sir Nicholas. Gideon needed to be sufficiently prepared for the meeting with his father. Not convinced he would get the full story from Sir Nicholas, she armed Gideon with knowledge of his own history. Retelling didn't get easier—it broke her heart each time because she took on all responsibility for the daughter she had failed.

"That explains a few things, doesn't it?" Gideon narrowed his eyes and crossed his arms. "What else did St. James's cousin have to report?"

Twitch answered on Lady Aurelia's behalf. "Rafe has his own methods and his connections. He did all within his power to see justice done for both your sister and the poor dairy maid but fell short. Brentmoor is too well protected by his peers. His reputation since the duel has become increasingly tainted. At the urging of certain circles of influence, he has removed himself from England. Rafe heard he opted for a prolonged visit to the West Indies under the pretense of inspecting a sugar plantation he won in a game of chance, sight unseen."

Scandal had been narrowly avoided thirty years ago and, miraculously, it had not come calling at Fernsby Hall after the duel. "Oakley Lightfoot" had done what he could about keeping that quiet, and Lady Aurelia did not question him. Gideon would have to be content, just as she was, in knowing vengeance belonged to the Lord, and Brentmoor would answer to the Highest Authority for his crimes come judgment day, if not sooner.

"Father is not coming home," Gideon stated. "We all know it. I am, therefore, honor-bound to see him in Florence. I can only pray he lives long enough for me to travel to him now, while he can still convey his wishes. For my part, I want explanation for expectations suddenly devolving upon me as his firstborn. I don't want to wait to learn them through his solicitor during the reading of his last will and testament.

I am no longer the second son. The current situation raises a conflict of interests as the 'one for the land' carries far different responsibilities than the 'one for the war' ever did."

Gideon cracked his knuckles. "I can understand why St. James feels inadequate to take on title and inheritance when unprepared for the involuntary assignment." His grin flashed. "Not that I, as Sir Gideon of Fernsby Hall, am of equal rank to Lord Oakleigh and Oakleigh Combe, mind you. He and I are not who we thought we were. We were raised second sons, bought commissions, survived the adventure of war. And now we inherit, ready or not."

Twitch sat back in his chair. "I daresay you'll each find a way to bear it, master it, and thrive."

"I like your confidence," Gideon said. "But this all starts with Father."

Lady Aurelia reached for a daybook, a number of documents tucked between its pages. "Letters of introduction, banking, transportation, and a character reference for the British diplomats at Genoa and at Florence."

"When the *Oceanna* next sails," Twitch said to Gideon, "you'll go with her. I am still working on final arrangements. It shouldn't take you long to close up this place if the staff comes out for an extra day or two of duty this week. Prepare to go to London, as you'll need to purchase traveling equipment more readily available there, and from there the *Oceanna* will depart for Italy."

"I almost wish St. James was going along," Gideon said. "Grandee, are you satisfied Marcus St. James is a good man?"

Twitch chuckled. "Good enough for Serenity, you mean?"

Lady Aurelia fluffed the lace trim at her right sleeve. "I would have investigated anyone for whom Serenity showed the slightest hint of proclivity. If you are asking me if I think she would make a fine wife for a viscount—well, it doesn't signify what I think. He must reach that decision on his own."

Gideon and Twitch both laughed.

"By definition," she added, "goodness manifests in varied levels in a myriad of circumstances. In my limited interaction with the man, I find St. James strong, kind, caring, and that he deeply loves what remains of his family. He reminds me of you, Twitch, in that it might be wiser not to be at odds with him. We have all come to understand he is a troubled man and his personal dilemmas require sorting and reckoning. He has not yet settled on what he will accept or how he will navigate his way forward in the life left to him. I pray for complete healing of his mind and body, spirit, and soul. The wounds he carries are not merely the physical variety."

"Mayhap Serenity took a piece of his heart, and he wasn't expecting that," Gideon dare said.

"There may be a grain of truth in that. If you chance to see him in London, perhaps you should inform him his suit would not be unwelcome."

The man might need a nudge—or a prodding—toward her granddaughter.

# Chapter 22

"Beg pardon, my lord, but I've taken the liberty of showing Atticus Bartholomew and Sir Rodney to the front parlour. They apologized for arriving without a proper appointment, but they stand ready to make amends, as the matter they wish to discuss seems to carry a sense of urgency."

Marcus struggled to refocus on the present when Featherstone interrupted his daydream. The mental image of Ravensworth's sister faded, and he offered a slow blink. "I'm sorry. Say again?"

"Atticus Bartholomew and Sir Rodney are here to see you, my lord. Front parlour."

"Very well." Marcus stuffed his arms into his coat sleeves, making short work of fastening the fabric-covered buttons. "Ask Jenny to—"

"I'll have Jenny bring tea, my lord."

"Thank you, Featherstone." Marcus clapped his steward-butler-valet's shoulder as he passed. Though he'd tried, he still couldn't get Featherstone to stop addressing him as the viscount he was.

Marcus slid the pocket doors open and left them so to aid the housemaid when she brought a loaded tea tray. "Welcome," he greeted his visitors. "To what do I owe the pleasure of your esteemed company?"

Sir Rodney started with pleasantries and belated holiday greetings, explaining how he'd crossed paths with Atticus Bartholomew at the Horse Guards coffeehouse during another between-class break. "I understand you are catching on with your new position by leaps and bounds."

Marcus shrugged at the praise. "I have started learning how to use a pantograph for duplication by accurate scale."

"You have gleaned a good deal since starting your role as draughtsman—your talent is a valuable commodity," Atticus Bartholomew said. "Something unforeseen has come up, however, and I should like to hear your thoughts on the matter."

Marcus braced himself. The recent wave of change still required adjustment, and he wasn't yet ready for the next crest.

"Might you have any interest in returning to the Colonies—Pennsylvania specifically?"

"Pennsylvania?" A fragmented vision of Fort Pitt with its trenches, fraise, brick retaining walls, and sturdy stockade flashed in his memory. "What for?"

Atticus Bartholomew produced a missive from one Benjamin Franklin of Philadelphia. Marcus was impressed. The renowned scientific man was an acquaintance through the Royal Society—a collection of natural philosophers and physicians who held the mission of recognizing, promoting, and supporting excellence in science, and encouraged the development and use of science for the benefit of humanity. Franklin's letter expressed an unusual request to send someone who might be interested in working with a survey team. Marcus accepted the pages Atticus Bartholomew handed over.

The colonies of Pennsylvania and Maryland shared a common border—a long and disputed border. To settle the decades-old feud once and for all, commissioners representing the Penn and Calvert families hired a team led by Charles Mason and Jeremiah Dixon to establish and document the official border. A sudden and unexplained change in plans created a vacancy. Franklin requested a replacement be sent as soon as may be.

"You are recommending me?" Marcus he didn't think he was qualified.

"You have firsthand knowledge of the terrain," Atticus Bartholomew said.

"I am not an engineer. I do not possess a surveyor's license. I am about to start my third week working in the Drawing Room."

Stroking his chin, Atticus Bartholomew argued away Marcus's doubts. "You are a quick learner and would make a fine assistant, license or no. Your education prior to joining the army provided necessary foundational basics. Plus the fact that you are a landowner, it would behoove you to know where the boundaries of your current holdings are or potentially mark boundaries of any future land acquisitions. 'Twould be an unparalleled experience for you."

"Will you at least think on it before saying no out of hand?" Sir Rodney asked. "I can imagine you pulling chains in the wilderness. A tad more exciting than day in and day out in the confines of the Drawing Room at the White Tower, eh, my boy?"

"Or mayhap I could fill in as an ax man or drive one of the wagons should the need arise." Marcus didn't miss the man's wink or the blatant insinuation of *what have you got to lose*. "For how long?"

"A crew is preparing even as we speak—have been doing so since Mason and Dixon arrived at Philadelphia back in November. If you could arrange to leave in a fortnight, it might very well be the end of March before you crossed the Atlantic. Your first step, I imagine, would be to secure passage," Sir Rodney said.

Inwardly, Marcus jolted. One of Twitch Kerrigan's ships would sail at the end of this month. What level of personal torture would it be to spend weeks at sea with Serenity on board, only to have to wrench himself away from her once more? *God, I surrender. Again. What do You want of me?*

Jenny appeared and delivered the tea service, remaining long enough to pour, then departed until summoned again.

Curiosity sufficiently piqued, Marcus listened with intent as the conversation resumed. It was agreed he didn't possess enough technical knowledge to fathom all the astronomical and mathematical significance of the endeavor, nor had he practiced celestial navigation. But as an assistant on the survey crew, he could take and follow orders. And learn. Atticus Bartholomew was right—the skill to accurately survey his crown-awarded land in the Ohio River Valley, should he be granted the two thousand acres owed him, would be useful indeed. Anything else would be up to the Almighty. Marcus prayed with repetition for direction as he faced an option he hadn't even known existed.

"I need to think on it." Marcus drummed his fingertips on his thigh. He neither accepted nor rejected the offer. "May I have three days?"

"Certainly. After all, this is a decision of some magnitude," Atticus Bartholomew agreed. "The survey will take time."

Time. Risk. Danger. Adventure. A reason to go back to America. A chance to ... No. Impossible. Marcus dismissed the outlandish notion of trying to find Wakwi before it gained a foothold. His thoughts raced his pulse. And Serenity. He would be most willing to reestablish the foundation there for the courtship that stalled here. Being on the same side of the Atlantic would provide a more favorable likelihood for shared proximity.

Should he agree to the terms of the proposition in Benjamin Franklin's letter, Marcus would need to be single-minded about the job expected of him. He would not want to disappoint Atticus Bartholomew or Sir Rodney or have them regret placing their confidence in him. His off-duty time, however, would be spent at his own discretion.

Atticus Bartholomew departed first, after confirming they would meet again in three days at the Horse Guards Barracks coffeehouse.

Sir Rodney lingered. "What are you thinking, my boy?"

"I don't know what to think. It seems ... sudden, coming from out of nowhere." Marcus pressed his fingertips to his temples and sighed. "Is this your idea of forcing me to move on? Get over my grief?"

"You will never be free of the memories of your father or brother—good or bad—God rest their souls. But it does make me ponder how the Almighty may have spared you for a singular purpose. You are wise to weigh the choices. What would prevent you from accepting? What would induce you to accept?"

"That is what I have to figure out. In three days."

The voice in Marcus's head insisted it wasn't about Wakwi. No. It was about investigating if he'd truly lost those two thousand acres of land beyond the Allegheny Mountains or if there was any avenue for recompense. Could this be the next right step? *God help me— Scripture says without faith it is impossible to please You.*

"Would you regret it if you didn't give it a try?" Sir Rodney asked.

"If you were approached with this position, would you?"

"I think I might."

"I had a feeling you were going to say that." Marcus nodded. "Do you know this man Franklin?"

"Heard of him," Sir Rodney answered. "His experimentation with electricity, his inventions, his musical glass armonica. He's a self-made man who wrote almanacks under the pseudonym 'Poor Richard' and retired from the printing business. I've heard it said Philadelphia would not thrive without him."

Marcus recalled a drawing he'd seen while in the Colonies, one credited to Benjamin Franklin's design. A snake severed into separate parts labeled with the abbreviations of the individual Colonies.

The head representing New England, followed by New York, New Jersey, Rhode Island, Maryland, Virginia, North Carolina, and South Carolina. Beneath the snake, the words "JOIN, or DIE" appeared. During the war against the French and their Indian allies, the message to the Colonies had been a call to join together for a common defense. Yet the Colonies were not united, as betwixt them existed too much squabbling, such as this border dispute between Pennsylvania and Maryland that needed a permanent decision.

"Will I meet him?" Marcus asked. "Mr. Franklin."

"'Tis my understanding he prefers the address of 'Dr. Franklin' by virtue of his honorary doctorate degrees from Oxford and St. Andrews, awarded for significant achievements. Atticus Bartholomew will send you with a letter of introduction and instructions on how to contact him, should you decide to go."

"I have much to consider."

"No one is forcing you."

"And yet you thought well enough of me to bring it up."

"You are young, intelligent, and brave. I daresay, my boy, the end result of this survey might prove more far-reaching than we can see in this moment. You could be part of something big, noteworthy, lasting—at least as noteworthy as the maps by Byrd and Mayo or Fry and Jefferson. I shall leave you now. To ponder and decide."

Featherstone brought the post in the wake of Sir Rodney's departure. The silver salver bore a pair of letters—one from Johnna, the other from Twitch Kerrigan. Marcus broke the seal. Kerrigan wrote, in part, concerning a delay that necessarily pushed back departure of *The Raven's Lady* by another week. The *Oceanna* would depart on schedule—tide permitting—to sail Ravensworth to Genoa, then continue to the Colonies. A berth was available, should Marcus find he had such a need.

Marcus inhaled his prayer and reread the missive. The penned words did not change. For all intents and purposes, it seemed God meant to provide safe passage through Kerrigan and the *Oceanna*. Another puzzle piece snapped into place.

⌒

*Lady Aurelia's Townhouse at the King's Circus, Bath*
*February 1764*

"Surely Twitch is not restricting you to only one trunk?" Madelaine's teasing laughter attested to the miracle that would warrant. This morning she'd brought three new traveling dresses— recently fitted and hemmed—to be packed with Serenity's collection of fine garments stored in the mahogany clothes press and wardrobe, which stood guard on either side of the door connecting Serenity's bedchamber to the private sitting room.

In the boxwood-hedged parterre below, two ravens vied over a fresh kill, alternately shredding a carcass into ribbons of raw flesh and fur. The imposing corvids had been at their task long enough to render the rodent species indistinguishable, leaving a diminishing pile of bloodied strings and sinews. Those ravens that traveled with them from Fernsby seemed to be settling in well enough after the move, accepting of their new aviary at the back of Grandee's townhouse.

"I— No." Serenity shook her head, prying her gaze from the grisly scene beyond the glass panes and the garden below. "Amos merely insisted Twitch said as much because the little jester knows he is the one who will have to help haul whatever I bring on board *The Raven's Lady.* I suppose I shall have to bake a batch of sweet buns for him to make up for it before we sail.

"Truth of the matter is Uncle Twitch advised I bring as many of the gowns you have made for me as we can fit. His wife, Susanna, wrote in her last letter she has several customers interested in fashionable English-made frocks. While I must keep in mind storage will be at a premium aboard ship, he will permit three trunks. He has a full load of textiles, salt, nails, pins, and shoes, although some of the cargo might be traded away as needed should an order of Madeira await him when we put in at the Azores."

"Susanna sounds like an astute woman of business." Grandee positioned herself at the wardrobe in Serenity's bedchamber, eyeing each dress stored within as if she herself were a prospective buyer. "'Tis my understanding she sells out of fabric within but a few days of unloading after Twitch docks with merchandise at Philadelphia."

"Part of me wishes I could go with you." Madelaine expressed the wistful confession as she examined a pencil-sketched map from the bureau top. "To see for myself the places he tells of, the ocean that still holds him in its clutches, the Colonies. There are those who infer the population little more than provincials, but he says they are just as British as we and avenues for opportunity are more readily available there than here in England. There is a measure of pride in being a citizen of the vast British empire, is there not?"

"And yet citizens here in England continue to gather in mobs and riot in opposition to the tax Lord Bute levied on cider production or so Gideon says." Serenity unlatched the first trunk. "Since the war's end, England is obligated to protect its acquired territory—Canada from the French and Florida from the Spanish. British command keeps a standing army in the North American Colonies. During peacetime. And loyal citizens—both at home and abroad—must pay for said protection."

Grandee arched one of her silver-grey brows. "That is not news, dearest. It is known and such opinion bears influence of your soldier-brother. Is it your way of thinking as well?"

Madelaine paused in her study of the map.

"Should not the Colonies provide for their own defense?" Serenity wondered and read a headline bearing complementary sentiment from a less-than-current edition of the *Bath Chronicle* before wrapping a fragile, framed looking glass with the printed sheet. "What, Grandee? Do you not think it prudent I learn a bit about where Amos and I are going?"

"It is indeed wise to be prepared, dearest. I would rather you glean enough knowledge not to be caught unawares." Grandee added a pair of dresses to the "going" pile. "I pray daily Gideon will not get called back there. He has more than enough to claim his immediate attention on this side of the Atlantic."

"This map." Madelaine tapped the creased parchment with enough force to lure Serenity's attention. "Did St. James draw it for you?"

"Yes, he did. Before he left last month." Marcus's gift of the detailed map was thoughtful, and appreciated, and came with a final "thank you" before he'd departed. He had been somber, unsmiling, while he'd administered an incremental perusal from the top of her beribboned cap to the tips of her green leather slippers. Memorizing her? When she'd asked him what he was thanking her for, he'd merely pressed a hasty kiss to her forehead and whispered, "For all of it." He'd straightened his cocked hat, squared his broad shoulders, and turned on his heel to ride back to Oxford with Johnna and Corinna in the traveling chariot.

Serenity could no longer deny Marcus St. James had absconded with a fair-sized piece of her heart. The harder thing to accept was the uncertainty of how long before she might see him again. Madelaine and Grandee each held suspicions with regard to the depth of her attraction for Gideon's troubled friend, though neither seemed concerned about the fact he should be styled a viscount while she was a mere baronet's daughter.

Propped against pillows and barricaded by more on either side, Jessa whimpered and pulled on one ear, clearly unhappy while gnawing on the miniature horse Amos had made for her.

"What ails you, my sweet?" Serenity applied a gentle touch to Jessa's brow and wiped drool from her chin with a soft cotton cloth. "She feels warm to me."

"She's cutting teeth again." Madelaine inspected the interior of Jessa's mouth. "Two front bottom teeth have made their appearance and will be soon joined by two more on top. For the past few days, she's been feeling poorly, not sleeping or eating well."

"Grandee, do we still have ... "

"We do indeed." Grandee offered an ornate silver whistle to Madelaine. "I failed to bring this when we visited of late. But as you were coming this morning, I made it a point to set it aside. This teething toy has been stored away since Amos had no further need. I wondered if Jessa might get some benefit from it, so I cleaned it for her."

Madelaine accepted the polished toy with gratitude. Visible indentations on the neck of the whistle—likely inflicted while Amos was teething—marred the otherwise smooth surface. Four bells attached to the hollowed silver tube made a pleasant chiming when shaken like a rattle. A nub of red coral for chewing on capped the bottom end. Jessa's attention focused briefly on the shiny toy before intuitively putting the coral into her mouth and biting down with swollen gums.

"She is perhaps a little overwarm." Maternal concern swam in Madelaine's eyes.

Grandee tapped her deeper well of experience. "Asher survived. Jessa will too. All part of the growth process."

Before long the little girl was fussing again, still agitated.

Serenity collected Jessa from amid the makeshift pillow fortress, dabbing away drool and tears. *All part of the growth process.* Though Grandee had directed those words to Madelaine, Serenity felt their impact. They added a layer of balm to her weary and anxious heart. She didn't have to go to the places on Marcus's map. Grandee had reminded her, in their conversation the previous evening, that she could still change her mind and elect to stay in Bath. Grandee, along with Madelaine and Jessa, would be most content to keep Serenity company while all her brothers were distant and abroad.

However, as the date of departure approached, Serenity's yearning for the impending change solidified. Mayhap as part of her own growing process, she needed this impetus to go forth and find out what would happen next. For her, time in Bath was at a standstill since Jonathan had returned to Balliol and his studies, Marcus was ensconced in the White Tower Drawing Room with his maps, and Gideon was planning his quest to Italy to find and confront their father in Florence. Amos grew quite animated whenever he talked of new adventures in the part of Britain's empire that lay across the vast western ocean. Another such prospect for Serenity might not come again, and therefore she reconciled her clouded view of the future to taking the next right step. To going ahead and following through. Come what may.

Grandee pulled several more outfits from the wardrobe, spreading them on the duvet.

"Are you regretting this decision?" Madelaine asked.

Serenity rubbed Jessa's back in a soothing motion while shifting from one foot to the other. Not meeting her friend's penetrating glance, her attention instead raked the multi-hued pile of silk, satin, taffeta, muslin, and merino. "Not regretting per se, so much as questioning the wisdom of it all." She mustered a slanted smile and forced a weak laugh. "Ask me again in a year."

Madelaine, Grandee, and Serenity—with the help of the lady's maid—carefully packed and distributed Serenity's belongings among the three trunks. Exquisite stylish gowns of Madelaine's design and skill, plus serviceable day dresses. Shifts, nightclothes, clocked and wool stockings, garters, lace-trimmed fichus, pockets. Under, over, plain, and quilted petticoats. Jackets with long sleeves and short.

Aprons, gloves, scarves, kerchiefs, mitts. Half boots and low-heeled slippers. Day caps, ruffled caps, market bonnets, and wide-brimmed straw hats. Inherited jewelry, silk ribbons, feathery plumes, hat pins, and straight pins.

Upon Grandee's recommendation, Serenity packed a day's attire along with a few personal items into a smaller-sized leather portmanteau. "'Tis more than the three-trunk allotment, but if you keep it with you in your cabin, dearest, I doubt Twitch will throw it overboard."

"Have you ever met Susanna Kerrigan? Has she never come to England with Twitch?" Madelaine asked.

"No, unfortunately. But not for sheer lack of inviting her to come," Grandee said. "In the few letters we have exchanged over the years—which lead me to believe Twitch's savvy business acumen laid the foundation for their association, prior to any romantic inclinations on either of their parts—Susanna sounds capable, knows her own mind, and is not afraid to share her good opinion or leave any doubt where she stands on any given subject. He trusts her, and as you well know, that is saying a good deal. Once you reach the Colonies, I have every confidence her genuine nature will come to your aid in any means necessary. She, it seems from this distance, has a heart equally as good as his."

Before fastening the portmanteau's buckles, Serenity put in her embroidery, Bible, journal, ink vial, raven's feather quill, hairbrush, hand mirror, ribbons, and a few other trinkets and feminine necessities. A cameo brooch her mother bestowed on Serenity's seventh birthday. A miniature of Grandee. To assuage her penchant for reading, she slipped in her copy of *The Art of Cookery Made Plain and Easy* from Nancie Heath, along with a supplemental volume on herbs for medicinal purposes. There was no space for any works of fiction by Henry Fielding, Samuel Richardson, or Eliza Haywood. Only a battered copy of *The Life, Adventures, and Piracies of the Famous Captain*

*Singleton* by Daniel Defoe, plucked from a low shelf in Father's study. "For Amos," Serenity said, "as reward or change of pace from working at his lessons in *Cocker's Arithmetick* and *The Child's New Spelling Primer* while we sail across the waters."

"I shall count on you to write." A rush of tears filled Madelaine's eyes. She hugged Serenity and whispered, "I am already missing you and you've not left yet!"

"I shan't be gone forever." Serenity hugged her friend, a lump in her throat because her leaving exacted a heavy toll on her loved ones. "Count on that."

"You have my prayers, there and back again," Madelaine promised with a tentative smile. "You may count on that."

"I will keep you in my prayers as well, dearest." Grandee's beringed hand caught Serenity's as she absently toyed with her bezel pendant in nervous anticipation. "I suggest you conceal your sovereign coin safely out of sight while you travel. No need to offer any temptation. Keep it close." Grandee cupped the side of Serenity's face before leaning near to bestow an emotional kiss upon her cheek.

Obedient, Serenity tucked the antique gold coin beneath her stays and adjusted the necklace chain under her fichu. "I will, Grandee."

*Cornhill, London*

Ducking into a narrow alley, Marcus emerged in a closed and cobbled court. He pushed his way through the door of Simpson's Tavern with new resolve, determined to locate his cousin among the crowd of patrons.

There he was. Rafe had arrived at the busy chophouse ahead of Marcus. Remnants of steak and oyster pie revealed his choice of menu special for luncheon, which had been presided over by the Chairman at precisely one of the clock. He was, by this point, well into his dessert of stewed cheese and toast.

Rafe had secured two facing seats next to a wall at a table lit by outside light sifting through the window. Two gregarious gentlemen exited the wooden stall, which allowed Marcus to slide into the communal booth. They then filed in behind him again, effecting no interruption in the discussion floating across the table with the two men occupying corresponding space on Rafe's bench. Their discourse over a recent news item in one of the London papers continued while they consumed blue Stilton and drained glasses of port.

The swirl of political dialogue concerned another riot in the West Country, sparked by the 1763 Cider Tax, before switching to the repeated refrain of Parliament contemplating enforcement of regulations and taxing British citizens in America to raise revenue to pay down England's war debt.

Marcus deposited his hat in the overhead rack, his long legs uncomfortably confined in the limited space beneath the cluttered table. Proximity must have spurred Rafe's choice of meeting place, as privacy was not to be had.

"You're late," Rafe complained between bites, his somber glance cautioning Marcus not to speak too freely in the company of those who shared their booth.

"With reason." Marcus wondered why Rafe had chosen the overcrowded chophouse, located nearer the White Tower than to Bow Street, if they weren't going to be able to talk. "I stopped at the Jamaica Wine House across the way to obtain a copy of the shipping notices. I'll likely go back for coffee once we're through here." He slid an envelope across the table toward Rafe. "Letter from Johnna. Once you read it, we have things to discuss."

Marcus perused a column of the tri-weekly *St. James's Chronicle*, then examined a shipping advertisement in *Lloyd's Evening Post*.

"What is this about Ian being dismissed at Balliol?" Rafe sopped up cooling liquid cheese with a corner of toasted brown bread, taking a hearty bite.

"Part of what we shall discuss. Amongst other things."

Rafe studied Marcus for a long moment. "What are you up to?"

Marcus pushed a tankard of small beer aside. "Putting things in order. It will be some time before I return."

"You're truly leaving?"

"Yes." Marcus had come back from war when he hadn't expected to, and one thing he'd learned was that life held no guarantees— merely opportunities to be ready and know without doubt where his soul would go should his body meet an untimely demise.

The odd bits of conversation drifted to where Marcus and Rafe sat.

"Rampant smuggling ... and now the customs duties are being enforced."

"And why shouldn't the colonies pay for their own defense?"

"What say do they have without any Parliamentary representation in the House of Commons? They've essentially been left to governing themselves all the way over there."

"And make some of us rich over here."

Contrived chuckles punctuated the observations, but Marcus tuned out the polemic opinions of the nearby diners, quelling any wonder if the conversational fragments held merit. He had a great many other things on his mind.

"Ravensworth!" Rafe spotted Serenity's brother before Marcus did.

Turning, Marcus banged a knee against the table support. One of the things on his mind had indeed been a Ravensworth, but not this one. "Thanks for joining us," Marcus gritted, rubbing his smarting joint.

"Good to see you again." Rafe offered an outstretched hand to Ravensworth. "What brings you to London?"

"Good day, St. Jameses." Ravensworth tossed an affable grin at each cousin in turn, shaking their respective hands. "Family business brings me, but I'm here only temporarily. Kerrigan will join us soon. He stopped in at the Jamaica Wine House..."

"For a copy of the shipping notices." Marcus held up his own. "Could have saved him the trouble."

The gentlemen patrons deliberating taxes and riots departed when Kerrigan arrived, freeing up seats for himself and Ravensworth. The tavern settled into a between-meal quiet, and these four remaining tablemates' discussion lengthened to cover the better part of an hour. Tankards and trenchers emptied. Tea and shortbread disappeared.

"I'm for Italy then." A palpable air of new purpose was plain, and resolution glinted in Ravensworth's eyes. "Florence, by way of Genoa."

"Never had time for a Grand Tour myself," Rafe said, "and I've never been to Tuscany, though I've heard of Michelangelo, the exceptional food, and vineyards."

"I'm told the convent—*il nosocomio*—is outside the old city walls. It's run by an able staff of nuns who implement instructions administered by an overseeing physician. It is where my father is receiving treatment for his consumption," Ravensworth said. "I pray I am not too late."

"We shall pray the same," Kerrigan said.

"I continue to pray for your sister, Ravensworth." Marcus braced for a glib reaction to his admission. "Her heart's desire was to keep your family together, and yet there seems to be no stopping the scattering."

"Scattered like the dried leaves rolling across Fernsby's parkland, driven by the force of the wind." Sadness tinged Ravensworth's observation. "Serenity—and Grandee before her—did what she could. Events beyond her control changed things and people."

"We grow up, learn from mistakes, take the good with the bad." Rafe pooled his own nostalgia with Ravensworth's.

"And trust God will make straight the path He intends for us. He does not change. From age to age, He remains all-knowing, all-caring, always." Marcus began drawing in a quarto-sized sketchbook. The map was not to scale, nor in great detail, save for a few symbols. It would serve as a reminder of where his friends and family would be stationed in the months to come. His prayers would have a lot of ground—not to mention an ocean—to cover: Bath, Oxford, Florence, Chipping Campden, London, Philadelphia, and the Virginia colony.

Ravensworth traced the points of interest. The farthest, western-most label read *Fort Pitt*. He shot a piercing glance at Marcus.

"Point of reference, nothing more," Marcus said.

Kerrigan's elbows rested on the tabletop. "If you sail with Ravensworth to Italy, you'll have little, if any, time to linger. The *Oceanna* will have to turn around and immediately head toward the Colonies in order to get you there in time to rendezvous with the survey team."

"Finding Benjamin Franklin is my first order of business." Marcus patted his breast pocket and the letter of introduction from Atticus Bartholomew. Map forgotten, the four hashed out in great detail preparations for departing England and sailing to the Mediterranean Sea.

# Chapter 23

Marcus heard his name. Urgent. From a distance. He dared not answer. Must hide. Before his stalker found him ... and finished him. Like Lucas. His heart thudded in cadence. *Which way? Which way? Which way?* His legs refused to run, and his knife offered scant protection against a predatory foe, but it was all he had. Hard pressure encircled his wrist. His ragged breathing stopped, terrified to be caught.

"St. James!"

Blinking, open eyes reacquired focus. A lantern on the cabin wall. A suspended hammock stretched across the space. Primal dread receded. Marcus's chest rose and fell with shallow panting, and his pulse slowed. He blinked again, aghast with comprehension—his knife's sharp blade angled below Ravensworth's chin. And Ravensworth's tight clamp on his wrist stayed the knife.

"Everything in order, friend?" Ravensworth stood immobile in front of the swaying canvas hammock, his voice even, calming. "Now, had I been wearing a neck stock, the degree of bite might be less imperative. Blade against flesh, however, that's a different kettle of fish. Let's not spill any blood tonight. Agreed?"

Marcus groaned and leaned back against his too-short bunk, staring at the low ceiling. "Agreed." He turned the knife loose into Ravensworth's keeping.

Ravensworth laid aside the sharp-edged weapon, sinking down into the nearest chair. "I should not have tried to shake you awake. I didn't think that all the way through. I only wanted to dislodge the nightmare since you didn't seem able to. I meant no harm."

"Sorry, man." Marcus rasped a shaky apology and dragged a cuff of his damp shirtsleeve across his sweaty forehead. "I didn't hurt you, did I?"

"No." Ravensworth tossed an affable grin. "Dealing with you, however, is a bit more precarious than comforting Amos after a bad dream or forestalling Jonathan from walking in his sleep." He picked at the open V of his own shirt and straightened the garment along his shoulders.

Sighing with wary relief, Marcus shook his head. There was no pattern to when the nightmares came roaring back to taunt him with the horrors relived in his mind's eye of a blood-soaked landscape strewn with mutilated dead. "I will be all right."

Ravensworth arched a brow, yet unconvinced. "Hmmm. Shall we talk about that?"

Marcus took another swipe at his forehead and used his sleeve to mop his face. "I'd rather not." Ravensworth had shown little regard for his preferences on previous occasions—mostly to Marcus's benefit, if he would admit it.

Ravensworth ignored his declination. "The dreams—they've returned with increased frequency. You have not slept through a single night since we departed London. Why is that?"

"I don't know."

Crossing his arms over his chest, Ravensworth voiced his suspicion. "I know you better than most. It's the first mate. He sets you on edge. We can all see the tension rolling off you, but they don't understand why he disturbs you."

The fingers of Marcus's right hand circled around his left bicep in lieu of a vocal reply.

Ravensworth tipped his head from side to side and stretched his neck. "So, I confess. Curiosity got the better of me. I asked Captain Van den Bosch about him, about the tattoos. What tribe was he from. His family is native to Delaware, but he grew up west of Philadelphia. He's been in the employ of Kerrigan Shipping for the last three years."

Marcus swallowed hard. "Part of me cringes, and anger burns hot with the memory of the Ojibwe and Sauk. Their baggatiway game was just a ruse. It's not easy to forget the murderous things they did to annihilate the English at Michilimackinac."

Ravensworth waited.

"The first mate has no scalp lock or nose ring. Mayhap his tribal markings stir a reminder. Yet something about him also reminds me of Wakwi—and she wasn't out to kill me. She helped me live."

Challenge ignited in Ravensworth's eyes. "Why are you going back to America?"

Serenity's lovely face surfaced. "I told you ... to see about my land in the Ohio River Valley. To be part of the survey team."

"Forgive me, but I don't believe that is the whole of it. If the opportunity came about, would you attempt to locate that Ojibwe woman Wakwi?"

Marcus's grip around his upper arm clenched tighter. "I'm fairly certain finding her would be impossible, even if I wanted to. To what end?"

"I don't know." Ravensworth shrugged. "Explain it to me. I'm still trying to figure out your line of thinking in this case. 'Tis not entirely logical."

"I don't know either." Marcus struggled with reconciling the massacre's aftermath, interspersing details he knew with those he'd been told, still absent of what he couldn't remember. Shaking his head again did not dispel the image of Serenity's ginger-brown eyes, fighting her way to the forefront of his thoughts.

"If the opportunity came about, I hope foremost you would find Serenity. If she matters to you, and I believe she does, you ought to think about giving her an apt reason to not forget you. If she doesn't matter enough, I rely on your good sense to be honorable and for you to walk away."

Oh, but she mattered a great deal. A concurrent contributing factor to his already cloudy confusion. The portrait miniature of Serenity given to Marcus by Lady Aurelia before he'd left Fernsby resided in his inner coat pocket—but he withheld that bit of private intelligence from Ravensworth. It was Marcus's own secret.

Eight bells chimed on the deck above them, marking the end of one shift and the beginning of the next.

Marcus scrambled up from his bunk, hastily dressed, and fastened his pea coat. He pulled a tasseled knit voyageurs cap down over his ears. "It's time. I'm assigned morning watch."

Before Marcus could make his escape, the first mate descended the ladder, his mumbled greeting terse and tired. He handed an envelope to Ravensworth. "When we were at Gibraltar for supplies earlier today, a mail bag from a British ship departed from Genoa was delivered to Captain Van den Bosch. He finished sorting through it and found this one addressed to you."

"Much obliged."

"You're up, St. James. Captain's waiting for you." The first mate's brisk nod was followed by a low command.

"I'm going." Marcus disappeared through the hatch overhead.

How long had the stealthy-footed first mate been there—and how much had he overheard?

*Port City of Genoa, Ligurian Sea*

"Had we arrived in summer, we'd have met 'with roses, carnations, jessamine, and all manner of colorful flora splashed throughout the town.'" St. James stopped reading the guidebook essay.

A pang of homesickness expanded in Gideon's chest at St. James's casual mention of the namesake flower. Along with dear little Jessamine, Gideon's imagination conjured a parade of faces—Asher, Madelaine, Tyree, Jonathan, Amos, Grandee, and Serenity—each tugging at his heart-strings. St. James was not staying. Gideon would be on his own once the *Oceanna* set sail and reversed course, destined for the Delaware River and Philadelphia—a world away. St. James had yet to embark on his own looming journey.

Clearing his throat, Gideon opted to credit the hot sting of tears as caused by the sea breeze and salt air, though it was subterfuge. He'd banish this feeling again, as he had done before. In North America, meeting and serving with St. James in prescribed military routine had reduced the severity of the dull ache, and all sentimental chords had severed the instant Gideon was thrown into the fracas of his first battle. Nostalgia was a peacetime luxury or, at the very least, something to indulge in around a campfire or in one's tent at day's end.

During his first assignment as leader of a small detachment, he'd further honed his focus, paired with a strong desire to fight to stay alive in order to return to England and his loved ones. By the grace of God, he'd dragged with him a surviving St. James in tow.

The bustling Italian port hosted numerous ships off-loading cargoes of silks and spices from distant Arab and exotic Far Eastern markets. Even without flowers in bloom, late-winter sunbeams illumined Genoa's brightly painted buildings of medieval and succeeding period architecture, spilling up and across the western slope of the Apennine Mountains. The *Oceanna*'s blissfully noneventful voyage from London was perhaps due in part to the overt presence of swivel guns spaced evenly on both starboard and port railings—a deterrent aimed to keep notorious Barbary pirates at bay. But Gideon knew enough about answered prayers to attribute their current level of safety to God Almighty Himself.

"Genoa. Birthplace of explorer Christopher Columbus." St. James licked his thumb and first finger and turned another page in the guidebook. "Some maintain the Holy Grail was brought here after the Crusades." He pointed out the tall lighthouse-fortress standing guard on a rock, the *Capo di Faro* at the base of the San Benigno hill. "Genoa has a long maritime history. Originally, bonfires lit the way into the harbor, and, in the sixteenth century, *La Lanterna* was rebuilt of brick and stone rather than wood. A large copper lantern with clear Venetian glass crowns the top of the terraced tower, reaching almost four hundred feet above the surface of the Ligurian Sea." He craned his neck and shielded his eyes against the descending sun. "From here, you still have nearly a hundred and fifty miles to travel overland to reach Florence."

"You really ought to add guide duties to your surveyor endeavors," Gideon teased, referencing St. James's proffered knowledge of the boot-shaped country comprised of city-states, kingdoms, and Papal states, but the solemnity of the moment caused his attempt at banter to fall flat. A muscle ticked at his jawline.

"Why such a morose countenance? You are starting off on what might be your only chance at a Grand Tour—or at least a partial one."

Gideon leaned against the ship's glossy rail and locked his elbows. "I had no wish to see Calais or Paris—not after fighting against the French with their Indian allies in America. Going over the Alps at *Monte Censio* by sled or sedan chair didn't hold much appeal either. As an Englishman in foreign territory, I am not entirely sure I'd be welcomed by the French, so I shall strive to be ever charming and diplomatic with the Italians instead." He skimmed the shoreline of the port city. "Colson would be rolling over in his grave if he knew I was going places he only ever dreamed of. But this is no Grand Tour."

"It might be as close as you'll get, so why not enjoy the sights, learn the traditions, and partake of the cuisine, as Kerrigan suggested? You carry with you documentation corroborating you are the firstborn of a baronet. Doesn't that make the Grand Tour a traditional rite of passage for someone of your social rank?"

"I could ask the same of you, Lord Oakleigh." Again, the attempted humor did not play out well.

St. James shot a quelling look. "If not an abbreviated Grand Tour, then certainly a business trip—given the short amount of time. You have the documents from the solicitor in Bath?"

"Aye." Gideon slipped his hand under the flap of the leather document holder tucked in his coat's breast pocket, reaffirming the collection of papers prepared by Alton Grierson. "I need to locate this Dante Olivadotti, whom my father trusts to meet and accompany me to the convent."

St. James's eyes crinkled at the corners. "Does your father anticipate trouble of some sort with you here?"

"I don't see why he would." Gideon shrugged. "I'm an amiable enough chap."

"And a humble one too," St. James declared. "Maybe he just wants to ensure your safety—an Englishman in an unfamiliar place, and all."

Gideon nodded. "We're not staying long, and as you said, there are things to be accomplished."

"What time are you to appear at the residence of the envoy here in Genoa?"

"The invitation is for tea, discussion, introduction, and dinner to follow. Why not come with me? If the wind is favorable and the

*Oceanna* sails on the morrow, this might be your only chance to see anything in this port city."

As former junior officers in the King's service, Gideon and St. James had supped when required with ranked military and civilian officials, some with titles and some without. Dispensing a nonchalant shrug, St. James accepted.

Gideon mulled the magnitude of the circumstance in silence. Once the *Oceanna* cast off her last mooring line, neither friend could know for certain when they would see each other again.

On shore, not far from the lighthouse, the signal of three bells faded, and an Italian gentleman approached. *"Mi perdoni."* He halted and switched to accented English, addressing Gideon directly. "Pardon me, but I wonder if you are the son of *Signore* Nico Ravensworth?"

"I am the son of Sir Nicholas Ravensworth."

*"Sì!* You resemble him." The Italian's dark eyes reflected heartfelt thanksgiving. *"Grazie a Dio*, you have arrived safe." Shaking Gideon's hand with warm exuberance, he introduced himself. "I am Dante Olivadotti. Signore Nico has been most anxious ever since we learned of your intended visit."

"I received your letter at Gibraltar," Gideon affirmed.

"Then you understand Signore Nico enlisted me to meet you here in Genoa to be your guide to the convent where he is staying outside of *Firenze*."

"Sir Nicholas still lives then?" St. James returned Olivadotti's handshake, also recipient of a warm and genuine welcome.

Olivadotti's nod bespoke his positive enthusiasm. "Signore Nico seemed to rally when the report came declaring the impending arrival of his son." The Italian turned to Gideon. "He has much to share with you. If you have no objection, we should depart straightaway, not linger in Genoa. If all goes well and the roads stay dry, it will take us until the end of the week to reach Florence.

We have sturdy conveyances and swift horses. Guns and powder. Better safe than sorry should it come to an encounter with any *banditti*."

"We"—Gideon motioned between himself and St. James—"are invited to the envoy's residence for supper. St. James and I planned to return to the ship afterward. I can be ready to leave with you come morning."

"I too acquired an invitation from the British diplomat." Olivadotti patted his jacket pocket. "I'm told tonight's gathering is not a ball on grand scale. However, due to another recently arrived Englishman and his entourage, there will be dancing and entertainment with cards after the meal."

Gideon chuckled over the groan St. James failed to stifle.

Olivadotti smiled and resumed his briefing. "There are others who will travel with us when we set out—my nephew Gregorio Lazzaro and Antonio Ventresca, who married my sister Lucrezia. You will meet them soon. Lazzaro and Ventresca have secured lodging nearby and will be ready to leave as soon as you give the word, Signore Ravensworth."

"So long as my father lives, he is still rightfully Signore Ravensworth. I am just Gideon."

Olivadotti accepted that, falling into step beside Gideon as they walked along the cobblestoned piazza, with St. James bringing up the rear. "Forgive me, Signore Gideon. Decorum would have me offer condolences for the recent loss of your brother, no?"

"No." Gideon waved off the sympathetic platitude. "If you know my father at all, you surely understand my older brother's passing was not a loss by any stretch of definition."

Olivadotti nodded but touched his forehead, chest, and each shoulder in the sign of the cross. "'*Nihil nisi bonum*—let us not speak ill of the dead.' Signore Nico hinted this particular circumstance proves beneficial to more than just yourself."

⌐

Solely to placate Ravensworth's entreaty, Marcus acquiesced to make an appearance at the home of the British envoy. He would have preferred to forgo the diplomatic invitation and return to the *Oceanna*. Socializing was neither one of his strengths nor a favorite pastime. As a habit, he avoided situations that required he engage in superfluous conversation with strangers or feign politeness toward aristocrats he'd likely never encounter again.

As the supper hour drew nearer, the stronger Marcus's hunger pangs became. He felt like Amos, being governed by his belly when Ravensworth predicted a menu of something other than familiar British fare. If this was indeed his only outing in Italy, at least he would sample a taste of the country.

Supper featured appetizing local dishes prepared and served with great flourish. In addition to fresh-caught seafood, he enjoyed every bite of buttered *tagliatelle* with dried tomatoes and grated cheese. Dipping another slice of flatbread in oil, he faced a difficult choice between lasagna or ravioli with pesto sauce, and he decided to test both.

Savoring the bruschetta, Marcus noted the deliberately downplayed identity of the young man seated nearest the envoy. Ravensworth cast a conspiratorial nod toward the man in question. If Marcus wasn't mistaken, they dined in company with the younger brother of their sovereign, King George III.

The woman seated next to Marcus confirmed the royal's identity. She, the niece of an ambassador, repeatedly patted Marcus's sleeve and leaned too close, thereby exhibiting her obvious charms. In November, she shared, Prince Edward, the Duke of York and Albany—traveling under the alias title "Earl of Ulster"—had arrived in Italia along with his entourage. His emphasized naval career garnered less pomp and circumstance than his princely status, so that by all appearances the journey was for pleasure, curiosity, and culture.

The guests nearest Prince Edward conducted genial discussion about a recently performed theatrical production and something about a violin concerto by an Italian composer named Antonio Vivaldi called *The Four Seasons*, introduced in Amsterdam four decades past.

As an appointed member of the King's privy council, the "earl," as one might expect, could not escape undercurrents of duty in play. Historically, this part of Europe had seen conflict at various times and in various combinations between the Austrians, the French, the English, and the city-states on the Italian peninsula. Diplomacy required a balancing act.

Olivadotti had been correct. Following dessert servings of gelato or tiramisu, the musicians tuned their instruments for the evening's ensuing entertainment.

Marcus's mind drifted back to Bath, to Serenity, and by his inattention found himself maneuvered into a dance with the ambassador's niece by one of the persistent bejeweled matrons. Grinding his molars stemmed inconsiderate comments. At least he didn't have to speak. The woman rambled on in a lengthy monologue.

When he caught the dip of Gideon's chin and the tilt of Olivadotti's head, each indicating the direction of the exit door, he danced the set to its conclusion. He bowed with hasty apology, returned the niece to her chaperone, and escaped with his own brand of diplomatic aplomb to counter appearing boorish. Muttering under his breath something less than flattering where manipulative females were concerned, he tugged at the sleeves of his frock coat as he sauntered off to join Gideon and the Florentine guide.

He bent his knees and slouched his shoulders, bringing him level with Ravensworth's shorter height. "Can we get out of this crush now?"

"Indeed, I think we should." Ravensworth chuckled, allowing Marcus to retreat ahead of him. "Before she can set her sights on you again."

Grinning, Olivadotti put himself between Marcus and the ballroom, stating the obvious, "The *signorina* will be ever so disheartened to learn you arrived in country and left again before she could sink in her talons."

Ravensworth stifled a laugh, giving Marcus a purposeful shove toward the arched door. "Crack on, man. I've got your back."

While he appreciated his friend's loyalty, Marcus failed to appreciate Ravensworth's jesting. The Buxtram episode in London was still raw and recent.

Olivadotti walked with them through the *Piazza di Ferrari* on their return to the waterfront and promised to collect Ravensworth come morning.

In the cabin below the *Oceanna*'s main deck, conversation with Ravensworth continued unhindered by the schooner's slight rocking. Marcus voiced the question that had been eating at him. "Do you trust these men?"

Ravensworth's demeanor matched Marcus's seriousness. "Enough. I have little choice but to do otherwise. The letter from my father's solicitor spelled it out. Olivadotti, Lazzaro, and Ventresca were retained to fetch me and bring me to my father under safe conduct. I feel easier knowing I'll go with people who know the land, language, and customs." He pulled a monogrammed linen kerchief from the pocket of his breeches and handed it to Marcus. "Open it."

Marcus peeled back the fabric to reveal a signet ring. The engraved flat oval bore the Ravensworth crest. "Your father's?"

"Now mine." Ravensworth slipped the ring onto the little finger of his right hand. "Olivadotti brought it as a token of good faith. I don't know the Italians well—yet." A flintlock pistol and sheathed dagger next to his satchel served as reminders he knew what to do with the weapons should he need to defend himself. "That will likely remedy itself in the time it takes for us to get to Florence."

"*Firenze*," Marcus mimicked, practicing his dialect.

"What of you? You have Kerrigan's word his crew will deliver you to the Colonies. I'd say an equal level of trust is being required of you, as it is of me."

"We are placing our lives in their respective hands. Therefore, we must trust God even above that," Marcus said.

"St. James?"

Marcus met Ravensworth's intense eyes.

"Should it become a question, you have my blessing where Serenity is concerned."

Marcus opened his mouth to argue and closed it again. He sighed, resigned. "I thank you. If said circumstance manifests itself, 'twould be my honor to be the means of uniting our families. In time. Perhaps. However, it is not only my heart involved. Your sister would have a say, and I would honor her wishes."

"I leave it to your judgment. Time and place notwithstanding, either side of the Atlantic."

Unable to rein in his meandering thoughts, Marcus listened to the snoring of the off-duty Dutch sailors and Ravensworth. He didn't need to light a taper to envision the words in his Bible. During his devotional reading that morning, the Scripture seemed to jump from the section in Isaiah, as if the Lord had spoken directly to him. *I, even I, am he that blotteth out thy transgressions for mine own sake, and will not remember thy sins.*

Lady Aurelia's parting commentary came to him again: *The forgiveness is there, Marcus, because Jesus bled and died to offer redemption for each of us and bestow life eternal in Him. He loved us that much and more than we can fathom. However, it is up to you to accept His provision. No one else can do so on your behalf. Acceptance is on you alone.*

⌒

Kerrigan's Dutch captain, Gerrit Van den Bosch, issued commands to his crew. The schooner separated from the dock.

Marcus raised a hand in farewell to Ravensworth and to the three-man Italian contingent who'd come to the harbor quay to see the *Oceanna* off. Their horse-drawn calash and wagon would travel the hundred and fifty miles overland to Florence.

The port city receded, and the travelers diminished as the distance from shore lengthened. *Godspeed them on their way.* In the open water, trimmed sails caught the wind. A few days back to Gibraltar—a British outpost on the tip of Spain, which served as gateway to the Mediterranean—then westward to British North America. Marcus's petition to the Almighty included safety across the leagues and fathoms, and cooperative weather for the *Oceanna.* By this time, *The Raven's Lady* should have set sail out of Bristol. Serenity might well be riding the same briny waves, headed in the same direction.

That night, after the sun dipped below the horizon and the blue-black sky shone with countless pinpricks of shimmery light, Marcus imagined Amos teaching Serenity how to find Polaris, the North Star. The trustworthy lad would follow through as Marcus had instructed, and until he saw her again, he would hang his thoughts of Serenity there.

Van den Bosch offered a steaming mug to Marcus on deck. "Ravensworth will be in Florence for some time?"

"Until the business with his father is settled or Sir Nicholas passes—whichever happens first."

"My *vader* went to sea when I was eleven. Never came back."

"Mine was killed last year. Pontiac's Rebellion."

Van den Bosch scratched his dark-blond head. "Life's never quite the same once a vader is gone."

Marcus nodded in mute reply. He still felt the ache from the hole wrought by his father's death, doubly so coupled with the death of Lucas too.

"Kerrigan shared a little of your history—not to be telling tales so much as to give a better understanding to those of us who have to put up with you for the next couple of months."

Marcus managed a grin. "Then you have the advantage."

"I make it my business to know something about those sailing under my command. Long distances, close quarters. It goes better to address unease with immediacy and head on." The Dutch captain let the admonishment settle before he asked, "How's the arm?"

"Healing. The strength is returning by degrees." Marcus rotated his shoulder and fisted his fingers closed, then opened them and repeated the motion. "Not fully restored yet, but neither is it hanging limp from the socket like it was a few weeks ago."

"Kerrigan says you can be useful in other ways, if not pitching in with loading or unloading on this voyage. He indicated you're the curious sort. Do you know anything about navigation?" Van den Bosch asked.

"No."

"You may find it useful. Our first mate can teach you. He's skilled at it and knowledgeable about the stars."

Marcus swirled the coffee in his mug, avoiding suspicion in Van den Bosch's wary eyes. It was wrong to harbor ill feelings against someone who held no part in the grievance.

"Is there a problem?"

"No." Marcus cleared his throat, squared his broad shoulders, and resigned himself to the next right step. "No problem. I'll speak with him at the next shift change."

Van den Bosch nodded in the affirmative. "He's hard to miss. Rangy fellow, not quite equal to your height but nigh unto close. He's the one with the turtle tattoo down the side of his neck."

"I know who you mean." Marcus tasted chagrin. He didn't like that his aversion to a man of obvious native origins had been evident despite his attempt to hide it. Van den Bosch was right. The *Oceanna* was too small a ship for dissention. Marcus ordered himself to release what was behind him or it would plague him without end. And if he was to make the effort to work on that, he should resolve to straightening out the situation with Serenity. "What is his name?"

"Nagatamen," Van der Bosch said. "Lenape. Or at least his vader was." Reflective, the *Oceanna*'s captain took a long swallow from his mug. "Vaders are interesting creatures, *ja*? Some good, some aren't. Some strong, some don't have it in them. Some have influence, some you wish didn't. And the consolation is there's not one on this earth who can compare with God the heavenly Vader, the Holy One of the universe. He out-loves everyone ever. For whatever. Forever."

"Are you anyone's father?" Marcus asked.

A jolly chuckle ripped from Van den Bosch. "*Ja*, to six of my own, and Opa to two more. I told Kerrigan I'm getting too old for this. But his incentives are too tempting to turn down."

"How long have you worked for Kerrigan?"

Van den Bosch squinted. "Summer of seventeen and forty-three, maybe? Forty-Four? Hard to remember so long ago. How do you know him?"

"We met when we sailed from Alexandria in the Virginia colony back to Bristol. Ravensworth found out he was there and somehow manipulated arrangements for us to go back to England with him rather than wait for the troop transport to return. I was wounded and was recovering then too. You might say it's been a rough year from a physical standpoint."

"Yet you're still here."

Van den Bosch echoed Sir Rodney, as had Lady Aurelia too. And Serenity. Marcus looked up again at the nebula dusting the heavens, locating Polaris at true north, then Orion's starry belt. God's handiwork illuminated the dark sky, His presence nearly palpable—not out there where Marcus couldn't differentiate between liquid horizon meeting distant atmosphere. Closer. Within. He rubbed his chest, felt the kindling warmth of the Holy Spirit, and admitted he needed to pay attention or he might miss what God wanted to teach him. For his own sanity, Marcus decided he'd rather learn the hard lessons once without having to repeat them. If he had anything to say about it.

# Chapter 24

*Deck of* The Raven's Lady, *Bristol Docks*

The first two months of seventeen and sixty-four dwindled as rapidly as an hourglass's sand flowed from top to bottom. The designated day on the calendar suffered a slight delay, but the adjusted date was no longer looked forward to—it was upon them.

In those intervening weeks, Serenity divided her time between Grandee's townhouse and the Northcrafts, making frequent conversational encounters with Uncle Twitch. The gruff pirate-looking man cared deeply for those he allowed in his familial circle, although he didn't always express it in a genteel manner. His rough edges were part of his understated charm. Orders were orders, whether for his crewmen or those closest to him. He treated both sets equally, favoring neither group above the other, the mark of his expectations high.

Whipping wind hastened the good-byes at the Kerrigan Shipping warehouse. "I shall see you when I see you, dearest." Grandee held her close during their final tearful farewell hug. "You have my love and prayers. Be of good courage. And write."

Raucous foul language of irreverent tars working along the wharves burned Serenity's ears. The assaulting smell of fish and salty wet ropes made her nose wrinkle in protest. Uncle Twitch followed her up the gangway onto the deck of *The Raven's Lady*, where activity buzzed in anticipation.

"When we are underway, you can come back on deck if you like, but for now, let's get you out of the cold. Later, I'll introduce you to the crew," Uncle Twitch said.

The crew cast quick nods and polite smiles at Serenity as she passed. She was the only woman on board, which didn't bother her, having grown up in a houseful of brothers, but some sailors flatly refused to sail with one in their midst. Uncle Twitch didn't hire that sort. He exercised a sensible nature, putting little stock in superstitions. He'd traveled across the waters with women passengers enough times to discharge any validity that having one on board was akin to courting ill luck on a voyage.

Once, he caught a runaway disguised as a newly hired crew member. Upon learning her dilemma, Uncle Twitch had vowed to keep her secret to help her elude an abusive husband vowing to kill her. After the late war, he'd transported widows of soldiers killed in action back home to family in England.

A number of women passengers had sailed on *The Raven's Lady* over the past few years. Uncle Twitch remarked, "Lady Aurelia has been a longtime investor in Kerrigan Shipping. Her influence is more land based, I grant you, but even she embarked on a jaunt at my invitation to Edinburgh and Dublin."

"Don't forget shopping excursions with Madelaine to London," Serenity laughed.

"Aye, her ladyship and my Madelaine brought home with them twice as many trunks to Bath on their last visit to London as you're departing with. We should be so thankful—isn't that right, young Amos?"

Amos and one of the crew, Obadiah Welles, carried the smallest of Serenity's three trunks between them, waiting for her to descend into the lower realm of the schooner so they could follow and allow her to direct where she wanted each one placed.

"Turn around." Uncle Twitch swirled a finger near his right ear as his left eye narrowed. "First thing you're going to need to learn," he said to Serenity, "unless you plan to don breeches, is how to navigate that ladder, both up and down, without looking, and not get your feet caught up in your hem."

Serenity recognized the practical advice for what it was. She scooped her hem with one fist and raised her skirt high enough to clear her ankles. Facing the ladder, her fingers firmly grasped the varnished handrail, and she lowered the toe of a half boot until it met the successive stair below. She repeated the motion with the opposite foot to gain the next lower rung, until after seven repetitions, she was standing in the narrow passage under the main deck. She looked up. Uncle Twitch gave a curt nod, signaling his approval concerning her level of agility. Stepping aside, she motioned for Amos to descend.

The square patch of fading light outlined Amos's lanky form against the purpling atmosphere of day's end. One by one Serenity's trunks were transferred from deck to master cabin, which Uncle Twitch had voluntarily given up so she would have a private space to herself for the duration of the voyage—unless, of course, he had need to retrieve any of his atlases, navigation charts, instruments, or maps.

Beneath the skylight, Serenity seated herself on one of the four chairs chained to the rectangular table bolted to the master cabin's floor. Uncle Twitch possessed a collection of bound and loose maps, most printed rather than hand sketched. She traced the edge of the island kingdom of England on one and took a fortifying breath. Like the whisper of parchment, a wistful sigh escaped. Reaching into her pocket, she assured herself St. James's map lay exactly where she'd left it. She fidgeted with her gold sovereign pendant, thinking of him and saying a quick prayer for him, wherever he was.

Gideon had teased her, insisting St. James, as viscount, would need to marry the "Lady Oakleigh" of his choosing to bear him an heir. But perhaps Gideon hadn't been entirely in jest, for he maintained St. James was more than fond of her.

Equal to the height of Serenity's chin, a single row of windows lining the stern let the last of the daylight pour into the master cabin. Darkness would be upon them soon. Already the lanterns reflected on the moving surface of the water, and the images of ships moored along the dock swayed in watery distortion.

Uncle Twitch guaranteed the crossing would be a learning experience for Serenity as well as Amos. "You'll learn about tides, ride the waves, and grow accustomed to the squawking of gulls trailing behind the ship, looking for food sources—be they swimming in the water or discarded and thrown overboard." Amos promised to teach her how to find the North Star.

The schooner rocked. Voices shouted commands as the crew coordinated their actions and responsibilities in quick obedience as the vessel slipped away from the dock.

The ship's motion disturbed her equilibrium. Serenity spent her first night on board as she had her last in Bath, drenching her pillow with muffled tears before drifting into exhausted slumber. She had no wish to think of all she was leaving behind, and she wasn't yet ready to be appropriately enthused by what lay ahead.

Serenity awoke drained. Drawing the draperies aside from the row of master cabin windows, she saw nothing but water and a thick flock of gulls tagging along behind *The Raven's Lady*, her red flag with a Union Jack in one corner unfurled and snapping in the tug of the breeze. Stiff wind filled the canvas sails. Serenity's stomach rose and fell with each corresponding swell. Determined to battle the lethargy, she tied on a clean apron, secured her cap and cloak, and stepped into the passageway.

On either side of the master cabin were two smaller compartments, one designated by a sign marked *Lieutenant* and the other bearing a nameplate reading *Doctor/Chaplain*. Serenity thought Uncle Twitch stowed his wool travel bag in the second cabin. The remaining members of the six-man crew—plus Amos—bedded down in bunks with pocket-door enclosures or hammocks suspended with ropes secured on hooks from port side to starboard. Two closed pocket doors indicated sailors asleep before their shift assignments, so she quietly climbed the ladder to the main deck. Time to become acquainted with her new routine for the next ten to twelve weeks.

Uncle Twitch did not serve in capacity as full-time captain on this trip, delegating most duties to his able lieutenant, although remaining available for consultation as needed. Release from his usual obligations afforded him stretches of time to spend teaching Amos, and that one's lessons began on the very first day *The Raven's Lady* set sail.

This being Serenity's first crossing, she wasn't sure she would have enough to do on board to keep herself occupied, given the amount of time Amos spent with Uncle Twitch. That proved a false assessment. When not with Uncle Twitch, Amos was with her for lessons in reading, spelling, and arithmetic. She listened to his recited Scriptures and a daily chapter of the novel they read together. She'd brought embroidery along and dabbled with practical mending when needed by the crew.

Five days beyond the Severn Estuary and Bristol Channel and out into the Atlantic, Amos dragged Uncle Twitch to find her standing at the schooner's railing. "Sis?"

Serenity smiled at her brother. "Yes, Amos?"

Uncle Twitch's eyes filled with concern. "How are you doing? Have you kept anything down today?"

"A little."

Amos clapped his hand over his mouth to stifle his laugh. "I am sorry you're feeling so poorly, Sis. But we have something to take your mind off that."

"The cook, Teaspoon, burned his arm," Uncle Twitch said.

"So I volunteered you for the job. I explained to the crew you make very tasty sweet buns." Mischief saturated Amos's smile. "In fact, you owe me a batch for helping haul your trunks aboard. That was the deal, was it not?"

"Yes, Amos. That was the deal."

"Bribing him again?" Uncle Twitch smoothed his whiskers, hiding a chuckle.

"For as long as I can get results, I'll continue employing such tactics." Without shame in her proven methods, Serenity headed to the galley kitchen.

Introducing herself to the ship's cook, she offered to assist with dinner preparations that night. Teaspoon was grateful, as he'd been struggling to dice vegetables for fish chowder with only his uninjured hand. The crew too were thankful she was willing to feed them all. When they tasted her offerings, they expressed a collective request to have the experience repeated. Often.

After dinner's cleanup, Serenity consulted her herb book. She alternated poultices of houseleek and turmeric, and also applied honey to Teaspoon's burn, with noticeable results. The Scottish cook, dubbed Teaspoon by his shipmates, possessed the inexplicable habit of adding a teaspoon of random spices to whatever he was preparing—whether the receipt called for it or not. His nonchalance for the sake of sheer experimentation resulted in every meal seeming an uncharted adventure. No one was quite sure how his creations would taste from one meal to the next—and some days were better than others.

The number of days for his recuperation extended for so long Serenity doubted the success of her ministrations. Until the ship's carpenter assured her it was not Teaspoon's medical condition that was slow to heal but his reluctance to confess that, like the rest of the crew, he preferred her cooking to his own.

Cooking was the only ship's duty with which Uncle Twitch allowed Serenity to assist. Before the end of the first month, Serenity had quietly assumed culinary duties three days a week to the unspoken delight of the crew, though Serenity sensed their appreciation. There were never leftovers on those nights, but neither did anyone want to insult Teaspoon. They still had to eat on the days when it was his turn in the galley.

Ever since the men had overheard Amos talking about the Chelsea-style buns, they'd entreated Serenity to make them with regularity for as long as the supplies would last. She had done so each Friday since putting to sea.

Serenity gained additional practice as she cooked for the crew, and menu items met with more triumphs than not. The men willingly overlooked any near calamity because it meant one less meal of Teaspoon's burgoo.

Amos mentioned, in no uncertain terms, he believed her attempts had much improved since they'd left Fernsby Hall and Grandee's townhouse, given what she had to work with. "Nancie Heath would be proud," her brother assured. He rubbed his satisfied tummy and squealed when Serenity tickled his ribs.

Her little brother's enjoyment encouraged her more than he knew.

⌒

*The Villa near Convent Santa Magdalena, Florence, Italy*

*Dear Jonathan,*

*St. James is on his way to Philadelphia, and I am here, in Italy. Father sent Dante Olivadotti, Gregorio Lazzaro, and Antonio Ventresca to provide company and security for the overland miles between Genoa on the coast and Florence on the River Arno. Italian*

*roads have highwaymen, like English roads do. Thankfully, we did
not experience any unsavory dealings with banditti along the route.
You would appreciate the history in this place. Florence is bisected
by the Arno, but the bridges keep both sides of the community united.*
Ponte Alle Grazie, Ponte Alla Carraia, Ponte Santa Trinita.
*The most elaborate arched bridge here is called* Ponte Vecchio, *built
in 1345. The Benedictine Abbey, called Badia Fiorentina, was
founded in 978.*

*The convent next door to the villa where our father has lived since
arriving with his diagnosis, is not as old as that. During the past
two years and a half, he has resided here under the watchful eye of
his physician and of Signora Lucrezia, Olivadotti's sister and wife
of Ventresca. She has been diligent in caring for him according to the
physician's instructions and they have accepted him into their family.
They call him Signore Nico and, being his son, they have taken me
in as well.*

*I am learning the ways of the convent and its frustratingly lei-
surely pace. Meal schedules, chapel services, including vespers and
Mass, general time spent in the garden or in the workshop, tinkering.
Naps in the afternoon—*La Pennichella *or* il riposino pomeridi-
ano. *If something gets accomplished, well done. If not, then there is
tomorrow...*

*The day I left Genoa with the Italians, St. James and the*
Oceanna *sailed away without me, and I again questioned the
soundness of what I am doing. Yet I hold resolute, even with no fixed
diary or precise schedule. I have come this far and still have questions
requiring answers.*

*Our calash was not the only carriage departing Genoa that
day—the Earl of Ulster with his entourage also departed for their
itinerary's subsequent destination. It makes me laugh to think about
sharing a table with the incognito prince at the envoy's residence. It
has altered my perspective, for now whenever I find myself humming*

*"O'er the Hills and Far Away," I have a keener awareness than before, that that man's brother is England's own sovereign, the one, as the song says, issuing the commands, while we soldiers—and citizens—obey.*

*How go the studies? Any update on Ian FitzGerald's reinstatement at Balliol? And your tutoring sessions with Henry at the Eagle and Child? Will you make time to visit Grandee and the Northcrafts or observe Resurrection Sunday?*

*For my part, I find it easier to pray for other people more than for myself. My list might contain the same names, and perhaps comparable requests as yours, so I hope God hears your prayers if He isn't listening to mine.*

*I am still not sure what I'm hoping to prove, but maybe that will make itself manifest before long. I arrived with a sick feeling in my stomach and a rather large grudge marring my outlook, incredulity burning in my gullet and righteous indignation searing my heart. I dragged a veritable satchel full of whys and whatever-were-you-thinking type sentiments ready to sling during interrogation on Day One.*

*This is Day Two. Alas, I have not yet seen Father. Prior to my arrival, he suffered a "bad night," according to Signora Lucrezia. It took an extensive dose of laudanum to settle him, and the harsh coughing spasms have subsided. He sleeps. Therefore, I wait.*

*Perhaps tomorrow. If he makes it through this night.*

*I shall send word when there is something to share. I came here uninvited, against his wishes, and I'll stay until I get answers—one way or the other.*

*Until then I remain your affectionate and duty-bound brother,*

*Gideon*

*P.S. When I return, we will revisit that stupid poem once and for all—not only for Amos's sake, but for all of us. I wish it had been buried with Colson, but it was not and it has a residual effect. Though he is no longer here to enforce his twisted point of view on our lives or rightful heritage, his unlamented absence results in us three remaining Ravensworth brothers each moved up a rung in the birth order. Colson's demise might have altered what our respective positions are, but it doesn't change who we are. Not in the least. Crack on and Godspeed.*

# Chapter 25

The Raven's Lady, *Atlantic Ocean*

No land in sight—at least none Serenity could see—only an endless stretch of undulating grey-green waves. Beneath a bright-blue sky studded with clouds, pewter-colored on the bottom and fluffy cotton white on top, the sails billowed, full of the ocean's breath.

Seven weeks out from Bristol, the continuous sound of water lapping at the hull and the rocking motion of the schooner's deck was not so noticeable unless white-capped swells multiplied and grew, which they sometimes did. Serenity had learned how to ride out tempest-driven lurching firsthand. A veteran of two wicked storms—both deemed relatively smooth, according to Uncle Twitch when compared to previous squalls he'd been all but swallowed up by—Serenity felt very small so far from anywhere out in the Atlantic waters.

As of Thursday last, Uncle Twitch's nautical navigation calculations had *The Raven's Lady* in closer proximity to the coast of the Colonies than of England. She did her best to concentrate on something other than not seeing shore for days on end, and only a rare vessel in their vicinity displaying the colors of the British Navy. Fact of the matter was, they were still weeks away from land on either side.

"If I take the wings of the morning, and dwell in the uttermost parts of the sea; Even there shall Thy hand lead me, and Thy right hand shall hold me." Her recitation of a particular bit of Psalm 139 dissolved into earnest prayer. *I thank You, Heavenly Father, for holding us in Your hand. For Your continued protection. And thank You, again, for the opportunity You have created for Amos, and for me. Please also continue to be with Grandee, Gideon, Jonathan, the Northcrafts ... and Marcus St. James, wherever he is.*

Her stomach listed, as it had the tendency to do whenever she observed her youngest brother clambering up the rope ladders.

"Captain Twitch!" Amos hailed from the unnerving height of the crosstree, fingers flattened to shield his eyes from the sun. "Another schooner!"

Curious, Serenity collected her needlework and made her way toward the stern. Uncle Twitch consulted with the helmsman at the tiller. Sails of a second ship appeared and followed in their liquid path. From this distance, she couldn't make out the colors but suspected the vessel flew a friendly flag—elsewise the crew of *The Raven's Lady* would be manning their posts at the swivel guns lining the fore and quarter decks.

"Is it one of yours?" she asked Uncle Twitch.

"Yes, it is indeed a schooner of the Kerrigan fleet. She's the *Oceanna*." Uncle Twitch lowered his spyglass, offering it to Serenity. "She'll have come by way of Genoa, where she deposited Gideon. Then on to swap out cargo at St. Eustatius in the Dutch West Indies, and finally headed to Philadelphia ahead of us."

Serenity peered through the telescopic glass as Uncle Twitch continued, "She flies the banner of Kerrigan Shipping, adorned with a raven and a shamrock. If you see the Kerrigan banner with the British Red Ensign and its Union Jack canton, that means we've encountered friends."

She nodded, appreciative whenever Uncle Twitch shared bits of sailing and shipping knowledge when she needed to know them, and took pains to alleviate any apprehension.

Since leaving England, she and Uncle Twitch cultivated their mutual friendship. Upon better acquaintance, unexpected aspects of his character clarified her perception of him. Yes, the merchant sea captain was customarily shrewd and oftentimes wily. Someone to be reckoned with and wiser not to cross. Amos's innocent comment in passing had her agreeing that when provoked, Uncle Twitch might be as fearsome as Blackbeard or Captain Kidd. In common dealings though, Serenity discovered him grounded, just, well-read, determined, and dedicated. She admired his decision to live out his convictions as a God-fearing man. No wonder Grandee esteemed him as she did.

Serenity had patched together a mosaic of things she knew about him but which hadn't been revealed in their occasional chessboard conversations. She combined her own compiled surveillance with Grandee's stories about him, and Madelaine's, and chided herself for initially dreading his assistance on Amos's behalf. She now viewed him as a good and influential mentor, a blessing she hadn't grasped until recently.

"Will she catch us?" Serenity wondered.

"Do you want her to?" The bushy brow over Twitch's left eye arched and a mischievous glimmer sparkled.

In this moment, she was convinced Uncle Twitch guarded a secret, his private mirth splitting the space between his moustache and beard, revealing a knowing smile. His expression made Serenity believe he held back from laughing at her expense, for surely mischief was afoot.

Raising the spyglass to cover her eagerness, she squinted for a second look. Though the ship appeared closer in the glass, she could not make out any faces of the crew.

"That could be arranged, providing the ocean remains relatively calm," Uncle Twitch said. "Might even provide a learning experience

for young Amos. I'll send him over with a supper invitation when
they get close enough."

"How large a crew is aboard the *Oceanna?*" she asked. New faces
would supply a diversion and bring fresh conversation.

"Six, plus one passenger. But that one pitches in where he's
able."

Serenity handed back the glass and tucked the flapping end of her
scarf into the buttoned collar of her red woolen cardinal. Unable to
restrain her wide smile, she excused herself. "I shall inform Teaspoon
we may be having guests for supper tomorrow or the next day."

One passenger. And she was fairly sure she knew who that was.
She started praying for *calm enough* as it pertained to the water—and
to her heart's anticipation.

⌒

Heralding the morning, early light broke through a dense bank
of hovering clouds. Peeking between the thick curtains covering the
stern windows, Serenity witnessed streamers of pale pink, gold, and
orange as the reflected sunrise gilded the wavy water. She viewed
the dawn as another display of God's brilliant finger-painting. The
*Oceanna* sailed within shouting distance of the starboard side of *The
Raven's Lady.* If he was there, she couldn't see him—and if he was,
could he see her?

Following breakfast, Uncle Twitch orchestrated a new lesson for
Amos. He barked a series of commands the crew hastened to carry
out and, in short order, he and Amos were in the small boat bob-
bing atop the rippling water. Heart in her throat, Serenity's wide
eyes stayed locked on Amos the entire time it took for them to row
between the two schooners. Was a supper invitation worth the risk?
But she needn't have worried. Uncle Twitch's firm instructions guided
the boy and the small boat toward a lowered rope ladder. With the

small boat secured, Uncle Twitch followed Amos's agile ascent to the *Oceanna*'s main deck.

The strength of the gusts caused Serenity to shudder and the unnerving feeling of being watched unsettled her. Shielding her eyes, she scanned the men at the *Oceanna*'s rail aiding Uncle Twitch and Amos to safely board. Her brother paired an enthusiastic wave with a triumphant grin. Serenity reciprocated both his actions.

She returned to her mending to keep herself from thinking too much, but such was only good in theory, not practical application. She continued praying under her breath every second until Amos and Uncle Twitch again had their feet planted on the deck of *The Raven's Lady*, bringing word that at least three, maybe four from the *Oceanna* would join them for supper later this evening—weather, wind, and water permitting.

That perceptible feeling of being watched disturbed Serenity's tranquility while she sat in the afternoon sun, picking at a torn seam in the shirt on her lap. The angle of the sun cast shadow over the majority of the other schooner's deck, and she could not discern the source or location of the heavy glance she felt sure was trained upon her.

Serenity slowly swept the *Oceanna*'s decks with the helmsman's borrowed spyglass.

There! A bright circle of light danced crazily across the *Oceanna*'s jib sails, then descended to a point above the head of a mariner. Next, a flash of sunlight glinted on the barrel of a spyglass held in the large hands of a long-legged, bearded man sporting a pea coat and voyageur cap, who undoubtedly had her in his sights.

Serenity's mouth formed a surprised "Oh" when the seaman collapsed his glass and tossed a jolly salute.

Marcus St. James.

Her heart skipped. Then raced.

Marcus retrieved his shaving kit but decided against using it. Not all sailors let their whiskers grow while at sea. However, between these two crews, more than half did—including Kerrigan and Van den Bosch—and Marcus took the liberty of following their example. Though his elbow was mending, some stiffness and limited restriction in the joint lingered. He elected to forgo the risk of cutting himself shaving due to his unsteady arm or the constant motion of the schooner. With no crewmates about, he pulled his soiled shirt over his head, making a quick swap for a fresh one. He wanted no questions should one of them appear at the ladder and spy his feather armlet tattoo.

He caught himself missing Featherstone as he brushed his vest and coat, and ran a comb through his wind-mussed hair before employing a narrow strip of black leather to secure his queue. Expelling a breath, he turned from the mottled looking glass, abandoning further improvements to his reflection. He slung his canvas bag over his uninjured shoulder. "Go before me, Lord. May I find favor in Your eyes. And in hers."

An even exchange involving six men commenced. Three of the crew from *The Raven's Lady*, including Obadiah Welles, traded places with Van den Bosch, Nagatamen, and Marcus when they left the *Oceanna*. Ahead of the appointed hour for supper, the two small boats crisscrossed the waves between the schooners, leaving both fully manned should any unforeseen need arise.

Amos was first to greet each at the rail as they ascended the rope ladder.

"Goodness, but you've grown at least another inch," Marcus proclaimed. "Maybe even two. You're going to need longer breeches sooner rather than later by the looks of it." He remembered all too well growing out of his clothes at a rate that alarmed his mother. He and Lucas had often suffered a gap between the cuff of their breeches and the tops of their stockings.

Amos tugged at his breeches to cover his knees. "I didn't tell her."

"She knows," Marcus whispered back. "She saw the light from your signal mirror and we saw each other through the spyglasses."

Arms crossed, Amos tipped his head to one side, as if pondering why they would bother. "You were spying on each other?"

"Something like that." Marcus flashed a grin.

"She's going to think you look like a pirate."

"No, not entirely." Serenity approached, scrutinizing Marcus's features with exaggerated deliberation. "No parrot on his shoulder, no patch over one eye, no timber toe, and his trim whiskers are nowhere near long enough to fashion in true Blackbeard style."

"She's been reading to me about pirates in a story about a Captain Singleton."

"Authored by Daniel Defoe," she said.

"Ah." Marcus wriggled beneath the intensity of her inspection and the curious stares of sailors from their respective duty stations. "Miss Ravensworth, it is a pleasure to see you again." He held her fingers, drawing them to his lips as he bowed over her hand. "You are looking remarkably well. I take it the sea air agrees with you."

"I— I thank you, Mr. St. James." Color high on her cheeks, Serenity's soft bite against her lower lip betrayed the same nervousness Marcus experienced. "I confess, I am doing much better having grown acclimated to the constant motion."

He detected the *What are you doing here?* question snapping in her eyes, but he didn't answer in front of their audience. He relinquished her hand to gesture to the two men who'd accompanied him in the *Oceanna*'s small boat. "Allow me to introduce my shipmates. Captain Gerrit Van den Bosch and first mate Nagatamen."

Van den Bosch executed a polite, gentlemanlike bow. The tattooed Lenape greeted her in like manner. Serenity dispensed an amiable curtsy, displaying neither hesitance nor distaste. Perhaps exposure to Marcus's indelible feathers during his surgery had served to alter her perspective, alleviating any residual shock or foreignness such tribal markings might have otherwise caused. He credited her adaptive manner as a positive trait. Neither did it surprise him to learn she performed hostess duties as graciously here aboard ship as she'd done in Bath.

Introductions established, the *Oceanna*'s captain and first mate excused themselves to join Kerrigan near the foremast.

Alone, save for Amos's tag-along presence, Marcus faulted himself for her sudden shyness, she seeming as tongue-tied as he. Their last encounter had ended in awkward stalemate. He'd wanted to kiss her, not just hold her, when they were in the kitchen at Lady Aurelia's townhouse. Common sense gave Marcus pause. He and Serenity hadn't been moving in accord before. Were they now? Happiness lit her candid expression at seeing him, ready as he to savor this incredulous gift of shipboard time spent together.

She accepted his offered right arm and he smiled into her luminous ginger-brown eyes before turning his attention upon her brother. "Are you enjoying all this then?" he asked Amos.

Amos rattled off a litany of specifics gleaned from Kerrigan's proficient tutelage. "He's not the captain this time, you know. At least, not all the time. Otherwise he would be too busy to teach me." Palm up, the boy held a small shaving mirror for Marcus's examination. "He's teaching me how to use a signal mirror. And he might teach me how to play a fiddle because when he's the only musician, there's no one else to play, so he doesn't get to dance."

"Fiddle? That could be useful," Marcus agreed. This animated side of Amos was one he'd not witnessed before and given the look in Serenity's eyes, it pleased her as well.

"Uncle Twitch knows someone in Charles Town who might have a fiddle for sale," Serenity said. "South Carolina will be our first port of call."

"I'm learning how to use a sextant for a dead reckoning," Amos added, "and I can find the North Star. I even showed Serenity how to locate it, as you asked me to do. Right, Sis?"

"Yes." Serenity's light laugh rippled like a wind chime. "We have delayed retiring to our cabins on many cloudless nights, staying on deck until we locate Polaris—offering a prayer and a wish when we do."

Marcus made a mental memorandum to himself to not tell Amos anything he didn't want Serenity to know.

"Has your arm healed?" she asked.

"Getting better." Marcus rubbed a hand over the elbow joint that ached less and less as the days went by. She was kind to give him grace to cover their previous meeting, choosing to attribute his changeable demeanor to his injuries. "I adhere to Dr. Graham's prescribed regimen of exercises, as I hope to regain full use of it again. I can lift a four-gallon pin in my own strength, but not yet a firkin." He tapped the toe of his boot to a metal band circling the bottom of a much larger hogshead-sized barrel. "I am determined I will before the end of the voyage."

"It does me good to see you recovered, and I am most thankful that bullet is no longer lodged against the bone."

"The swelling has decreased a good deal." Marcus recalled the distressing amount of blood expended when Dr. Theophilus Graham had fished out the spent ball and sewed up the resulting hole in his flesh. His current condition might well be his healthiest—he'd been hurt in some form or fashion from the day he met her. He very much wanted her to care for him in his own right, not wounded or ailing or in dire need of her capable nurturing. He couldn't stop staring, drinking her in.

She administered a gentle squeeze to his arm. "Mayhap that is true about the swelling, but I suspect your coat sleeve is still tight now that you are regaining strength."

His hand covered hers as he stood close to share warmth and block the wind tugging at her hooded cardinal. His fingers itched to touch escaped tendrils blown loose from her ruffled lace-edged cap, and he took the liberty of pressing his lips to the pink line of the residual scar on her forehead. Her familiar lavender-vanilla scent permeated the sea-salt laden air. He prayed in earnest that if she harbored any bad memories of the night she was injured, they were as faded as her scar.

Amos's brow bunched as he observed them and his inquisitive expression combined with a wrinkled nose. Marcus emitted a low chuckle and a blush stained Serenity's fair countenance. It would be a while before the lad appreciated the difference between placing an innocent kiss upon the cheek of a baby girl compared to bestowing a kiss on the cheek of a pretty lady whose trust he longed to win.

"And what have you learned on this voyage thus far?" Marcus asked Serenity.

"Oh, lots of things, including how candied ginger and peppermint tea go a long way to sooth a seasick constitution. Those first few days sailing were rough, yet I have prevailed. By the grace of God."

Teaspoon motioned to Serenity from the shadowy passageway.

"I beg you will please excuse me, Mr. St. James." She disentangled her arm from the crook of his. "Teaspoon and I are laying supper in the master cabin, and he must have the first course ready to serve. Amos?"

"Yes, Sis?"

She handed Amos a piece of grid-lined paper, and he listened to her careful instructions. "Go down to the master cabin. Get a pencil from the top drawer of the dressing table beside the bedstead. In each corresponding square, record exactly where the chess pieces are on the board. Uncle Twitch and I will have to finish our game later where we left off. Then close the chess table and push it back against the cabin wall. We'll put the extra serving dishes and cutlery there—be sure to count enough forks and knives, will you?"

"We can manage that easily enough, can't we, Amos?" Marcus bowed, taking his leave, her little brother in tow.

At Marcus's departure, Serenity pressed a hand to her stomacher, able to breathe again. She felt as if she'd run a great distance through Fernsby Hall's parkland—or spent too much time in front of Nancie Heath's bake oven. Recalling the lodestone Uncle Twitch had demonstrated to Amos during lessons, she could not deny the magnetic pull toward Marcus St. James.

The master cabin seemed to shrink with five men plus Amos crowded around the rectangular table set with pewter, wood, horn, and sputtering lantern light. No china, crystal, or silver, and no pretentious identifying placards or need for precedence, as each merely dropped onto the nearest chair. This was no fancy banquet hall supper. All that mattered was the food was hot in their trenchers and consumed in company she wouldn't trade. She found herself tucked in between Marcus and the man called Nagatamen.

The Lenape's markings graced his neck, part of one cheek, and both arms from wrist to elbow, visible for all to see—distinct yet different from Marcus's concealed tattoos. She wondered if they might represent a story or Lenape legend.

She pushed bland vegetables around with her fork, unsure what type of meat Teaspoon had prepared and she wasn't adventurous enough to ignore the mystery. If she couldn't identify what it was, Serenity wasn't about to put it into her mouth.

"May I ask what your name means?" she addressed Nagatamen.

"One who can be trusted," came the resonant reply.

Marcus halted sawing the "meat" with his knife, jaw and hands clenched.

Nagatamen waited, candleflame reflecting in his light eyes.

Serenity didn't comprehend the underlying meaning of the look that flashed between them, only that it had something to do with the subtle strain radiating from each. Both were warriors. Their exchange didn't seem so much challenge as perhaps dared acceptance. Or an olive branch?

Knowing what she did about him, she imagined Marcus's reticence traceable to his horrific experience in the Great Lakes Territory at Fort Michilimackinac. She sent a prayer heavenward, beseeching the Almighty to prod Marcus into taking a step that might promote a deeper healing than his residual surface scars. Those invisible wounds might have begun to heal but they were tender still.

For several minutes, there was no sound in the master cabin other than the mantel clock's swinging pendulum, the splash of waves, and the groan of creaking wood.

Marcus dipped his chin in a single nod and Nagatamen offered a hand, which Marcus willingly clasped.

Across the table, Serenity saw Van den Bosch and Uncle Twitch exchange a silent glance. A matter of poignant significance bridged an understanding.

⌒

Under a three-quarter moon, Van den Bosch and Nagatamen rowed back to the *Oceanna* after supper, their small boat again crisscrossing with that of the three sailors returning to *The Raven's Lady*. Kerrigan insisted Marcus stay and return to the *Oceanna* come morning. Conscious of Serenity on the other side of the common cabin wall, they kept their voices low so she would not discern the substance of their conversation.

"I am not in need of client banking services," Marcus began, "but I could use your assistance with power of attorney. The solicitor and my uncle Kent have all the contingencies back in England, but we are a long way from London or Oakleigh Combe.

"If something were to happen to me while working for the survey team—be it wild animals, accidents, sickness, attacks, or raids—and I don't make it back out of the wilderness, may I impose my trust for you to clean up my affairs and contact my family with news? Such seems a little more urgent with the viscount title in the mix now. Before ... my family would certainly care if I lived or died, but there would be fewer complications at stake."

"I believe this an example of overt caution, but in truth, we're all one breath away." Kerrigan handed Marcus a quill and pulled the stopper from the ink bottle. When the drawn-up documents bearing each of their signatures dried, Twitch folded and inserted them into a thin leather case. He tied the string enclosure. "One more thing, St. James."

Marcus braced for the next volley. "Captain?"

Kerrigan stopped drumming his fingers against the tabletop and folded his arms across his barrel chest. "I want to know what you aim to do about Serenity."

Direct hit. Marcus sat up straighter in his chair, contemplating his response. "Before leaving Genoa, Ravensworth told me I should do something meaningful, something she'll remember. I'm not certain she knows how much I care for her."

"Have you tried telling her?"

Sheepish, Marcus flashed a crooked smile. "You think that might aid my cause?"

Kerrigan burst out laughing. "Good night, St. James! You need me to spell it out for you? Very well. Gideon may be close to the mark. You and Serenity have not experienced a routine courtship. You're at an impasse. End it. Do something about it, without exceeding boundaries."

Marcus heard Kerrigan's words but Johnna's voice.

Kerrigan sighed and pinched the bridge of his nose. "Serenity deserves a reason to believe you'll come back for her but only if you mean it. You speak the words, you will be held accountable. A good, sound kissing might serve to knock some sense into each of you."

Surprise shot Marcus's brows upward. "That is not at all what I expected you to say."

"You and I have endured life from different angles and drastic circumstances. Let's revisit that part about being a breath away. Loved ones die. I regretted much in the wake of losing Amaryllis. The good Lord gave me a second chance with Susanna. I endeavor to tell her what is on my heart every time before I sail away. I would admonish you to not leave things unsettled with Serenity. Establish the foundation, then build from there." Kerrigan's pointed finger delivered warning. "Do not lead her astray. Nothing untoward, no scandal. Actions speak louder than words."

"I'm much obliged for your counsel." Marcus needed to ponder and to pray. "I shall take your suggestion under advisement—and all it implies."

"See that you do." Twitch cleared the spent candles. "Dawn's approaching. Get some rest, if you can. We'll soon send you back to the *Oceanna* so you can be on your way to Philadelphia."

⌒

But Marcus did not sleep before sunrise. Rest eluded him as he tossed and turned and prayed and pleaded for guidance. Searching for the next right thing to do—for Serenity's welfare and his own—come what may.

Amos sought him early, accepting that a long time may transpire before they would be in each other's company again. The lad was developing insight.

Finishing his turn during the latest round of Shut the Box, Amos passed the dice to Marcus.

A six and a three. Marcus reached into the stained hinged box, turned down the carved wooden tab bearing the number nine. He shook again, then once more dropped the dice onto the green felt-lined interior. His second roll showed a three and a two, but his attention strayed from the game to the comely figure ascending the ladder.

"Good morning." She chucked Amos under the chin and tossed a saucy smile at Marcus.

She was a welcome sight to his bleary eyes. "Where are you off to?"

"Hopefully, she's going to make cornmeal hoe cakes with honey for breakfast," Amos called after her, loud enough for his suggestion to be made known. A few minutes later, the lad was disappointed because Teaspoon had made oatmeal and, though there was brown sugar and maple syrup left, neither was enough to mask the scorched flavor resulting from being over the flame too long.

Marcus's spoon stood at attention in the thick grey ... porridge?

"I thought today was yours to cook, Sis." Amos curled his lip in disdain, complaining to Serenity and pushing aside his untasted bowl.

"Amos, be kind." She smoothed his windblown locks for naught. "I didn't intend to oversleep, and Teaspoon knew the men would be hungry, so he started without me. I put three loaves of sourdough in the bread trough and there will be chicken stew for luncheon."

"Are you staying long enough to eat, St. James?" Amos consulted the skies above. "Looks like a storm building, but that could be hours away yet."

"Let's talk about that." Kerrigan joined them on deck. "As it does indeed seem those clouds are getting darker, lower, and nearer. Today might prove another opportunity to practice how to reef your sails. Keep an eye out."

Kerrigan wrapped an arm about Amos's shoulders, guiding him to the master cabin.

"They will review atlases or charts to make calculations for the morning's lesson. Practical application for shoring up the canvas and rigging will come later, it appears."

"He's getting on swimmingly, isn't he?" Marcus turned from watching the lad and settled his glance upon Serenity.

"Uncle Twitch has him ever watching, observing, practicing. Amos will be writing eventually, but at present drills and exams are verbal in nature and Amos's learning mainly experiential. His eagerness is contagious. Like a sponge, he soaks up knowledge."

Marcus acknowledged her evident delight with a nod, but without comment he recalled the stranglehold Colson had once brandished over the Ravensworths. Thank God those manipulations had ceased. For all their sakes.

"You and Uncle Twitch had a fair amount of business to discuss last night." Serenity made it a statement, but really it was a question.

Kerrigan had assured him they wouldn't be heard through the cabin wall. She seemed to know there had been conversation, though not its content. Marcus extended his hand, palm up.

With implicit trust, she placed her hand in his. He led her to the awning rigged above the tiller, casting a nod to the helmsman, who doubled as an informal chaperone. They sat on a cushioned bench seat, and she shivered as the breeze picked up. Marcus curled an arm around her shoulders, allocating shelter and warmth.

"Tell me about Nagatamen. Something significant happened at supper, yes?"

"He's Lenape. From Pennsylvania. His mother was a white captive."

The disclosure produced a heavy pause before she said, "His markings are not the same as yours."

Marcus swallowed. "Different tribe."

"You still dream of the massacre." Serenity's hand rested against his pea coat, level with his heart, which marched at the double quick.

Every muscle in his body tensed. "This is not what I brought you out here to talk about."

Her eyes brightened with a teasing light and she mimicked his deep voice. "Next you'll say, 'Leave off, Ravensworth,' or grumble about my being related to my brother. Marcus, you must know with certainty by now Gideon and I wouldn't pester you if we didn't care." She held his big, callused hand between her smaller ones. A fraction of his tension dissolved.

"Enough of that," she said. "Did you and Uncle Twitch talk about anything of import?"

"You."

She flushed a becoming shade of rose pink. He pulled her close and leaned his bearded cheek atop her head. "We discussed business first. I supplied Kerrigan with instructions in the event I don't come back out of the forest with the survey party."

"But you will come back." She sat up straight. "I— We ... "

He raised her knuckles to his lips, brushing them with his moustache. "Yes, I plan to come back. God willing. I— We ... " Like her, he had difficulty stringing together coherent sentences. He raised her chin. "The last time you and I had a private conversation, I assumed we were not headed in the same direction, wanting the same things. I find I was wrong. My feelings now are more focused than they were then. I care for you deeply, yet I still grapple with certain issues. I just ... I need more time. Will you grant me a bit?"

"How long?"

Hers was a fair question, for which he didn't have a ready answer. "I don't know. I suspect I will learn more when I get to Philadelphia."

Tears welled in her eyes, but longing snapped beneath the tears and in their ginger-brown depths he saw his own ache reflected.

"Will you trust me?"

"I do." She nodded without hesitation. "I trust you will come back to me."

He cupped her jaw with both hands and lifted her face, thumb swiping away an escaped teardrop. "You have my word. Within my power and the Almighty's good favor, I will come find you." No regrets. He searched her expectant expression and touched his lips to hers in a soft, gentle, tentative exchange—until she kissed him back.

More than anything, he desired to follow her statement of trust with a more imperative question, but asking her if she loved him wasn't fair. He wanted an honest declaration of her own volition, not one he'd coerced from her in uncommon circumstances under duress. She cared, and that he could live with. For now. Their stormy situation wasn't favorable at present, either the literal one approaching across the waters or the figurative one binding them together.

"Marcus?"

He heard her plaintive intonation—*Mar-kiss*—and he had the blessing of her kin. His arms encircled in a tighter embrace, and he administered another kiss—something to remember him by—even as the helmsman behind the tiller no doubt looked on.

She clenched the lapels of his coat and instinctively leaned into him. With reluctant effort, he broke away. *Boundaries. No scandal. Promise.*

His breathing was as choppy as the waves surrounding the schooner. "Serenity..."

She shuddered and stared at him until a wide-eyed smile overtook her. "Oh, Marcus." She touched his lower lip with her fingertips.

He pressed her palm against his mouth.

The helmsman cleared his throat. "Sir?"

Marcus and Serenity jumped.

"Beg your pardon, sir, miss. But I wasn't sure you'd seen the small boat from the *Oceanna* on its way over."

"To fetch me." Marcus muttered his discontent. Menacing clouds rolled nearer, obscuring the sun. "Time and tide…"

"…tarry for no man," the helmsman completed a version of the proverb.

Marcus didn't want to leave her bereft but wanted to remind her he would be back for her. He drew Serenity into his arms again and whispered near her ear, "Until I return, don't give up on me. Please?"

"I will not give up on you."

His heart thundered—or was that the dense cloudbank above? She mustered her tenacity for his sake. And he appreciated tenacity.

"I shall look for you in Philadelphia." He caressed her cheek. "It means a good deal to know you care. We'll have that to look forward to." He curbed the temptation to share one more kiss with her, since Amos approached toting Marcus's canvas bag and Kerrigan shouted orders.

"I will keep praying for you." Serenity deposited a chaste kiss on his whiskered jaw, hugging him tight before turning him loose. "Go!" She pushed against his chest and her brave smile flashed as the first raindrops splattered the deck.

Nagatamen waited impatiently in the small boat. Hasty farewells to Amos and Kerrigan. Serenity maintained her smile.

Lowering himself down the rope ladder, Marcus heard Amos ask, "Sis?"

"Yes, Amos?"

"Was St. James kissing you?"

# Chapter 26

*Philadelphia, Pennsylvania Colony*
*Spring 1764*

Susanna Kerrigan's directions to the Tun Tavern had been precise. Marcus left her brick rowhouse in Gilbert's Alley, made a right on Front Street, and kept walking. He should cross Chestnut, but if he missed Tun Alley and came to Walnut Street, he'd gone too far.

Atticus Bartholomew's letter felt like a lead weight in Marcus's frock coat pocket. *Father God, if Dr. Franklin does not show, I trust You will provide another means to verify this is indeed the path You intend me to pursue.*

Marcus's apprehension was for naught. Dr. Franklin stood at the top of the tavern's galleried porch steps, leaning upon his cane.

The older gentleman's shoulder-length hair was both receding and greying, and in stature he missed the six-foot mark by at least three inches. He'd grown a bit soft around the midsection, as evidenced by the tautness of fabric where buttons and their corresponding holes met, yet the man's frame was sturdy. The care-worn and lined face lacked a wry grin, though a hint of sardonic wit lurked beneath the sage's surface seriousness.

"Good day to you, my good man. I daresay I am the one you seek." He extended his hand as a gesture of welcome and introduction.

"Benjamin Franklin, retired printer. You, I venture, are the young gentleman sent at the behest of our mutual acquaintance, Mr. Bartholomew."

"I am, yes." Marcus released the proffered hand and accepted the unspoken directive to follow.

Entering the noisy tavern and passing the caged bar, they were shown to a corner table near a window offering a view of Front Street as well as warmth from the fireplace. Settled into imported Windsor chairs, their conversation centered first on their common connection.

A frequent customer at Tun Tavern, Franklin's drink preference came delivered in a pewter tankard without needing to be ordered. The barkeep gave Marcus a choice. "Cider? Ale? Madeira?"

"Cider will do, thank you." Marcus laid his hat on the empty chair to his left. Franklin occupied that to his right. When the barkeep delivered a flagon, Marcus indicated he'd have the pot roast to Franklin's root vegetable soup.

"Have you heard much concerning the Cider Riots in England?" Marcus asked.

"Smattering here and there." Franklin stirred the turnips, celery root, parsnips, and carrots floating in a hearty beef broth. "'Tis a situation that bears watching. Conjecture has been voiced over Parliament's need to re-examine the issue, especially as demonstrations and riots grow louder among the affected populace. From what I've read in the London papers, the militia has so far been able to control occasional flares of contrary opinions and summarily quell unruly actions of the more vocal protesters."

Marcus knifed a hunk of beef, chunks of potato, and slices of onions and carrots into smaller bites. "Talk of increased taxes and ensuing after-effects takes up quite a bit of conversation on both sides of the Atlantic these days."

"One of life's few guarantees, taxes." Franklin sipped from his tankard and nodded. "And death, of course. But neither are the reason we've come here to speak of. We're here to see you embarked on this new adventure. According to Bartholomew, you display a marked penchant for drawing maps."

"My grandfather taught himself cartography and surveying. I credit him for passing to me his mapmaking skills, instilling an interest in the art. He surveyed all our family's holdings, and I used to watch him record measurements that provided his successors a clear point of reference for the acreage and its corresponding responsibilities."

"In addition to the drawing, do you possess an equal fondness for mathematics and geometry?"

"You could rightly say I favor the former more than the two latter," Marcus said, "though they are necessary. During the Atlantic crossing, I occupied time acquainting myself with Mr. Love's *Geodaesia* and Mr. Wyld's *Practical Surveyor.* Both manuals claim the art of land measuring made easy. Easy might be a relative term—I'm still studying." Marcus benefited from Nagatamen's patient instruction, and he added, "The first mate of the schooner I came over on introduced me to celestial navigation."

"Well done." Franklin dipped a wedge of crusty bread into his bowl.

Over tankards and trenchers, their discussion touched on the recent eclipse observed on the eighteenth of March, followed by the scope of the Maryland-Pennsylvania border project, the date the survey party had departed Philadelphia, and how long it would take Marcus to catch up with them.

As conversation waned, Marcus fished in his pocket for payment to cover the expense of their repast. He also extracted an embroidered linen kerchief and an exquisite miniature portrait.

Franklin stayed Marcus's hand. "No need. Keep your coin. This round was on me." Franklin retrieved Serenity's likeness from where it lay on the scarred tabletop, and the conversation recommenced on a divergent topic. "Hmmmm ... Is this what's awaiting you back in England?"

"I pray she's willing to wait, but she's not in England. She's actually here in the Colonies. Virginia, by last report. The schooner she sailed on anchored at the town of York about the same time mine arrived here in Philadelphia. If she's not there, then she's gone to the capital city at Williamsburg."

"And you are walking away into the woods by choice?" Franklin's eyebrows rose in twin arches above the curved brass frame of his bifocaled spectacles. "Excuse my curiosity on such short acquaintance, but what would possess a man in his right mind to leave so handsome a young woman, choosing raw wilderness for months at a stretch over spending time with her?"

Marcus traced a mug ring stain on the table. "Our families are in favor, but we have no stated understanding between us at present."

"More's the pity." Franklin pushed aside his empty soup bowl. "But there is mutual affection?"

A cherished memory of Serenity—ginger-brown eyes alight with yearning and rosy lips swollen from shared kisses on deck of *The Raven's Lady*—produced a broad grin. "Aye, we are fond of each other." *Quite fond.*

"Then take the well-meaning advice of an old man: Don't squander that. Consider carefully, while you're out there marking chains and plotting maps, some sacrifices are worth swift implementation. Regret can be a bitter pill, my friend."

"I'll keep that in mind," Marcus affirmed.

Franklin folded his hands atop the cap of his cane. "Don't give her reason not to think of you. Left unattended, long distances can ofttimes stretch too far."

It sounded to Marcus like the voice of experience.

As they continued with their meal, Marcus discovered Franklin was a storyteller and eagerly listened to his narrative concerning the city. Within the past fifteen years, Philadelphia had surpassed Boston's population and was the second largest port in the British empire, behind London. The Colonies were thriving, providing resources that made British merchants flourish as men of means. The Colonists—a high percentage of whom were proud British subjects and displayed dogged loyalty to the Crown—were willing to trade goods and livelihoods to benefit under the protection and equitable rule of King George III. Marcus contributed to the welfare of the empire by virtue of his service—and shed blood—to the King. He desired to partake in the spoils his efforts had earned him, while he was still alive to do so.

Marcus enjoyed the former printer's tales, including that of how he'd fled Boston and come to Philadelphia, an environment that had irrevocably captured his imagination when a younger man. Many of Franklin's ideas for the betterment of the citizens had taken shape in the creation of public services, including a police force, a fire department, a circulating library, an academy, a hospital, street lighting and paving, a postal service, and roads. He'd also invented a more efficient stove that used less firewood, had better air flow, and generated more heat. Along with his network of influential friends, members of what he termed the Junto Club used their beneficial connections to aid one another's businesses, while at the same time instituting changes that profited all. No wonder people here had no desire to ever go to London, as there was little need for them to do so.

Marcus did not, however, enjoy the drift in subject to the horrific tale of the Paxton Massacre of mid-December 1763.

"A narrative pamphlet appeared concerning the details describing the events at length." Franklin's retelling was brief but all too descriptive, and he quoted, "'The Blood of the Innocent will cry to Heaven for Vengeance.'"

Marcus's disquiet concerning the massacre belatedly registered with Franklin. That subject, summarily dropped, was replaced by further discussion of the upcoming survey endeavor. Then Franklin's commentary shifted to the recent reinforcement of old restrictive revenue acts and the creation of new ones in the name of paying down national war debt. Such was becoming an increasingly prickly topic in polite and public debate.

Changes in British policy as applied to the Colonies in America grew incrementally irksome. But compared to the report of the massacre of the Conestoga Indians, taxation seemed a mere seed Marcus couldn't dislodge, uncomfortably stuck in a tooth. Irritating, but a thing that would eventually work itself out, like the rankling inaccessibility of his awarded land.

Franklin strolled with Marcus back to Susanna Kerrigan's narrow house on the cobbled street of Gilbert's Alley. "Mrs. Kerrigan's husband has an order of Madeira for me, I believe. I must check to make sure I have a zero balance on my account or I'll have to pay whatever is owed in full before she'll release it to me."

In parting, Franklin said, "I shall forward specifications for when and where you will meet the wagons assigned to the encampment. You should catch up and start work with the survey team at or near the Harlan farm."

"Thank you, sir. I appreciate the opportunity."

Franklin angled his head and peered through his spectacles. "I wish you well, Marcus St. James, and sincerely hope this endeavor will spark your education, as well as provide at least some of the answers you seek." Shifting his cane from one hand to the other, Franklin clasped Marcus's in a firm grip. "Write her—before you go."

"Yes, sir. I will do that." Marcus nodded with a compliant grin. "Rest assured, I will."

ᔕ

*Capital City of Williamsburg, Virginia Colony*
*Late May 1764*

> *Dearest Grandee,*
> *Uncle Twitch thought to complete his transactions in Williamsburg*
> *in a matter of days, but we have been here for more than a sennight.*
> *After unloading goods in the town of York and then deliveries here to*
> *two local merchants—Mr. Prentis and Mr. Tarpley—a crack was*
> *discovered in one of the masts. It likely started in the last storm before*
> *we docked in Charles Town, worsened by strong winds. By the time*
> *we put in at the York wharf, needed repair was obvious.*

Serenity's raven-feather quill hovered above the sheet of foolscap. The storm had been violently cantankerous, the cause of hasty
farewells that had sent Marcus with Nagatamen rowing back to the
*Oceanna* only marginally ahead of the building squalls.

That night, she'd dreamed of being wrenched from Marcus's
embrace by furious wind and waves, straining against rising water
and whipping gales to reach him. But slender copper-hued arms
gathered him before she could, and dense forest undergrowth swallowed his form whole.

Her hand trembled. An errant drop of ink landed on the paper.
She blotted at it as best she could, but it absorbed too quickly into the
rag content. Exasperated with her own inattentiveness, she ended up
writing around a stain the size of a shilling.

> *Uncle Twitch sent word to the Steward Shipyard on the West*
> *River near Annapolis, inquiring after a replacement spar for the*
> *mast. We shall be leaving by the end of next week, he said. The delay*
> *will preclude our stopping at Alexandria. He is anxious to get the*

*repair completed on* The Raven's Lady *as soon as may be and proceed north to Philadelphia, to his Susanna.*

*York is the name of both town and river. The town is situated directly across from Gloucester Point, where the width of the river is at its narrowest. As a tribute to Queen Anne's son, the high street in Williamsburg is called Duke of Gloucester Street. Williamsburg and York boast varied populations of better than two thousand souls apiece, and their respective busyness relies on distinct circumstances.*

*York's significance is its designation as tobacco inspection port. Amos went with Uncle Twitch to declare imported goods and pay the corresponding duties and required fees. The Custom House agents are charged with discovering smugglers and putting a halt to their illegal practices. The officials are generally successful in this endeavor but other times not. Shops and businesses are located on the main street atop the bluff and also line the swath of land between the bottom of the bluff and the waterfront. Houses here are built of wood or brick and well-maintained. York was founded in 1691, not yet seventy-five years ago, and by comparison to English history, is practically new. The gardens contain a profusion of brilliant colors this spring.*

*Uncle Twitch frequents the coffeehouse and habitually partakes of the chocolatier's wares. He is adamant the drinking chocolate here is a better receipt than that blended in England and it nicely pleases the palate. He sent me to the mantua maker for a new frock—something pretty I could dance in.*

*We lodged three nights at the Swan Tavern in York until relocating to Williamsburg. In a time past, there was debate on where to place the capital of this Virginia colony—Williamsburg or Jamestown— and once Williamsburg was settled upon, businesses and buildings sprang up and have continued growth in population and prosperity. A wave of improvements in these last few years are similar to con-struction conditions in Bath. Williamsburg's busyness is owed mainly to the House of Burgesses and everything associated with those inner governmental workings, plus all the entities that support it. The capital city occupies the peninsula halfway between the York and James Rivers. Either because of court days or assembly sessions, the ebb and flow in Williamsburg has it near to bursting at the seams with the swell of visitors added to the local dwellers in and around town. Lodging and dining are in perpetual demand, with increased expense to board horses and carriages and wagons.*

*Uncle Twitch owns a lot on Francis Street, and when the party to whom he let his house departed, we moved in. It is an easy distance from the Capitol. We have dined at Chowning's, at the Raleigh, and at Shield's Tavern. The Palace Green in front of the Governor's Palace is the place to be seen, walking or riding. We've not yet been to the theatre but have attended one subscription ball, Amos included. He is nearly as tall as some of the shortest men, and he is turning out to be quite a good dancer.*

*So far, it strikes me that in Charles Town, York, and Williamsburg, the inhabitants strive to emulate our English ways, including dancing—and why not, since these are British colonies and by extension England. The country dances are ever so popular, but also sets with the minuet and allemande. I danced with a government clerk who informed me he'd only recently started lessons with a dancing master. He apologized ahead of time for stepping on my toes. "Beg pardon, miss, that my feet are so large." Uncle Twitch had me reduced to giggles by the time we finished a Scottish jig. I could not keep up with him. He loves to dance to fiddle tunes, not just play them.*

*Amos has outgrown his breeches and we have made the acquaintance of a tailor, Mr. Nicholson, whose shop is across the street from Uncle Twitch's house. When the fitting was finished, Amos insisted on visiting the Public Gaol, where—Mr. Nicholson told him—a number of Blackbeard's men had been incarcerated prior to being tried and hanged for their acts of piracy. We read Defoe's* Captain Singleton *on the crossing, and it piqued his young imagination. I shivered to see where actual pirates—not those of a merely fictitious nature—had their necks stretched as judgment for their dire crimes.*

*The College of William & Mary is another source of busyness. The needs of the students contribute to the thriving trades and shops. Bruton Parrish Church is the prominent place of worship. We, of course, have been in attendance each Sunday in Williamsburg, although when in York of a Sunday we attend Grace Church instead.*

*I pray for all of you, even when not in church. Please keep us— and St. James, wherever he is—in your prayers.*

*Shall you accept the offer to go visit the St. Jameses at Oakleigh Combe near Chipping Campden? Have you had any word from Gideon since he arrived in Florence? Is Jonathan fine? Be sure to tell Madelaine I miss her. Hugs to Jessa and Asher. Greetings to Tyree.*

*This bears all my love and hopefully will be in your hands to be read by you soon.*

*Your dearest granddaughter,*
*Serenity*

# Chapter 27

*The Villa near Convent Santa Magdalena, Florence, Italy*
*June 1764*

An early morning breeze ruffled a stack of papers and sent loose sheets cascading. Gideon padded across the sun-warmed terra-cotta tiles, reached under the table to recapture the pages, and returned them to their proper order. Several of the documents had necessary signatures of legal witnesses and official wax seals affixed to them. He rested a travel guide on top of the small mountain of foolscap to keep it in place and out of his sight for a little while longer.

Sipping from the mug in his left hand, he shifted his weight from one bare foot to the other and braced his right forearm at ear level against the doorjamb. He inhaled the damp morning dewiness, then exhaled, attempting to savor the scene. In a manner of speaking, he was involuntarily undergoing a variation of the physician-prescribed *lana, letto, latte* treatment to which his father adhered. In Gideon's case, the *lana*, or warmth, came in hot summer temperatures. *Latte* in delicious and plentiful food. It was the *letto* part—quiet and rest—that chafed most.

Accustomed to activity, Gideon accused time of coming to an utter standstill. Nothing productive was accomplished. He craved regimented drill, regular exercise and riding—not the villa's tortoise-like pace. Since his arrival in Italy, he'd been bound to wait on decisions made for him by others. As a guest, he worked on appreciation of generous hospitality in combination with the beauty of the land. He repeated self-directed orders, reminding himself to enjoy this leisure time free from responsibilities. Inevitable change knocked on his door and his carefree youth evaporated into the past.

On this morning, creeping fog dissolved in bright daylight. The convent's olive grove and vineyard-covered ground sloped toward the Apennine foothills. The view out his window displayed bridges spanning the River Arno, like giant hand-sewn stitches connecting the two halves of Florence.

From the cloisters, children's laughter mingled with a chorus of birdsong. On the hour, bells sounded—near ringing from the convent's belfry and distant ringing from several towers in the town long ruled by the Medici family of bankers, princes, and merchants. Afterwards came the collective singing of nuns, routinely treading their path toward the chapel like clockwork.

Intermittent sips of cinnamon-laced coffee punctuated Gideon's detached deliberation. He contemplated afresh what he had learned about his father, his mother, and himself in the weeks since his arrival.

"*Buongiorno, giovanotto.*" Signora Lucrezia entered Gideon's first-floor room bearing a serving tray.

Abandoning his mug to tug up the waist of his breeches, Gideon pulled his shirt on. He'd asked his father to translate *giovanotto* and was told it meant "handsome young man." As it turned out, Signora Lucrezia called all her nephews, cousins, brothers, son, grandsons, and male in-laws by the same endearment, whether they were younger than Gideon's one and twenty years or decades older. Sir Nicholas was not left out, though he was neither young nor handsome anymore. The sapping lung ailment leeched all hint of natural color from his complexion and caused the purplish circles beneath his dulling eyes, giving them a hollow, vacant look. Breathing—shallow or deep—was painfully audible and progressively labored.

Gideon pulled his shirtsleeves up past his elbows, inspecting the breakfast tray. He selected a diminutive pot of yogurt over a generous slice of crusty buttered bread, stirring in a mixture of berries and jam. "*Grazie*," he said. The longer he abided here, the more Italian words and phrases he recognized. "Is my father still abed?"

Signora Lucrezia waved away his gratitude, smile faltering. "Signore Nico took another bad turn last night." She dabbed at her red-rimmed eyes with the hem of her apron and sniffed. "It pains me to tell you, giovanotto, he will not be strong enough to visit Sir Horace Mann's house or to keep the appointment the diplomatic minister has made for you to see the private gallery of art at the *Uffizi*. He said for you to go on ahead and come back and tell him about it later."

Cautious alarm coursed through Gideon. He banked his initial reaction and asked to make sure he heard right. "That's what he wants me to do—go see the local sites?"

She nodded. "He said he will wait for you."

Gideon's resignation did not come easy. He'd worked so hard to break through his father's walls of self-preservation and, once breached, establish a rapport man to man that transcended their tentative father-son relationship. His father was putting deliberate distance between them. Again. His sigh signaled defeat. "Fine. If that's what he wants."

"I shall tell him." Signora Lucrezia picked up the empty mug.

A racking, hacking cough echoed between plaster-covered hall walls.

Gideon changed his mind. "Give me five minutes to dress. I'm coming with you."

Olivadotti matched his steps to Gideon's pace—almost at the quick march—respecting the silence between them. Ventresca and Lazzaro would be following at a watchful distance, as was their habit. Though never stated outright, their presence was felt for what it was—guard duty. His father issued the command that they protect him. From something. Or someone.

Gideon's mood waxed dark, frustration mounting. Their protection was there for his physical safety, but it filtered the truth as well. If the Almighty decreed today as his father's last day on earth, he would rather have spent it with him than pretend to care about centuries-old religious paintings or naked marble statues inspired by heroic biblical characters or mythological gods and goddesses. *David, Mary Magdalen, Nicodemus, Mary, Jesus, Perseus, Medusa, Neptune.*

On the good days, which had been considerable in number over the past month, Gideon pushed his father's invalid chair along concrete pavers and lumpy cobblestones, escorted by Olivadotti and shadowed by Ventresca and Lazzaro. Lively music made by *zampogna, ghironda, organetto,* and violin accompanied after-dinner strolls along piazzas, alleys, and streets in the heart of the place the locals called *Firenze.*

Sporadic excursions with his father and reading through the guidebook St. James had left behind gave Gideon an appreciation for the Italian city. Florence's historic origins in banking and the widespread standard of florin coin usage affected trade transactions both domestic and foreign. Lauded for its contributions in art, literature, and science, Florence was a center of rebirth, pushing past the constraints of the Dark Ages into revolutionary new ways of thinking.

It was also a town filled with tradition and churches, and the churches were filled with wood, marble, gold leaf, stained glass, frescoes, tapestries, and famously painted crucifixes and altar panels.

Beyond gilded doors called the Gates of Paradise, scenes from the Bible and Jesus on judgment day adorned the interior of the octagonal Baptistery of San Giovanni. The mosaics depicted how, according to their deeds and their standing with God, the faithful were rewarded and the damned rejected.

Forgiveness, Gideon reflected, must be requested and received, two separate procedures leading to the same result. The free gift of salvation required acceptance to be activated. As Grandee had said many times, all actions had consequences. Without forgiveness there was no freedom. In order for a person to partake of the joy and hope of life everlasting, one must let go of guilt's oppressive weight. Gideon perceived the letting go achievable with divine aid for the asking, not in his own strength.

One thing Gideon had accomplished was satisfying Lazzaro's blatant challenge—climbing with him the more than four hundred steps to the top of the red-tiled dome of Brunelleschi's *Duomo*. Their confined ascent in the ever-narrowing spiral stairwell had seemed to take forever, until at last the final door had opened to an outdoor platform encircling the uppermost lantern. The memory of it made Gideon's heart pound. After the feat, descended and partaking in refreshing cups of gelato, Gideon had conceded that the incomparable view had been worth the temporary shortness of breath. From the lofty height atop the Duomo, they had looked down on the marble-faced Bell Tower of Giotto's design. The *Palazzo Vecchio* too had appeared a fraction of its grand stature.

In letters addressed to Grandee and Serenity, Gideon had failed to adequately describe the panoramic landscape more beautiful than any painter's rendering. Purple-blue mountains formed the backbone of the Italian Peninsula, and morning mist often hovered above the snaking ribbon of river. Outlying farmsteads studded tilled fields, vineyards, gardens, and orchards.

The longer Gideon stayed, the more comprehension deepened as to why the Tuscan countryside and Florentine architecture held such allure for his father. Within a week Gideon had given up on trying to keep the many cathedrals and palazzos straight. He could differentiate Palazzo Vecchio in the *Piazza della Signoria* only because the extraordinary image of David—sculpted by Michelangelo in 1501—stood in front of the battlemented medieval fortress. The white Carrara marble statue measured a colossal seventeen feet in height. The David sculpture, a study in silent and methodical rumination, inspired observers to stand up to their own figurative Goliaths.

Gideon pushed aside remembrances of visits with his father to the Medici tombs, *Santa Croce*, and *Santa Maria Novella*, concentrating instead on his foreseeable future. Once his father passed, he would not linger in Italy. With forethought, Olivadotti dispatched a rider to Uncle Twitch's agent in Genoa to learn when the next Kerrigan schooner might be in port.

⌒

The Ponte Vecchio bridge was a favorite of artists, tourists, and residents alike. According to Olivadotti, the bridge, originally open and lined with butcher shops below and dwellings above, had been covered. An elevated corridor comprised part of a communication passageway designed for the Medici family to maneuver between the Palazzo Vecchio, where they worked, and the *Palazzo Pitti*, where they lived. The stench of slaughtered meat from the butcher shops permeated the corridor and were replaced by gold and silversmiths with corresponding jewelry and trade shops.

*Uffizi* was Italian for *office* and the top floor of the municipal building housed the renowned art collection, which had been left to the city by Anna Maria Luisa, last of the Medici family line. With the assistance of Sir Horace Mann, the local British resident, Olivadotti secured an invitation for Gideon to see the art collection by appointment.

Several buildings in Florence reminded Gideon of those Tyree Northcraft had added his craftsmanship to in Bath. The two towns shared architectural features, like Palladian windows, glazed tiles, columns, and balconies. He tamped down another rise of residual homesickness while observing the Uffizi's colonnades.

Concern for his father had not diminished. He squinted against the afternoon sun's strong glare. Something unnerving about one of the two men ascending the courtyard stairs made the hair on the back of his neck rise. A door shut behind the men before Gideon could vouch identification. He met Olivadotti's quizzical glance and shook his head. He reasoned the particular man in question, while bearing a disturbing resemblance to The Lord Brentmoor, couldn't possibly be him.

"What is amiss, Signore Gideon?"

"We have a phrase to describe a sudden unease—a prickling sense of awareness or foreboding. We say someone has walked over our grave."

"Ah, and someone has done some grave walking here?" Olivadotti scanned the empty courtyard.

"A passing feeling." According to the thief-taker's last missive, the intelligence St. James's cousin had collected confirmed that Brentmoor had departed England, destined for the Sugar Islands. The strain of the past few months was finally catching up to Gideon. He'd partake of a double dose of lana, letto, and latte once they returned to the convent.

Walking his antique gold sovereign coin across his knuckles and back again, Gideon bounced one knee, not disguising his impatience the longer he and Olivadotti sat waiting in an antechamber near the long top-floor gallery. Tardy for more than a quarter of an hour but not yet half, the British diplomatic resident, Sir Horace Mann, joined them, clearly agitated.

In hushed overtones, Sir Horace haltingly explained the unexpected appearance last evening of an English baron with his traveling companion. "As they are only staying in Florence long enough to have their carriage repaired before continuing to Naples, they asked if it possible to see any of Florence's famed sites. Someone divulged I was bringing another Englishman here to the Uffizi. My first inclination was to decline accommodation for such a late request with little by way of introduction. But when the man learned your identity, he insisted, claiming an acquaintance with you or your family by way of some business connection. Are you acquainted with The Lord Brentmoor?"

The illusion Gideon talked himself out of identifying earlier resurrected into the reality now standing before him.

Unflinching and with conjured civility, he countered the baron's mockery. "Regrettably, yes, my family is acquainted with Lord Brentmoor." Gideon's fingers fisted around the gold sovereign. "What's happened to the plantation in the West Indies? Did you lose it in a hand of cards as easily as you won it?"

Lord Brentmoor's chortling ceased. "No, no, the plantation on Montserrat is still mine—for now. Who knew rum distillation could be such a profitable avenue of commerce, what with a veritable stream of contracts to supply the British Navy for sailors' rations."

"Then why aren't you on Montserrat overseeing your personal empire?"

"I retained a savvy overseer and he handles everything on my behalf. Why disturb something that's in good working order? He recently reported our production earned more than double the amount of your brother's gambling debt." False benevolence laced Brentmoor's sneer. "I have elected not to pursue collection of that sum since I no longer need it any more than I need your delectable little sister's dowry."

In a blurred flash, Gideon smashed his fist into Brentmoor's jaw. The small tea table in the center of the antechamber could not bear his weight, and it, along with the crystal flower vase, became casualties.

Appalled at the ungentlemanlike exhibition, Sir Horace rushed to examine the damage, collecting broken bits of the crashed vase. "My lord! Mr. Ravensworth! Do remember yourselves!"

Ventresca and Lazzaro materialized from the shadows to flank Gideon, not protecting him from Brentmoor but the other way around. Gideon reined back the roiling surge of anger within.

"I already have one dead Ravensworth to my credit." Brentmoor regained his feet, brushing away bedraggled flower stems and excess water not yet saturated into the expensive fabric of his breeches or the weave of his stockings. "Your baseborn brother's demise improved your lot in life," he scoffed. "Maybe I should kill you too and shake up the birth order even further."

The nameless man attending Brentmoor put a hand on the baron's shoulder, a firm gesture of scrupled caution. Gideon recognized him from the hunt and supper at Fernsby Hall. He wondered if this was the man Jonathan deemed fair in his standing as Brentmoor's second throughout the duel. Perhaps even now he served in the role of self-appointed bear-leader for the baron. If so, Gideon did not envy him the task of preventing the baron's intentional mischief.

Brentmoor ignored the associate's hint, extending his acidic invective. "Does Serenity still have her dowry or has your soldier-friend staked his claim to her for her money? Second sons are generally expected to marry well if they want to live in the standard to which they are accustomed."

Brentmoor's canine countenance turned more wolfish in appearance, a glinting, feral light in his eyes. "Oh, my mistake. For upon Colson's demise, you became the heir, not merely the spare. You are 'the one for the land,' and said inheritance falls to your purview. You ought to be able to seduce—I mean induce—an innocent to share your new title, if not your bed. For some wenches, a little goes a long way. Stupid girls but they satisfy a need. Your sister would have had a certain usefulness in producing a handsome heir."

"Stand down, Brentmoor." The associate did not suggest but commanded. "Do not tarnish the Colson Ravensworth affair by your present course. That incident was closed with satisfaction and good faith. Leave it."

Brentmoor shook off the warning. He moved to grab his walking stick, but Ventresca beat him to the weapon, wasting no time in pulling the cap apart from the stick and pointing the slim, balanced blade tip against Brentmoor's snowy cravat.

During years of diplomatic service, it was known Sir Horace had rendered aid in the unsavory business of extricating young Englishmen from inopportune circumstances. His wary glance darted from Brentmoor to Gideon. Brentmoor possessed the higher-ranking title, but Gideon held the truth.

In his modulated accent, Olivadotti disclosed to the British resident, "The incident between Lord Brentmoor and the Ravensworths happened several months ago in England. Lately it is said Lord Brentmoor needed to vacate Montserrat in haste—before a neighboring planter's daughter identified him as her seducer. Is that not accurate, my lord?"

Brentmoor's face mottled not with repentance but sheer regret for having been caught in a repeated pattern of intrigue.

Sir Horace cleared his throat. "I see. Well thankfully, no harm is done to any irreplaceable antiquities. The vase was not terribly old and another tea table can be acquired. No call for swords for two—do I make myself clear?"

Lord Brentmoor opened his mouth to retort but his associate stepped forward and expelled a guttural *"Haud yer wheesht"* to accompany a silent order for the baron to say nothing and stay put. He assured Sir Horace there would be no further inconvenience. "We shall depart for Naples the moment our carriage is travel-worthy once more."

Sir Horace assumed the obligation to do whatever was in his power to speed the process of getting Brentmoor well away from Florence as soon as possible.

Gideon walked out with Sir Horace, who graciously accepted Gideon's apology, offered for the sake of polite honor. Olivadotti, Lazzaro, and Ventresca followed.

"How long do you plan to stay in Florence, Mr. Ravensworth?"

"Not much longer," Gideon affirmed. "When I arrived, I was told my father's death was imminent, possibly a matter of days. Now he is fading and could slip away at any time."

Sir Horace nodded. "Should you wish to have the gallery appointment rescheduled, I will see it arranged."

"Unnecessary, Sir Horace, but I thank you for being willing to represent on my behalf." Cancelling the Uffizi visit caused no great disappointment, only that he wouldn't be able to write Serenity and Grandee about the gallery or *Tribuna* in a later report.

Brentmoor's associate intercepted Gideon in the shadow of a colonnaded walkway. "A word, Mr. Ravensworth?"

Gideon locked his hands behind his back as a preventative measure, aware Olivadotti was nearby and that Ventresca and Lazzaro would likely swoop in from the courtyard at any sign of trouble. "I never got your name."

"If it were essential for you to know, I would give it," the man said with a suppressed hint of Scottish brogue. "In this instance, it is not. It's enough you recognize me."

"What do you want?"

"Nothing. I only respectfully request you give my compliments to your brother Jonathan, as well as to your sister. I hold no ill will toward any of you Ravensworths. Brentmoor's quarrel was not mine, but I had a job to do. As far as I am concerned, the episode in Bath was settled to satisfaction. Brentmoor was—is—the guilty party. Rest easy, we will be leaving Florence. Today. Had I known before arriving you were here in this place, I'd have steered our driver to seek repairs elsewhere if possible. It was happenstance, running into you."

*Happenstance?* Gideon contemplated. *Or divinely ordained?*

"Brentmoor is lucky he didn't have to face you on the field of honor," the associate said. "Had you been the second instead of Jonathan, I believe you'd have been the end of him. He's too much a jingle brains to realize, the good-for-nothing coxcomb."

Crossing his arms over his coat buttons, Gideon waited.

However, the associate stopped shy of elaboration and instead said, "We are headed to Naples for Carnival, then on to Pompeii."

"You serve in the capacity of his traveling companion—why? It does not appear you have any particular regard for him. Are you not friends, then?"

"Not even by a very flimsy definition. Our fathers were brothers by marriage, not blood. We have known each other all our lives, but Brentmoor is the perfect antithesis. He is in no way to me what St. James is to you." The associate's words were smooth, but anger smoldered. "I cannot change what your sister suffered at his lordship's hands. But barely a week following the duel with Colson, I caught him replicating the reprehensible scenario. I travel with him to assure myself that your sister remains safe—and that he's no longer in a location to be taking advantage of mine."

The associate implied an unspoken truce.

Gideon accepted. "Godspeed your way to Naples."

The man cracked a malicious grin. "Would that Mount Vesuvius erupt again and swallow Brentmoor into the lava ruins."

A messenger from the convent engaged in earnest conversation with Olivadotti, Lazzaro, and Ventresca under the portico. Gideon instinctively deduced from their somber demeanor his father's end was met. "Tell me."

"Signore Nico is gone." Olivadotti clapped a sympathetic hand upon Gideon's shoulder. *"Grazie a Dio,* he suffers no more of that wretched disease."

Gideon shuddered and expelled a shaky breath, a prayer on his lips. *God, please, grant me wisdom.*

He'd arrived in Italy a man driven by impetuous determination, but in his heart he was a boy searching for his father. Angry and hurt that Sir Nicholas had not asked or required Gideon's presence so close to the end of his life, Gideon had wrested the opportunity to know him while there was still a chance to do so. Gideon was glad he'd acted on that inclination.

Sir Nicholas had been a complicated man. In his younger years, he himself had been deeply hurt, had plans thwarted, withstood hushed humiliation, dodged open scandal, and endured an array of obstacles. There were things he refused to talk about. He admitted he was not perfect. He would not waste time on regret. Once he made a decision, he only moved forward, rarely looking back.

Up to this point, Gideon had no say in matters familial or financial. All Sir Nicholas's arrangements were in tidy order—legally assigned and acknowledged to eliminate any doubt or plausible argument, along with a formal, witnessed declaration for submission to the Committee for Privileges, should the Lord Chancellor require supporting evidence. The solicitor back in Bath had instructions to execute Sir Nicholas's wishes to the letter.

Misapprehension and dispossession—brought on in part by second-son standing and partly by not recognizing Colson's lies for what they were—gave way to a brittle but peaceable acceptance.

"Signore Gideon?" Olivadotti's voice held concern and condolence.

He refused hot tears, then lifted his head. "Can we just . . . walk a bit?"

"As you wish, signore. I am here to serve. It was important to Signore Nico that we look after you. My assignment does not end because he has." He fell into step at Gideon's side. "Come. Sir Horace also arranged permission for a visit to *Giardino di Boboli* behind the Palazzo Pitti by way of the corridor—neither open to the public. What harm is there to see them before you go? One of the finest examples of grand gardens in all of Europe, plus a whole host of distinguished portraits by more famous artists."

Gideon allowed a small smile. Making the most of opportunities was something he and his father had discussed at length. There were days Gideon felt older than his years, but he was still a young man and the responsibility for Fernsby devolved directly on his squared shoulders. He had Grandee and Serenity to look after. By necessity, he would give up the army and sell his commission. Shares in Kerrigan Shipping would earn additional income, but he'd need to consider how to continue being a beneficiary to the Blue Coat School, albeit at a reduced rate. He had enough options to get by on without having to hawk his sovereign coin.

In the elevated corridor above the Ponte Vecchio, Gideon paused at a round window, taking in the river below, dotted with fishing boats in both directions and bustling marketplaces on either side of the Arno. The descending sun was on the far side of noon.

Sir Nicholas had also suggested Gideon find a woman of good character to take to wife, not merely a pretty one, although a lady in possession of both attributes would be so much the better. Being heir included an obligation to sire the next heir. Gideon had that in common with St. James now too. He could have used his friend's counsel. St. James understood as few other would.

At the impressive hillside garden, birds did more chirping than he and Olivadotti did talking. They roamed the amphitheater, ascended and descended terraced stone stairs, passed through the topiary hedges. They went through gates, over bridges, and skirted freestanding fountains. At the top of the hill, depicted in Roman garb, a female statue called *The Abundance* held a bouquet of wheat in her raised left hand and carried a basket of produce in her right arm.

Abundance—meaning "more than enough." Pertaining to his newly acquired inheritance, it was not an altogether applicable word. "Just barely enough" was more apt. Sir Nicholas had put in motion safeguards to protect his original fortune. He'd had no means of preventing Laurenda's entire allotment—save for Serenity's dowry from Grandee—from falling into Colson's greedy clutches. In the past three years, Colson had wagered a lot of money—an absolute sickening abundance, to be sure—and he'd somehow gotten it into his head that Fernsby was entailed, though it wasn't. Gideon carried the rank of baronet, and the bulk of Fernsby's property was now his to do with as he desired. He intended to establish an account with something set aside for each of his younger brothers post-haste. Jonathan and Amos each had their own sovereign coins from Grandee as collateral, but Gideon determined it shouldn't come to that. He imagined Colson's nasal whine: *Sir Nicholas is dead. Long live Sir Gideon.*

The tower bells tolled the lateness of the afternoon. As shadows angled and lengthened, Gideon felt the absence of Ventresca and Lazzaro.

"They have gone back to the villa to assist with preparations. Signore Nico's remains are to return with you to England," Olivadotti said quietly.

"Oh."

"He feared while you were here, Brentmoor might try to have you killed."

Gideon arched a brow in askance. "Which he threatened this very afternoon."

Olivadotti nodded. "When Signore Nico received word you were on your way, he did not try to stop you, but he was determined to see you protected."

"So you were all on the lookout for Brentmoor even though Oakley Lightfoot reported he had left England."

"Brentmoor did leave. But then you left England to come here. Beyond the shores of England, the risk increased, and that your *nonna* and *Cattaneo* Kerrigan wouldn't ignore. I had my orders—you were to return home where you belong, alive and in one piece."

At that Gideon laughed. "Oh, that sounds very much like Grandee, brooking no argument and expecting her directives to be obeyed."

"You will return to England and to Fernsby then."

"Aye." But the looming image in Gideon's mind foretold an empty manor house devoid of laughter, love, and family. If he were honest, he would confess he regretted the one who broke his heart—"given him the two of spades," as Lazzaro might have quipped. Though his own family structure had fractured, blood ties mattered. Even more, since Gideon witnessed the Italians and their demonstrative affection for one another. It sparked a notion akin to that held by Serenity. He too craved love and belonging, a family of his own.

Sailing for home was the right course. Gideon was sure Grandee wouldn't object to allowing him to stay at the King's Circus in town for a bit, at least until the proverbial dust settled. Once Sir Nicholas's remains were interred, Gideon would begin with Fernsby's tenants and grounds to see what on the estate most needed doing. Pursuing a wife and begetting an heir would wait.

# Chapter 28

*Home of the Kerrigans in Gilbert's Alley, Philadelphia*
*June 1764*

Serenity held fast to Uncle Twitch's arm as they ascended the incline from the Delaware River wharf to Front Street, then onward to Gilbert's Alley. They had finally arrived in Philadelphia and she was all astonishment. Her breath caught on the swell of realization, thinking of all the leagues, fathoms, and miles between where she found herself in this moment compared to where she had been in England just a few months ago. Hand to her heart, she tamped down her giddiness. In body, she'd survived crossing the Atlantic. In spirit, she was anchored by the Almighty's grace.

At a three-and-a-half-story brick dwelling, not as long and hardly as wide as a Kerrigan schooner, Uncle Twitch turned the handle on the bottom section of the Dutch door. Into the cozy front room, he dropped Serenity's portmanteau against the enclosed stair door and bellowed a greeting. "Susanna?"

"Hello, love." Susanna came from the rear of the skinny house, tying on a clean apron. When she spotted Serenity, she pulled up short. "Oh! Miss Ravensworth . . . I—"

Uncle Twitch tipped his head. "Everything all right?"

"I didn't know you'd be here this soon. I thought . . . well . . . usually you take care of the unloading at the warehouse first . . . "

"Aye, and I'm headed back to the wharf now that I've delivered Serenity to you. I didn't think she would enjoy waiting when she could be here having tea with you and getting acquainted." He pulled Susanna into a hug and kissed her. "I've missed you."

"I'm glad to have you back."

Here was another facet to the man Serenity hadn't expected but it suited him.

He cleared his throat. "Serenity, meet my wife, Susanna Kerrigan."

Serenity dipped a polite curtsy but formality was soon discarded. "It is my honor." She hugged Susanna. "Grandee wanted me to make sure I delivered her best wishes to you just as soon as we met."

"I'll leave the pair of you now so we can finish up at the warehouse and be back in time for dinner." Uncle Twitch settled his tricornered hat.

Susanna put a hand on Uncle Twitch's arm. "Where is young Amos?"

"Still aboard *The Raven's Lady*. He's got a short list of things to accomplish upon arrival. But he'll be along as soon as he is done."

"My brother looks forward to meeting you as well." Serenity offered a sincere smile.

Out the door, Uncle Twitch turned back on the top step of the stoop. He winked at Susanna. "Obadiah Welles will unload Serenity's trunks and bring them here."

"Mr. Welles—very good. We shall watch for him." Susanna shooed her husband away. "Hurry and be done. Dinner will keep until you and Amos get here."

Sauntering toward the waterfront, Uncle Twitch indicated he heard her with an overhead wave.

In Uncle Twitch's absence, each nervously waited for the other to initiate conversation. Serenity folded her hands at her waist and pressed against the edge of her stomacher. "Uncle Twitch speaks very highly of you and I have very much been anticipating this meeting."

With a less than steady hand, Susanna tucked an errant blond strand back under the edge of her cap and rocked on her heels. "Twitch has spoken of your family so long and so often, I feel as if I should know you already."

They shared an airy laugh and Susanna issued a cordial invitation. "Never too early for tea, if you ask me." Wispy steam spewed from the kettle's spout. She wrapped her apron around the handle and moved the copper vessel from the Franklin stove to a heart-shaped iron trivet.

Serenity stepped forward to make herself useful in the small kitchen at the back of the house. "Where does one find bowls and saucers?"

Susanna collected spoons and other tea accessories. "One cabinet to your left."

On tiptoes, Serenity reached two Meissen cups with handles and matching saucers, rimmed in gold and hand-painted with floral sprays. To the German-made dishes on the table, she added linen napkins while Susanna set down a bud vase with fresh cut flowers and a plate of ginger biscuits.

They sat on stools at the diminutive table in the brick-walled hearth room adjacent to the kitchen. As the tea steeped, Serenity and Susanna traded timorous smiles, mirroring each other's shy nerves. Susanna abruptly crossed from kitchen to main room to close the top of the half door at the front of the house. The action resulted in less light but also less volume from bustling foot traffic emanating from the cart path called Gilbert's Alley. She returned to her seat and their spoons scraped in synchronized circles against the porcelain cups.

Susanna snipped sugar from a cone wrapped in thick blue paper, except she laid her spoon aside without sweetening her tea. "I'll just say it plain—I am altogether surprised you are here."

"So am I." Serenity's self-directed laughter held a note of hesitation. "Until I stepped across the gangway at Bristol, I debated and prayed every day whether I should come or not. Should won out because all things considered, given what I could lose compared to what might be gained, I judged it a worthy risk."

Serenity kept her many enquiries momentarily in check as she didn't wish to seem impertinent by prying into matters none of her business. She stifled a yawn. "Forgive me. It's not the company, I assure you. I have not slept well on board and I am looking forward to a mattress that will be blessedly unmoving."

"These two feet of mine fancy terra firma." Susanna's gentle humor eased the reserve in her eyes.

Serenity blew on the steaming black Congou tea. "When Mr. Welles delivers my trunks, you shall see how Madelaine, Grandee, and I packed as many gowns in as we could possibly fit. Uncle Twitch indicated you have customers who might be interested in viewing and purchasing the latest fashions. Several of my gowns are Madelaine's own design. You are welcome to sell them, if there are any takers, as she can sew replacements for me when I get back home."

Susanna reached for a biscuit but didn't take a bite. A wistful tone crept into her voice. "If I had a showroom, we could unpack the gowns there and pour out a tea party. Invite prospective clients and likely buyers to come sample fresh English fashion, direct from Bath."

The two shared a quiet laugh over such a scene but Serenity fueled the notion. "Is that something you hope to do, open a showroom?"

"I've bandied the idea about on occasion, though haven't done anything about it." Susanna shrugged. "Twitch says he'd be all for it, if that's what I wanted to do."

"Then perhaps you ought to think on it at length. I'd be happy to help, if there is anything I can do." Serenity hadn't yet settled on how she would pass the time in Philadelphia, any more than she had in York or Williamsburg. She preferred being useful and lamented empty, pointless days.

"I shall think on it." Susanna clasped her hands together on her lap. "I know we don't know each other well, but this is a small abode. Twitch says the main deck of any of his ships are longer than this house is wide. Here, we are stacked in the vertical, though not uncomfortably so. As we will be dwelling together for the short term at least, it may be in our best interest to become better acquainted. There are days when I put forth more effort into being genteel than others. I'm rough around the edges and know I can be blunt, so if any of my questions make you squirm, please do let me know. It is not my intent to step on toes or press too hard. Chalk it up to rabid curiosity."

Gratified by the overture of camaraderie, Serenity removed restrictions. "No, please, ask anything you like. For I have questions of you as well."

Susanna possessed a merry laugh. "Now you've given me leave and I don't even know where to start."

"Then I shall." Serenity sipped her tea. "I balked at this outlandish plan at first. I did not want my youngest brother to come to the Colonies with Uncle Twitch."

"Why ever not?"

"I—" Serenity gathered her thoughts. "I love my brothers, but I cannot stop them from pursuing their own paths. It was naïve of me to think I could keep them all together in one place—to essentially have time stand still and things remain as they were. In that I utterly failed. We none of us are together—we are scattered abroad."

She held her tea cup with a hand cold in spite of the sticky June temperature. "I did not know Uncle Twitch well and had not yet learned I could trust him. He is often gone from England but having sailed with him, I know a bit more about him and his business now. I understand that with your blessing, he is doing a remarkable thing for Amos. And Amos is thriving again." Serenity rested her open palm against her embroidered neckerchief, blinking back tears. "I am grateful Uncle Twitch—and you—are willing to make a way for my youngest brother. My oldest brother was making us all miserable."

Susanna contemplated Serenity. "What would make a baronet's daughter quit her lovely little life in England to brave an ocean crossing?"

"I—" Serenity fingers curled around the gold chain of her sovereign pendant. "I did not think it all the way through. The move was impulsive on my part. My brother Gideon and his friend would say my tenacity got the better of me."

"Needed a change of scenery? Or nurturing hopes of encountering a certain gentleman mapmaker?"

Serenity stilled, recalling with a nod. "Ah yes. You have met him already."

"Marcus St. James." Susanna bit into her biscuit and chewed with exaggerated deliberation. "There's a lovesick man if I ever did see one."

"What makes you say that?" Warmth suffused Serenity's cheeks and heart.

"Those oh-so-sad eyes and the dimming of his smile when I told him you'd been delayed, owing to the repairs at the shipyard near Annapolis. Broke his heart he couldn't stay to wait, much as he wished to." Susanna retrieved two envelopes marked with Serenity's name, in care of Captain Twitch Kerrigan at Kerrigan Shipping in Philadelphia, Commonwealth of Pennsylvania. "Once you've written your replies to those, I'll walk with you to the post office so you can better get your bearings and I'll take you to the print shop, the bookstore, and the grocer, along with the chandler. It will make a good start. It's not a difficult city to get accustomed to once you learn the streets and alleys. The warehouse and wharves line the Delaware River, though I would recommend not going there alone. 'Tis safer to apply caution and not invite any unwanted attention."

Of their own volition, Serenity's thoughts drifted to the night of Gideon's homecoming.

With kindred compassion, Susanna said, "You know a bit about trouble and temptation firsthand too, I'll wager."

Serenity refocused and parried. "Have you never wished to come to England?"

"No." Susanna emphatically shook her head. "I've never even been as far as Baltimore, let alone Alexandria or York. Please understand—I appreciate the ships that bring goods to sell or haul them away to trade, but it doesn't follow that I must prefer for myself the mode of transportation that gets the barrels and crates to their respective destinations."

"Grandee has tried to contact you, issued a standing invitation to come to Fernsby Hall."

This time Susanna nodded. "Do you have any idea how intimidating it was to receive a sealed wax letter on such fine stationery from the daughter of an earl? The Lady Aurelia McCandless herself. Twitch holds her in high esteem and has spoken of her for years."

"Grandee is all that is good and kind and likely only ever wanted to make it known you are welcome. Long ago she was able to contribute to Twitch's success. Now the two of you are in similar position to help Amos. Prior to my leaving Bath, she explained how Uncle Twitch is bound to my family by his good heart, and she is of the opinion that you would have a good heart too or he wouldn't have been drawn to you."

Susanna's cheeks pinked. "Twitch Kerrigan rescued me."

A sharp knock at the kitchen door sounded behind them. "Mistress Kerrigan? Now a good time for me to come with them trunks?"

Susanna held a finger up to Serenity, bookmarking their conversation to be resumed after the interruption.

A seaman pulled his hat off, revealing coarse black hair cropped close to his head. "Have you decided where you want me to put them trunks, ma'am?"

Susanna followed him into the main room, and Serenity joined them. "Thank you for the delivery, Mr. Welles."

Serenity's brow furrowed. "Mr. Welles?"

"Y-yes, miss." He shot a worried glance at Susanna, but she countered with a confident smile.

"Oh, of course! You would have met Obadiah Welles while you were on *The Raven's Lady*."

"Yes, but ... " Serenity searched the man's dark face, unable to put her finger on what seemed different about him.

Obadiah Welles blinked, looking askance at Susanna.

Susanna filled the awkward silence. "Mr. Welles, if you'd be so kind as to move the trunks down to the cellar, we'll be able to preserve the little bit of space available in the front room and get to the unpacking later. Isn't that right, Serenity?"

Serenity belatedly nodded, wondering, as something didn't add up.

"Yes, ma'am. Thank you, ma'am." Obadiah Welles excused himself to do Susanna's bidding. For him, moving the trunks required little effort. One at a time, he lugged them out the front door and down the exterior cellar steps to the storage area below the thin house.

"Thank you, Mr. Welles." Serenity attempted to engage him in conversation after his haul to make him look at her so she could see his face again.

"Miss. Ma'am." He readjusted his voyageur's hat, eyes averted. Task complete, he retreated down the alley in all haste.

"Serenity?"

"That was not the same man as the Obadiah Welles I met on *The Raven's Lady*."

"Do you honestly not recognize him?" Susanna led Serenity back to the hearth room, then selected another biscuit and broke it in half.

Doubt sputtered as Serenity pondered. She hadn't had as much communication with him as some of the other members of Uncle Twitch's crew because he'd drawn a disproportionate number of middle and morning watches—watches covering shadowy nighttime hours, not bright sunlit hours. Was the land Obadiah Welles as tall as the ship Obadiah Welles? This one's face seemed thinner, but the tattoos at the wrists were similar. In the not-so-distant past, Serenity wouldn't have notice details like that.

"He didn't mention the sweet buns I planned to make for the crew once we were ashore—borrowing your kitchen, if you would allow it. That was our final conversation, about baking one last batch for them. He consumed his fair share on the voyage." If she remembered rightly, he was one of the crew who crisscrossed in the small boats between *The Raven's Lady* and the *Oceanna*.

Susanna's glance held cool warning. Serenity yielded, deciding not to continue with her interrogation over the dark-skinned crewman but rather save it for Amos later.

Redirecting their conversation, Susanna's bluntness cut through Serenity's musings. "What are you running from in England?"

Serenity's determined gaze matched that of her hostess. "Some days I cannot decide if I am running from something or to something. But I do enjoy an intriguing story, and I should like to hear yours, if you will share it with me."

Genuine surprise ignited Susanna's expression. "Intriguing? Perhaps. Ugly and disagreeable may be more apt." Her attempt to fan away the humidity failed. Instead she folded shaking hands atop the checkered tablecloth. "There is good that came out of it, but the redemption doesn't come until much, much later."

Serenity selected another ginger biscuit from the plate and settled in for the telling.

"I am two and forty. My birthday came and went while Twitch was away this last time, and I've told him if he's not here to witness them with me, they don't count. His silvering whiskers are an indictment to his aging—whereas I choose to gratify my own silly vanity a bit longer."

Serenity offered an understanding giggle.

"Twitch wrote to explain family business was taking longer than anticipated, additional matters required his personal attention. And he would be bringing Amos back with him on the next crossing. Except for shipping, the two halves of his life seldom intersect. He was born in England, though I think the Colonies suit him better.

"I was born here, in Pennsylvania. By my own choice I did not participate in the Church of England, as a good British citizen generally would. I attended sessions with the Society of Friends at the Quaker Meeting House every now and again, but that wasn't for me either. Most often I worship with the Moravians." Susanna took a settling breath to curtail her rambling and continued more on point. "My uncle was a gambler and a cheat."

"I— Oh, no . . . " Serenity covered her mouth with her hand, sympathetic dread rising in the back of her throat.

"His losses, by cards and horses, mounted beyond his ability to pay back in full the jeopardized account. He borrowed too much. His lender renegotiated but the reduced demand was still more than he could raise. He was given an ultimatum—pay with his own life or sell something of value that would fetch a high price. When I was sixteen, I was sold as an indentured servant to satisfy his debt."

Empathy flared in Serenity. "This plot is more common than it should be, even with tragic variations, and it always ends badly."

"To quote a wise man"—Susanna traced the checked tablecloth pattern with her spoon handle—"there's nothing new under the sun."

"And a purpose for everything under heaven," Serenity whispered.

"Often the purpose is not evident until after, when one has endured and come through the trial to the other side." Susanna set the spoon down. "It was a four-year contract. I would not be free again until my twentieth year. I prayed I would survive until then.

"I served a family consisting of a devious master, his jealous mistress, their two haughty daughters, and the overindulged son away in Europe. For the first three years, I managed to keep my head down, do my work, and fade into the background. Until the son returned. I was attending the girls' rooms when I heard the son and master in the hall, discussing me by name. 'Quite a misfortune for her to be born so handsome.'

"Those words set me on my guard. From that point I did my best to never be alone without another of the servants in close proximity. I went out of the house with the lady's maid every chance I could. To the milliners or dressmakers, picking up the daughters' finished garments, ribbons, baubles. During one such outing, a ginger-haired sea captain crossed my path. He'd seen one of the wrapped parcels of my load drop and was kind in retrieving it. He balanced the stack for me to prevent any of the other packages from falling."

Serenity's smile blossomed. "That is how you met Uncle Twitch?"

"Met?" Susanna tapped a finger against her lips, constraining a grin. "We barely exchanged a handful of words. 'There you go,'" she said in a deep tone, then replied to herself in her own voice, "'Many thanks.'

"The next time I saw him, he tipped his hat and asked after the health of myself and the lady's maid. With my attention focused on the sea captain, I did not see the master's son across the street watching us from the Christ Church gate, but the lady's maid had, so we hurried along." Susanna sighed.

"If you would rather not continue . . . "

Susanna's eyes sparked. "I haven't dredged up this part of my life in years. Less than a handful of people know the whole of my story, but I feel you may understand."

Serenity reached to squeeze Susanna's hand and she continued. "Six months before my contract expired, the housekeeper sent me on an errand to the upholsterer's shop. The ginger-haired merchant sea captain was delivering an order of fabric from England for draperies and bed curtains. Before we parted, he pressed a bag of shillings into my hand and told me if I ever needed help for any reason, he stood ready to assist."

Serenity recalled Uncle Twitch's confession. *I have a wife in Philadelphia whom I adore.*

"The butler and housekeeper, the lady's maid, and a footman took note of the increasing attentions by the master's son and knew I did nothing to encourage him. They did what they could to run interference for me. But fighting off his advances proved more and more difficult. His patience wore thin and anger over my rebuffs replaced his smug teasing. He cornered me on the stairs. I was so frightened that I knocked over the mistress's favorite five-finger creamware vase. I didn't care my final pay distribution would be docked.

"Dear Cook gave me her sister's address, so I had two resources once I was free. But the day before my discharge, the undersheriff was summoned by a report of theft—while polishing the silver, the butler had noticed two spoons gone missing. All the staff were questioned, rooms searched. The spoons, and Twitch's shillings, were discovered in my satchel."

"Susanna." Serenity chafed the cold hands of Uncle Twitch's wife between her own. "The son—he lied and framed you for spurning him?"

"That or the jealous mistress had seen the way both her husband and her son looked at me, and she stood her ground between me and her men. She locked me into the schoolroom at the back of the house until they could decide what was to be done with me.

"Before she died, my mama taught me letters and numbers. The schoolroom had books on every shelf. I read everything I could sound out on my own while I waited. One day more and I would have been free. Instead of crying, I prayed and I practiced writing my name, Susanna Apphia MacDougall, over and over, all neat and legible." She brushed her hands together, as if ridding her fingers of long-ago chalk dust.

"Cook brought a supper tray and news I was to appear before the magistrate. The next day, even though my contract had ended, the undersheriff locked shackles about my wrists and led me away. Cook repeated, 'Just pray. All will be well.' I doubted her at first because municipal authorities were more apt to take the word of a socially superior family over that of an urchin like me but she was right. As I was escorted into the hearing room, Twitch, the butler, and the footman exited the magistrate's office. To this day, I don't know what was said or done. The charges were dropped. I was dismissed from my contract, shackles removed, and my satchel and shillings returned to me."

"Almighty God sent Uncle Twitch to rescue you." Serenity dabbed away tears.

"It wasn't the last time he did so."

Serenity lost track of the number of cups of tea consumed between them and the ginger biscuits completely disappeared. She continued listening as Susanna told how by the time she worked up enough nerve to go to the warehouse to thank Twitch Kerrigan for his part in her rescue, she did not meet with him because he had sailed for England and would not be back until after hurricane season.

"Sad to have missed him, I returned to Cook's sister's home by way of the London Coffee House, where business dealings are conducted between ship's captains and other merchants over handshakes and tankards fortified with a brew stronger than coffee alone.

"Quite by accident, certainly without meaning to, I attracted the roving eye of a fine-looking and prosperous merchant who, in but a few weeks of our acquaintance, sold me a boatload of pretty lies and expressed a desire to wed me. He was a peacock of a man who persuaded me to believe he needed me. He turned a blind eye to my past and proved willing to cover me with his name. I gained respectability as a married woman, *femme covert*, and with him away at sea at least half of each year, I was content to stay here in Philadelphia and run his business in his absence. In peace. Which held great appeal. I can report his shipping office business did well. It was I who did not.

"Twitch returned from England and the man I'd spoken with at the warehouse informed him I'd come to call. When Twitch could not find me at the home of Cook's sister, he delved deeper to track down my whereabouts until his search revealed I had married his stiffest competition. I had known nothing of the contention between them or that it existed beyond their business dealings. I also did not know, until it was too late, that behind closed doors the peacock was a wife-beater. Twitch saw too much, the bruises I tried to hide. His anger kindled and boiled. He had words with my husband—issued a stern warning just shy of a full-fledged threat. I didn't understand his concern for me and, though I was grateful, it cost me. Twitch was everything respectable, discreet in checking on my well-being. Instead of thanking him, all I could do was harangue him in public, discarding all overtures of his kindness because the jealousy of my husband was such that he made me pay for conversations with any other men, including daily business transactions."

"What happened to your peacock?" Serenity wound her napkin into a knot.

"There are those who will tell you I killed him. When he drank, he was the personification of mean. He brought me to the docks to show off his newest sloop—bigger and faster than any of Twitch's schooners. We argued over something trivial and I lost the argument—along with a child. While I lay bleeding and befuddled on the deck, the peacock—drunker than drunk—fell overboard into the river and I failed to raise the alarm."

"Vengeance is mine, saith the Lord. In His mercy, He was with you and took care of what needed to be taken care of." Serenity believed the same as applied to the circumstances Colson had orchestrated, which had resulted in his own demise.

"Oh, but I don't know why I am telling you any of this." Susanna lowered her head.

Serenity understood the acute embarrassment, a resurfacing of shame because she'd experienced a measure of the same. She released her agitated grip on her sovereign coin and, with compassion, said, "Mayhap because I asked and you needed someone to listen."

"Twitch Kerrigan is the only piece of redemption in a story I'm not proud of."

"I know how to keep a confidence."

Susanna did not argue. "You seem the sort who would guard secrets well."

"I am taking that as a compliment."

"As it was intended."

"I thank you for your trust and for honoring me by answering my questions." Serenity's fingers curled around her bezel pendant again. "Now it's your turn. What may I answer for you?"

"You have yet to tell me what you are running from—what provoked the tenacity to make you leave a home and family you love?"

"I was grasping for a way out of my own bad situation. What happened to me could have been far worse had I not been rescued from the clutches of a powerful, titled man used to getting his own way. Our experiences share overlapping threads, too many similarities to be mere chance."

"I told you, there's nothing new under the sun."

"'He that loveth silver shall not be satisfied with silver; nor he that loveth abundance with increase: this is also vanity,' says Ecclesiastes." Serenity added, "Like your uncle, my oldest brother incurred more debt than he had means to repay. The man to whom Colson owed a great amount wanted my dowry in exchange for settling my brother's account. He vowed to have me in the bargain, with or without the benefit of marriage."

A dawning lit Susanna's features as she fit the pieces together. "And that's where Marcus St. James enters your story. He's the one who did the rescuing."

Serenity hugged her elbows, her nod affirmative. Her thoughts often were filled with Marcus and the survey team working to establish the commissioned border line. In the bright light of day and, with so many weeks passed since the night of Brentmoor's attack, she recognized the Almighty's fingerprints in the outcome. "God sent the ravens at the right time. And the ravens directed Marcus."

Susanna listened with reciprocated sympathy. "God's providence has been with each of us—through the hurt and intended harm—in the form of our respective rescuers being on hand when most needed."

Overcoming forged an uncommon foundation for their friendship. The therapeutic clearing of the air was a good thing for both their sakes.

"You, at least, have learned how to forgive—much sooner than I did," Susanna said. "Sometimes I still struggle with that."

"The forgiveness I gave Colson was more for me than it was for him. He needed divine forgiveness but rejected it outright. My choosing to forgive placed the burden back in the Almighty's able hands. He carries it for me. I am not strong enough." Serenity shook her head.

Susanna's lips quirked in half smile. "Oh, I beg to differ. The good Lord equips us to fight whatever battle He calls us to. He has promised, and His promises are faithful and true."

# Chapter 29

On board the Bluebird, *within sight of The Rock, Strait of Gibraltar*
*August 1764*

*Dearest Sis,*

*I suppose we are the definition of orphans now, but we remaining Ravensworths have the love of each other and of course, that of Grandee. We are blessed.*

*I wish I could report that I enjoyed my Italian sojourn—my mock Grand Tour—but aside from the food and meeting with kindness from strangers, I had no desire to stay once Father passed. When we are together again, I shall regale you with the tales, the good and the less so. Beautiful country, but not my cup of wine. Signore Olivadotti sent word to Kerrigan Shipping and the first available bunk was aboard the Bluebird. We are docked in Gibraltar for supplies. Captain Welles estimates we'll put in at Bristol by the end of the month.*

*What a horrid disease the white plague is. The wasting away, the racking coughs. It may take a while for the residual memories, both audible and visual, of Father's harsh death rattle to fade— not altogether unlike instances where soldiers breathe their last on a battlefield. It serves a poignant reminder that it is best to be prepared to enter the next life, the eternal realm, when this life is done. We are not guaranteed tomorrow, yet we live to make plans and hope for our future. Signora Lucrezia was adamant my coming did indeed cheer Father, for he rallied and lasted longer than anyone—his physician included—thought he would. He didn't want me to see him that way and I can't rightly blame him for that. I might feel the same were I to ever find myself in his boots. I am thankful I arrived in Florence with time enough to make our peace. It was worth the battle of wills—his, mine, and the signed parchment documents—to assure myself a measure of understanding, not that it changes anything. We none of us can go back and do things differently, especially those things that happened before any of us were born. But I am inescapably changed by it, and, going forward, I choose to apply the lessons of others if it means I can alleviate suffering the same mistakes. I have determined what kind of father and husband I never want to be. I vow I will be better at both, should those opportunities become mine. I would not delay in expressing to my wife or our children that I loved them—and would strive to do so with everything in me—to foster no doubt, only to find out at the end, when it was almost too late, how deep the emotions ran. I have no idea what you remember of him, as he was absent many years. But try, if you can, to retain something of the good. He loved us to the best of his ability.*

*When I am returned to Bath, there are several things that will need resolution, the main one being the undisputed fact that Colson's deceit and mismanagement all but ruined the Ravensworths. Mother's money is entirely gone, but Grandee's dowry for you remains untouched. From Father, I have inherited a title and some land, and that is the extent of it. To generate a significant amount of investment capital, I've decided the first thing to do is have the solicitor arrange for a buyer for Colson's sovereign coin. When sold, I will put our oldest brother's share of inheritance money to good use rather than foul, with application toward maintenance. St. James's uncle Kent may also have some plausible ideas concerning estate management. I have much to learn but I will not burden you with all of that at present.*

*Speaking of St. James, I trust you were able to see him at least once before he headed out on his adventures. He and Twitch were plotting a scheme I'm sure pertained to you, and I'd speculate it was perhaps a rendezvous in the middle of the Atlantic with romantic implications? I expect he'll waste little time to find you—either in Philadelphia or Williamsburg—come late autumn. Surveyors can't work over snow-covered ground, you know.*

*Has Amos acclimated to his surroundings? Please let me know how he fares as Twitch's shadow. By the time this letter reaches you, half the agreed-upon year may already be spent, and then in six months' time, more decisions will require the making. I earnestly pray it is working out more favorably than you anticipated. I know it was not your first choice for Amos. Do you concede it the better one, for his sake?*

*I'll sign off here. A British ship headed for Philadelphia is in port and will take mail westward. I am well, and I will write again when I've settled in at Fernsby.*

*With love and affection from your brother,*
*Sir Gideon*

*(I only wrote that to make you laugh, which I imagine you are doing, and that would in turn cause me to smile.)*

⌒

*Home of the Kerrigans in Gilbert's Alley, Philadelphia*
*September 1764*

Weeks passed and, not unlike being on board *The Raven's Lady*, unfamiliar became established routine. Reading, writing, spelling, arithmetic, and Scripture lessons translated from ship to shore without alteration. Amos followed Twitch by day, taking care of merchandizing matters at the warehouse. Following supper, Serenity read with him before going upstairs to a dormer window to see over rooftops and ship masts to locate the North Star.

Serenity did not miss Fernsby Hall or Bath as much as she thought she might. Very likely because it wasn't the places that mattered—it was the people.

Traffic in Gilbert's Alley thinned by late afternoon but didn't dissipate altogether until after dark. The crispness of autumn overtook the hot summer nights, when windows remained open for air circulation and noises of both shop and home life carried along cart path-turned-street. Narrow two- and three-story homes of Georgian architecture stood cheek by jowl. Some shared walls. Bricked passthroughs divided others, leading to small backyards in the rear of the lots. John Gilbert's name might be attached to the alley but the landlord owning the most rental properties along its length was Jeremiah Elfreth.

None of the trinity houses were identical. They shared similarity in structure but distinction in character, a veritable stew of colors, and not every lot was built upon. Front doors had stoops or stairs, others transoms or pediments, and a number boasted shiny brass knockers and boot cleaners. Shutters or turnbuckles embellished small-paned windows and here and there boxes for flowers and greenery underscored lower sills. Exterior access to cellars by way of angled double doors and ground-level windows provided additional light for basement storage or living quarters. Walls and chimneys displayed a variety of masonry designs, including Flemish bond patterns. The alley exuded a blended ambiance of desirable residential quarters and productive artisan commerce.

Neither Twitch nor Susanna made further reference to the mystery of Obadiah Welles. Amos had no details either. The man had ostensibly vanished after delivering her trunks and, for the time being, Serenity let the curious matter drop.

Serenity had latched on to Susanna's mention of a showroom and together they'd fabricated plans to implement a hosted afternoon tea for clients and showcase the fashionable gowns Serenity had brought across the ocean with her.

Invitations were couriered to a half dozen select repeat customers of Susanna's acquaintance. All six eagerly accepted on the same day as receiving the calligraphed cards.

*By Invitation*
*Please join us for an Exclusive Showing*
*On Tuesday Next*
*Of Gowns, Accessories, and Slippers*
*Recently arrived from the spa town of Bath in Somersetshire*
*And to take part in tea and polite conversation*
*Your response is requested—please reply to*
*Mrs. Taggart Kerrigan*
*In Care of Kerrigan Shipping*

"Where did this come from?" Serenity uncapped a brown bottle of distilled lavender water, sniffing a hint of vanilla in the mix. She had been rationing her supply since starting to run low, saving it for the yet unknown day of Marcus's return.

"I described your fragrance to Mrs. Kerrie, a tradeswoman who operates a still for oils and tinctures. She has experimented with lavender and mint, but this was her first attempt adding vanilla instead. I think it's lovely. No wonder St. James is partial to it."

"He told you that?" Serenity's brows bunched in question.

Susanna laughed, plucking the brown glass vial from Serenity's fingers. "Not in so many words, but were he to get a whiff of that fragrance somewhere along the line, I'm guessing your comely image would pop into his mind. You wear it well."

"Thank you."

"I know it's still a bit warm this afternoon but do you think you could manage the forest-green brocade?"

"I shall wear whichever you think best, since you agreed to take the robin's-egg blue silk." Serenity held up matching ribbons. "You go on up. I'll be right behind you to help with your hair."

Their showcase tea proved a brilliant success. After cleaning up, the drying of washed teacups and spoons gave way to counting the proceeds of sold gowns, gloves, buckles, and bolts of chintz. Susanna decided, having consulted the schedule Amos kept on his own calendar for estimated stock arrival of Twitch's next shipment from England, that their next event should be held at the end of November. That would give purchasers of raw fabric enough time to have apparel made by their preferred seamstress or dressmaker's shop, finished and ready with time to spare before Christmastide balls and Twelfth Night celebrations.

Serenity wished again for Madelaine's presence. Such an event would be a boon to her business as well. She would write her about it in her next letter. She hadn't heard from Madelaine or Grandee in a long while, and that bothered her. She prayed all was well, that nothing was amiss for them.

Three weeks later, a letter from Madelaine did arrive, bringing with it the latest news from home.

*My Dear Serenity,*

*You'll please forgive me. I feel I'm only able to write one letter for your every three—or maybe it just seems such a ratio due to the delay whenever the post is delivered from the Colonies. I appreciate your faithfulness in keeping up our correspondence. Believe me when I say it's not that I don't think about you, but rather I fall asleep if I'm still for even five minutes at a stretch. I am tired and so many things have happened since I last picked up my quill, but I will catch you up with the happenings as best I can.*

*We are in receipt of the melancholy news of Sir Nicholas's passing. Gideon has returned to Fernsby a little older and wiser, I think, and he is embracing the new responsibilities that give him purpose.*

*Tyree has two new commissions for finish work on townhouses in the same section of the King's Circus as Lady Aurelia's. He, his journeyman, and Asher have a constant source of income for the next few months at least. That is a blessing. Tyree's master craftsmanship is spreading by word of mouth and he is in demand for his quality woodworking skill.*

*Mr. Craddock has been keeping my needle busy. I'm grateful for the extra work the tailor sends my way, but the days fly in a blur and I feel like I need another set of hands to keep up with the ever-growing list of things that need to be done. There are nights I just can't keep my eyes open when Asher wants to read together. Since your mention of the book about Captain Singleton, he's had a hankering for adventure stories. What else are you and Amos reading together?*

*I am bracing myself. Jessa has started pulling up to her feet and giving serious consideration to taking those first steps. She hasn't quite comprehended that until she lets go of either her J initial block or the little horse Amos carved for her, she can't steady herself with both hands. She still uses the silver rattle whistle whenever a new tooth appears. That coral tip has been a relief through the process, to be sure. When she shakes the bells, I can hear her in whichever room she has crawled into.*

*Should Amos inquire, you might let him know she has been attempting to say his name when I show her his miniature portrait. She always smiles when she sees Mr. Gainsborough's painting of him, but then her brows furrow in confusion because she looks about for him and can't find him. Yesterday after her nap, she woke up and patted my pocket. When I pulled out the miniature, she smiled her dimpled smile and said "May-mos" while pointing at his face. I know Amos was concerned she would forget him while he was away.*

*I don't think that's the case. He made a lingering impression before he went and she misses him, as Asher does.*

*I am not sure if Lady Aurelia has written of late, and if she hasn't, I'm willing to stake the reason is because she has not yet told you of her recent fall. Do not be alarmed—she is healing, albeit more gradually than she would wish or command. She accepted an invitation from the family of The Viscount Oakleigh to stay with them near Chipping Campden. Incidentally, did you know St. James was a viscount?? How did I miss that? You must fill me in on that part later. At any rate, Lady Aurelia went to Oakleigh Combe, coordinating her visit at such a time as when Johnna FitzGerald and her husband, Ian, were also there with their daughter, Corinna. That little one is not far behind Jessa in age and development. Johnna and I have been comparing notes about our girls on each instance she stops by my workshop since moving to Bath. But let me back up so I can explain.*

*Johnna's husband lost his appeal to continue working at Balliol due to his married status. He tendered resignation from Oxford and has taken an instructor's position, which includes fund-raising and publicity at Bath's Blue Coat School in Saw Close. He has talked Jonathan into volunteering at the charity school, and Jonathan, after weighing his options, agreed to accept the challenge. Therefore, we are seeing Jonathan with increased frequency while he juggles his studies and keeps tutoring the boy at the Eagle and Child, and now Ian FitzGerald is priming him to be the next chaplain—however, that position won't come to fruition until Jonathan completes his degree and is ordained.*

*Lady Aurelia and Johnna were strolling about the gardens at Oakleigh Combe, which I'm told are both beautiful and extensive. Lady Aurelia tripped over a flagstone paver and went down hard, jamming her wrist and spraining her ankle. It was an unfortunate accident and has slowed her considerably, but the timing turned out* to be fortuitous because the FitzGeralds were able to bring her back with them. They lived with her for a few weeks until they found a place of their own to let. Lady Aurelia offered them the use of Fernsby Cottage but Johnna prefers town, she being more of a social creature.

Between Nancie Heath and me, we kept an eye on the ravens during Lady Aurelia's absence, though in truth they fend well enough on their own. I've brought butcher scraps to Nancie Heath a few times and, while I don't possess the courage to go into the aviary to leave them, Nancie Heath does. Those ravens tolerate us at best only because they are clever enough to know who feeds them—canny birds.

Lady Aurelia is returned from the house party at Oakleigh Combe and has established temporary lodgings in the sitting room on the ground floor of her townhouse. She maneuvers well enough with the brass-capped cane Rafe St. James lent her, but she will not be satisfied until she can master the stairs without assistance again, I trow.

Oh dear … It has been four days already since I started writing, and while nothing else remarkable has transpired in that amount of time, Mr. Craddock requested another batch of shirts. I finished them this afternoon. And now I will finish this letter, praying it will sail away to you sooner rather than later.

I ask that you would pass along my sincere greetings to Twitch and his Susanna.

Ever your steadfast friend,
Madelaine Northcraft

P.S. At week's end, Jonathan came to visit us here in Bath. Gideon came from Fernsby to check on Lady Aurelia and get an update on her progress from Dr. Theophilus Graham. Your brothers stayed for cards and a lively debate ensued with Ian, while Johnna's played Vivaldi on the pianoforte. It was pleasant to see them and Lady Aurelia's stamina is reviving. She does not tire as easily this week as she did last.

*This letter will be posted today! I'm already melting the sealing
wax and as soon as the ink is dry, will fold it up and be done with it.
Have you heard anything of Marcus St. James's whereabouts?*

⌒

*Home of the Kerrigans in Gilbert's Alley, Philadelphia*
*Late November 1764*

Marcus ascended the three steps of the rowhouse nearest the river
and paused on the pedimented stoop. Muffled fiddle music stayed his
hand as he reached for the brass lion-head knocker on the Kerrigans'
front door. Straining to listen to the duet, he could hear the marked
improvement Amos had gained after many long hours of practice
under Twitch's instruction.

Susanna Kerrigan sat writing at the kitchen table. He didn't see
Serenity through the window but that didn't mean she couldn't be in
one of the rooms on another level.

Amos spied him and his bow screeched to a halt, disrupting the
lively song. The boy scampered across the yellow pine floor, yanked
the Dutch door open to allow Marcus entrance into the main living
room and pitched himself into his arms with evident delight. "You're
come at last!"

It made Marcus's heart happy to know his presence was anticipated. "I told you I'd be back in my last letter. Did you not receive
it?"

"Aye, so we did but you failed to declare an exact day, only an
estimated week." Twitch transferred fiddle and bow to his left hand,
gripping Marcus's hand in welcome with his right.

"'Tis a pleasure to see you again, Mr. St. James." Susanna came
from the kitchen, wiping smudged fingertips on her ink-stained
apron. "I confess, we didn't tell Serenity of your anticipated when, as I

didn't want her disappointed in the event something might alter your plans. She is out running an errand, picking up more cards and envelopes from Deborah Franklin at the print shop, but that's only a few blocks away. It is my understanding she's not one for surprises, but in such a case as this, I do believe she'll make the exception for you."

"I hope you're right." Marcus matched Susanna's grin, adding a wink.

Upon arriving in Philadelphia, Marcus had gobbled a hasty dinner and secured lodging at the Man Full of Trouble Tavern. When Susanna encouraged him to stay for supper and offered a cup of hot drinking chocolate, he refused neither.

The tall case clock in the corner indicated the better part of an hour passed and still there was no sign of Serenity.

"She probably ducked into the bookshop for shelter when it started raining," Amos said. "She promised to look for something new for us to read since we finished *Gulliver's Travels* and *Pilgrim's Progress*. Shall I go fetch her home?"

"No, let's keep you here. Should you miss her, at least we still know where you are. She'll be along. She knows we start making ready for supper within the next half hour." Susanna put her hands on her hips. "You didn't say anything to her about plans for Virginia?"

"No." Amos shook his head. "You told me not to."

Marcus bit back a grin. Young Amos was learning how and when to keep a secret. That could be useful.

"We cannot leave any sooner than Wednesday next. I promised Susanna. She and Serenity have another customer tea party scheduled for Tuesday." Twitch stowed his fiddle case and added two more logs onto the fire. "Meaning Serenity, Amos, and I will be free to depart by the end of that week."

Susanna showed Marcus an invitation marred by an ink splotch. "Our first showcase tea did so well we started planning this one almost immediately before we learned you'd be released for the winter."

"If you deem it expedient, I could go on ahead, arrive in Williamsburg before you, and put necessary arrangements in order for the next few months."

"There's a capital idea." Twitch crossed his arms, tapping his finger against his lips. "Would you be willing to deliver a message to Obadiah Welles for me? All you have to do is leave it for him at the front desk of the Swan Tavern in York. No questions asked. He'll be anxious to know I'll have need of him on the next voyage to England."

"That's an easy assignment." Marcus nodded. "Before I head south though, I'd like to see if I might meet with Benjamin Franklin."

"I heard Franklin sailed for England three weeks ago as representative for the Assembly of Pennsylvania. Surely you haven't been so far in the wilderness to have not heard the continued rumblings of the mounting call to tax the colonies for the late war debt." Twitch drained the last of his chocolate. "The Sugar Act was passed in April. Massachusetts merchants have voiced concern about enforcing duties on foreign molasses to the American colonies while cutting the domestic duty fees in half to three pence per gallon. The furies in Boston allege harm to their—*legal*—trade prospects with the West Indies as well as an invasion of their charter rights for self-government."

Twitch Kerrigan was a merchant, trade and commodities his lifeblood. "Will this affect Kerrigan Shipping business?" Marcus asked. "I didn't think you dabbled in molasses or sugar or slaves."

"I do what I can to stay clear of the Triangle Trade due to my own personal convictions. I will not deliberately turn a profit on human bondage if I am able to avoid it outright. Anyone who has commercial dealings with Kerrigan Shipping knows that."

"Not everyone shares—or appreciates—your principles."

"That is between them and God."

"Not all circumstances are in your control."

"I do what I can." Twitch reiterated his position, left eye atwitch. "Representatives and lawyers in Boston are pointing out Colony charters include granted rights to govern themselves and that dominions under the protection of the Crown should not be taxed without their consent. These are grave matters. It is hoped Parliament is aware of the contents of the language and spirit of meaning those charters entail. I understand having to pay for a war but with more than three thousand miles between King George and his thus-far faithful Colonies, there must be a way to accomplish these measures within acceptable parameters. There has already been introduced in the House of Commons what is being called the American Stamp Bill. Lord Grenville tabled it when certain representatives raised objections, suggesting the Colonial governments ought to be brought into the discussions and consulted."

"They—we ... " Marcus amended. "Aren't we all British citizens with the same rights as those who dwell in England? These are His Majesty's Colonies of *British* North America. Our regiments fought and died to force France out of *British* territory. Why would Parliament not see them—see us—as equal?"

"That, St. James, is a question begging to be answered. At some point, it will no longer be enough to claim the Colonies only when most beneficial. The monarchy and its Parliament either need to accept and grant representation or they need to come over here and see how things are done. The Colonies are Britain's biggest customer base. As a merchant, it's part of my job to take care of my customers."

Marcus pondered that. Citizens on both sides of the Atlantic were subjects of the Crown. They were Englishmen. He'd bled for his country ... That had to mean something.

The front door opened and the sound of Serenity's voice bubbled with enthusiasm. "Susanna? I brought the cards. And I found a new book for A—"

In that instant, all notions of current political issues disintegrated for Marcus. He stood, gave a single-shouldered shrug, and opened his arms to her.

His name formed on her lips, and she uttered *Mar-kiss* as a mere whisper. A hitch in her breath preceded the muffled squeal, laughter offsetting her tears. Like her little brother, she barreled headlong into his embrace. "Oh, praise be to God! I am so glad to see you!"

"And I you." He brushed a happy tear from her cheek with his thumb, studying her, keenly aware of their observant audience.

Serenity extricated herself from his warm hug and gave the parcel she carried to Susanna. "I had to wait for the cards to be cut. Then I stopped in at the booksellers for just a moment."

"See, I told you she'd be at the bookstore." Amos flashed a simpering grin.

Marcus noted the top of Amos's dark curly head reached just shy of Serenity's shoulder, and the boy said to her, "And I told you he'd be back."

Amos faced the Kerrigans. "Can I tell her about Virginia now?"

Serenity ruffled her brother's locks. "Cat's out of the bag, wouldn't you say?"

"Oops." Amos covered his mouth with both hands. "Sorry."

She administered a light-hearted swat against his arm. "Come help put another leaf in the table. Susanna and I will have supper ready in a little bit. In the meantime, you can tell Marc—Mr. St. James—all you and Uncle Twitch have been doing at the warehouse."

"And after supper, I'll read my poem."

"What poem?"

Amos shook his head. "Uh-huh. Cat's not out the bag on that part yet."

"Come on, you." Marcus beckoned to the boy. "Where does Mistress Susanna hide her extra table leaf?"

Serenity joined Susanna in the kitchen, leaving the men to rearrange the furnishings, fitting the wider table and an extra chair in the center of the main room. As she passed by carrying cutlery for five, Marcus winked at her, breathing in. "You smell good."

She blushed again. "Thank you." She seemed to revel in the knowledge he was having a difficult time paying attention to anyone else but her. "How long will you stay in town this time?"

"You missed the beginning of our earlier discussion about Williamsburg. The survey crew has been furloughed, and I am at my leisure until I must report back in the spring. The perpendicular line between the Delaware colony and Maryland has been recorded with the Commissioners. Measurement for the western line between Maryland and Pennsylvania is the next stage of the project."

"This is good news indeed." Her shy stammer made him smile. "Most welcome news."

Susanna caught Marcus watching Serenity's retreat to the kitchen and he was unapologetic. No one in this room didn't already know he cared for her; therefore, he felt no compunction to hide the fact.

When all were sated and the room put back in order so they could relax and enjoy one another's company following the evening meal, Twitch suggested Amos play the song they'd been practicing—"Merrily Kissed the Quaker's Wife"—from start to finish.

At the tune's conclusion, Amos dodged the applause. He sat on the Chippendale settee next to his sister, across from Marcus, and laid his head on Serenity's shoulder, hardly able to bridle his building mirth.

"He has a handful of songs in his repertoire now," Susanna smiled. "And the more he practices, the better they sound. Good job, young man. I'm proud of you."

"What is this about a poem?" Twitch stretched and locked his fingers behind his neck. "Something of your own creation?"

Amos pulled a piece of paper from his waistcoat pocket, explaining for Susanna's benefit more than anyone else's. "Colson used to quote an old poem he always said was like us Ravensworth brothers. Well, since Colson is dead, things have changed. Gideon told Jonathan we should revisit the poem—make something up to match our improved circumstances because things are different than they were." His shoulders lifted in a shrug. "I wrote a new verse. One more fitting."

"Are you going to recite it for us?" Marcus prompted but then halted with a wary pause.

Amos's mischievous grin reappeared. The imp reread the scrap, folded it into his pocket, and, with amplified exuberance, made a show of clearing his throat. He first took a sidelong peek at his sister, then slid a crafty glance to counter Marcus's arched brow. Facing collective anticipation, he delivered his rhyming oration:

"The 'one for the war' became the 'one for the land'
The 'one for the church' made a brave stand
The 'one more' at business tried his young hand
Now three brothers wait to see Sis love a husband."

# Author's Historical Notes ... and Inadequate Thanks

I write historical fiction augmented by weaving in factual research gleaned from study and travel. I strive to produce an engaging story that delivers a glimpse into the time period. I also like to have readers finish and say, "Hmm, I never knew that before."

Once the challenge of writing another story registered, switching time periods brought a requisite need for a new knowledge base. I did a lot of digging to attain a fledgling grasp of eighteenth-century chronology, historical figures, fashions, food, locations, relationships, daily life, religion, holidays, and prevailing attitudes—all carrying distinct differences compared to what I learned during my study of the 1860s. My comprehension of America and England in the 1770s was limited. Before I could write about the American Revolution, I had to learn its backstory. How did we end up breaking off with the Mother Country? What grievances over taxation and citizens' rights caused a movement for "Independency"? Until 1776, we were all British. That realization lured me back to the 1760s to explore what served as catalyst for the upheaval to come. Therefore, this story starts after the Seven Years' War before approaching the road to revolution.

Details, details...I could write pages and pages about my research. I have created more than a dozen photobooks chronicling various road trips. I will share a few interesting tidbits here and for those who want to know more, please visit my website at www.telizabethrenich.com. I also invite you to author Laura Frantz's and my private Facebook group, Gorgeous Georgians, for more interesting facts from the Georgian era (1714-1837).

- The poem outlining English primogeniture law has multiple versions but I have not yet found a solid citation for reference aside from Anonymous.
- A King Henry VIII Gold Sovereign (monarch on the front, crowned shield of arms on the back) was worth £24 when minted in 1545. That's somewhere in the $20,000 range in today's currency.
- John Wood the Elder and John Wood the Younger were prominent architects in Georgian-era Bath and their building projects contributed to the spa town's renovation. I've visited twice (2017 and 2019 with Julie Klassen's tour groups) and want to go again! Thanks to Julie and Brian for sharing photos from their visit to the Palladian Bridge at Prior Park for the visual details.
- The British called it the Seven Years' War but it was known in North America as the French and Indian War. The conflict spanned from 1754 to 1763, followed by Pontiac's Rebellion (1763-1766). Math is not my forte—words are—but by my calculations, that's more than seven years of consecutive fighting.
- Colonel George Washington had Fort Loudoun constructed on high ground north of Winchester, Virginia, as a defensive post on the colonial frontier. There are varying views on how long the fort—manned by militia not British Regulars—actually stood. In *The James E. Taylor Sketchbook* (1864), the fort lay in ruins. However, portions remained for a time before building materials

were repurposed. I left out Dr. James Craik's name as the surgeon who treated Marcus's wounds. Dr. Craik had served with Washington but after his marriage, he moved to Port Tobacco, Maryland, and it is uncertain when exactly he might have split time between there and Winchester after that.

- Long known and frequented by area tribes, the "Warm Springs" (also referred to as "Medicine Springs") of western Virginia appear on the 1753 Fry-Jefferson map. Originally named for the resort town of Bath in England, the location switched from Virginia to West Virginia when the latter seceded from the Confederacy and gained statehood in 1863. Bath is to this day the official name of the town but the U.S. Postal Service assigned the name Berkeley Springs, which is how it is listed on modern Google maps.

- Wakwi is a girl's name found on www.babycenter.ca. In the Ojibwe language, the word means "cloud."

- Pea coats have been worn by European and American sailors for more than two hundred years and remain fashionable. Ladies' red woolen hooded cloaks were called *cardinals*.

- Small things: smallclothes in the 18th century refer to men's breeches and shirt, a state of undress without a coat. Small beer is a brewed beverage with low-alcohol content, as it wasn't always safe to drink city water in the 1700s.

- In Philadelphia's Old City, Elfreth's Alley is a three-hundred-year-old residential street but it wasn't until the 1780s when it became known by that name. It appears as "Gilbert's Alley" on the 1764 Library of Congress map. Twitch and Susanna Kerrigan live in a Gilbert's Alley rowhouse closer to the Delaware River than Second Street.

- Benjamin Franklin studied what came to be known as the Atlantic Ocean's gulf stream. It factored into why sailing from England to North America took longer than America to England.

- It took the commissioned survey crew led by Charles Mason and Jeremiah Dixon nearly four years (1763-1767) to measure and map the border between Pennsylvania and Maryland. It wasn't called the Mason-Dixon Line until 1820.

- Williamsburg was Virginia's capital city until 1780, when Thomas Jefferson, then governor, had it moved to Richmond. York was Williamsburg's nearest major port and in 1774, had its own tea party. It was known more commonly as Yorktown following the American Revolution.

Many thanks to so many living historians/interpreters, rangers, guides, docents, staff, and visitors' centers for assistance, information, and direction. They willingly let me pick their brains and welcomed my many questions.

- **DC**: International Spy Museum, National Archives. **MD**: Annapolis, Fort Frederick, Frederick Town Barracks, Schooner *Sultana*. **MI**: Colonial Michilimackinac, Elmwood Cemetery, Fort Mackinac. **NJ**: Monmouth Battlefield, Morristown NHP, Old Barracks Museum. **NC**: Charlotte Liberty Trail, Guilford Courthouse NMP. **PA**: Benjamin Franklin Museum, Betsy Ross House, Bushy Run Battlefield, Christ Church, City Tavern, Elfreth's Alley, Fort Ligonier, Fort Necessity, Fort Pitt Museum, Independence Hall, Museum of the American Revolution, Powel House, Valley Forge NHP. **SC**: Historic Camden Revolutionary War Site, Cowpens Battlefield, Kings Mountain NMP, Ninety Six Historic Site. **VA**: American Revolution Museum at Yorktown; George Washington's Ferry Farm; George Washington's Mount Vernon, Distillery & Gristmill; George Washington's Office; Hanover Tavern; Hugh Mercer Apothecary Shop; Jamestown Settlement; John D. Rockefeller, Jr. Library; Historic Kenmore; National Museum of the Marine Corps (Tun Tavern Café); National Museum of the United States

Army; Rising Sun Tavern Museum; St. John's Church; Schooner *Alliance*; Scotchtown; Tall Ship *Providence*; Thomas Balch Library; Watermen's Museum; Yorktown Battlefield. **WV**: Museum of the Berkeley Springs, Renaissance Spa (Warm Springs).

*Continuing Education*: My eleventh-grade U.S. History class with Coach Witte was too long ago, so I took online classes and zoom lectures through the Museum of the American Revolution and George Washington's Mount Vernon. I also accessed Jenny L. Cote's "Epic Order of the Seven" online workshops and homeschool classes based on Jenny's books (taught by Beth Cuvelier, with zoom-classmates Maggie Long and Carey Talevski). I attended an 18th Century Woodworking Conference at Colonial Williamsburg, and the School of Instruction for 18th Century Surveying hosted by the Department of the Geographers.

*Resources*: The internet, Google, YouTube, and Amazon are game changers as compared to researching for writing my Shadowcreek Chronicles series back in the day. Modern technology has made information readily accessible, though it still needs authentication.

* Apps—*Blue Letter Bible, Etymology Online, National Park Service, Word Hippo*.
* Books—*5 Love Languages/Military Edition* by Gary Chapman with Jocelyn Green; *Attack at Michilimackinac* (Diary of Alexander Henry) edited by David A. Armour; *Colonial Williamsburg: The Story*, by Edward G. Lengel; *Colonial Williamsburg's Official Guide Book*; *Drawing the Line* by Edwin Danson; *Gentlemen of Uncertain Fortune* by Rory Muir; *Rebels at Sea* by Eric Jay Dolin; *Surveying in Early America: The Point of Beginning* by Dan Patterson and Clinton Terry; *The Art of Cooking Made Plain and Easy* by Hannah Glasse; *The Compleat Housewife* by Eliza Smith; *The General and*

*Mrs. Washington* by Bruce Chadwick; *The Journal of Charles Mason and Jeremiah Dixon* introduction by A. Hughlett Mason; *The Ravenmaster* by Chris Skaiff; *The Royal American Regiment* by Alexander V. Campbell; *The Vulgar Tongue* by Francis Grose

- Facebook Pages—Breed's Hill Institute, Colonial Williamsburg, Daily Dose of American Revolution, Gorgeous Georgians, Inspirational Regency Readers, Minute Man NHP, and Regency History with Andrew and Rachel Knowles
- Movies/Mini-Series—*Beyond the Mask, The Crossing;* HBO's *John Adams; The Patriot,* PBS Liberty! Series; PBS The War That Made America Series; *TURN: Washington's Spies; Williamsburg: The Story of a Patriot*
- Music/Artists—Baroque Essential Collection, Colonial Williamsburg Songs, Donna Nomick, Hesperus, Jim's Red Pants, John Mock, soundtracks ("Beyond the Mask," by Jurgen Beck; "The Patriot," by John Williams; "Pirates of the Caribbean," by Klaus Badelt, select tracks by Two Steps from Hell)
- Podcast—*HTDS* (Professor Gregg Jackson; early episodes cover the American Revolution)
- Websites—
  - Historical Marker Database (www.hmdb.org) – Use this site all the time. Have contributed twenty-eight entries, and counting.
  - Correct Forms of Address (http://www.chinet.com/~laura/html/titles12.html) –Bookmarked and referred to frequently. Ongoing learning for "rules" for my titled English characters. Any mistakes are mine
  - Founders Online (www.founders.archives.org) – Digital collection of writings by Washington, Franklin, Adams, Jefferson, Hamilton, Jay, and Madison.
  - The receipt for the Chelsea-style sweet buns at Colonial Williamsburg's website https://www.colonialwilliamsburg.org/learn/recipes/how-make-chelsea-buns/.

- YouTube Channels—Falconry & Me, Townsend's 18th Century Cooking

I have an incredible huddle of supportive friends, family, and co-workers who supply encouragement and prayers. I don't have words enough to thank them for everything here, but I am blessed because the LORD put them in my path and grateful for their respective contributions to my project. I would not have made it this far without them:

American Christian Tours – Betty Anderson – Dan Brisco – Cornerstone Chapel in Leesburg & Tuesday Night K-Group at the Milburns – Jenny L. Cote – Laura Frantz – Joann Geslak – Judy Gillette – Sue Goedken – Bobbi Graffunder – Michelle Griep – Sarah Hamaker – Dori Harrell – Marilyn Heath & Peter Johnson – Matt Jones & Jones House Creative – Jill Kemerer – Julie Klassen – Hannah Linder – Ramona (St. James) Martin – Libby Carty McNamee – Bernadette Murphy – Melanie Radcliff – Dave & Nancy Renich – Nathan & Vanessa Renich – Cynthia Ruchti – Jan Tornell – Traveling companions on Liz Curtis Higgs' 2016 Scotland trip, and those on the 2017 and 2019 tours to England with Julie Klassen – Erica Vetsch – Karla Wachenheim – Jaime Jo Wright – Beth Zarin.

- Extra special thanks to Ryan Kerrigan, Sarah Northcraft, and Kirk Olivadotti for lending their names. (Of course, they're good characters!)
- Before he died, Daddy knew I was going to be published again with my "Cancer is a Team Sport" chapter in *She Writes for Him: Stories of Living Hope*, but I wish Momma could have seen how this Sovereign Liberty Series came into existence. She (like Bobbi) would have claimed the backstory a story in its own right—punctuated with God's fingerprints all along the way.

*Dear LORD, I do not always see or understand what You are doing but I surrender to wait and watch as Your ways are higher (Isaiah 55:9) and You are Sovereign. Blessed be the Name of the LORD!*

# About the Author

T. **Elizabeth Renich** has written four Civil War novels, worked for two NFL teams, and visited all fifty United States of America. International travels have found her in Germany, Japan, Ireland, Israel, Scotland, and England. She hunts historical markers and shares hope as an ovarian cancer survivor. Her love of photography is evident as she documents research trips and life, giving glory to God for the great things He has done.

Additional information can be found at her website https://telizabeth.com, on Facebook https://www.facebook.com/telizabethshadowcreekbooks/, or Instagram @telizabethrenich

She also co-hosts the Gorgeous Georgians private Facebook page with author Laura Frantz at https://www.facebook.com/groups/305339915561627